Yvonne M.

Dear Reader,

What would you do if everything you held dear in the world was suddenly gone? Would you have the courage and sheer grit to pick up the pieces and build a new and different life for yourself?

Intriguing questions like this seemed to fuel my creative engine when I began to think about the plot for this book. In *Never Tell*, as always, I've plunged my heroine into a kind of hell where she'll need courage, self-reliance and, yes, sheer grit just to survive. I promise that her plight will touch your heart, and her struggle to overcome the truly dreadful hand she's been dealt will leave you feeling that there is always hope after tragedy. There are enduring friendships to be treasured. And there is always love to be found in the world…if we just open our hearts to receive it.

I hope you enjoy this book as much as I enjoyed writing the story. I would love to hear from you! If you would like to be part of my mailing list, please write me at P.O. Box 141, Pearland, Texas 77588-0141. Or visit my Web site at www.authorkarenyoung.com.

Happy reading!

Karen Young

W9-BMN-383

KAREN YOUNG
NEVER TELL

MIRA®

MIRA®

ISBN 0-7783-2143-6

NEVER TELL

www.MIRABooks.com

Printed in U.S.A.

ACKNOWLEDGMENTS

I owe thanks to several people for their generous support and suggestions during the development of this book. To Emilie Richards and Erica Spindler for the brainstorming session in Santa Fe. To Joanna Wayne and Gloria Alvarez for one of those "why-didn't-I-think-of-that" ideas. To Barbara Colley for keeping me focused. To Jon Salem for...well, he knows why.

Warm and loving thanks to Alison Simmons for her generous donation of time and ideas on a part of this business of writing that seems to come naturally to her, but not to me. Thank goodness she works cheap! And finally, to my editor, Valerie Gray, whose thoughtful insights are always right on.

In loving memory of Linda Kay West

One

The telephone shrilled the fourth ring, but Erica Stewart resisted coming fully awake. Let it go to voice mail, she thought, while a part of her still struggled to finish the dream. The phone rang again and Willie, her cat, nudged her hand with his head. Purring loudly, he climbed on her chest and pawed at the blanket. With a sigh, she raised herself on one elbow and looked at the caller ID, then groggily reached over and picked it up. "What?" She knew she sounded grumpy, but she wasn't at her best before coffee and all her friends knew that.

"Good morning, sunshine."

"This had better be good, Jason," she grumbled, falling back against her pillow. "It's Sunday. You know it's the only day I can sleep in."

"You'll forgive me when you hear this," her business partner and quintessential morning person said. "Have you seen the Sunday *Chronicle?*"

"You woke me from a sound sleep, Jason. I'm still in bed. And thanks to you, Willie's now meowing to be fed. So, no, I haven't seen the newspaper."

"Wait'll you see the article in *Zest,* sugar. It's fantastic.

It's gonna mean success with a big *S* for us. Get dressed," he told her. "I'm coming over."

"Can't you just—" She stopped, realizing the line was dead. Grumbling, she threw off the covers and glared at Willie, who was wailing now. "I'm up, I'm up."

When Jason knocked on her door fifteen minutes later, she'd barely had time to brush her teeth and throw on a pair of jeans and a T-shirt. He had a bakery box in one hand, a newspaper under his arm and a cardboard tray holding two cups of Starbucks coffee in the other. "Here, straight house blend, no frills, just the way you like it," Jason said, thrusting the coffee at her. Then, waggling his eyebrows suggestively, he offered the box. "Kolaches. Mixed varieties."

He knew she had a weakness for the delicious pastry stuffed with everything she shouldn't eat. Why was it some people preferred to skip breakfast altogether when for her it was the best meal of the day? And irresistible. With a sheepish groan, she grabbed the box, turned and led the way into her kitchen.

The table in her breakfast nook was littered with fabric scraps, scissors and parchment-paper patterns. Sitting in the midst of that was her laptop. She remembered looking at the clock around 2:30 a.m. and thinking she should shut down and go to bed. She did, finally, about an hour later, knowing it was Sunday and she would be able to sleep in.

"Whoa, somebody's been busy," Jason said, looking at the mess on the table.

"Until the wee hours," Erica said, setting the coffee and kolaches on a countertop nearby. She collected the material scraps and dropped them into a box, tossed the paper patterns into a tall trash can she'd placed beside her chair and shoved the computer to the opposite side of the table. "But it was worth it. I finished the design for Jill McNeal's evening jacket. I'm really happy with it, Jason. I think she'll be pleased."

"Have your coffee first," he told her. "And sit down. We'll look at the design and pig out after you look at this." With a flourish, he snapped the fold from the newspaper and spread it out on the table.

Erica removed the plastic lid from her coffee cup and sat. Then, tucking a strand of dark hair behind one ear, she turned her attention to the paper. Her gray eyes went wide. The first thing she noticed was her own photo on the cover of *Zest,* the *Houston Chronicle*'s Sunday magazine. Small but prominently displayed at the top, it was a teaser for a feature article inside.

"Wait'll you see the article," Jason said. "It'll blow your mind. We couldn't pay enough for advertising like this, Erica." Not waiting for her to find it, he leaned over and flipped the pages until he located it. He straightened and stood back to gauge her reaction. "Have a look at that, partner."

He was right about one thing. They could never afford to pay for advertising at this level. She was pictured arranging the display in the front window of the shop in the Village. She remembered the day she'd worked on the display. She'd wanted the fabric she'd used in the jacket to coordinate with the quilt, another of her original designs. She'd draped the quilt over an antique chair, which she'd borrowed from a shop located a couple of doors down. On the floor beside the chair was a tall urn containing a few gnarled and leafless limbs she'd collected on the side of a country road. River stones had been strewn over the floor to look as if they'd been cast out carelessly, adding a last artful touch to the oddly eclectic grouping. She'd had some doubt about the photographer's request to shoot her at work in the window, but the result was more than interesting.

Jason grinned with delight. "Is it great, or what?"

"It's nice." The article wasn't about Erica alone. It was a piece showcasing the unique personality of the Village, a favored location for merchants, upscale and otherwise, some selling unique merchandise while others offered chain-store quality. When Erica and Jason decided to open a retail outlet for her jacket and quilt designs, they'd chosen the Village as much for its personality as for its location near upscale River Oaks.

"Nice?" Jason propped his hands on his hips. "That's it, just nice?"

"It's really terrific."

"You know what this means, Erica." He sat down on the cushioned seat of the bay window, but he was so energized that he was instantly up and pacing again. "It's going to make us a household word. You've already made a name for yourself in Houston and this article is simply icing on the cake. Circulation for the *Chronicle* takes us throughout the whole state of Texas and beyond."

"First Texas and then the world?" she teased, smiling while savoring the taste of the coffee. Jason's expectations were anything but modest. He really believed Erica Stewart was destined to become a label as well known as Kate Spade or Cynthia Rowley. He was so certain that sometimes Erica almost believed it herself. This morning, however, her expectations were firmly grounded. She needed a couple of seamstresses to work full-time on the jackets and quilts, but so far she'd found only one who met her exacting standards. Her creations were pricey, unavoidably so, as they were labor intensive. She wanted anyone who bought a jacket or a quilt to get full value for their money.

"I'm not the one in denial," Jason said, biting into a kolache. "You are." Then, chewing on the pastry, he pointed to the article. "Do you think they do these feature articles for just anybody? Hell, no. Even if you can't believe you're destined to be a significant player, sugar, other folks do." He tapped the article with a forefinger. "Now all we have to do is make the most of what's been handed to us on a silver platter."

"Uh-huh." Erica rose and rummaged in a wire basket where she'd stashed recent mail. "If you're excited over that article, you'll really love this." When she found what she was looking for, she handed it to Jason, who gave it a quick once-over. Then, doing a double take, he reread it.

"This isn't a joke," he said, looking at her. "You wouldn't do that to me, would you?"

"No, Jason. Where would I get letterhead with a *Texas Today* logo? It's real."

"You've been named one of Twenty Women to Watch in Texas," he said in a tone of wonderment.

"I know. I've read it," she said dryly.

"Do you have a clue what this means?"

"I've got friends in high places?" But she was smiling, knowing Jason would get almost as much pleasure from the honor as she did. Maybe more.

"We agreed we couldn't find enough money to buy the *Zest* article, but this knocks that right out of the ballpark."

She licked raspberry filling from her finger before grabbing a napkin. "Hey, maybe we'll find the money to hire another seamstress."

"I'm serious, Erica. This is…this will…" He shook his head. "I'm speechless."

"Now, that is a first." Taking the letter from him, she sat down again and reread it. "I'm flattered, Jace. And you're right. This is a once-in-a-career boost, and yet…"

He looked at her in disbelief, propping his hands on his hips. "And what, for Pete's sake? You can't possibly find anything negative in this. You said the *Zest* article was a fluke, and that if our shop wasn't in the Village, and they didn't just happen to be featuring businesses there, we would never have been included. And when you got that order for jackets from that boutique in the Galleria, you called Christopher Crane to make sure he meant it for Erica Stewart and not our competition in Dallas. It was legit and that's because you're good. Chris Crane doesn't just run his finger down the yellow pages and pick a designer at random to feature in his shop, darlin'. You're good, you're better than good and I wish to hell you believed it as much as I do."

"Okay, okay." She gave a weak smile and rubbed her forehead with two fingers. "I get a headache when you start to lecture."

"You should," he said with no sympathy. After a beat or two, he dropped into a chair opposite her. "I don't get why you keep trying to downplay your success, Erica. If I were in your place, the Astrodome wouldn't be big enough for my ego."

She studied his face with affection. They'd been friends since meeting in an art class in college more than twelve years ago. He'd been the male model that day. It was later when Erica learned he was actually an art student, and that he'd volunteered to model because it was just the zany kind of thing Jason sometimes did. He was physically beautiful. No other word fit. He had every natural asset needed for a career as a male model. His hair was a thick, glossy near-black, his eyes were startlingly blue and he had cheekbones to die for. Added to all that, his tall, hard-muscled body looked delectable in clothes. In fact, he'd briefly pursued modeling as a career, but quickly abandoned it as being, in his words, "soul-destroying and shallow beyond belief." In his bones he was a serious artist, but unlike Erica, he hadn't been able to support himself with his art.

To tell the truth, Erica wouldn't have been able to support herself with her art, either, if Jason hadn't come up with the bright idea that the two of them should collaborate. In his opinion, her fabric designs had commercial appeal. He'd pitched the idea at the darkest time in her life. She'd been holed up in her house popping antidepressants, stashing away the jackets and quilts she designed in a closet in the cluttered room where she created them. Had it not been for Jason and his dogged determination to save her from herself, Erica wondered how long it would have taken her to decide to reenter the land of the living. So, with her designs and Jason's ability to promote and sell anything except his paintings, he persuaded her that going into business together would be a good thing. And indeed it was. With hard work, plus a lucky break or two, they'd achieved quite a remarkable commercial success.

"I just have this feeling, Jace," she said, moving a finger over the *Texas Today* logo. "I know you think it's my insecurity talking, but every once in a while I just feel as if that success you're crowing about has been helped along by some outside force. I don't know how else to describe it, but it's there."

"Here we go again." He rolled his eyes. "That is total bullshit, Erica. You're a talented artist and that's why the world is noticing you." He chose another kolache from the box and added, "Helped along by the somewhat brilliant promotional contributions that have come from me, if you'll excuse me saying so."

"I've had to excuse a lot more than that since you nagged me into opening the shop," she reminded him dryly.

"Your lucky day."

She smiled and gave in. "Okay, okay. Between the two of us, we're enjoying a little taste of success."

"And it's sweet indeed."

"So I'll stop looking for a worm in the apple."

"Good. Because there isn't one." Grabbing a pen, he got ready to do what he did best: seizing opportunity and running with it.

"More coffee, Morton?"

Lillian Trask lifted the decanter from the server and waited to pour. Along with coffee and juice, the breakfast cart was laden with scrambled eggs, bacon, croissants and a collection of gourmet jams and jellies. For herself, she preferred only fruit and yogurt to start the day, but her husband liked a hearty meal. After a moment, he grunted a response and she refilled his cup.

He held a cell phone to his ear with one hand while he scanned the pages of the Sunday edition of the *Houston Chronicle* with the other. Open and within easy reach was his trusty Blackberry, on which he received and sent e-mail, retrieved information, accessed his address book, noted the weather and even picked up breaking news. Since sitting down to breakfast twenty minutes ago, he'd been focused on the Blackberry or talking on his cell phone. She'd once tried to declare mealtime a no-business zone, but she'd been instantly overruled. Only if they had guests did she expect conversation with a meal. When they were alone, Morton was too busy talking business to talk to her.

Actually, it was rare that they breakfasted together. When she came downstairs in the mornings, more often than not, he was already out of the house, headed downtown to the offices of CentrexO. As its CEO, he was never separated from the company, not even when he was in

Galveston, where his boat was docked. She hated going out on the boat, or rather, his yacht, as he constantly reminded her. The luxurious Bertram was equipped with every convenience to live aboard for days—even weeks—at a time. But she tended to get seasick, and nothing was worse than being miles offshore with her head spinning and her stomach revolting. At those times, Morton was utterly unsympathetic. He, of course, was never seasick.

They owned a condominium overlooking the Gulf and she could spend a weekend there if she wanted, but she seldom did so. It was a seventh-floor corner unit with a great view, but when she was there, she felt lonely and isolated. There was no magic in watching a stunning sunrise or sunset alone.

She finished her breakfast, listening with half an ear to Morton's conversation with a business associate. Maria, the housekeeper, appeared to clear the table, and when that was done, Lillian turned her attention to the stack of mail she hadn't gotten around to opening yesterday. She didn't hear Morton addressing her directly until he barked her name for the third time.

"What? Oh, I'm sorry, Morton. What did you say?"

"That was John Frazier in Washington," he told her testily as he entered something in his Blackberry. It irritated him when he didn't have her full attention. "He's at the airport on his way back to Houston."

"John Frazier." She repeated the vaguely familiar name but couldn't place him.

"You met him at the fund-raiser last month," he reminded her.

She thought a minute, then remembered Frazier as a tall, thin man with a practiced smile. "He manages one of those PACs, doesn't he?" It would be impossible to guess which one, as Morton was a heavy contributor to several political action funds.

"Yeah. And listen to this. He just left a breakfast meeting with some VIPs who have the ear of the president." He finished entering data and looked up at her as he shut down the Blackberry. "According to John, I'm definitely on the short list for an ambassadorship. I was reasonably certain it would happen, but these things can slip away with the slightest turn of the political tide."

"Ambassadorship?" she repeated, starring at him in stunned surprise.

"Is it so astonishing? I've contributed a goddamn fortune to those jackals in Washington. It's the least they can do."

"You mean we'd leave Houston?" And everything and everyone she held dear?

"I can hardly serve as an ambassador from my office downtown." He was gleeful as he picked up the newspaper again. "I've got a short list of posts I'd prefer. How does Costa Rica sound?"

"Hot and humid," she murmured.

"So? Houston is hot and humid, too." And with that, Morton dismissed her reaction. "Think of it this way. You won't have the bother of shopping for new clothes. You already have the right wardrobe." He snapped the newspaper open before adding, "It won't necessarily be Costa Rica. I just mentioned that country as a possibility. I could be placed in any of half a dozen other locations."

"What about the company?" He couldn't be serious. Nothing took Morton away from CentrexO for any length of time.

"Not a problem. I've been grooming Alex Winfield to take over, just in case. The experience will open other doors for me, as well, Lillian. There could be something in Washington. There would definitely be something in Washington," he added, idly paging through the paper.

"I'd make some valuable contacts, and after getting back to the States with the ambassadorship under my belt, I'd be able to write my own ticket."

Lillian put a hand to her throat. He was serious, and it sounded as if the decision was final. She was to have no say in it.

Still heedless of her reaction, he said, "I admit I didn't expect to hear so soon, but it's good to know that, for all practical purposes, the deal is done."

"I knew nothing about this, Morton," she said, dismayed. "I don't want to leave Houston."

He lowered the newspaper just enough to peer over it. "Why, for God's sake? There's nothing you're involved in here that you can't find elsewhere. If we wind up in Washington, there are museums and charity causes to fill up your time, plenty of hospitals where you can volunteer." He disappeared again behind the paper, adding, "As for the other, after a few weeks in a new country as wife of the American ambassador, you'll adjust. Give it a chance before going negative. You might even enjoy yourself."

She gazed down at her spoon. Not if it meant leaving Houston and her work in the arts. As the wife of a powerful and visible CEO, she was in a unique position to assist the arts community. But even without her commitment to the arts, there was Hunter. As she thought of her son, her gaze strayed to the window and the center of the immaculate lawn, where a cherub poured water from a jug into a tiny pond. It was painful to remember how close they'd once been. He tolerated a rare lunch date with her now only out of a sense of duty. She sighed, able to pinpoint the moment when their relationship had begun to deteriorate. But then, so much of the downward spiral of her life was marked by that moment. She set her spoon and yogurt aside, untouched. Between the demands of Hunter's business and his preference for spending his free time at the ranch, she rarely saw him. If she went out of the country for any protracted length of time, she could lose touch with him altogether. As for Jocelyn, she had so little contact with her daughter that it probably wouldn't matter if they were posted to China.

For a long moment, she watched the sparrows fluttering in the water. She was drawn to the ranch herself, but it was awkward explaining to Morton why she wanted to spend time there. He found the place dusty and hot. Totally urbanized, he didn't ride and was repulsed by the dust, the torturous Texas heat and the smell of horses. So, they didn't go.

With another sigh, she chose another envelope from the stack of mail and slit it open. Perhaps she'd survive a brief tour in a foreign country if she could look forward to returning to Houston and the life she'd built for herself, but if Morton had his eye on something in Washington, it was unlikely they would ever live in Texas again. She didn't think she could bear that.

"Anything in there from Jocelyn?"

She quickly scanned the rest of the envelopes but saw nothing. No surprise there. Jocelyn wasn't much of a correspondent. The best she could manage was a phone call to her parents once a month. "I don't see anything," Lillian said. "The last time we talked, she was so excited about this new job. That's probably why we haven't heard from her. She's very determined to make a career for herself, Morton."

"By reporting for some sleazy tabloid in Key West?" He folded and set aside a section of the newspaper before picking up another. "I don't think so. Not unless we see a big change. She doesn't stick with anything any longer than she sticks to her husbands. Twenty-five years old and two divorces, for God's sake."

"One divorce and one annulment. And good reasons for both," Lillian argued. "The first was a silly, rebellious prank, and that awful Leo person was addicted to cocaine. Would you have wanted her to stay with either one of them?"

"No, but I also didn't want her marrying either of those bozos…not that she consulted me. She's spoiled rotten, Lillian. And it's unlikely to change as long as you keep stepping in when she screws up. What she needs to do is grow up."

They'd had this discussion before. Jocelyn did have a string of broken relationships behind her. In an act of open rebellion, she'd eloped on the night of her eighteenth birthday with the golf pro at the country club. Morton had been livid but had managed to avoid a major scandal by paying off the bridegroom and arranging an annulment. To the dismay of her parents, however, that first debacle established a pattern and it had been one disaster after another since, including a hasty marriage to a druggie. She seemed addicted to destructive behavior, and after so many years, Lillian wondered if her daughter would ever settle down and be happy.

"I can't just ignore her when she needs me, Morton."

"Give her a chance to feel the consequences of her screwups and she'll soon straighten out," Morton said grimly. "If she'd consulted me when the time was right, she would be set up fine and dandy on a decent career path at CentrexO, and not down in Key West consorting with who the hell knows what kind of riffraff." He snapped out another section and scanned it through his bifocals. "But what's the use closing the barn door after the horse is out. I'm more concerned about the present. I want you to call her and get it through her head that she'd better be on her best behavior for the next few months. I don't want her mixed up in a scandal that would cause the president to kill my appointment."

He was right, of course, not that she'd admit it to Morton. Their daughter was spoiled, indulged to a fault and constantly setting herself up for failure. And, unfortunately, the time was long past when she would consider consulting them about anything in her life. Morton might rant on and on about Jocelyn's tendency to make mistake after mistake, but the blame wasn't hers, it was theirs.

She looked up when Morton made a choking sound, sputtering into his coffee. "Did you see this?" He shoved a section of the newspaper across the table. "They do a feature article on those hokey shops in the Village and they choose hers to put front and center? This just proves my theory that they're desperate to find anything newsworthy today."

Lillian set an invitation to a charity function aside, then looked at the article, bracing for what she would see and the quick, sharp stab of conscience she would surely feel. Artist Erica Stewart had been photographed in her shop, intent on arranging the display in the front window. Her face was in profile, but Lillian needed no reminder to know exactly what Erica looked like. She recalled everything about her with cruel clarity, her storm-gray eyes and dark, curly hair that stubbornly refused to be tamed. Her face, with its strong features, was not quite beautiful; still, it was an arresting face, young and vibrant. As always, Lillian was unable to bear looking. She glanced quickly away and said without any emotion in her voice, "I wouldn't call her shop hokey."

"That whole damn neighborhood is hokey." He made a grumpy sound. "She's probably sleeping with somebody with clout at the newspaper to get this kind of play in the Sunday edition."

"Actually, I think she's quite reclusive." The moment

the words were out, she wished she'd kept quiet. This was a subject that, by tacit agreement, both avoided.

He looked up with a sharp frown. "How do you know that?"

She sighed. "I hear things, Morton. I attend an art class. I sponsor young artists. They talk."

He held her gaze for another long moment, then disappeared once more behind the newspaper, this time with the sports section. "If she's all that solitary, her success strikes me as even more unlikely. It takes capital to set up a business and make a go of it. I bet if we knew more about her we'd find she has a sugar daddy somewhere. Artists do that kind of thing."

But Lillian did know about her. She knew everything there was to know about Erica Stewart, but she'd never tell Morton that. She could not remember a time when Erica hadn't been a presence in her life even though they'd never met. It had been out of desperation that she'd found ways to be helpful to Erica without her ever knowing it. And, in doing so, had helped ease the pain of her conscience. But it had taken years. This feature article in the *Chronicle* was just one of several times when Lillian had been in a position to boost Erica's career and she'd acted to do just that. Of course, it helped that the young woman was a wonderfully creative artist. And when she'd opened the shop in the Village with her friend Jason Rowland, between the two of them—Erica's talent and Jason's gift for sales and promotion—they'd really needed no help from anyone. Getting the article on Erica was one of those moments when Lillian had been in a position to help. She'd learned from a contact at the paper that a feature article about the Village was in the works, and she'd suggested Erica and her shop as a good example of the kind of thing that was proving so successful in the Village. Simple, really.

"She has a business partner," Lillian said, continuing the conversation and giving in to some perverse urge that pushed her on when the prudent thing would have been to drop the matter before Morton lost his temper.

He lowered the paper to look at her. "Don't tell me, the partner's silent and well heeled."

"I don't know how silent he is or what his financial situation might be." An outright lie, but with the bit in her teeth, she seemed bent on a headlong dash to the finish. But something—Morton's arrogant announcement to pull up stakes and leave—drove her on. "It's Jason Rowland," she said.

Morton put the newspaper down slowly. "Jason Rowland? Not Bob Rowland's son?" Now it was his turn to gaze out the window with a puzzled expression. "The one who's an artist, right?"

"I believe so."

"Well, I'll be damned."

"Yes."

He was busy mulling it over and missed the irony in her voice. "Well, I was right about one thing. He's probably the one bankrolling the shop in the Village, but I guess that shoots my theory about her sleeping her way to success."

Lillian sighed. "Please, Morton."

"At least, not with Jason," he said, smirking. "The boy's gay, isn't he?"

"I wouldn't know," Lillian said stiffly. "And he's hardly a boy. He's almost as old as Hunter."

"Well, he is gay. Everybody knows it. Not that Bob's ever mentioned it. And I see him at the club frequently. As a matter of fact, we played golf last week. Naturally, he doesn't mention Jason much, but—"

Lillian rose abruptly. "I need to talk to Maria about lunch," she said. Not waiting to hear him out, she left the room.

Two

To Hunter McCabe, a week when he didn't make it to his ranch was a week that sucked. For the past seven days, he'd divided his time driving on Houston's clogged freeways between two construction projects forty minutes apart where everything that could go wrong had. He needed to breathe something besides exhaust fumes and city smog. So it was barely daylight when he left the parking garage at his high-rise condominium and headed west out of the city. Making good time, he'd be at the ranch just as Theresa was dishing up breakfast.

It was a few minutes past seven when he finally turned off a state road onto the ranch—two hundred and eighty acres of prime Texas land. As he drove beneath an iron arch with McCabe-Colson forged in large letters, his mood improved. The ranch was a legacy from his father and one that Hunter cherished. Bart McCabe had purchased it thirty-five years ago with his business partner, Hank Colson. According to Hank, they'd bought it mostly as a tax write-off, but with hopes of raising cattle on a large scale in the future. But those plans had died when Bart went down in the crash of a small plane, leaving Hunter fatherless at age two and his mother a widow. Driving past grassy pasture now, he blessed the impulse that had moved Hank and his dad to purchase the land, whatever their motivation.

Once out of the car, Hunter breathed deeply, taking in the smells of the ranch—fresh-cut grass, wood smoke and horses. In the south pasture, a young mare stood cropping winter rye while her foal nursed vigorously. A prize Appaloosa in the pasture opposite spotted Hunter and whinnied, but he resisted the temptation to head that way. There were a couple of things that needed tending before he could escape to the stables. A weather front had brought rain yesterday and the cold, crisp day was perfect for what he had in mind.

He braced for the wild welcome from the chocolate Lab who rushed toward him, barking joyously. Charlie was aging, but somehow in greeting Hunter, who'd raised him from a puppy, he seemed to forget his aching joints. Laughing, Hunter dodged the dog's tongue and enthusiasm, and only after he'd given him a good rub did Charlie fall in beside him, tongue lolling happily. He was up the steps onto the porch in two strides, pausing to stamp the dampness from his boots on the welcome mat at the front door before going inside.

The man who met him before he cleared the threshold might have stepped right out of a Remington sculpture. "Thought I heard you drive up," Hank said, handing over a steaming mug of coffee. "If you'd headed to the barn first, I was coming after you and I wouldn't be offering coffee."

"I missed you, too." Hunter took the coffee, knowing it would be hot and strong, and inhaled deeply.

Tall and whipcord lean, Hank was on the downhill side of sixty but still as fit as a man in his forties. He had a face made of sharp angles and shadowy planes and a generous mustache as gray now as his eyes. And in spite of the fact that he always wore a hat, his skin was still richly tanned and weathered.

Hunter tossed his hat at the rack by the door, ringing it squarely. "Before you light into me, hear me out. I plan to look over that lease agreement you've been nagging about right away. Not that I need to. If you're satisfied, I'll sign it and we'll be done with it."

"This is a partnership, Hunt. I'm not signing anything that ties us to a contract for five years without you blessing it."

Hunter tasted the coffee with caution. "I know as much about growing pecans as you do about building a high-rise," he said, wincing over his blistered tongue.

"It's not about growing pecans. It's about your land and—"

"Our land, Hank. We're equal partners here. You keep forgetting that I was only ten years old when you had the idea to plant a thousand trees on ground that was growing nothing but grass and scrub. Left to me, it would still be grass and shrub, as long as there was pasture for the horses. So, if you say you want to lease more acreage to plant more pecan trees, why would I argue?"

"We're lucky the land butts up to ours and that Billings is willing to lease it out," Hank said. He watched Hunter give the collection of mail on the table a quick glance, then lose interest before adding, "I'm thinking if we offered enough, he'd probably let us buy it. 'Course, he'd want an arm and a leg per acre. His wife's the one holding out for leasing."

Hunter leaned against the table, smiling. "Thinking you can afford to pay an arm and a leg?"

"Thinking we both can," Hank said.

Hunter studied the older man, knowing that if and when a deal was done, it would be to the advantage of McCabe and Colson no matter how grasping Billings's wife was. Hank had keen business instincts. He and Bart McCabe, who'd been a pilot, had started up an air-cargo business back in the sixties and it was thriving at the time of Bart's death. When Lillian remarried, Hank bought out her share and continued to run it with truly phenomenal success until about eight years ago. Then he'd surprised everyone by announcing his retirement. That was the year his daughter, Kelly, was accepted into the veterinary program at Texas A&M. Hank set her up in an apartment in College Station and moved into the ranch house after enlarging it enough so that Hunter wouldn't feel crowded when he dropped in. It was after his retirement that he'd developed a keen interest in the lucrative crop, and it was not long afterward that he'd decided to get into growing pecans in a big way. In five years, he had more than a thousand trees in varying degrees of maturity and varieties. He'd taken to the role of planter enthusiastically and was now highly regarded in that field.

"Just let me know what you decide," Hunter said, and pushed away from the table. "Now, can we have breakfast? I'm starved."

He could smell bacon frying. Theresa, the ranch's longtime housekeeper and cook—and surrogate mother to Hunter—would have a mouthwatering spread waiting. Heading for the kitchen, he glanced around the place with a sense of homecoming. It was clearly a masculine abode decorated with a strong Western influence. The man-size furniture was upholstered in leather, the end tables were wrought iron and wood, the chandelier was made of a wagon wheel and deer antlers, and over all lay the smell of cigar smoke and lemon wax. The place was orderly and spotless, no thanks to Hank or Hunter. Theresa ran a tight ship.

She was stirring something on the stove when they entered the kitchen, but she paused to hug Hunter. "It's about time," she said, inspecting his face with the familiarity of one who'd changed his diapers. She was a tiny woman with hair as black now as it had been when Hunter was three. Her bones felt as frail as a bird's, but he knew she was as tough as a pine knot. Theresa was always up and about at daylight, and if she ever sat down during the day, no one ever saw it.

He swung her off her feet and kissed her soundly before setting her down to inspect what she was cooking. "Whatever it is, bring it on. I've been saving up for this."

"Sausage gravy for your biscuits," she told him, giving him a shove toward the table. "Scrambled eggs and bacon are on the table. Sit down and get started. Hank, leave him alone until he's done with his breakfast. You know he's not about to dispute your plans, so give him a minute to eat in peace."

"He can listen while I fill him in on the details." Hank reached for a folder and opened it before Hunter took a seat.

"Do me a favor," Hunter said, heaping his plate. "Skip the details. Just hit the high points."

With a sigh, Hank closed the file and picked up his coffee. He watched Hunter tackle the food, then gave him the bottom line. After stating the costs, he added, "I'm considering some new hybrids recently developed at A&M. I figure I can plant at least five hundred trees on the land."

Hunter paused, buttering a biscuit. "Are you sure you want to take on the responsibility? You know I can't get up here except on weekends, plus you're supposed to be retired. Adding five hundred trees to what you've already got isn't my idea of retirement."

"You let me worry about that. Best thing about growing pecans," he said, taking a sip of coffee, "it's not labor intensive like, say cotton or corn, crops like that. 'Course, we won't get any return on these trees for years yet, but when they do come in, they'll be cash in the pockets of your kids…if you ever have any."

Tucking into his breakfast, Hunter chewed slowly. He knew Hank believed it was time he settled down with a wife. And here lately Hunter had found himself thinking the same thing. If he'd been asked when he was in his mid-twenties whether or not in ten years he'd still be unmarried, he would have dismissed the possibility out of hand. Of course he'd eventually marry and have kids. Most of his friends had done exactly that. One by one, he'd watched them find the "right" woman and head happily for the altar. It hadn't happened for Hunter. He'd had relationships—even some lasting a few years. He'd just never felt compelled to marry. He now figured he wouldn't ever experience the crash-and-burn-type passion like his friends had, and was resigned to settling for something else. There was a lot to be said for being with a woman who shared the same goals.

"And speaking of family," Hank went on after failing to get a response from Hunter, "you didn't forget Lily's birthday, did you?"

Hunter's knife and fork clinked against his plate. "Damn, I guess I did." Frowning, he glanced at the date on his watch face. "Today's the third. I've got a couple of days. It's the sixth, isn't it?"

"You should know your mother's birthday, Hunt. Yeah, it's the sixth. And I had a feeling you'd forget."

Theresa reached to remove an empty platter from the table. "Maybe if you weren't so ready to remind him," she said, "he'd get in the habit of remembering on his own."

"And maybe he wouldn't," Hank said.

"I guess we'll never know." Ignoring Hank's grumpy look, she spoke to Hunter. "I told him you had a calendar at work. You'd eventually see it and go out and buy her something nice. It might be a day or two late, but it would happen."

Hunter nursed the last of his coffee and wisely said nothing. Taking sides between Hank and Theresa would be inviting trouble. The truth was that Hank had nailed it, saying he'd probably forget if he wasn't reminded. Theresa was right, too, saying sooner or later he'd realize it and get his mother a gift.

Hank stood up. "Bottom line, you haven't done it yet. You'll be at work tomorrow morning up to your ass in alligators and last thing on your mind'll be shopping for Lily's birthday. Lucky for you, half the job's done. Wait here."

Clueless, Hunter looked at Theresa as Hank left the kitchen, but she only shrugged with a who-knows expression. Both knew what it was that drove Hank to remind him of his mother's birthday, and it wasn't to prevent Hunter forgetting it. It was Hank's own partiality for "Lily," as he called her. It had been plain to Hunter for a long time that Hank had a soft spot for Lillian. Both Hank and Bart McCabe had been married forty years ago when they went into business together. But when Marguerite Colson died of cancer, Hank's interest in Lillian grew beyond friendship. She'd remarried by then, but as a boy, Hunter had often pretended that Hank, and not Morton Trask, was his stepfather. He definitely felt more of a kinship to Hank than he ever had to Morton.

"Take a look at this." Hank was back, shoving a section of newspaper at him.

Front and center on the *Zest* magazine was a photo of a woman doing something in the window of what appeared to be one of those trendy little shops in the Village. Hunter's interest in the newspaper was usually confined to the sports section first and the front page next. *Zest* covered arts and theater stuff and he often skipped it. It was always the first thing his mother pulled out of the *Chronicle*'s Sunday edition. He glanced up at Hank. "Give me a hint. How is this related to Mom's birthday?"

"I've heard Lily mention this artist, Erica Stewart," Hank said, paging through to find the article. "She designs quilts and stuff and she's good. I bet Lily would appreciate something from her shop. You've been traveling between those two jobs day in and day out. Not twenty minutes out of your way to detour over to the Village and choose something."

Theresa had risen to stand at Hunter's elbow and study the article. "Hmm, anything in that shop'll be pricey, count on it."

"He can afford to spend some money on his mother," Hank said testily.

"I'm not arguing that," Theresa said, then pointed to an item in the window. "You want my opinion, go for one of the jackets. The quilts are probably gorgeous, but not exactly Lillian's style. Now, if those jackets are as elegant as they appear in this picture, I think she'd be thrilled to get one."

"I'll check it out." Hunter got up, taking the *Zest* article with him. He was relieved not to have to spend time he didn't have browsing in the Galleria. Clapping a hand on Hank's shoulder, he moved toward the door. "Thanks. I appreciate it, Hank." Passing the sideboard, he took a couple of apples from a bowl and headed for the door to get his hat.

Once out of the house, he took a deep breath and followed the path leading to the barn. The air was sweet, the sky was already as blue as only a Texas sky can be and the birds were singing. The sun, high now on the east horizon, had burned off traces of morning mist. A perfect day for what he had in mind. Near the barn, Cisco, one of the two regular ranch hands on the payroll, was climbing onto the seat of a tractor hooked up to a trailer loaded with hay bales. Hunter raised his hand in greeting as Cisco headed out to pasture.

The noise faded as Hunter entered the barn. Taking in the familiar smells of hay, horses and manure, he welcomed the hush. A soft whicker came from the first stall. Jasper, an Appaloosa stallion Hunter had bought a year ago, lifted his head and flicked his ears back in recognition. Hunter pulled one of the apples out of his jacket pocket.

"Hey, boy. Ready for a ride?" Standing outside the stall, he fed the apple to the horse, rubbed him behind the ears, then reached for a bridle hanging on a hook. Jasper crunched the crisp apple and blew out a soft, gentle sound, stamping a foot. Hunter grinned, recognizing impatience as he slipped the bridle into place. "Looking forward to a good workout, huh? Well, me, too. Just let me get that saddle and we're outta here, buddy."

The gear was in the tack room at the rear of the barn. As soon as he saddled up, Hunter planned to spend the next few hours skirting the perimeter of the ranch. Cisco and Earl were paid to see that the fences were in good shape, but Hunter liked to check himself from time to time. After the week he'd endured, he looked forward to a few hours to himself.

"I knew I'd find you here."

Hunter turned with the saddle in his hands. Kelly Colson stood in the doorway. Blue-eyed, slim as a boy in boot-cut jeans and a baseball hat on her auburn head, she looked more like a teenager than a thirty-three-year-old veterinarian. "I thought you'd be sleeping in this morning," he told her, hefting the saddle onto his shoulder.

She stepped aside to let him pass. "Is that why you didn't call me?"

"I drove in early. Hank hit me at the door with paperwork. I only escaped ten minutes ago." He hadn't thought to call her, but he wasn't about to admit it. "You're up early, too."

"I never went to bed," she said. "Tom Erickson called around midnight. His prize bull got out and was hit broadside by a teenager in a pickup. I didn't get away until a few minutes ago. I spotted your car as I was passing on my way home."

"Not that bull he imported from Colorado?"

"Uh-huh."

Hunter pushed Jasper's stall door open. A man could buy a whole ranch for what some prize bulls cost. "Were you able to save him?"

"Luckily nothing was broken, so he'll survive." She caught Jasper's bridle as Hunter put the saddle blanket on his back. "He won't be doing his job for a while, but when he's called on to perform in a week or two, he'll do his duty."

"Poor baby."

Kelly specialized in large animals, which is why she'd chosen to set her practice outside Houston. There was opportunity galore to practice in the city, where there were plenty of youngsters whose parents could afford the expense of a horse, but like Hunter, Kelly preferred breathing country air. It was one of many interests they shared. They had a lot in common, from a love of horses and country living to family history.

She watched him pull the cinch tight around the horse

and then reach to adjust the stirrup. "Looks like you've got plans for the day."

He glanced over at her, picking up something in her voice that made him proceed with caution. "At least, for most of the morning," he told her. He and Kelly had drifted into a relationship of sorts lately. She'd stayed overnight at his condo once in a while when she was in the city, and they were often together on weekends when he made it out to the ranch. But today he craved a few hours by himself. "I thought I'd check the fence line," he said, and bent back to his task, hoping she wouldn't want to mount up and go with him.

They'd been friends since childhood, which was understandable seeing the close connections of their parents. It was when Kelly finished her training and returned to establish her practice near the ranch that he realized she wanted them to be more than friends. She was an up-front, direct kind of woman who went flat out for whatever she wanted. And she made it plain that she wanted Hunter. He admitted he hadn't put up much resistance; even so, he'd felt a little uncomfortable the first time they'd wound up in bed. Not that the sex wasn't good, it was. Kelly didn't seem to feel any qualms and had settled happily into their affair. What he couldn't quite figure out was why—to him—something didn't feel exactly…right.

"Isn't that Earl's job?"

"Riding fence?" He'd almost forgotten what they were talking about. "I do it for the fun of it. He indulges me." When she failed to smile, he reached for the reins and she let go. "I've been fighting traffic and breathing interstate exhaust night and day for two weeks, Kell. Once I'm out of the barn, it's just me and Jasper and open air. You know the feeling."

"I guess that means you don't want company."

He had Jasper out of the stall now. He put his foot into a stirrup and mounted up. The stallion danced and snorted, eager to be moving, but Hunter held him in check for another moment. "You've been working all night. Get some sleep. I'll come over later. We'll drive into Brenham and get something to eat."

"Did you even think of calling me, Hunter?"

Since he wasn't sure in his own mind why he hadn't, he wasn't in a mood to admit or discuss it now. "See you around seven tonight."

Three

Erica's Art was the name of her shop and Erica loved it. She loved stocking it with her designs and watching customers pick and choose from the collection of quilts and jackets and then leave pleased to own something she'd created. It surprised her that she was a good merchant. As an artist, she preferred solitude to produce her creations, and she was shy when she had to assume the role of salesperson. That was Jason's thing and he was so good at it that she didn't often have to actually deal with a customer. Everything else about the shop she loved, even the end-of-month accounting. It was satisfying to run the numbers and find they were solidly in the black.

Today, she had holed up in the office at the rear of the store preparing tax records for their accountant. Finally done, she closed the books just as a ping sounded, announcing a customer. She glanced up, caught a glimpse of a tall man entering the store before he moved from her line of vision to browse. Jason had returned from a lunch date a few minutes ago, which relieved her of having to drop what she was working on to go out and sell. She knew it was silly that she found it awkward standing by while perfect strangers fingered her quilts, or squinted critically at her jackets. She had no problem accepting that what she created and stocked in the shop wouldn't appeal to everyone, but it was so…well, awkward pretending that it wasn't somehow personal, when creating every design was, in fact, somehow *very* personal.

Turning to a shipment of fabric that had arrived an hour ago, Erica tore the wrapping from material intended for a series of jackets still in the design stage. She pulled yardage from the first bolt and ran a palm over the weave, pleased with both texture and color. She itched to get started, but she'd have to wait until Jason could help her take the shipment upstairs to her studio to begin cutting. She made all originals of her jacket designs herself before handing the pattern and fabric to the two women who sewed the numbered replicas. She never authorized more than six of a single design.

"Psst! Erica, come out here for a minute." Jason stuck his head around the door, doing funny things with his eyebrows.

She frowned at him. "What?"

"You'll see," he hissed. "Just drop that and walk out here on the floor."

"Not until you tell me why." She'd been on the receiving end of his practical jokes before. Refusing the bait, she reached for a second bolt.

He gave an exasperated sound but had to withdraw when someone—the customer, she assumed—called, "Hey, I'm on my lunch hour here."

"Sorry, I was just consulting with the designer," Jason said, giving the man a boyish smile, one that was usually effective in softening up the most hardened sales-resistant browser. As she tore at the wrapping, she heard Jason launch full bore into his sales pitch. Apparently the customer's choice was narrowed to one of the evening jackets. Dismissing them, she removed silk shantung in a stunning shade of crimson from the packing material. She held the length of silk up to the light, visualizing a beaded design. Jet beading, she decided with a forefinger pressed to her lips. With a long black skirt or skinny black pants, it would make a fabulous holiday outfit. She reached automatically for her sketch pad.

"Why don't we ask Erica to help us out." Jason was again at the door, but this time he'd dragged the customer with him.

It took her a moment to bring them into focus. She looked beyond Jason into dark eyes deeply set in an unshaven face of chiseled angles and shadowy planes, a bone-deep tan—which she knew did not originate in a tanning booth—and hair a rich, sun-streaked, tobacco-brown. He was tall with an athlete's build and wore a battered leather jacket and black T-shirt. He looked tough and not quite housebroken. She noted all this with her artist's eye before realizing with an unsettling start that he was studying her, as well. Setting her sketch pad aside, she said, "What's the problem?"

"No problem." Jason glanced at his customer as if dishing him up on a platter for Erica. "This is Hunter McCabe. He's thinking of buying his mother a jacket for her birthday. Hunter, meet the artist herself, Erica Stewart."

"My pleasure." Hunter leaned around Jason and extended a hand.

"Hello." With no other option, she put her hand in his and found it as hard as his jaw. She quickly withdrew hers. He definitely did not spend his days behind a desk.

"From Hunter's description of his mother," Jason said, beaming at the two of them, "she's probably about your size, Erica. Am I right?" he asked Hunter.

"Yeah, but that's pretty much where the resemblance ends."

Erica flushed as his gaze held hers a heartbeat too long, before dropping to her chin, then drifting down past her midriff all the way to her feet. Her bare feet. She had a habit of kicking off her shoes while she worked. It irritated her that she hadn't remembered to put them on after getting up from her desk and tackling the new shipments.

"Erica's a size six," Jason said helpfully. "I know it's difficult to judge one person's size by another, but if you think she's about Erica's height and weight, we should be safe in choosing a size six."

Standing with his arms crossed, Hunter cocked his head, considering. "I'd know for sure if you'd put on one of your jackets."

"Great idea." This from Jason.

"Jason, I don't think—" But he was off like a shot. "Excuse me," she said to Hunter, then turned to find her shoes. Something about the way he was looking at her made her feel stripped as bare as her feet. Which was a ridiculous reaction, she told herself, gazing around the tiny room. Where the heck had she put her shoes?

"Looking for these?"

She turned to see him pluck her shoes from beneath the pile of wrapping paper on the floor. "Yes, thanks." She took them and stood on one leg to put them on, thinking she must look like a flamingo. That done, she took a deep breath, straightened, tugged her sweater down over her jeans and met his eyes. He was openly amused.

"Do you always work in bare feet?"

"It's a habit and a silly one," she said. "I somehow shed my shoes once I get caught up in what I'm doing." What was keeping Jason?

He leaned one shoulder against the door frame, as if settling in. "If that's the secret to your creativity, then I'd forget trying to break it. I don't know much about quilts or fashion, but I'm told an Erica Stewart label is the hottest thing going."

"We've been very fortunate," she said, and went back to her desk before looking at him again. "Tell me something about your mother, her hair, eyes. Just because we're the same size doesn't mean our style and color should be the same. Does she tend to wear subtle colors or bold ones?"

"Her eyes are blue and her hair is blond. She tints it to cover the gray, I think. Not that I've ever seen a gray hair."

She put a hand to her own wild and curly mane. No matter what she did, her hair tended to take on a life of its own in Houston's humidity. "And colors?" she prompted.

"Not too much bold stuff. Subtle, I guess." His gaze went to her black T-shirt and jeans before wandering back to her face. "She hangs out with a lot of artists, but she doesn't dress like one. She doesn't look like one, either," he added.

Jason returned just then. "The champagne silk, I think." He displayed the jacket over one arm with a flourish. "Size six. How tall is she? Erica's five-six. If your mother's around the same height, this should be just perfect. Come out from behind that desk and try it on, Erica. He needs to see it on to get the full effect."

"His mother's a blond and she has blue eyes," Erica said, staying put. "The champagne should be right for her. There's no need—"

"Champagne is right for anyone, sugar. What Hunter needs to see is whether it fits. Come on."

Before coming out from behind her desk, she shot Jason a dark look, promising retribution. Nevertheless, she allowed him to help her into the jacket, noting with a quick glance at Hunter that he was clearly enjoying the whole charade.

"You should be the model for your designs," he said, looking her over. "You'd sell those things faster than you could make them."

"We're already selling them faster than we can make them." Head cocked, Jason studied the picture Erica made wearing the jacket. "And you're absolutely right, Hunter. Wearing that little number with those black jeans, she strikes just the right note of sexy sophistication, don't you think?"

"Damn straight."

With a huff of exasperation, Erica took the jacket off. The man was a potential buyer, so she bit back a tart remark and conjured up a professional smile. "If your mother is not pleased with the color or style, we'll be happy to exchange it for something else."

"Trust me, she'll love it. And can I wait while you gift wrap it?"

"Certainly. Jason will take care of you." Back behind her desk again, she picked up the sketch pad and folded her arms around it…for some reason. "Right, Jason?"

"Right, sugar. I live to gift wrap." Jason held the jacket up and studied it with a critical eye. "I'm thinking something in that pearlized cream paper and possibly the pale gold ribbon, the gauzy stuff, Erica. What d'you think?"

"Fine." She again made the mistake of looking into those dark, amused eyes.

"Cream and gold sounds perfect to me," he said, grinning.

Beaming, Jason moved toward the door. "Your mom will absolutely love this, Hunter. And be sure to tell her to look at the next issue of *Texas Today.* Erica's been named one of the mag's Twenty Women to Watch." Jason's smile flashed at Erica. "She's one terrific gal, our Erica."

Grinding her teeth, Erica said, "You'll want to start wrapping that, Jason. Mr. McCabe is on his lunch hour."

"You betcha." With a saucy wink, he left them.

Hunter moved from his position at the door into her office. "I saw the article in yesterday's paper. Your stuff looked good, but I don't think the real impact of your work was captured in a newspaper spread. Have you considered printing up a catalog? Those quilts would look great in full color, but the jackets would really pop out. It pays to advertise."

"Are you in that line of work?"

"Advertising? No, I'm an architect."

She couldn't help giving him a quick once-over. In jeans and a leather jacket over a dark T-shirt and scuffed boots, he didn't look like an architect. He looked like a man who worked outdoors. "Really."

"Cross my heart." He said it with a slow smile. "I'm dressed for fieldwork today. I've got a couple of jobs going and I like to keep close tabs on any work in progress." He glanced at his boots. "I just left a job where the crew struck a waterline and flooded the whole site."

"So you'll need to get back, I imagine."

"The situation's under control," he said, sitting on the edge of her desk. "Tell me about the *Texas Today* thing. Something like that doesn't just fall into a person's lap. Congratulations."

"Thank you. As I said, Jason and I have been—"

"Fortunate. Yeah, but it's you who's been named, not Jason. You're the artist. You're the designer." He paused, looking at her. "At least, I assume the designs are yours exclusively, right?"

"They're my designs, but Jason is a talented artist. And he's absolutely tops in promoting our shop." She put the sketch pad down on the desk. "Mr. McCabe, I don't want to seem rude, but I still have a lot to do here." She glanced at the drape of red silk spilling over her drafting board. "There never seems to be enough hours in a day to get everything done."

"I hear you." He stood up and looked at her ringless left hand. "Is there a Mr. Stewart?"

Not anymore. The thought came quickly and with its usual swift, piercing pain. But her reply was simply "No."

The look she gave him was usually good at discouraging even the most determined man. Something in the tone of her voice or the look on her face usually put them off. It worked now with McCabe.

"Okay," he said, moving to the door. "I'll let you get back to it. Nice meeting you."

"Thank you. I hope your mother likes the jacket. As I said, if she's not pleased or needs a different size or color, have her bring it in. We'll do our best to find something she likes."

"She's never returned anything I've ever given her, but I guess there could be a first time."

"Yes, well…be sure to pick up a card on your way out, so she'll have our phone number." She picked up the sketch pad again.

He glanced at it. "Something new?"

"Just some raw sketches. If I don't make some effort to save them, they go out of my head and are lost. I try to keep—" She paused, caught herself up. She could hardly get her work done if she kept chatting with him. "I don't want to be rude, Mr. McCabe, but I really have a lot to do."

He smiled. "Hunter. Mr. McCabe is what my accountant calls me."

"I'll just check to see if Jason's finished." She moved from behind her desk even though she had to brush past Hunter to leave. Jason must be done but was probably dawdling over wrapping the gift in a very unsubtle attempt to prolong conversation between her and a man. He never tired of trying to stimulate her social life even though he knew she had no interest in developing a relationship. That part of her life was over.

"Okay, he was a hottie and don't you try to tell me you didn't notice." Jason stood with one foot in the door of the office and an eye on the floor of the shop where a couple of customers were browsing. "Also, he did not wear a wedding ring."

"Which means nothing. Nowadays, not wearing a ring is almost de rigueur for some men," Erica said, tearing the wrapping from a bolt of electric-blue fabric.

"Yummy, I love it when you talk sexy."

"Oh, would you look at this color! I love this blue. I think a lining in just the right shade of green, clear bottle-green…" Her eyes went unfocused as she visualized the effect in her mind.

"He's just the kind of guy you should be dating," Jason persisted, ignoring the possibility that McCabe was married. "He was driving a sixty-thousand-dollar SUV and his boots cost at least half that. If your libido didn't perk up at just being in the room with Hunter McCabe, I'm gonna give up. It means you're dead."

"The best part of that sales pitch is you're thinking of giving up."² She tossed the blue bolt aside and ripped open another one. "I think those customers are ready to check out."

He glanced at the two women who were trying to make a decision about a quilt. "They're not even close. I'm serious, Erica. I saw the way McCabe was looking at you, as if you were crème brûlée and he'd just been told he could have dessert."

She placed a bolt on the growing stack behind her, then fixed him with a direct look. "Jason, how many times do I have to tell you that I am not interested in dating? And don't start with that your-life-is-incomplete-without-sex line. I'm very satisfied designing clothes and quilts. You know yourself I don't have enough time left over to grocery shop, so when would I have the time to have a relationship with a man?"

"If you gave yourself a chance to fall in love again, you'd make the time. It's normal. It's natural. All human beings need the physical and spiritual connections that come from a sexual relationship."

"Speaking of that," she said, tearing into another package, "what happened when you went to see your dad?"

"Same as always. Two minutes after I got there, he started. If we hadn't been at a restaurant, it would have been a huge scene. As it was, Susan stopped him, midtirade. She handles him better than my mother ever did, which makes me wonder how it came about that he married someone who doesn't ask how high when he says jump. My mother always rolled right over under his overbearing ways. Anyway, Susan threatened to dump her coffee in his lap if he didn't calm down. You can imagine how lovely the rest of the meal was. If it hadn't been for her playing mediator, I would have left in the middle of the meal. The man can be a real jerk."

"Maybe you should cut him some slack until he comes to terms with your lifestyle, Jace."

Leaning against the door frame, Jason got a stubborn look on his face. "That is such bullshit, Erica. He's known forever that I'm gay. Just because I never said it, he's trying to pretend it's not a fact. The only reason this came up is he happened to run into Stephen and me at that restaurant and he was with a couple of VIPs he does business with, like he was so afraid they'd guess my little secret. Like it has anything to do with him, damn it. Next time, maybe I'll bring Derek Kingsley," he threatened darkly. "See how he reacts to that."

"Speaking of jerks," Erica put in dryly. "It's Derek Kingsley, not your father, who comes instantly to mind."

"Which is exactly the point. And until Dad accepts me for who I am, I'm going to devote myself to pissing him off."

"Very mature of you," she told him. "And that should make the next family gathering just lovely. Here, make yourself useful." She shoved two of the fabric bolts into his arms. "Help me haul this stuff upstairs. I've got several ideas for using it and you've got merchandise to sell."

Hunter hoped to avoid seeing Morton when he took his mother's gift to her on the evening of her birthday. He planned to stay long enough to have a drink and watch her open the gift, then cut out before Morton showed up. The older he got, the less Hunter was able to handle Morton with his gigantic ego and his callous attitude toward Lillian. Tonight, for example, she would be wined and dined royally, which was Morton's style, after which she would be relegated to the background of his life until some other event required him to turn his attention to her again. At which time he'd do something else lavish and over the top, all in keeping with his public image, of course, then go back to ignoring her. Hunter had long since stopped trying to figure out why she hadn't walked out years ago. There was apparently something that kept their relationship together, but what it could be was a mystery to him.

Could be his disgust with Morton was plain, old-fashioned jealousy, he admitted, not of the man's success in his career, but of the place he occupied in Lillian's life. There had been a time when Hunter and his mother had been as close as any parent and child could be. In spite of the fact that Lillian had remarried after the death of his dad, Hunter had known he was first in her life. Even after Jocelyn's birth, he and his mom still had a special bond. When exactly that had all changed he wasn't quite certain, he thought now, frowning. He simply knew that he'd realized one day that their special bond was gone. She'd somehow turned into a ghost of herself and he had yet to figure out why. What wasn't hard to see was that Morton was suddenly front and center, placing Hunter—and Jocelyn, too—as distant also-rans.

But today was his mother's birthday and he should have outgrown old resentments. Besides, giving her the jacket as a birthday gift offered him a chance at maybe finding out a little more about Erica. If his mother had any passion besides fulfilling her role as the perfect wife to Morton, it was her participation in the arts community in Houston. If, as Hank said, she was familiar with Erica's work, she would probably know something about the artist herself.

He couldn't remember when he'd been as intrigued by a woman as he was with Erica Stewart, a woman he'd barely met and about whom he knew nothing. When he'd left the shop after buying the jacket, all he knew was that he wanted to see her again. In fact, for a couple of days he'd tried to think of an excuse to go back to the shop, but she'd been anything but encouraging in the few minutes he'd spent with her, and he found himself oddly unwilling to chance an outright rejection. He wasn't sure why he was so intrigued. She was beautiful, of course, but there was something else. Those big gray eyes looked as if they held deep secrets, and her jumble of dark curly hair invited a man's hand. But it was her mouth that he liked best—

wide and bow-shaped—entirely at odds with the serious-ness of her eyes and attitude. Downright sexy, it was. Hell, thinking about how she'd taste, he'd been on the point of asking her out before he remembered Kelly.

Probably a good thing the feeling wasn't mutual.

His mother's face lit with pleasure when she opened the door. "Hunter, darling, it's so good to see you."

"Happy birthday, Mom."

She made a face. "Don't remind me." Lifting her cheek for his kiss, she caught his arm and pulled him over the threshold. "I've got your favorite, Maker's Mark. And I wish you'd join Morton and me for dinner. He's taking me to Annie's. You know you'd enjoy it."

"Too much to do after I leave here," he told her. "I've got a couple of hairy jobs going and the weather hasn't co-operated." It had rained hard the day before and the sites were still soaked. The construction boss had been forced to send the crews home on both jobs. More rain was fore-cast and construction on both projects was not far enough along to do any inside work. "I'll take a rain check, so to speak, okay?"

"I should hold you to that, but I won't even try because I know you don't mean it."

"Did you hear from Jocelyn?" he asked as they left the foyer. "Where is she, incidentally? Last I heard, she was in Key West trying her hand at journalism, but to be hon-est, the newspaper sounded more like an underground pub-lication than a bona fide newspaper. Let's hope the guy who claims to be the editor doesn't turn out to be a jerk."

"She called to wish me a happy birthday this morning, but she wasn't very forthcoming as to how the job was going. The last time we talked, she couldn't say enough about her editor, but today she barely mentioned him or the job. I know what you're thinking, Hunter, and I agree.

The last thing she needs is to get involved in another rocky relationship. Of course, I can't discuss it with Morton."

If there was anything of consequence his mother could discuss with Morton, it would surprise him, Hunter thought. He made a mental note to check on Jocelyn. His half sister did not need another aborted relationship to add to the mistakes she'd already chalked up.

Lillian led him down a hall to the darkly sumptuous den. He deliberately avoided looking in the eyes of the massive ram that was mounted over the mantel. Morton was an avid big-game hunter and it pleased him to show the world what he shot and killed. The den was the only room in the house whose decor didn't reflect Lillian's gracious, tasteful influence, but it looked exactly the way Morton wanted.

Stopping at the bar, she poured Maker's Mark in a short glass and handed it over. "Actually, Morton's upstairs now and should be down soon to join us for a drink. He was able to leave the office early today."

Hunter kept his reaction to that off his face and lifted the glass. "Here's to a beautiful lady."

"Thank you, Hunter." She took a sip of wine from a glass she poured for herself, then brightened as he produced the gift-wrapped box. "Oh, what a lovely package. Hmm, this is probably going to be something wonderful. Dare I ask where you got it?"

"At a shop in the Village," he said, and relaxed against the bar as she set her wine aside to open it. "And before you brag about my good taste, I'll tell you it was Hank's recommendation. The artist was featured in Sunday's *Zest* and he seemed to think you'd appreciate something done by her."

"Really?" Some of her pleasure seemed to fade and a tiny line formed between her eyes. But before he could question her, Morton appeared.

"Hunter. Glad to see you." Smiling and jovial, he held out his hand and they shook. "Your mother's looking fantastic for an old lady of fifty-seven, don't you think?"

"She is," Hunter said, lifting his drink. Lillian was studying the signature wrapping paper on the package. "Go ahead, open it, Mom. I have it from the designer herself that it'll suit you."

"Who's the designer?" Morton asked on his way to the bar.

"Erica Stewart," Hunter said as Lillian pulled at the gauzy bow decorating the box.

He was looking at the gift, so he almost missed a wordless exchange between Lillian and Morton as he said Erica's name. He thought Morton muttered an obscenity, but when he glanced at the older man, he was busy pouring himself a drink from the bottle of whiskey. "Do you know her? Hank said you'd mentioned her work. He seemed to think you'd like anything she did."

"I'm sure it's lovely," Lillian murmured, removing the lid from the box. The jacket, a creation of champagne silk lavishly trimmed with Austrian crystal, was nestled in a froth of creamy tissue. Light from the chandelier overhead reflected off the crystal as Lillian stared at it, then quickly reached for the lid and covered it. Hunter thought she seemed a little pale as she set the box on the bar, and it was with some effort that she smiled. "Thank you," she managed to say in a shaky voice. "It's very nice."

"You can exchange it for something you like better," Hunter said, frowning. "They were insistent about that."

"They?" Lillian reached for her wine and quickly took a sip.

"She has a partner. He was in the shop when I bought the jacket." Still trying to make sense of her reaction, he added, "Do you recognize the artist?"

Lillian perched on the edge of the sofa, her knees tight together and her wine clutched in both hands. "Yes. She's…I think…local."

"Mom, is something wrong? You're pale as a ghost and you look upset."

"No, I'm fine. Just a little light-headed." She blinked a couple of times. "I skipped lunch and shouldn't have." She set the wine on the coffee table in front of her. "I shouldn't—"

"Maybe you should have a piece of cheese or something before you head out for dinner." He glanced at Morton. "There's something in the kitchen that she could have, isn't there?"

"I'll get it," Morton said.

Lillian waved a hand and looked distressed. "Really, it's nothing. I—"

"Humor me, Mom. While he's gone you can tell me what you know about Erica Stewart. She was…well, I guess I didn't know what to expect. She was kind of reserved but really helpful in choosing your gift. You're about the same size, so she tried this one on to give me an idea whether I thought it would fit." Her image came instantly to mind and he smiled. "She was in this black T-shirt and black jeans and she's got this curly hair—real dark—that she kept blowing to keep off her face. And big gray eyes. I was there just as she was opening a shipment of the stuff she works with and she kept grabbing up her sketch pad and scribbling in it." His chuckle was soft as he gazed into his drink. "She was po-lite—I guess she has to be—but she made it plain she wanted me to get the hell out of there so she could go back to work."

"Sounds like you got a pretty good fix on her," Morton said, returning with a plate of small cheese squares, which he handed to Lillian. "I don't know how your mother could add much to that character sketch, except to say we heard she's going to be recognized in the next issue of *Texas Today*." He reclaimed his drink. "She's named as one of their Twenty Women to Watch in Texas, if you can believe that."

"After seeing her shop, I can believe it."

Morton was shaking his head at the inexplicability of it. "Proud of it, is she?"

"But modest," Hunter said. "She went out of her way to credit her business partner. Seems he has a flair for marketing and promotion."

"Credit should probably go to more than her business partner," Morton said, taking a piece of Lillian's cheese for himself. "There's a sugar daddy somewhere, mark my words. She's auctioning something at the symphony fundraiser your mother's friends have drummed up. You need to know somebody to get in there."

"Someone like Mom, I assume," Hunter said, wanting to knock the smirk off Morton's face. He wasn't sure why, but he felt a fierce desire to defend Erica. He didn't like the idea that Erica might compromise herself for a shot at publicizing her art.

"Considering the success of her label, the auction committee was lucky she was willing to participate," Lillian said quietly, nibbling on a bit of cheese. "And I'm not a member of that committee." There was some color in her cheeks now, but she still seemed not quite right to Hunter. It was always like this when he had to be around the two of them, a tense undercurrent with Morton throwing his weight around and Lillian holding her breath for fear that her son and her husband would get into a row. But Hunter wasn't in the mood tonight.

"Is Erica going to be there or is she just donating something for the auction?" he asked.

"Why, can we stick you with a couple of tickets?" Morton said, rubbing his hands together. "Your mother's always looking for takers. And it'll take some of the heat off me. I warn you, though, they're overpriced."

"Hunter isn't interested in charity events for the symphony," she said softly.

"Somehow, I can't see Erica at an event like that," Hunter said, smiling at the memory of her standing barefoot in her office amid a sea of wrapping paper. "Won't everybody be wearing shoes?"

"What?" With cheese suspended in midair, Lillian looked at him, frowning.

"She has this goofy habit of kicking her shoes off." Hunter headed to the bar to refill his drink. Morton intercepted him and did the honors while Hunter took the lid off the box to get another look at the jacket. "Are you sure this is okay, Mom? There are quilts as well as these jackets. And there're other things from some pretty spiffy designers in the shop. I don't know anything about this stuff, but Jason was pretty proud of what they carry. Me, personally, I liked Erica's stuff best."

"Jason Rowland," Lillian murmured.

Hunter gave her a quick glance. "You know him?"

"He's Bob Rowland's boy," Morton told him.

"Who's Bob Rowland?" Hunter asked.

"One of Morton's business acquaintances." With a look at Morton, Lillian got to her feet, setting the cheese aside. Then, to Hunter, "I could never be disappointed in any gift from you, dear. Thank you. It's simply beautiful and I'll treasure it."

"If you're sure…" He still felt something was wrong here, but he didn't have a clue what it was.

Morton set his glass down with a thump. "Well, our reservations at Annie's will be lost if we don't leave soon. Hunter, you sure you won't join us?"

"Thanks, but I've got some paperwork on my desk that I can't ignore."

Lillian touched his arm. "When will I see you again, Hunter?"

"Not sure. I'll call you." He bent and kissed her cheek. "Happy birthday, Mom."

Lillian returned to the den to find Morton studying the jacket, still in the box, its decorative trim twinkling like so many diamonds. "What are the chances he'd choose her shop from all the places in this town to buy a gift, babe? Damn thing looks expensive, too. She's making a killing selling that flashy stuff."

"I can never wear it."

"No?"

"No." Lillian stood with her arms tight around herself. "And it's not flashy, Morton. It's quite beautiful, really. I just—I mean, it's not…possible for me to wear something Erica's designed. I'd be afraid lightning might strike me dead."

"Oh, get a grip. You don't even know the woman. And go get whatever jacket you intend to wear tonight. I meant it when I said they wouldn't hold our reservations. We've got twenty minutes before they go to someone else."

With a sigh, she turned to do as she was told.

Four

Erica scribbled her signature at the bottom of the umpteenth document put in front of her and tossed the pen on the table. "Well, I hope that does it, Michael. My fingers are cramped from all that signing."

"It's the last for a while." Her financial adviser collected the documents from her desk, tidied them up and slipped them into his briefcase. "We'll watch both the stock and bond markets and if we decide you need to move some of your assets, I'll give you a call."

"Tell you what," she said, standing up. Her shoulders were tight and she put a hand up to massage her neck. "I appreciate your advice, Michael, but I've been keeping pretty close tabs on my investments. I'll give you a call when I'm ready to make other changes."

"Erica, Erica, Erica..." He was shaking his head. "I know you feel quite confident in some of the choices you've made on your own recently, but—"

"I'm happy with all the choices I've made recently, Michael," she said dryly. It irritated her that he thought he needed to guide her like a blind person through the mysteries of money management.

He gave a pained smile. "Well, of course, but these are precarious times in the financial world and there are pitfalls that you may not be aware of. If you'll allow me—"

"I'll call you, Michael." She'd relied on Michael Carlton's expertise to manage her money at a time when she had little or no interest in whether it grew or not, but that had been a few years ago. She was now quite capable of managing on her own with occasional professional advice…when she asked for it.

As Michael snapped the locks on his briefcase, she came around from behind her desk to escort him out of the shop. She would have to let him out, as it was a few minutes after closing time and Jason had left for the day. But instead of following her out of her office, Michael put out a hand and stopped her.

"Since business is done for the day, how about having dinner with me?" he said. Michael was a man of medium height, dapper and exquisitely coordinated in his Brooks Brothers suit and tasseled loafers. But even features and a flair for clothes didn't quite disguise the fact that he was about as interesting as a financial prospectus. Dinner with him would probably include a lengthy analysis of the day's market activity.

"Thank you, Michael, but I'm working on some new designs and they've kept me up several nights in a row. I think I'll have an early night."

"You have to eat something, don't you?" To her surprise, he reached out and brushed a stray curl from her cheek. She withdrew slightly, resisting the urge to actually slap at his hand. Was the man making a pass?

"I'll get takeout," she told him, her hand on the doorknob.

"Then a drink. You have time for that, don't you?" His tone lowered and his blue eyes roved lazily over her face.

He moved in a little closer and she took a matching step back against the open door. "You'll be nice and relaxed, then you can have that takeout and snuggle in for the night. Better yet—" he gave what he probably assumed was a sexy smile "—I'll snuggle with you."

She thought she heard the faint tingle of the shop door and with a sigh of relief realized that Jason must have forgotten something. The tension she felt eased and she said laughingly, "Michael, you can't be serious. What are you doing?"

Now he had both hands on her waist. "I'm making a move, Erica, something I've wanted to do for a long time. But I knew you weren't ready." He pulled her a little closer and touched his lips to her temple. "You're beautiful, but it's like you don't realize how beautiful. You drive me crazy."

"Oh, please, Michael. If that's a line, it's a ridiculous one."

"See, you think you have to deny it." He sniffed her hair and it was all she could do not to laugh. Wait'll she told Jason. He'd get such a hoot out of this. She was startled when he suddenly pulled her close enough that she felt just how aroused he was. "I love your hair. I'd like to just lose myself in it," he said.

"Michael, stop. I mean it. You don't want to cause a scene, do you?" Until now, she'd had both hands on his chest and felt reasonably certain she could shove him away. But suddenly he had both his arms locked around her and she couldn't break his hold. And now he was trying to kiss her! Repulsed, she averted her face.

"Stop it, Michael!"

"Just one kiss, Erica," he muttered, rooting around in the vicinity of her ear. "You're the sexiest woman I've ever known. Jesus, I want you."

"Well, get over it," she told him, still straining away from him. A kiss from Michael Carlton wasn't going to be pleasant, but with his arms like a vise around her, she was afraid she was going to get one if Jason didn't appear soon. The man was much stronger than he looked. She'd have to get rough, she supposed. Wiggling against him was doing more harm than good. And then, somehow, he forced her up against the door and was fumbling under her skirt. In no time, he'd found her panties and next thing he'd have his hand where no man had touched her in nine years!

"Michael, stop it! I mean it." Outraged, she tried to push away from him, but he was fully aroused and now working at his zipper. My God, she thought, did he think they were going to have sex right here in her office…standing up, with her resisting in every way she could think of? There was a name for that. With a mighty heave, she shoved him back and aimed a kick between his thighs. It missed, but landed on his kneecap, knocking him off balance and giving her time to scramble out the door. She slammed it shut and twisted the lock.

For a moment, she stood outside breathing hard, thanking fate that Jason had had the forethought to install a lock on the office door to keep nosy customers out when neither of them occupied it. Just then, Michael rattled the doorknob. When nothing happened, he gave a quick, hard rap on the door. "Erica, let me out."

"After you've cooled off."

She heard a low chuckle behind her and turned, ready to light into Jason for waiting until things got out of hand before showing himself. But it wasn't Jason standing a few feet away with his arms folded over his chest and looking mightily amused. It was Hunter McCabe.

"Are we having fun yet?"

She shoved her hair back from her face with both hands

and realized that she was trembling. "I thought you were Jason."

"Not even close." Grinning, he moved his gaze to the door where Michael was now kicking and banging and cursing.

"Damn it, let me out of here, Erica!"

Hunter winced. "If this is the way you treat interested suitors," he said, "it's no wonder you're still single."

"I have no interested suitors and that's the way I like it," she said. Ignoring the racket Michael was making, she told herself she hadn't felt so much threatened as outraged. And it was adrenaline making her a little shaky, not fear. "And how did you get in here?"

"I came in the front door."

"That's impossible. Jason locked up."

"This is crazy, Erica. Open the door this instant!"

Controlling his smile, Hunter glanced at the door. "I think he means business."

"And I think he can stay in there until hell freezes over, which is what he deserves."

Now grinning, Hunter asked, "Will you let him out before morning?"

"I suppose I'll have to." She didn't want to admit it, but she was just now realizing that opening the door to let him out might be a bit risky. He'd revealed a surprising streak of aggression. But he could hardly do anything with Hunter here. With a look of disgust, she flipped the lock and took a hasty step backward as the door was flung wide. It brought her up against Hunter's solid, male frame.

Breathing hard and flushed with fury, Michael opened his mouth to say something, but Hunter firmly cleared his throat, and whatever it was died unspoken. Settling for a dignified retreat, Michael said stiffly, "That was totally unnecessary, Erica. You completely misunderstood my intentions, but we can discuss it another time."

"I don't think so, Michael."

Hunter stepped around them to pick up Michael's briefcase. "Are you going to introduce us?" he said, handing it over.

"My *former* financial adviser, Michael Carlton," she said, then added in a frosty tone, "On your way out, leave the papers I just signed on the counter, Michael. The only thing we have to discuss is whatever arrangements are necessary to dissolve our association, which we'll do first thing Monday morning by phone. Don't—" she put up a hand as he tried again to speak "—don't insult me further with a lame explanation for what you did. Just consider your apology offered and be thankful I don't mention this to your father. Goodbye."

"His father?" Hunter repeated as they watched Michael skulk out.

"Stanley Carlton. He's a senior partner in the firm and the person I originally consulted."

"How'd Michael get in the picture?"

"After a while, Stanley began to suggest that Michael fill in for him. Since I knew Stanley was still overseeing everything, I didn't particularly object." She breathed out a long breath and resisted an urge to wrap her arms around herself. "It just never occurred to me that he had anything like *this* on his mind," she muttered, looking around in a distracted way for her keys. She was more than ready to go home. "All he ever seemed interested in was how to increase dividends and shelter money."

"I don't know why you'd assume that," Hunter said, taking her jacket from a coatrack. "He was handed a golden opportunity, he's male, he's apparently not gay. I, for one, am not surprised."

She swept up her keys and snapped off the light. "If you're suggesting that he has an eye on my portfolio, you don't have to draw me a picture. I get it. Now." She paused, looking over the interior of the shop to be sure no other customer had wandered in after closing hours. Seeing no one, she allowed Hunter to help her into her jacket. "It just irritates me that I was caught off guard. I didn't have a clue what he was thinking."

"I can't help feeling a little sorry for him," Hunter said.

"You're kidding."

He shrugged. "Seeing you on a regular basis and being forced to keep your relationship strictly businesslike must have been torture for the poor bastard. And I wasn't suggesting he had designs on your portfolio. I was suggesting he had designs on you, 'the sexiest woman in the world.'" He made quotation marks with his fingers.

Okay, he was amused again, at her expense. But now Erica was beginning to see the humor in it, too. She made a disgusted sound and laughed. "You heard that?"

"It's a good line."

"Well, I never gave him any sign that I'd welcome that…or any line." She sighed and looked at him. "And I should apologize that you were dragged into something so distasteful." She paused, wondering now at his reason for stopping in. She glanced at the counter, expecting to see the gift box with the jacket he'd bought for his mother. Except for the papers that Michael had left, the counter was clear. "I assume you're here to exchange your mother's gift?"

"Why would I do that? She loved it."

"Oh. Well—"

"I was driving by and realized it was closing time. I thought you might let me buy you a drink. My mother went speechless when she opened that box. Do you get that reaction often?"

Erica stuffed the financial papers in her purse. "We

haven't had a problem selling that particular style. I'm glad she liked it." She was also glad that Jason had adjusted the lights into overnight mode so that the place was dimly lit. The way Hunter was studying her face, he'd be able to tell she was a little flustered. It was beginning to dawn on her that if she hadn't managed to slam the door and lock Michael in her office, he might very well have finished what he started.

She blinked when, with a finger beneath her chin, Hunter tilted her face up. "He didn't hurt you, did he?"

"No." She shifted away from him, looked down at her keys. "It was just that he surprised me. I wasn't expecting anything like that and he's always seemed so…well, harmless."

"No man's harmless in a situation like that. He's probably been fantasizing about you for a while and thought he'd take his chances. I'm glad I happened to show up when I did, but to tell the truth, you didn't look as if you needed much help."

"Well, he made me mad. I told him to stop and he didn't." The adrenaline rush was fading a little now, and standing alone in her shop with a man like Hunter gave her an entirely different feeling. "Maybe the next time a woman tells him no, he'll believe it," she said with a militant look in her eye.

"I think he got the message," Hunter said dryly. "If not, his bruised knuckles will remind him."

She smiled in spite of herself. "He was banging pretty hard on the door, wasn't he? I hope he has trouble typing on his stupid computer."

Grinning, he propped an elbow on the counter. "Seeing how ticked off he was, I'm wondering how you were going to let him out of there. Did you realize you had a tiger by the tail?"

"Not until I slammed the door. I owe you for arriving when you did."

"Then how 'bout that drink? I'm thinking a margarita, top shelf. Cuervo Gold."

She felt a new rush of nerves. "Oh, I don't—"

He straightened up with a pained look. "Please don't say it. You don't drink."

"I do, but—"

"Good. There's a quiet little bar about three blocks away. You can follow me in your car or I'll drop you back here when we're done."

A few minutes ago, when she'd turned and found Hunter and not Jason at her back, she'd been surprised by her reaction. In his battered leather jacket, his worn jeans and boots, he'd looked a lot more dark and dangerous than Michael, who'd just assaulted her. But it wasn't fear that had streaked through her. Just the opposite. Something more elemental and exciting. She wasn't used to reacting to a man in that way, and had almost forgotten what it was like.

"I'll follow in my car," she said. And without giving herself time for second thoughts, she walked with him to the door.

Five

Hunter picked a booth toward the back of the bar for its privacy. This was his first opportunity to spend one-on-one time with Erica and he intended to make the most of it. Since buying the jacket, he hadn't been able to put her out of his mind. He wasn't sure what it was about her, but sitting across from her now, he knew he didn't want to be anywhere else at the moment.

When their margaritas were set in front of them, he lifted his, waited for her and then touched his glass to hers. He'd like to say something she'd find sexy and charming, but he had a feeling she was a woman who wouldn't appreciate anything that sounded like a practiced line, and besides, she struck him as needing a slow hand. He had a feeling, too, that it would be worth the wait. "To a new financial adviser," he said.

"Absolutely." She took a dainty taste. A bit of salt clung to her lip and she licked it off. As he watched her, it was all he could do not to reach out and maybe run his thumb over the enticing curve of her lower lip, then bring it up to his lips for a taste of her.

"Hmm, that's good," she said. "Tart-sweet and smooth as silk."

"It hits the spot," he agreed.

"The margaritas are so good here. In fact, Jason and I often stop after we close the shop. I can only have one, though. Two and there's no way I would be able to do any work when I get home."

"What kind of work is waiting for you at home?"

"New designs. For the jackets, there's always next season to be working on. The quilts are not seasonal, but I can duplicate a design only a few times, so I have to keep coming up with new ones. I've been amazed at how well they sell, but it means I feel pushed to keep ahead of the demand."

"Couldn't someone else work at the shop? Besides Jason, I mean. That would leave you free to create new designs during the day."

"Not really. My studio is upstairs, which is where a lot of the actual physical labor is done and, to tell the truth, it doesn't seem like work. But I don't like selling so much. That's Jason's thing." She shrugged and smiled. "I'm cranking out the product and he sells it. For us, it's been a winning combination."

"Let me get this straight," he said, hitching his chair forward. He'd like to take her hand, but he sensed she'd shy away from anything approaching intimacy. "You spend your days at your studio above the shop, then you work on creating new designs in the evenings at home. When do you have time to socialize?"

"I guess I don't have much of a social life." She was sitting with elbows on the table, holding the margarita loosely in both hands, but as he leaned closer, she eased back, pushing at her dark hair and tucking a strand behind one ear. "It's not the way many people would choose to live, but it suits me."

"My mother mentioned one of your creations will be auctioned at the gala next weekend. That should generate even more demand."

"It's incredible. I don't know how that happened, I really don't. I had a call from the auction chairperson just out of the blue. I was thrilled as it certainly is a golden opportunity."

"No inside connections, huh?"

"At the symphony?" She smiled. "No. I haven't even been to the symphony in years, not since—" She stopped and, with a stricken look, quickly reached for the napkin and touched it to her lips. When she raised her eyes to his a moment later, they were calm and clear. "Are you a fan?"

"Not really. My mother used to nag me about going, but I liked baseball better." He decided not to try digging out the reason for whatever that look meant, at least not right now. "You'll be there when they auction your jacket, I assume?" When she nodded, he added, "Do you have a date?"

"A date?"

"An escort. You're not going alone to the gala, are you?"

"Oh, no. Jason and I are going together. He's almost as excited as I am."

"You and Jason are very tight."

"We are." She twirled the stem of her drink and smiled. "He's not only my business partner, but he's also my best friend. In fact, the shop was his brainchild. I'd still be designing in the spare bedroom of my house and squirreling everything away in a closet if he hadn't practically shoved me out of that house and back into the real world."

"What was going on that you'd retreated from the real world?"

She stopped and actually pressed her fingers to her lips. "I'm talking too much. I don't—it's the margarita." She fiddled with her napkin, hesitating so long that he thought she wouldn't say any more. He guessed she'd probably gone through a rough divorce and he wondered at the stupidity of a man to let a woman like her get away.

"It was a dark time for me," she explained finally. "I'd thrown myself into designing to keep from…simply dying." She gave a soft laugh. "That sounds pretty melodramatic, but that was how I felt at the time."

"Was it a nasty divorce?"

Her face went quiet and sad. "No." After a second, she looked up at him. "Could we change the subject?"

"I have an idea."

She gave him a skeptical look. "Okay, so long as we change the subject."

"It's changed." He held up both hands. "You come to the gala with me and let Jason find himself a real date."

"Thanks, but I think I'll stick with my original plan." She gave him a smile as if to take the sting out of her refusal.

"Why am I not surprised?" he said dryly. Leaning back, he laid an arm over the back of the seat. "But just so I have the full picture here, you're not involved with anyone right now, are you?"

She took a tiny sip of her drink. "Under the circumstances, anyone who was seriously interested wouldn't be very long, would they?"

"Depends on the circumstances."

Her smile faded as she studied the remains of the margarita in her glass. "My days are crammed with the demands of my work and the shop, Hunter. That's my life now and I like it as it is. It only makes sense that good relationships blossom when a couple has the luxury of time to spend together, don't you think?"

"Yeah, I guess that does make sense." Kelly and her expectations flashed in his mind. He wasn't spending enough time with her for a relationship to blossom—to use Erica's word—and he wondered at his lack of motivation to make that happen. He wondered at the strength of his desire to get to know Erica and knew his curiosity about Kelly had never been as keen. The thought made him uncomfortable. Just being here doing what he was doing made him uncomfortable, but he was doing it, anyway.

"Mom mentioned you're going to be named one of *Texas Today*'s Twenty Women to Watch," he said. "Congratulations. I know a few professional women who would kill for that."

"Well, I don't think I'd commit murder for it, but I was pretty happy." Taking a sip of her drink, she again licked a tiny salt speck from her lips. She looked away, her gray eyes thoughtful. "*Speechless* would be a better word," she told him dryly. "I don't know how it happened and I'm not sure I deserve it."

Was she serious? He studied her face. Or was she simply being modest? That wouldn't surprise him, but there seemed something more than simple modesty behind her words. "What does that mean? Of course you deserve it. They don't come up with that list by pulling names out of a hat. You've earned it with your art and the commercial success you've made marketing it."

"With Jason's help, don't forget," she said with a tiny smile. Then, as she traced the rim of her glass, her smile slipped away. "He says I'm imagining things, but from time to time, I've felt that more than a couple of the lucky breaks I've had are—" She gave him a quick look. "Don't laugh, but it's almost as if I have an unseen patron, someone who, every now and then, gives me a little boost."

"What counts as 'a little boost'?"

"Well, the auction opportunity at the gala, for example.

And the spread in the Sunday paper is another. You don't get those perks out of the blue."

"Word of mouth is a powerful thing. Your art is upscale, which means it appeals to an upscale crowd, people with taste like my mother. Hank said he heard her mention how much she admired you, which is how I decided on the Erica Stewart jacket for her birthday. A word here, a word there, and your label is hot. Enjoy it while you can. Make the most of it."

"I—we intend to." She leaned back with her fingers linked loosely on the stem of the almost-done margarita. "Who's Hank?"

"You're not the only one with a partner and Hank's mine. Hank Colson. We're co-owners of a ranch near Brenham. Do you ride?"

"Sure, cars, planes and bikes," she said, reaching for a pretzel.

He chuckled. "Horses. Do you ride horses?"

"Not in a long, long time." The troubled look in her gray eyes was gone. Now he saw only amusement as she played with the pretzel.

"But you know how?"

"I do. In fact, when I was a teenager, riding was a passion. I actually had a horse."

"Was that here in Texas?"

"Right here in Houston," she replied, raking crumbs off the table onto her napkin.

"So you have family here?"

"Not anymore. When I was sixteen, my parents got a divorce and both remarried, Dad first, two years later. Keeping a horse takes time and effort. It turned out to be more bother than either of them could manage at the time." She glanced at her watch, quickly finished off her drink and stood up.

"And that's the last time you were on a horse?" He was on his feet now, too.

"That's it," she said with a wry shrug. "I missed it, missed Misha—that was her name. But I got over it…after a while."

"So, are your parents still here in Houston?"

"No. My father and his new bride moved to Austin, and as soon as I graduated from high school, my mother remarried and moved to Dallas. They both started new families."

"And where did that leave you?"

"Left behind?" She said it with a short laugh, but as she was turned from him, reaching for her jacket, he couldn't see her face. "Hey, it was no big deal. I got over it. Besides, blended families are the norm, not the exception. I survived."

"I bet it was about the time you had to give up your horse that you discovered art."

She gave him a startled look. "I didn't discover art when I was sixteen. Riding was a passion, but art was an obsession. And since I was dealing with a lot of pain then, it became more important," she confessed, then added ruefully, "To tell the truth, I probably would have glommed on to just about anything to escape reality. Little did I know—" She stopped, almost biting her tongue. "It's the margarita. And no lunch. That must be why I'm telling you all this," she said, with a look of chagrin. "I haven't thought about Misha in a long, long time, or what I felt when my parents divorced."

Judging by the look on her face, he guessed she'd revealed more about herself than she intended. It made her all the more appealing to him. He reached into his jeans pocket for his wallet, took out a couple of bills and dropped them on the table. "You say you were sixteen when you had Misha?"

"Yes."

"I'm guessing she was a mare, smallish?"

"Yes."

He reached over and took the jacket from her. "I've got just the mount for you at the ranch, lady. In fact, that's her name—Lady. Not very original, but she's a sweet-tempered little mare and she'll take you for a ride that'll be so smooth you'll think you're at home in a rocking chair."

"And when would I find time for that?"

"Sunday. Nobody works on Sunday." Taking his time, he settled the jacket on her shoulders, then did what he'd wanted to do from the moment he'd first met her. He lifted her hair from the collar of her jacket and let it curl around his fingers, just for the feel of it. And just for a heartbeat, he let himself breathe in the scent of it.

Then she was moving away, adjusting the jacket, brushing at the front of her denim skirt, settling the strap of her purse on her shoulder. At the door, when he moved to open it, she glanced up into his eyes. "We never got around to talking about your work," she said. "Does it gobble up as much of your time as mine does?"

"It would if I let it," he told her. "But I make time to go to the ranch. Nothing like being on one of my horses, my hat on my head, the wind in my face. God, it's heaven."

"Spoken like a true Texan."

"Born and bred."

They were on the sidewalk now. She turned and gave him her hand. "Thanks for a very pleasant hour. I don't usually talk so much."

"You didn't give me an answer about Sunday. Will you go out to the ranch with me?"

"I—"

"Don't say no. You've already turned me down for the

gala, but you can make it up to me by letting me pick you up Sunday morning, bright and early."

"After being up till all hours after the gala? I don't think so." She paused, seeing his expression. "I haven't been on a horse in at least a dozen years, Hunter. I don't even know if I still know how to ride."

"It's like riding a bike. You never forget. And we'll make it next Sunday." He tipped her chin up. "C'mon, you'll love it, I promise."

She gave a soft laugh, rolled her eyes and, for once, didn't pull away. "Okay. I guess."

His reaction then was instinctive. Looking down at her, at the curve of her pretty mouth and fantasizing how it would taste ever since she'd taken the first sip of that margarita, he just went with instinct. He bent and kissed her. He meant it to be quick and casual, a slightly less-than-serious salute to the hour they'd spent together. But that was before he found her lips so warm and soft…and tasting of margarita…and something a thousand times more potent. With both hands plunged into her hair and holding her just where he wanted her, he forgot to be brief. Or casual. And the fact that she fell right into the kiss with him made it worth the risk of rushing her. It also made it almost impossible to stop.

But they were on the sidewalk. All around them, bar patrons came and went. He broke the kiss…reluctantly. Set her down on her heels—she looked dazed, her eyes wide. He found he still held her chin and he rubbed his thumb over that tantalizingly curved lower lip before letting her go. But he took his time about it.

"I'll call you," he said, then watched her as she ran to her car.

He called his mother on his cell phone from the car. While it rang, he rubbed a hand over his mouth, where he could still taste Erica's lip gloss. He shifted in his seat to accommodate a helluva hard-on and gave a short, incredulous laugh. What the heck had just happened? It was a simple kiss, done on impulse. A spur-of-the-moment thing that had turned into more than he'd intended. If they'd been in a private place instead of on a public sidewalk, he didn't know what it would have led to. He only knew that he hadn't felt such a deep and elemental desire for a woman, especially one he hardly knew, since he'd first discovered girls in the eighth grade and fastened his adolescent craving for sex on Cindy Walker.

"Hello?"

"Mom." He shifted the phone to his other ear and signaled to enter the on-ramp to the interstate. "It's me, Hunter."

"I know. Caller ID is a wonderful thing." There was a smile in her voice.

"Mom, do you still have tickets to that symphony gala you mentioned when I brought your gift over?"

"Why? You aren't thinking of going, are you?" She was clearly surprised.

"I might." Glancing over his left shoulder, he crossed two lanes of the crowded interstate. "Can you get me a ticket?"

"Just one? If you're going, you'll want to bring someone, won't you?"

"Oh. Well, I guess. Sure. Two, then."

"I take it you haven't checked with Kelly to see if she's free?"

"No, but it's not her kind of thing. No horses." He kicked the SUV into passing gear to get around an eighteen-wheeler. "About the tickets. Do I need to pick 'em up before that night, or what?"

"I'll leave them with someone at the door. I'll let you know who when I get a name."

"Leave it on my voice mail, will you, Mom? It's this Saturday night, right?"

"Yes. And you have really left it late to ask Kelly." There was a note of concern in her voice. "I hope she's free. Oh, I'm just thrilled that you've decided to go. Some of my friends haven't seen you in ages, Hunter."

"Uh-huh. Are you wearing your Erica Stewart jacket? It's the kind of thing you'd wear to an event like this, isn't it? It adds a little pizzazz to wear something from an artist whose stuff just happens to be up for auction, don't you think?"

She took so long to reply that he thought he lost the connection. "Hello?"

"I'm here," she murmured. "And I haven't really thought too much about what I'll wear, to tell the truth."

"Well, that's a first." He merged smoothly into the exit lane. "I've spent a few years watching you get all decked out for occasions like this, and I remember you fretting for days over what to wear. Wear that jacket and you'll turn a few heads."

"I'm beyond turning heads by a few years, Hunter," she said dryly.

"No way, you're gorgeous and you'll still be gorgeous when you're ninety."

"Thank you, son."

He thought he heard a catch in her voice. "Gotta go, Mom. I'll send a check for the tickets. And hey, thanks."

Lillian clicked the phone off and stood with it in her hand, thinking. It was a toss-up to decide which was more unusual—Hunter's sudden and unusual interest in going to the symphony gala, or his interest in what she might be wearing, which was also sudden and unusual. He'd never before expressed the slightest interest in what she wore.

Like countless moms before her, she'd long ago become used to being almost invisible to her son as far as her physical appearance went.

It was that damn jacket.

"Who was that on the phone?"

She blinked and turned to face Morton, who stood in the arched entrance to the den with a half-finished drink in his hand. "It was Hunter." Realizing she still held the phone, she replaced it. "He wants tickets to the symphony gala. Two tickets."

"What's the problem? You've been trying to drag him to one or another of your artsy affairs for years, so now he's going. Why do you look as though it's bad news?"

"He wants me to wear the jacket."

"What jacket?" He watched her walk past him to the bar and pull a wineglass from a line of stems suspended from a rack beneath the counter.

"The Erica Stewart jacket he gave me for my birthday." After dropping ice into the glass, she poured only a scant shot of gin before adding a wedge of fresh lime. She was trying to limit her drinking. It's numbing effect had become too inviting lately.

"Is that what's making you look so glum?" Morton finished his drink and moved behind the bar to pour himself another. "You said you loved it when Hunter gave it to you. So, wear it. Make him happy. God knows, you've never hesitated to put Hunter's happiness above your own before."

His jealousy of Hunter was a familiar bone of contention between them, but Lillian wasn't in a mood to take him on just now. "He wanted two tickets, but I don't think the other one is for Kelly. When I mentioned he'd waited until it was pretty late to ask her, I had a feeling he hadn't even thought of asking her."

"Meaning he's got some other woman in mind," Morton said, recapping the whiskey bottle. "Doesn't surprise me. It's been your and Hank Colson's fantasy that those two would get together someday, but if that was what Hunter wanted, he'd have done it by now. No red-blooded thirtysomething puts off marrying if he's found the woman he wants." Using a swizzle, he noisily stirred the fresh drink. "Kelly's a nice gal, smart and fairly attractive, but I don't see him putting a ring on her finger."

"It's her. That's why he's suddenly interested in going."

"Kelly? You just said—"

"No. Erica." She walked to the window and stood looking out.

"Erica?" He stared at her, the swizzle going still in his hand. "You lost me. We're talking about Kelly, aren't we?"

"Erica Stewart. The artist. Didn't you hear it in his voice when he brought me the gift? He couldn't stop talking about her. He was…dazzled."

"Dazzled."

"I know what you're thinking," she said, following the lights of a neighbor's car across the street. "I'm imagining things. I'm seeing a disaster where there's nothing. I'm jumping to a ridiculous conclusion. But I just have this dreadful feeling, Morton. What if he—"

"Oh, for God's sake, Lillian, get hold of yourself. He's got tickets to bring a date, and if it was her, he'd have mentioned it since we could hardly shut him up when he was over here talking about her last week. You're right about that, at least. Besides, he'd only met the woman that day and she's been on the agenda for the symphony thing forever, which means she's had her plans made forever." He crossed the room and picked up the remote for the television set. "It's time for the news. Sit down and relax. Forget about Erica Stewart. The woman's ancient history as far as we're concerned." And with that, he clicked the remote, tuned in the local station and settled back to view current events in Houston and the crime of the day.

Six

Erica cocked her head and studied the look of a jacket she was designing for a client. "No…no…*no…*" she mumbled, reaching for an eraser. She carefully removed the neckline she'd sketched in a minute ago. Third try and it was still wrong, totally wrong, she thought with disgust. She sat for a minute, then took up her pencil again and drew a few more lines to see if a mandarin collar would work. She knew before she'd made half-a-dozen lines that it was wrong, too. With a muttered curse, she flung the pencil in a nearby tray, ripped the sheet from her sketch pad and crumpled it in both hands. It hit Jason in the chest, dead center, when he appeared at the door.

"What is the matter with you?" he demanded, wading through a sea of balled-up paper on the floor. "You've been in here scribbling and muttering to yourself all morning. Take a break. Make yourself a cup of tea. Chill out."

"Tea won't help," she growled, and shoved back off her stool. Looking around, she found the photographs of the client whose jacket she was designing. "Look at her," she said, thrusting the prints at him. "I've tried boxy, I've tried slightly nipped at the waist, I've tried classic blazer, but nothing seems right. She's expecting something nice, something flattering, and everything I've dreamed up looks like something she could have found on Harwin Street."

"Natalie Rodrigue," Jason said, studying a photo. "It's not the jacket, sugar, it's the client. Coco Chanel couldn't design a jacket to make the woman look good." He sat on her stool and crossed his legs. "It doesn't matter what you come up with, she's gonna be so proud to wear an original Erica Stewart that she'll think it's gorgeous. She'll think she's gorgeous."

Erica studied another photo. "Maybe no collar at all…" Then, with a curse, she flung it away. "I hate the fabric she chose, anyway. I wanted her to pick the flat black silk, but she wants brocade. It'll make her look as big as…as—"

"As she is?"

She gave a short laugh. "I guess that's the problem." She bent down and began gathering up wads of paper. "One of these days, I'm going to be brutally honest with a client and just say flat out, 'Spend your money on a piece of jewelry instead of a jacket that will do nothing to flatter you. At least you can pass diamonds on to your grandchildren.'"

"Okay, sugar, spit it out. What is wrong with you? And don't bother telling me it's nothing. I haven't seen you so agitated since we were negotiating for this building and the landlord forced a five-year lease on us."

"Because there was no guarantee we'd be in business that long and we'd both mortgaged most of our assets."

"Considerable for you, but peanuts for me."

"Which you had to borrow from your mother, God bless her."

"Off the subject, Erica. What's bugging you today? And don't give me that garbage about the creative process being stressful. You usually turn out jackets and quilts at the same pace as a rabbit giving birth. For which I'm thankful, as it's the source of our bread and butter, but you don't usually have a face like a thundercloud and you don't usually have any difficulty making a client look elegant."

She chose to interpret that as an insult. "Well, if my work is the next thing to assembly-line trash," she muttered, "maybe I should look for another line of work."

He actually turned pale. "My God, don't even joke like that, Erica. And you know that's not what I meant." Leaving the stool, he caught her by the arm and led her to a small couch set against the wall. After urging her down, he took a seat facing her. "Now, tell Daddy Jason all about it. When I left the shop last night, you were in a huddle with Michael Carlton." He stopped abruptly. "Oh, Jesus. Have you lost all your money? Is that it? Has that goofball blown your nest egg and you're penniless?"

"No, but that reminds me, Jason. Did you realize you failed to lock up when you left the shop last night?"

He frowned. "Did I? Let me think… Oh, now I remember. When I was closing out the register, I had another one of those crazy calls from the idiot who lives in the apartment next door to mine complaining again about my dog barking. I guess I forgot. Shit!" He smacked himself on the forehead. "I'm the idiot, aren't I? Why, did something happen? Is that what's wrong?"

"Michael hasn't mismanaged anything, and fortunately nothing happened when you left the door unlocked…unless—"

"Unless what?" As his eyebrows went up, the telephone rang. "Wait, hold that thought." Rising, he moved across the room and, with his back to her, answered the phone, then stood listening. After a minute, he turned with a gleam in his eye, raised his hand and pointed his index finger at Erica as if it were a gun barrel. "Yeah, good to hear from you, Hunter. Sure, she's right here."

Erica sprang off the couch as soon as she realized it was Hunter on the phone. Shaking her head and flapping her hands wildly, she mouthed, "I'm not here." She'd spent a long and sleepless night and Hunter was the reason. Nine years and she had avoided any attempt by a man to get close enough for intimacy. But she'd been almost seduced by their conversation in the bar, then rocked to her core by that kiss. She'd been so rattled that when she got in her car, she started making plans to call him first thing and cancel their date. So, why hadn't she?

To block her escape, Jason casually stepped in front of her, still chatting with Hunter. "So she tells me. And your timing's perfect. You interrupted the lecture she was giving me for failing to lock up last night. But I swear, I thought I locked the damn door."

He paused to listen, ignoring the motion Erica made to slice his throat. "Horseback riding, you say? No, she didn't mention it. But it sounds like fun to me." With his shoulder propped on the door frame, he crossed his ankles. "Nothing like country air and a horseback ride to clear away the smog and renew the spirit, I always say."

The only time Jason had ever been on a horse was when he'd modeled Western gear at the Houston Rodeo. Rolling her eyes, Erica reached over and took the phone from him. "Hello."

"Hi, it's Hunter."

Even braced for it, her tummy took a tumble at the sound of his voice. "Hi." She glanced over and met Jason's wickedly dancing eyes and instantly turned her back on him. "How are you?"

"I'm good. And you?"

"I'm fine. Busy."

"Yeah, I guessed that. Okay, I'll be quick. I realized after I left last night that I don't know where you live. We can be at the ranch by eight if we leave early enough on Sunday morning, but I need your address. Are you an early riser or one of those types that sleeps in on the weekend?"

"You didn't forget it's next weekend, not this Sunday?"

"Not unless I can talk you into changing your mind."

"Maybe I will at that," she said, bending over to pick up a wad of paper on the floor. "Actually, Hunter, I've been thinking—"

"Don't." He paused, then went on before she could speak. "Don't think of reasons not to come…just this once. If it turns out that you don't like Lady—"

"It's not that I won't like your horses, Hunter. I just have so much on my plate at the moment that I don't think it's a good time to do…this."

"You work hard. Give yourself a break. I guarantee when you get back home, you'll thank me." Then he seemed to run out of words, finishing with simply "I wish you'd come, Erica."

Was that uncertainty in his voice? A plea? She'd pegged him from the start as a supremely confident male. He'd definitely seemed in command last night. But whatever it was she heard in his voice now, it weakened her resolve more than flashy charm or blatant flirtation ever could.

"Well…okay. But I'll need to get back at a reasonable hour." She gave him her address.

"In that case, we'll get an early start. Is six too early?" he asked.

Yes, but if she was going to do this, she supposed she owed him the courtesy of going along with his plans. "Six is fine. I'll be ready…*next* Sunday." She clicked off quietly and replaced the phone in its cradle. It was only when Jason firmly cleared his throat that she turned to look at him. "What?"

He was gazing at her in amazement. "You've really

made a date? With a man who isn't selling fabric or insurance?"

"Don't you have a customer on the floor?"

"No. And any customer who has the bad timing to come into the shop right now will just have to wait." He waded through the sea of discarded sketches and sat down. "Tell me everything. Leave no detail out."

"There is nothing to tell." She bent and began collecting the discarded sketches from the floor. "Last night, Hunter came in just as Michael was leaving." She straightened up, arms full of paper. "He owns a ranch near Brenham and apparently he stables a few horses. I think he enjoys getting away from the city. He must, as he's there almost every weekend."

"So he just dropped by the shop and asked you to spend the weekend—" He stopped with a look of consternation. "You can't go this weekend. You have to be at the symphony gala Saturday night."

"I'm not spending the weekend with him. I haven't lost my mind. I told him it would have to be the following Sunday."

"Well, kiss my grits."

She stuffed an armload of paper into the trash can. "You are so not funny."

Jason leaned back with an innocent look on his face and crossed his legs. "I told you he was prime stuff, not that you've ever paid any attention to my opinion before. But at least now I know what's got your panties in a twist."

"Wasting a whole morning trying to get a design right is what's making me crazy," she said, scooping up the photos of her client. Then, frowning, she stood looking at them. "I don't know why I agreed to go. Maybe it was because Michael acted like such an idiot and Hunter appeared at precisely the right moment. Or maybe it was the margaritas. But I only had one."

"Whoa. Hold it. What margaritas?" He gave a wide swipe of his arm, taking in the small office. "We serve no margaritas in here, sugar. Did you actually have dinner with him?"

"One drink. At Monty's Bar."

"Uh-huh."

"But somehow I found myself talking about when I had Misha and how much I loved her. Next thing I know, I agreed to go with him to his ranch. Next Sunday."

He studied her in delight for a minute. "Well, it's about time some guy storms the citadel, but go back to Michael acting like an idiot. I agree he's dull and boring, but if he didn't bring news of a financial disaster, what makes him idiotic?"

"Having the gall to force himself on me." She shoved the trash can back in its place beside her drafting table with more force than necessary, still outraged. "Apparently, he thinks I'm beautiful and sexy and with a little foreplay, I might be willing. His idea of foreplay was to grope me in spite of the fact that I kept saying no. I had to wrestle my way out of the office and lock him inside to keep him from throwing me to the floor and having his wicked way with me."

Jason's good humor evaporated. "Are you serious?"

"I know it's hard to believe. He's always seemed so… geekish. I fired him as soon as I unlocked the door and let him out." Recalling the moment, she grinned. "You should have heard him yelling and kicking, banging on the door with his fists. If Hunter hadn't come in when he did, I would have left him in there all night cooling his heels."

"Our hero."

"Well, he was a welcome sight at just that instant." She

lifted her shoulders in a who-knows-why shrug. "Maybe that was why I found myself agreeing to go to Monty's for a margarita." And then making a date to go horseback riding. And then kissing him madly on a public sidewalk. But she wasn't about to tell Jason any more, not until she figured it out herself.

Seven

The symphony gala was well under way when Erica and Jason entered the lobby of the hotel and made their way up the wide staircase that brought them to the mezzanine level. She pulled the ends of a tasseled shawl around herself and edged a bit closer to Jason. She was nervous. It had been a long time since she'd attended an event where there would be music and dancing in a crowd of elegantly dressed people. That had been part of another life.

"I love a party," Jason said, taking her by the arm at the foot of the stairs.

"Tell me something I don't know," she said.

"Champagne, music, all these guys in tuxes, what's not to love?" He flashed a smile at a dashing couple strolling by. "I bet our snazzy little jacket will go for no less than fifteen hundred, what do you think?"

"I have no idea. I worry that it'll go begging."

"Not a chance. Wait and see."

At the entrance to the ballroom, the attendant took their invitations and they went inside. With her stomach in a knot, she stood looking over the crowd. Men in black tuxes, women dressed to the nines, a din of cocktail chatter and laughter, all so familiar, so much a part of a life that had stopped short nine years ago. Nothing short of the opportunity to promote the Erica Stewart label could have dragged her here otherwise.

Jason spotted a familiar face, gave her a gentle nudge in another direction and said, "Let's mingle, partner. You know more of these people than I do, even if you haven't seen them in years." And off he went.

Erica did indeed spot familiar faces, including the owner of the ad agency she used, several clients who'd commissioned various pieces of her art, her church's minister and his wife, and a professor from Rice University, where she'd spoken to art students. Nursing a glass of champagne, she drifted from group to group and found, after a while, that some of her tension had faded. As long as she didn't stop and give herself a chance to remember the last time she'd been here, she was fine.

"Erica! Erica Stewart, is that really you?"

She turned as someone caught her hand and recognized Lisa Johns, an attorney whose famous married client—a pro sports hero—was fighting a paternity claim by a stripper in a topless bar. "Hi, Lisa. Yes, it's really me." Erica returned her air kiss with a smile while her heart gave a little bump. Seeing Lisa would force her back in time whether she wanted it or not. It had been foolish to think—to hope—otherwise. "How are you?"

"Giving them hell every chance I get." Lisa squeezed her hand, then stood back, taking stock of Erica. In her little black dress, short and chic, her hair pulled to one side with a diamond clip and her strappy three-inch heels, Erica knew she looked her best. "Goddamn, you're as gorgeous as ever, more so. And making such a stir with your art. It makes my heart go pitty-pat. I'm bidding on that gorgeous jacket, not that it'll look the way it should on me. But what the hell."

Lisa, a defense lawyer, was as tough—and tough-talking—as any male counterpart and twice as smart. She had a reputation among lawyers for taking no prisoners. "It's good to see you, Lisa. You're making quite a stir yourself with your client. This time, he's got to be worried."

"I wish. Maybe then he'd keep it in his pants, but he's mine and until he runs out of money or I simply kill him myself, I guess I'll have to stay in there pitching. No pun intended."

Erica laughed. "As his attorney, should you be saying things like that?"

"Shit, you're family, darlin'." She paused, took a good, long look into Erica's eyes, and when she spoke, her tone gentled. "Tell me, how long has it been?"

"Nine years," she said quietly. Nine years since Lisa Johns had shared an office with Erica's husband, David. Nine years since those carefree evenings when Lisa and her current lover would pop in at Erica and David's house to drink wine and talk, plan and dream. Nine years since it had all ended.

"Yeah. God, how time flies. Nine years." Lisa grabbed a fresh glass of champagne from a tray-bearing waiter as he passed and took a good gulp. "You know, every now and then when I'm slogging away on a case, I'll come across something David wrote, or some research he authored, and it'll hit me in the tummy. It still seems so unfair, so senseless. If I could ever get my hands on the bastard who did that, I think I'd forget my calling as a defense lawyer. There's nothing mean enough to throw at people like that, you know?"

"I try not to think about it, Lisa."

"Jesus." She reached over and hugged Erica. "I'm an

idiot. I've had too much champagne. Let's change the subject, 'cause I haven't seen you in so long and when I spotted you across the room, I couldn't wait to get over here." She finished off the rest of the fresh glass, deposited it with another tray-bearing waiter and gave a big sigh. "I meant it when I said you're looking fantastic. And it's great your label is taking off big-time. I saw one of your quilts in a house a year or so ago. This gal had it hanging on the wall of her den, Erica. God, it was stunning, a piece of art in fabric. And those fabulous jackets you're designing are all the rage. I'm gonna have one, I swear."

"Come by the shop," Erica said, smiling. "I have a couple that would look wonderful on you."

Lisa cocked her head with a bemused look. "But I thought painting was your forte, not fabric design. I read the *Zest* article in the paper, but I didn't see any evidence of your art from the pictures they took of your shop. Which reminds me, when do you have time to paint?"

"Actually, I don't." She managed a smile and gave her stock answer to the familiar question. "What with the shop and keeping up with demand, I'm just too busy." Painting had once been as vital to her as the air she breathed, but that, too, was nine years past. She had discovered then that only a very few things in life were really vital for survival.

Suddenly, Lisa paused and looked about curiously. "Where's your date? You didn't come to this thing stag, did you?"

"No, he's around somewhere mingling, as he calls it." She turned, scanning the floor trying to find Jason in the crowd. And then her heart skipped a beat. Threading his way through the crowd—and the object of more than a few admiring female glances—was Hunter McCabe. Even half a ballroom away, she could see that he was heading directly to her. What was he doing here? She knew—*knew*—this was not Hunter's kind of thing.

"Well," Lisa said, following Erica's gaze, "I don't think I'd let that one mingle any farther than two feet from my side. Are there any more like him? I'm available."

"He's not mine," she murmured, but Lisa was right. He did look good in a tux.

"Then if I were you, I'd do whatever it took to remedy that."

Erica watched him with the eye of an artist, thinking he looked almost as good as he did in that battered bomber jacket and jeans. The truth was, he was a man who was so comfortable in his skin that he'd even look good in nothing. At that thought, she caught herself up short, because it was too incredibly easy to imagine him wearing nothing but confidence and that rakish grin.

"Hey, there." Before she realized his intent, he'd caught hold of both her hands and pulled her toward him in a move so natural that she never thought of resisting. "I've been looking everywhere for you," he said after kissing her cheek.

Flustered, she inhaled subtle aftershave and not-so-subtle male. "I didn't expect to see you here," she said.

"And I may not last much longer," he told her, looking over the crowd with something in his face—a subtle twist of his mouth—that told her she'd been right. This wasn't his kind of thing. So what in the world was he doing here? He glanced then at Lisa. "Am I interrupting something?"

"Not a bit," Lisa said, extending her hand with a speculative look in her eye. "I'm Lisa Johns, an old friend of Erica's."

"Hunter McCabe," he said. Then, after a beat, he recognized her. "Joe Crenshaw's defense attorney, right?"

"That would be me, yes. God bless cable TV."

He was shaking his head, smiling. "Crenshaw's something else. I can't wait to open the sports page to see what he's been up to next."

"Me, too." Lisa took a healthy swallow of her drink. "But, unlike you, I pray his antics are confined to the sports page and not the headlines."

"I hear you," Hunter said, still smiling. "I suspect you'd have to lock him in his room every night to keep him out of trouble."

"I keep thinking he'll grow up," Lisa said, "but when will it happen? He's thirty-four." She glanced beyond them and made a face. "Uh-oh, I see I'm being summoned." She flashed a smile at Hunter, then gave Erica a warm hug and whispered, "If he's not your date, sweetie, he should be. Bye now."

Erica watched Lisa make her way across the ballroom toward a tall man with iron-gray hair and an air of authority. She turned away, putting a hand over her tummy.

"What's wrong?" Following her gaze, Hunter frowned, looking over the crowd.

"It's nothing." The man who'd summoned Lisa was the firm's senior partner. And David's mentor. If Edward Kerr realized she was here, he'd probably feel honor-bound to speak to her. She couldn't allow that.

She turned to look at Hunter. "I've been circulating, as Jason calls it, for an hour. I'd like to get away from the noise for a few minutes. Would you excuse me?"

"A break sounds good to me, too. Let's try the mezzanine. C'mon." He settled a hand at her waist and made a startled sound as he encountered bare skin. Her dress had long sleeves and a boat neckline that came up to her throat in front, but in back it plunged almost to her waist. "Jesus, you almost gave me a heart attack," he said, eyeing the enticing line of her spine.

She knew the dress was a bit risqué, but Jason had persuaded her to wear it. This was her first appearance in public, he told her. She should make a statement. In fact, it had been Jason who had chosen the dress for her in a chic little boutique in River Oaks, telling her that if she refused to wear one of her own designs, she needed to wear something equally stunning.

Apparently, Hunter thought it was stunning.

Without another word, he guided her toward an area at the edge of the room. Several people recognized him as they wove through the crowd, but other than brief nods and even briefer smiles, he didn't stop until he reached the wide stairs that led to the mezzanine.

She sighed with relief as the noise of the party receded. "I can't go far," she told him. "The auction is due to start in a little while."

"I know," he said, pulling her behind a huge column. "I've spent the last hour talking to people I don't particularly like and listening to enough cocktail chitchat to remind me why I avoid these things. I need a minute to breathe something besides expensive perfume and hors d'oeuvres too pretty to eat."

She smiled and decided against resisting. "If it's that bad, why did you come?"

"I came because I knew you'd be here." His gaze drifted over her, lingering long enough to make her skin tingle. "You look fantastic in that dress…what little there is of it."

"I have a shawl to cover—"

He touched her lips with a finger. "Don't even think it. I thought you'd probably wear something you designed, but now I'm glad you didn't."

The way he was looking at her renewed her misgivings about him. Not only was he an extremely attractive man, but he was stirring feelings in her that she hadn't felt in years. She'd met many men and had had many opportunities to begin new relationships in the years since losing David, but she'd never been even remotely tempted. It shook her that Hunter threatened those defenses.

"Something upset you back there," he said, studying her face. "It was when Lisa left. Want to tell me about it?"

She'd already told him more than enough about herself. "It was nothing," she said, shaking her head. "I'm a little tense over the auction. I know it's a wonderful opportunity to promote the Erica Stewart label and I'm appreciative of the opportunity, but to tell the truth, I'll be glad when it's over and I can go home."

One wall of the mezzanine was all glass. He led her across the floor and they stood looking out over the city. "I've always admired Houston's beautiful skyline," she said. "Are you responsible for any of it?"

He moved his gaze away from her reluctantly and pointed to a cluster of buildings due east of downtown. "See the steeple on that church way over there? Look just to the left of it. I was the architect on that building."

"Only that one?"

"There are several others, but that's the only one visible from here."

"It must be thrilling to design something so…important and then to see it come to life."

"It's not so different from what you do, is it?"

"A quilt compared to a stunning high-rise?"

"Art is art," he told her. "As for importance, one of your quilts will probably be some woman's treasure a hundred years from now when my building is crumbling."

"You are very good for my ego," she said, smiling.

"I'm hoping to be good for a lot more than that," he said. Again she felt a quiver of alarm, but before she had a chance to respond, he glanced at the time on his watch.

"It's time we headed back. The auction will begin in a few minutes and Jason will be wondering what happened to you."

She let him take her arm and in moments they were entering the ballroom. Jason obviously had been looking for her. He looked relieved when he spotted her and hurried toward them. She turned to take her leave of Hunter, but he caught and held her hand.

"After the auction, there's someone I want you to meet," he told her, but Jason had reached them and she didn't have a chance to respond.

"Hunter." Jason extended his hand. "I thought I recognized you across the room earlier." He gave them both a mock scowl. "I leave Erica to work this crowd and next thing I know, she's disappeared and so have you."

"I needed a minute to breathe," she told him.

"I tried to talk her into running away with me," Hunter said, "but she kept talking about this auction she didn't want to miss."

"Yeah, and if we don't head over there right now, we will miss it. It's just starting. She's nervous, so she refuses to be up front and center," he told Hunter. "Luckily, I've staked out a good location where we can see the action and still be almost invisible." He turned to go, but Hunter held her in place with a firm hand on her waist.

"Don't let her leave after the auction, Jason," Hunter said. Then he tipped her face up and kissed her full on the mouth. "I'll find you after," he promised.

As they went their separate ways, nobody noticed Lillian watching from across the room.

Lillian managed a bright smile and pretended to listen while one of Morton's associates talked. Thanks to Hunter, she'd been functioning on sheer bravado for the last half hour. Her delight in having a rare evening in her son's company was gone. She realized, when Hunter joined her and Morton without a date, that he wasn't at the gala because he'd had a change of heart about these worthy events. No, from the way he kept looking about, scanning faces, moving restlessly to the bar and listening to conversations with only half an ear, she knew he was there to see someone. And when he spotted Erica Stewart and began making his way across the ballroom directly to her, she knew with a sinking heart, why he'd come.

"Be careful what you wish for," she murmured to herself.

That kiss hadn't been casual. She saw his face. Saw Erica's reaction. She knew Hunter had been intrigued by the artist from the moment he met her. She realized he could have been seeing her ever since. What a cruel twist of fate that would be, she thought, fingering the brooch pinned on her shoulder. But it wouldn't be surprising. Erica was a beautiful woman. Hunter was a man in his prime. No matter how much she and Hank wished it, there was no serious commitment on his part in his relationship with Kelly. Morton was right about that.

Murmuring something in reply to a remark by Morton, she watched Erica and Jason approach an area near the stage where the auction was beginning. She looked quite stunning, Lillian thought. The little black dress was chic and sophisticated and just right for the occasion. Many eyes would be on her tonight, and with her dark hair clipped to one side, her face coolly aloof, she seemed remote and mysterious. An artist whose inner life was hidden. She would be a big hit. Lillian sighed. Why wouldn't Hunter be captivated?

"Do you want me to bid on the spa weekend?"

Lillian blinked, realizing Morton had spoken. "What?"

"The spa weekend," he repeated with some irritation. "What's the matter with you tonight, Lillian? You've been off in la-la land ever since we got here. I don't know what John Molinara thought with you standing there like a mannequin. You didn't say ten words. Hell, I thought you'd be tickled pink with Hunter making an appearance for the first time in years. It's no wonder he disappeared. Probably remembered why he hates these things and left."

"Sorry," she said, still twiddling with the brooch. "I did hear you invite John and Rita to dinner. I'll make it up to them then."

"Glad to hear it." He took her arm in a firm grasp. "The auction's getting under way. Let's move a little closer. Neither of us is looking forward to this part of the evening, but take my advice and do what I'm doing, just close your eyes and don't look when they put up the Erica Stewart piece. And you never answered. Do you want me to bid on the spa weekend?"

"I'm not upset because something by Erica will be auctioned. I'm upset because I realize that Hunter is here because of her, Morton. The reason he disappeared is that they left together for a while, just the two of them."

"Oh, come on. You're imagining things."

"I didn't imagine anything. I saw them." She didn't tell him about the kiss.

Morton still scanned the room. "Where is he now?"

"I don't know, but I don't think he'd leave without telling me. I also don't see him having much interest in the auction…unless he wants to bid on Erica's piece." She touched her forehead. "This whole evening has been so stressful. I'm not like you, Morton. I just can't be around her and not be reminded. I'm not able to put this out of my mind and go on with life as if nothing happened. I never will be."

He finally lost his temper. "It's ancient history!" he hissed in her ear. "Stop dwelling on it, You talk about this to anybody—anybody, Lillian—and everything we've worked for is down the tubes. I mean it. I want that appointment from the president, and it's dead, lost forever, if I'm even touched by a breath of scandal."

"Don't worry," she whispered, with a catch in her voice. "I'm the last person to ever talk about it."

Eight

The auction was a huge success. People bid outrageous amounts, or so it seemed to Erica, for luxury items that included a five-day ski vacation in Aspen, a set of leather luggage, a sitting with a professional photographer, a weekend stay at a spa, five nights in Las Vegas, a seven-day cruise on a luxury liner. It seemed incredible to her that an Erica Stewart jacket was even on the list. Even more incredible was the final bid on the jacket.

"Twenty-two-hundred bucks," Jason said, openly gleeful that his estimate came up short. "Shows what I know."

"I'm glad it's over," Erica said. She admitted to feeling good at having made a contribution to a worthy cause.

"I guess you know who won the bid?" He was practically salivating.

"No, who?"

"Barbara Bush's friend. I was in River Oaks one day with Stephen and they were together, leaving the spa. He recognized them. Well, I mean, anybody would recognize Barbara Bush, but Stephen knew her friend from the hospital. She volunteers."

"I'm impressed." She was, really. But now her main

thought was to slip away as gracefully as possible, in case Jason had more networking in mind. "Don't even think about bullying me into more self-promotion, Jason. My feet say it's over."

Jason's gaze shifted to a point beyond her shoulder. "Look who's here."

"I wondered how long you could stay upright in those heels." Hunter's voice at her ear gave her a start. He edged Jason aside and took possession of her elbow. "Not that they don't do things to your legs that make me crazy. They do. But keep 'em on ten more minutes, please. There's someone I want you to meet."

"You don't need me," Jason said, dropping behind after giving her a wink that Hunter missed. "I'll meet you at the escalator on the mezzanine when you're done." He glanced at his watch. "Twenty minutes?"

"Give or take," Hunter said, already steering her away from the auction area. "This won't take long. I know it's late and you've had a big night." As they passed the bar, he nodded to a couple waiting for fresh drinks who tried to stop him, but he flashed an apologetic smile without slowing his pace. "I want you to meet my mother. She's wearing the jacket."

Erica followed his gaze across the room where a woman, blond, slim and elegant, stood close to a confident-looking man with thinning gray-blond hair and a florid complexion. Hunter's father? If so, she couldn't see any resemblance. He was shorter than Hunter, but only barely. He seemed familiar, but she couldn't place how or when she might have met him. The woman she'd never seen before.

"She's very attractive," Erica said of his mother, meaning it.

"I think so. She doesn't look familiar?"

Shaking her head, Erica added, "Why?"

"My mother has two passions. One is her husband, Morton Trask. You've probably heard of him. He's the CEO of CentrexO."

She instantly recalled why he'd looked familiar. "Anyone who reads the newspaper or watches the news has heard of him, but I wouldn't have made the connection with you."

"He's my stepfather."

She heard a slight edge in his tone and glanced up to see his face, but there was nothing to be read in his expression. Another half-dozen steps and they would be close enough for introductions. "And her other passion?"

"Art. And the arts community. She knows a lot of struggling artists, and I think she probably takes a particular artist under her wing from time to time. She's never admitted that, of course. She knows I think she's too naive to tell real artists from con artists. God knows how many times she's been duped."

And as Morton Trask's wife, she would be in a position to make a difference to talented artists who might never make it otherwise, Erica thought. CentrexO's influence was everywhere in Houston, but from the sound of it, Mrs. Trask's interest was more personal. If she used her position to benefit starving artists, Erica could think of worse things.

She studied the Trasks closely as Hunter guided her toward them, thinking they looked exactly what they were— the cream of Houston society. In fact, the woman in conversation with them now was Melissa Reynolds, a TV anchor at one of Houston's local network channels. Jason was right to be thrilled over the publicity value of tonight's event. It wouldn't hurt having her label mentioned on the nightly news as well as on the society page.

Hunter paused a few feet back to let the anchorwoman make her farewells. His mother reached over and air-kissed Reynolds's cheek, then turned and saw him with Erica in tow. Her moment of eye contact with Erica was brief, a mere nanosecond, but it was long enough for the practiced smile on her face to change. A hand flew to her throat and something like fear flashed in her eyes. But, with a quick intake of breath, she recovered just as quickly, leaving Erica thinking she must have somehow alarmed the woman.

"Hunter, here you are," she said, as coolly gracious as the wife of Morton Trask must always appear. "We wondered if you'd left early without telling us."

"Not before I introduced you to the artist who designed your jacket," he said, nudging Erica closer with his hand, warm and firm on her bare back. "This is Erica Stewart, Mom. I wanted her to see how terrific it looks on you. Erica, my mother, Lillian Trask."

With her fingers still spread wide over her chest, Lillian looked into Erica's eyes. "Hello. It's…I'm so pleased to meet you. Your art is…simply wonderful."

This was not a woman Erica would have expected to stammer over an introduction under any circumstances. She *was* unsettled, for some reason. Erica glanced quickly at Hunter and found he'd marked his mother's reaction, too. He was frowning. Puzzled, Erica extended her hand. "Thank you," she said.

Lillian Trask's palm touched hers in a contact so brief it almost missed. Then she turned to Hunter's stepfather. "This is my husband, Morton Trask."

But Erica didn't respond to that. She didn't hear it. Instead, her gaze was locked on a unique brooch that was revealed on the woman's shoulder when she moved her hand away to take Erica's. It was a starburst of diamonds radiating out from a single large fire opal, set in a nest of more diamonds and opals. It was the perfect accent piece for the pale champagne color of the jacket Erica had designed. But Lillian Trask's unerring sense of style in pairing the jacket with just the right piece of jewelry was lost on Erica. She was in shock, staring in absolute horror at the brooch. Her chest felt as if all the breath was crushed from it. Something, fear or dread—or both—rose sickeningly in her. The opal at the center of the pin winked fire and terror, and both came at her in waves that stole the strength from her knees and froze the blood in her veins. She felt she might be sick and reached instinctively for Hunter.

He took one look at her face and covered the fingers she'd locked around his arm with his own. "Erica, what's wrong?" His voice was sharp with concern.

His words were lost in the roaring of terror in her ears. With her gaze riveted on the brooch, sounds came at her as if filtered through a tunnel. The whole world had stopped as if a camera had captured a picture in a freeze-frame. Panic spiraled up from her center, mixing with the pain in her chest. She snatched her hand away from Hunter's arm and, with a strangled sound, turned in a desperate need to run.

He stopped her, clamped both hands on her arms and forced her to look up at him. "Tell me what's wrong, Erica," he demanded. "You're pale as a ghost. Are you sick?"

She shook her head, glanced again at his mother, at the brooch. And again was almost overwhelmed with terrible pain. "I…I don't know," she stammered. Pulling away, she put both hands to her cheeks. "I…it's…I just feel a little faint," she told him, coming up with a lie. "The evening…ah, the…everything has been a little too much, I think."

"I'll take you home," Hunter said instantly. "Let's go."

"No!" She put a hand on his arm and struggled to bring herself under control. "No, thank you. My…Jason will be waiting in the mezzanine." She'd always deplored the mistaken view that some artists were unstable or, at best, overly emotional. With her heart still beating wildly in reaction to that bizarre moment—whatever it was—who could blame them?

She forced herself to turn and face Lillian Trask. It meant resisting an almost crazed urge to look at the brooch again, but she kept her gaze locked on the woman's face. "Please forgive me for rushing away. I know my partner is wondering what happened to me." She forced a smile, thinking it must surely look hideous. She had never felt less like smiling. "It was a pleasure meeting you."

"Yes," Lillian replied, then added, "Congratulations on your success." Beside her, Morton remained silent.

"Thank you." Taking care to walk away with some semblance of dignity, Erica fixed her eyes on the exit doors of the ballroom. Hunter kept pace beside her, but shot frequent glances at her profile as they walked. He was clearly bewildered.

"I don't suppose you're going to tell me what that was all about," he said.

"I think it might have something to do with the fact that I haven't eaten all day." That was not quite true, but she had to come up with some excuse.

He stared at her. "Jason says you're not comfortable doing PR and you knew this would take a lot out of you, yet you still skipped breakfast and lunch?"

"Maybe it was the champagne." And maybe she should tell him to mind his own business, she thought. But she didn't. Why that was, she hadn't figured out yet. "I just felt faint for a moment."

"You looked shocked to your toes," he told her flatly. "Are you sure you haven't met my mother before?"

"No. Never."

"My stepfather?"

"No, I've never met either of them. I just had a…a moment when I felt faint. It happens, Hunter."

He gave a skeptical grunt. If he could hear the way her heart was beating, he would know for sure that she was lying, she thought, clutching his arm in a death grip. But she somehow managed to make it to the mezzanine level without her knees giving way.

Jason was waiting at the escalator in animated conversation with a friend and didn't see them approach. She was glad to see he had her shawl, as she was cold all the way to her bones. When he turned and saw her face, he stopped talking midsentence. His eyes shot straight to Hunter. "What's wrong? What happened?"

"You'll have to ask Erica," Hunter told him. Taking her shawl from Jason, he settled it around her shoulders.

She pulled it close, grateful for its warmth. "I was a little light-headed for a minute, that's all. It's nothing to be concerned about. I'll be fine as soon as I get home and can k-kick off these shoes and change into something soft and c-comfortable." She pressed her lips together, as she couldn't seem to stop them from trembling. "W-Willie's probably wondering what happened to me anyway."

"Willie?" Hunter repeated.

"He's a cat," Jason explained. "Gray and scraggly-looking, a Willie Nelson clone." Still watching her with narrow-eyed concern, he said, "You've never fainted in your life."

"Too much excitement mixed with champagne," she told him.

"She hasn't eaten anything today," Hunter said, with a frown of disapproval.

"I'll have a bowl of cereal when I get home." With the shawl to warm her up, she was feeling more normal now, but something had happened when she was introduced to Hunter's mother and she didn't think it was too much champagne. She'd experienced an avalanche of emotion, not when she looked into the woman's face or when she met his stepfather. It was when she saw Lillian Trask's brooch. Why had she been almost bowled over by a piece of jewelry?

Without thinking what he would make of it, she turned to Hunter. "Your mother's wearing an interesting brooch. Do you know anything about it?"

"My mother's brooch," he repeated blankly. "You mean that pin she's wearing?"

"You're asking about a piece of jewelry his mother's wearing?" Jason was looking incredulous. His eyes went sharp with suspicion. "How much champagne have you had?"

"It's not that. I think…I mean—" She gave them both a weak smile and shrugged. "I know it sounds crazy, but I just thought for a minute that I'd seen it before. Is it an antique?"

Hunter took a second to focus on what she said. He lifted one shoulder and said, "I don't know. She likes jewelry and she usually buys pretty good stuff. I guess it could be old." His gaze wandered to the arched doorway of the ballroom. Presumably his mother and Morton were still inside. "If it's important, I'll go back and ask her."

"No, no. Don't. It's not important. I just…you know how you get a feeling of déjà vu sometimes? When I saw it, I felt it wasn't just familiar, but that I'd seen it before and it had some special meaning. Which sounds a little nutty, I guess. I couldn't have, right?" Seeking more warmth, she drew the folds of the shawl more snugly around herself. "It just kind of…startled me. Maybe it belonged to me in another life." The joke fell flat because she couldn't quite manage a real smile.

Hunter rubbed the side of his cheek, now thinking. "She's had that pin a long time, I think. I seem to remember when I was a kid, she'd get all gussied up for one of these affairs and wear it. She's partial to estate sales. That might be where she got it."

Jason looked at Erica. "What, you think it was your great-grandmother's or something?"

"No, of course not." Her thoughts raced as she tried to make sense of her panic at the sight of it. Estate sales. She occasionally went, which could explain how she might have seen it before. But why did it give her such a shock? And it had been a shock. She'd almost passed out with the force of whatever emotion it triggered in her. Then again, maybe it wasn't the brooch at all. Maybe the stress of the evening had simply caught up with her at that moment. Maybe the whole thing was just a nervous reaction. The auction was a crucial event for both her and Jason.

Hunter touched her shoulder. "Go home and get some rest," he told her. "And take it easy these next few days. I just wish you'd reconsider and come with me to the ranch tomorrow. We don't have to wait until next week." He saw second thoughts gathering on her face and put a finger on her lips. "Don't even think it."

"What?" Jason asked, looking at them both.

"She's going with me to the ranch next Sunday," Hunter said, keeping his eyes on hers. "It's a week away, but I couldn't talk her into going tomorrow."

"Not at daybreak," she said, resisting the pleasure of Hunter's warm palm on the curve between her neck and shoulder.

"She's lazy in the mornings," Jason said, grinning. "But

to get her started, bring fresh kolaches and coffee and she'll follow you anywhere."

"Thanks, I'll remember that."

With Erica gone, Hunter was more than ready to go himself, but first he wanted a word with his mother. Instead of leaving, he walked back to the ballroom and stood for a minute at the arched doorway, searching the thinning crowd. There were still quite a few die-hard patrons of the arts lingering. If he knew his mother, she'd be among the last to leave. Morton would indulge her, not for any particular love of the symphony—or his wife—but because he liked the two of them to be seen at these events. He finally spotted her and Morton as they were separating from a couple he recognized as longtime neighbors of the Trasks' in River Oaks.

"Hi, Mom," he said, coming up from behind. "You about ready to call it a night?"

"Oh, Hunter." She gave him a smile that didn't quite reach her eyes. "You're still here?"

"For a few more minutes. I hoped to catch you before you left."

Morton made a show of studying the time on his watch. "We're meeting the Jensons' at their house for a nightcap in a few minutes. Is it important?"

Hunter wondered whether he and his stepfather would ever be able to exchange a word or two without wanting to argue. "I won't keep her long," he told Morton. "You're valet parked?"

"Of course," Morton said with annoyance.

"I'll be done by the time your car's brought up." He took his mother's arm and ushered her past the rest of the lingering crowd, leaving Morton to follow or do as he suggested and call for his vehicle. His stepfather was a control freak who usually manipulated a situation, not vice versa. He was irritated at being one-upped, especially by Hunter. It showed on his face as he stalked off.

Lillian sighed. "Was that necessary, Hunter?"

Probably not, he thought, but it was difficult for Hunter to resist jabbing at Morton whenever he got a chance. A psychiatrist would call it petty retaliation after being under the man's thumb for too many years, but there it was. "There's something I want to ask you," Hunter said, steering Lillian along toward the escalator. "What did you think of Erica?"

"Oh." She stumbled in spite of the firm grip he had on her elbow. "Is that why you waited around, to ask what I think of a woman who's caught your eye?" Her laugh was forced. Nervous. "You used to do that when you were a teenager, but never since then if my memory serves me."

"No, that's not the reason," Hunter said with a smile. He didn't bother to deny his interest in Erica. Lillian would have been clued in when he brought Erica over to introduce her. Hell, she probably guessed when he showed up at the gala without Kelly. "She's a beautiful woman, isn't she?"

"Striking, certainly. Very sophisticated. In person, she's nothing like I imagined her to be."

"How is it you've thought about her at all? She tells me you've never met."

She gave a nervous laugh. It *was* nervousness, he told himself, nothing real or spontaneous about it. "I wasn't speaking of her physical appearance, but her…demeanor, I suppose you'd say. I'm familiar with her art—many people are, as you've seen for yourself tonight. You tend to wonder about the artist when you look at a piece of art. At least, I do. That's all."

What she said made sense, but for some reason, Hunter felt there was more to her reaction to Erica than her usual appreciation of anyone with enough talent to create art. She looked unsettled and tense. Almost fearful. Why would a conversation about Erica Stewart be anything but casual? She didn't know her. Neither woman claimed to know the other. And yet...

He thought back to the moment when he'd taken Erica over to be introduced, a moment when he'd been puzzled by his mother's reaction. Nobody's social skills were more accomplished, but for a moment she'd seemed on the verge of losing her composure. She'd been...shaken. But why? There'd been no chance to explore her odd reaction as he'd been distracted by Erica's spell. She'd had a similar reaction when he'd presented his birthday gift to her—a jacket she instantly recognized as an Erica Stewart creation. In hindsight, he saw she'd not been thrilled over it. He'd been so taken with Erica himself that he'd been blind to anything except his own opinion.

"What I want to ask might seem odd," he told her now, "but Erica had a really weird reaction to that piece of jewelry you're wearing tonight."

"What?" She gave him a bewildered look.

"That pin." He reached out and touched it with his finger. Although no connoisseur of women's jewelry, he realized it was unique. Probably expensive. Definitely expensive, if those stones were diamonds, which without a doubt they were. More of them than he could count at a glance. And he didn't know about opals, but he knew about his mother's judgment in these things and he guessed they were valuable, too. Maybe the value of the piece was in its design, he thought, studying it closely. What the hell did he know about anything except the damn thing had spooked Erica. And he wanted to know why.

"What are you talking about, Hunter?" She brushed his hand aside and covered the brooch with her fingers.

"I know it sounds…funny, but when Erica recovered after her little spell, she talked about your pin, called it a brooch. Which was a kind of old-fashioned word to me, but that's what she said."

"You're not making any sense, Hunter."

He gave a short laugh. "I guess not. Anyway, she seemed to think she'd seen it before, maybe in an estate sale or something. You two have that in common, an appreciation of treasures of the past, you might say."

"This pin didn't come from an estate sale," Lillian said. "It belonged to my grandmother. It was an anniversary gift to her from my grandfather. It has been in my family forever. It was willed to me when she died."

"No kidding." They were in the hotel foyer now, heading for the revolving doors where Morton would be waiting. Hunter didn't want to explain his interest in Lillian's jewelry to Morton. Besides, he was still in the dark over the whole thing himself. He couldn't very well explain what he didn't understand. "Erica said the jewels are diamonds and opals. Is that right?"

She made a little sound of exasperation. "Really, Hunter, I'm not used to having my jewelry vetted by a complete stranger."

"I've made it sound cheesy, just asking about it, Mom. I apologize. Erica would probably flip if she knew I was asking all these questions. It's just—" Spotting Morton waiting in their Mercedes, he decided to let it go until he'd had a chance to think more about it. He smiled at his mother and kissed her on the cheek. "I hope you had a good time tonight. I sure did."

Standing on tiptoe she caught his arms, and it seemed to Hunter that she clung to him for a moment. "I was thrilled that you came, Hunter," she said huskily.

"Maybe I'll surprise you again sometime," he said,

wishing to make up for upsetting her. She was upset. He didn't know why, but he knew it had little to do with her jewelry and everything to do with Erica Stewart.

He walked her to the Mercedes, where a valet held the door open. "About that pin, Mom," he said. She stopped, studying him with a questioning look. "Is opal your birthstone?"

"Why, no. Why do you ask?"

"Oops." He grinned at her, hoping to lighten her mood. "Because I've heard that you should beware of owning opals if they're not your birthstone. They're bad luck. But since yours are a legacy from the past and it's no fault of yours that you own these, their power is kaput."

He had failed to lighten her mood he realized as he stood at the curb waiting for the valet to seat her in the Mercedes. She looked straight ahead as Morton pulled abruptly away, but it was a night with a full moon and when the car turned the corner, Hunter saw her face. Even with the tinted windows, he could see that it was ghostly pale.

"Okay, cut the bullshit and tell me what that was all about." At the wheel of his Nissan, Jason shot across three lanes of Southwest Freeway traffic and settled in at a nice, steady seventy miles an hour pace before adding, "And I'm not some dude who's got the hots for you, sugar, so don't give me that line about not eating and your stress level knocking you to your knees. I've seen you when stress is bad and I've seen you when *life itself* is bad. This was one of the latter, not the former."

Erica sighed and fixed her gaze on the rear of an eighteen-wheeler just ahead of them. "I don't know what it was, Jace. I just took a look at that piece of jewelry and it felt as if I was suddenly hurled back in time. A horrible time. I thought I was going to be sick."

"Maybe it was the shrimp."

"I was so busy networking, as you instructed, that I really didn't eat anything."

"No kidding?"

"Cross my heart."

Jason drummed his fingers on the steering wheel, thinking. "Maybe there is something about the jewelry."

"But what? I've never seen Mrs. Trask in my life. Her face was totally unfamiliar. Mr. Trask, yes. Everybody's seen him from time to time. You'd have to live in a time warp in Houston not to. But I barely remember even looking at him, I was so busy trying to keep from passing out with horror."

"You say you felt as if you were hurled back in time. What does that mean?"

"I don't know. You remember reading about Alice falling down the rabbit hole? Well, that's the best way I can describe what happened. Except that I didn't see anything or remember anything. All I felt was…emotion. I was terrified, Jace." She bent her head in her hands. "Those people must think I'm crazy."

"When you told Hunter and me about it, you said it felt like a déjà vu moment. A psychiatrist might suggest there's something buried in your memory bank and the pin was like a key unlocking it."

"Oh, please, Jason. That only happens in the movies. I wasn't an abused child, I didn't witness my parents doing something heinous, and my nanny didn't lock me in a dark closet. There's nothing traumatic in my childhood."

"What about the trauma nine years ago? Seems to me that qualifies as something you've buried in your memory bank."

For a beat or two, she couldn't speak. The pain of it could still almost crush her. And Jason was the only person in her world who would dare remind her. "I don't see how a silly pin could have anything to do with that," she said quietly. Then, turning her face away, she closed her eyes, ending their conversation.

That night, she had the dream again. But this time, she wasn't wandering aimlessly, but moving through a huge room, smoke-filled and crowded. The hotel ballroom? As she walked, people moved about, talking and laughing. She heard snatches of music, the clink of glasses, smatterings of applause. She glimpsed faces and felt people turning to watch her making her way toward…whatever it was. And with the familiar heady anticipation building inside her, she moved toward that something—something wonderful. Now she saw Jason, who seemed to urge her on, but when she wanted him to come with her, he simply melted into the crowd as if he had never been there. Then she saw Hunter standing in the arched doorway, smiling. Beyond him was his mother wielding a pair of scissors, cutting her new jacket into shreds. She wanted to tell Hunter to stop her, but now he was disappearing, too, swallowed up in nothingness just as Jason had done. And then, suddenly, the promised joy was gone and she felt only deep disappointment and pain. Terrible, terrible pain.

She woke up to find herself sitting straight up in bed with Willie pressed against her, purring. She buried her face in her hands and found it wet with tears. Shakily, she wiped them away and drew in a long, shuddering breath. She was suddenly cold, bone cold. She reached for Willie and lay back, pulled the blanket up and covered them both. The cat was warm. Holding him close calmed her, helped to banish the dream. In a minute, she turned to look at the clock on the bedside table: 3:10 a.m. Hours yet until daylight. She was never able to sleep after the dream, anyway.

She pushed the covers aside, kissed Willie on the top of his head and got up.

Minutes later, she was seated at her drafting board sketching. Her first three attempts were ripped out and tossed in the trash. Tonight, instead of the usual escape she found in work, she felt restless and distracted, her concentration completely off. Oddest of all, she was aware of the paint easel with its blank canvas that occupied an unused corner of the room. It had been two years since Jason had appeared with all the materials she needed to begin painting again—easel, canvas, fresh paints, an array of brushes and tools and art supplies. He'd gone about setting it up, placing the easel in just the right light, ignoring her protests that she could never paint again. Painting, she told him, was like other passions in her life, lost to her now.

"Well, just in case, everything's here when you rediscover that particular passion" had been his reply. And two years later, there they were, still unused.

But tonight, for some reason, she couldn't seem to ignore them as she usually did. Tonight, something drew her gaze to the naked canvas, where she visualized light and shadow merging into an image. Once, a long time ago, she'd acted almost instinctively on those flashes of inspiration, but now she shook her head, resisting. How long had it been since that part of her had worked? And why tonight? But the image was so vivid. As if still in the dream, she slipped off her stool and walked over to the easel. The compulsion was simply too strong to resist.

With the sketching pencil in her hand, she began to draw a rough outline of what she'd visualized in her mind. She sketched hesitantly at first, but she soon lost herself in the need to capture the image. Working intently now fiercely focused, she moved her hand swiftly, confidently. She took no time to survey the result, so urgent was her need to transfer to canvas what she saw in her mind. At one point, she groped in a tray for charcoal, necessary to add shading and depth. Still, she had no conscious thought of what was taking shape on the canvas. And when she was done, she stepped back to study what she'd created.

For a shocked moment, she stared in disbelief at a head-on view of a car with a shattered windshield. With her heart racing, she jerked the canvas off the easel and carried it to the closet. There, she shoved it deep into the back of the dark space and slammed the door. Shaken to the core, she braced against it and fought down sickening flashes of a moment in time that had been buried for nine years. What was happening? First, her reaction to Lillian Trask's jewelry, and now this. Both in one night. Trembling and weak, she slid down the wall and sat huddled with her head bowed and arms tight around her knees. She had been right to avoid taking up her brushes to paint again. Going back was too painful.

Nine

Erica wasn't the only person thinking the past was too painful. Lillian Trask's hands trembled slightly as she carefully removed the heirloom brooch that had caused such a stir and placed it in its almost century-old, satin-lined box. Craving a cigarette, she removed the jacket, which she now loathed, and hung it in the deepest, most remote region of her closet. Her one concession to her addiction to nicotine was that she never allowed herself to smoke in her home. If she just had to have a cigarette, she went out onto the patio, no matter what the time or the weather. At times, she'd suffered bone-chilling cold, driving rain or Houston's sweltering heat to enjoy the delicious seven minutes it took to smoke a cigarette. But no more tonight. She'd overindulged, as was her habit when stressed. Consequently, she had a bitter taste on her tongue and a raw throat to show for it. God knows, she was stressed tonight. And thank God, it was almost over. That last hour and a half of drinks and chitchat with the Jensons had almost pushed her over the edge, but she was finally able to see the end of this hideous night. Almost.

She could hear Morton in the bathroom going through

his nighttime ritual. Whether the hour was early or late, he never varied his routine. But once he was done, she knew she would be subjected to a third-degree about Erica Stewart. He would also demand an explanation for Hunter wanting a private moment.

She quickly slipped into an ice-blue silk gown, donned the matching peignoir and, still carrying the antique box, sat down at her vanity to begin her own nightly ritual. She would have loved going straight to bed for a few hours of sleep rather than facing Morton's interrogation, but that would simply delay the inevitable. Better now than tomorrow morning.

Her fingers fumbled a bit in removing the lid from a jar of costly cream expressly formulated for her by her dermatologist. Closing her eyes, she smoothed it on her carefully preserved skin, calmed for a few moments by the sheer familiarity of a ritual established when she was young and still kept religiously even now. She supposed, like Morton, she was a creature of habit, too. She didn't like thinking about the spontaneity that had once been a hallmark of her personality.

"What the hell is going on with Hunter?"

Morton scattered her thoughts with the abrupt question. "You knew he asked for tickets to the gala," she said, meeting his eyes in the mirror. "Your guess is as good as mine."

With a look of distaste, he emptied his pockets on a walnut valet stand. "You seriously think he's interested in that woman?"

They both knew which woman he meant. "I don't know if it's serious, but yes, I definitely think he's interested."

"Jesus." Muttering, he shucked his pants and tossed them over the valet. "Must be a quarter million women in this town and he picks her. One thing I'll hand him, she's a looker. That article in the paper last week didn't do her justice. I guess I still see her in my mind as she looked—"

"Please, Morton." She touched both temples with her fingertips. "I don't want to discuss that tonight."

He paused with a pillow in his hand. "You may not want to talk about it, but you're damn sure thinking about it. I know that look, Lillian. You're like an addict with an irresistible craving to beat up on yourself whenever something happens to remind you. I wish to Christ you'd get over it. It's done. It's past. Didn't we agree this is the way it would be?"

"You made that decision, Morton," she said quietly. "It's been easier for you to accept because in your mind you wiped it away, and from that moment life was a clean slate."

"It was a clean slate for your life as well as mine," he told her grimly. "Don't forget that."

Lillian knew that he was impatient with her inability to do just that. But for her forgetting was impossible. Morton, on the other hand, was a realist, a person used to manipulating people and situations that were unfavorable to him. He took quick and decisive action, and then he carried on. He got beyond unpleasantness by shutting down his memory bank and concentrating on getting on with his life.

Even now, as he tossed the duvet back and climbed into bed, he moved on to another topic. "What was Hunter up to that he needed to have a private word with you?"

"I'm not sure. It was…puzzling. He asked about my brooch."

"Come again?"

She swiveled around on her chair and faced him. "The brooch that I pinned on my jacket tonight. He said he was asking because of Erica's strange reaction when she saw it."

He frowned. "Was that what was wrong with her? She freaked out over a piece of jewelry?"

"He said she wondered if it had come from an estate sale. That she felt she'd seen it somewhere before."

He was still frowning. "Didn't it come from your grandmother?"

"Yes."

"Must not have been an original piece," he mused, then added, "Or was it?"

"I always thought it was, because you can clearly see the artist's initials engraved on the back. I was told my grandfather bought it for my grandmother in New York as an anniversary gift."

"Which doesn't mean the artist didn't crank out a dozen just like it."

"I suppose."

The room went quiet and Lillian turned back to her mirror, wondering if Morton's thoughts were going down the same path as hers. If the jewelry was an original piece and it had been in Lillian's family for more than three generations, where and when might Erica have seen it? What did it mean that she'd presumably recognized it and almost fainted with shock? And above and beyond those questions was another, more troubling one. Did Hunter's obvious interest in Erica mean that she was destined to enter their lives once more?

After seeing his mother off at the symphony gala, Hunter didn't go home to his condo but drove directly to the ranch. His plan was to grab a few hours' sleep, slip out of the house the next morning before Theresa was aware that he was there, saddle Jasper up and spend the day on horseback. If she heard him, she'd get up and insist on feeding him. Instead, he woke up to the smell of coffee brewing and bacon frying, and by the time he finished his shower, breakfast was on the table waiting for him. There was no hardship in spending a few minutes with Theresa and Hank, or in enjoying a man-size breakfast. And yet, he felt his spirits lift the minute he stepped outside, heading for the barn. Now, mounted astride Jasper with a thermos of coffee and a couple of huge sandwiches tucked in his saddlebags, he had the happy prospect of a whole day of solitude before him.

It was a glorious morning, crisp, cool and bright. For the first hour, he rode for the sheer enjoyment of it, on the lookout for anything needing attention. He found a break at a cattle guard and made a mental note of the location to tell Cisco. He spotted a limp in one of the mares let out to pasture. Dismounting, he approached her with care and finally managed to get close enough to inspect her foreleg. With his knife, he pried out a sharp stone lodged in her shoe and stood watching with a smile as she galloped away, joining two other mares heading for a stream. One of them, a richly colored chestnut, was the animal he had in mind for Erica when she came to his ranch next Sunday.

That was all it took to put Erica squarely in his thoughts. Ordinarily, he was so satisfied just to be at the ranch that there was nothing he needed to make his time there better. But today he caught himself wishing to jump ahead to their date next weekend. He wondered what kind of rider she'd be, whether she'd have the stamina—or desire—to stay in the saddle for several hours. He told himself he wouldn't be disappointed if she wasn't too keen on enjoying the outdoors as he was. She might be a real girlie-girl type. He had a sudden and vivid recollection of the way she'd looked in that little black dress last night. What there was of it. Nothing to be disappointed about there.

He had dismounted to let Jasper drink from the stream when he heard a shrill whistle. Turning toward the rise of a hill, he squinted into the sun and made out a figure on horseback. The slim and graceful rider he recognized instantly, as well as the Appaloosa she rode. Kelly had rescued it, half-starved and blind in one eye, from an abusive owner. She would have been justified in putting the animal down, but instead she'd used her vet skills plus a lot of TLC and brought him back from the near-dead. Barney was her favorite mount.

She drew up at the stream and slipped out of the saddle with the natural ease of a born equestrienne. Hunter tightened his hold on Jasper, who snorted and danced restlessly with the appearance of the other horse. "I thought I spotted your wheels at the house," she said, pushing her hat back to look up at him. "When did you get here?"

"I drove up last night," he said, putting a calming hand on Jasper's neck.

"After the symphony gala, I assume."

Damn. By getting the tickets from his mother, he should have guessed she'd talk to Kelly and assume Kelly would be his date. "Mom told you?"

"Your mother is the soul of discretion where you and I are concerned, Hunter." She played out enough slack on the reins for Barney to drink. "No, it was a well-meaning mutual friend who called me before breakfast this morning."

Shit. She was bound to hear that he'd gone sooner or later, but he'd counted on it being later. "It was a last-minute thing, Kelly." He gave her a quick grin, hoping to head her off before the temper he could see simmering in her eyes blew. "To tell the truth, it was as stuffy as I remember from all those years when I was a teenager and Mom made me suit up and go. You didn't miss a thing."

"And so, assuming I'd hate it, you didn't even bother to tell me about it?"

He could see the destruction of his day staring him in the face. "You would hate it, Kelly. You know that."

"Put it like this, Hunter. I generally like to make up my own mind about things. I don't like anybody deciding anything for me."

"C'mon, you know I didn't mean it like that."

"Okay, explain to me how you did mean it."

He stared longingly at the distant horizon. Whatever he said would just make matters worse, since he wasn't ready to talk about his attraction to Erica. Especially as he hadn't figured it out himself yet. Besides, with Kelly spoiling for a fight, anything he said was bound to set her off. "Can we talk about this later, Kelly?"

"What? You need to take a little more time to come up with a good story? You'd like that, wouldn't you?" She jerked the reins of the Appaloosa, who was edging closer to Jasper. "I didn't just get a call that you'd gone to the symphony gala, Hunter. I was told you spent the evening with some female artist who's big with that particular crowd. And I was told you even took her over and introduced her to your mother and Morton."

His own temper snapped. "How about the times I went to the john? And I guess she counted my drinks, too. Who the hell is this 'friend,' Kelly?"

She gave him a disgusted look. "Who it is doesn't matter. You're not denying what she said. So don't bother telling me it was stuffy and boring because it sounds to me like the reason you overcame a lifelong dislike and went was because you have the hots for another woman."

He sighed and rubbed the side of his face and wished

to hell he'd stayed in town. He owed Kelly an explanation, but he wanted to do it in his own time. "I know we need to talk, Kelly, but just not right now, today. I really need to do some thinking before trying to put into words what I haven't been able to get a handle on myself."

"It's that complicated?"

She said it with heavy sarcasm, but he didn't react in kind. "It is complicated, Kell. What's happened between us is complicated. I've always felt…conflicted about it. You've got to know that. I guess, just from a practical point of view, it seems right, like it ought to work. We share a lot of history. We like a lot of the same things. Our folks are close. It's almost as if we share the same parents. I know you've been good to go on this, Kelly. I'm the one with the doubts."

She turned away, gamely keeping her chin up. But he could see her throat working as she struggled not to cry and he felt like shit. She spoke quietly. "Are you… Have you been to bed with her?"

He resented being pushed to discuss Erica. What he felt was personal, deeply private. "I don't want to hurt you, Kelly," he said. "But I just don't want to talk about it right now."

Without another word, she mounted Barney, jerked the reins to turn him and galloped off.

Like Hunter, as soon as Lillian drove beneath the arched gate at the ranch, she felt a sense of homecoming. Something about the place spoke to her heart even though title to the ranch had passed to Hunter with Bart's death more than thirty years ago. She had lost more than a husband and the father of her son when Bart's plane went down. She had lost dreams and plans and a big chunk of her heart. Treating herself to an occasional visit was a way to remember those early days when life was bright with optimism and the future filled with promise. At the time, Hank had been married to Marguerite and the two couples had been close. Not only had they shared ownership of the air-flight business, but they were partners in the ranch. That kind of friendship forged special ties. The ranch and Hank were inextricably linked in her life. She could never make Morton understand that. Still, it was with a certain amount of risk that she succumbed to her need to see the place—and Hank. The last thing she needed was to feel even more dissatisfied with her life.

Sure enough, the tension that had her stomach in a knot eased as she drove the private road leading to the ranch house. It was still troubling to have her suspicions confirmed that Hunter was attracted to Erica Stewart, but a day spent at the ranch with Theresa and Hank would help to distract her...for a while, at least.

She parked her car outside the equipment barn, behind Hank Colson's pickup. As she got out, she noticed both Hunter's and Kelly's SUVs. If they were together, that was a good sign. Maybe she was misinterpreting his interest in Erica.

Hank was out on the porch before she made it up the flagstone walk. "Surprise," she said, spreading her arms wide. "I know I'm earlier than I said I'd be, but I didn't want to waste such a beautiful day in Houston. I hope I haven't interrupted anything."

"Nothing that matters." He met her on the steps, his hand extended. After kissing her on the cheek, he ushered her into the house. "I finished the newspaper an hour ago and the ball game got off to a bad start."

"It'll take a miracle for the Aggies to get in the play-offs this year," she said.

"Bite your tongue, woman."

She laughed, knowing that would get a rise out of him. The one thing that had divided Hank and Bart had been their separate loyalties in college sports. Bart was an alumnus of UT and a die-hard Longhorns fan and Hank loved the Aggies. Both had taken the time-honored rivalry to ridiculous levels, in her opinion. She was hardly a sports nut, but she loved teasing Hank about his beloved Aggies.

"Where's Theresa?" Usually the housekeeper met Lillian in the foyer bearing fresh coffee and something wonderful to go with it.

"Has a new grandbaby," Hank explained, gathering up newspapers from the couch. "Left this morning right after breakfast. 'Course, she fed Hunter first. He got here in the middle of the night, but as soon as he finished breakfast, he saddled Jasper and we haven't seen him since. Acted like something was on his mind, but it was more'n my neck was worth to try and get him to tell it."

"I saw Kelly's SUV. Are they together?"

"She rode out to find him a while ago, but she came back about an hour later ridin' that Appaloosa hell-bent for leather. She's in the barn now. I went out there to see what was up, but she tore into me so ferocious-like it seemed smart to let her cool off on her own. She never welcomed any advice from her daddy, anyway." He took Lillian's denim jacket, then waited until she was seated on the couch before he lowered himself into his big leather club chair. "Something's sure got her in a snit. Her red hair was practically crackling when she was takin' the saddle off that horse."

"Do you think she's upset with Hunter?"

"Why, has he done something to make her mad?"

Lillian sighed, crossed her legs and locked her hands on one knee. "He had two tickets for the symphony gala last night and I naturally assumed he would take Kelly. Instead, he came alone, no date at all."

"Can't see why that'd make her mad. But why'd you think she'd be up for something like that anyway? She hates that kinda thing." Looking thoughtful, he rubbed the brass studs on the arm of his chair with one big, weather-gnarled hand. "Puzzles me why Hunter was there. If it's the symphony, it'd be black tie, wouldn't it? A tux and all the geegaws to match?"

"Yes."

"Must be more to it. He hates a formal shindig like that way more than Kelly."

"One of Erica Stewart's creations was auctioned. She's an up-and-coming artist. I think Hunter's interested in her, Hank."

His eyebrows rose in surprise. "Is that the gal featured in the paper a week or so ago? Makes spiffy jackets and quilts?"

"Yes. He bought my birthday gift at her shop."

"I guess I'm responsible for that. I remembered you mentioning her and I thought you'd like something with her label on it."

"I suppose he met her then. She was at the gala, naturally, and he spent a lot of time with her. At one point, they disappeared together. Afterward, when she was gone, he couldn't stop talking about her."

Hank stroked his mustache, letting her vent.

"He *kissed* her, Hank!"

"Uh-oh."

"It wasn't just a peck on the cheek, either."

"Well, if Kelly got wind of that, it'd be enough to set her off like she was just now. She'd probably be foolish enough to chase him down and throw it back at him. She's always been the one doing the chasin' for Hunter and not the other way around, Lily. She's my baby girl and I love her to pieces, but she's a little too pushy for her own good sometimes."

"She's a darling and I want her to be my daughter-in-law."

He reached over and gave her a sympathetic pat on her knee. "We can't always get what we want in this world, Lily. If Hunter wanted Kelly as a wife, he would have a ring on her finger by now. He's a man who makes up his mind without much dilly-dallying. The fact he hasn't given her a ring and set the date tells me he's not sure. You don't want them marrying if he's not sure, do you?"

"No, of course not." *Just, please, don't let Erica Stewart be the one.*

He settled back and crossed his legs, showing a battered boot as it rested on one knee. "So, what's the problem with Ms. Stewart that you're all in a panic? She's not a married woman, is she?"

Not anymore. Lillian drew a deep breath. "No."

"Then what, Lily?" Hank studied her closely. His inner radar was always ultrasensitive where she was concerned. Lying to him made her feel even worse than her fear that Hunter would get involved with Erica.

She managed a smile. "I suppose it's hard to give up a dream, isn't it? For years I've wanted Hunter to settle down, and when Kelly returned and set up her practice so near the ranch it just seemed a match made in heaven." With a grimace and a shrug, she smiled again…weakly. "We can't micromanage our kids' lives and it's silly to be disappointed because we can't."

"Hunter's got his head screwed on right, Lily. He won't choose a woman that's not fine daughter-in-law material." He smiled. "Frankly, I'd think you would be tickled he's got eyes for an artist, considering the fact that you've been a helping hand for more than a few arty types here in Houston. So, what's the problem if he likes Ms. Stewart? She's talented and successful. Pretty, too, judging by that newspaper. Look at it this way, darlin'. You could have a grandchild to steal your heart away."

She stood up abruptly, hoping to keep him from seeing the horror his words conjured up. "I don't suppose Theresa left any coffee in the kitchen, did she?"

After a keen look at her, Hank stood up, taking his time. "It's right here in one of those thermos carafes. I should have offered right away, and if you tell on me, Theresa will give me grief over it." He lifted the carafe and poured each of them a cup of coffee. "So, what's Morton doin' today?" he asked casually.

"Oh…golf, I think. He set it up with Tom Jenson last night."

"And last weekend he was on that big yacht he's so proud of, wasn't he?"

"Yes."

"I gather from Hunter that he's been out of town a lot lately." He passed the coffee across the bar to her.

"Yes. Something about a merger. One of the smaller satellite holdings, I think. I don't know. It's always something." She took the coffee but didn't go back to the couch. With both hands wrapped around the mug, she moved to the window with a view, not of the barn, but of the opposite side of the ranch property where rolling hills, trees and a limitless sky was a feast for the eyes. "What's really got him excited is something else entirely. He's on the president's short list for an ambassadorship, Hank."

Behind her, Hank whistled. "Does that mean it's a done deal?"

"He must think so. He's practically told me to pack my bags."

Hank moved so that she was forced to look at him. "Pack your bags to go where, Lily?"

"Some place yet to be named. The bottom line is that

I'll be leaving Houston," she added bitterly. "He didn't even tell me this was a possibility until he knew it was almost a certainty. It would take something really scandalous to kill it now."

"Goddamn it!" Hank set the mug down with a thump. "If you think he's taken you for granted in the past, Lily, just wait until you're in some foreign country where you don't have your work with artists or your busy social calendar to fill the void in your marriage." He stopped, stared at her hard. "I assume you're not even thinkin' of tellin' him you won't go?"

She rubbed her forehead wearily. "How can I?"

Exasperated, he hit the bar with the flat of his hand. "Why not, for God's sake? Why do you stay with him? It can't be the money. You inherited more money from your family than you'll ever spend in this lifetime. And don't think I don't know that played a big part in the bastard marrying you. You were rich and beautiful, a young widow with impeccable family connections in Texas. He was an opportunist then and he's still on the lookout to add to his résumé. This ambassadorship is just one more step up the ladder." He was pacing the floor as he ranted. Finally, he stopped and looked at her. "You've been unhappy for years, Lily. Why don't you do something about it?"

Lillian smiled sadly. "Why don't you tell me what you really think, Hank?"

"Jesus." Hank rubbed the back of his neck in chagrin. "Listen to me. I'm an idiot, Lily. It set me off, the thought of you leaving Houston. Pure selfishness. I spoke out of turn, darlin'."

Silent for a moment, both stood side by side at the window. Lillian fought a need to turn and let him take her in his arms. He would, in a heartbeat. He loved her. He'd never said the words, but she knew. There would be solace and comfort in his strong embrace, but she dared not. Doing so, she risked letting him discover her secrets. With tears blurring her eyes, she wrapped both arms around herself.

"What does Hunter have to say about this?" he asked quietly.

"I haven't mentioned it to him. I'm not supposed to be talking about it to anybody. Please don't repeat it. If Morton lost the appointment because of me, he'd never forgive me." She felt him looking at her, but she kept her gaze fixed on the horizon.

He spoke finally. "You don't have to go, Lily. I'll stand behind you if you need help telling him. Just remember that."

A few minutes later, when Hank received an important phone call, Lillian went outside to walk off some of her misery. She was going to have to get hold of herself, she thought. Obsessing over the thought of leaving Houston would change nothing. Morton's mind was made up and her reaction would only irritate him. And panicking over Hunter's interest in Erica was just as pointless. He'd reached his midthirties without needing her advice about the women in his life and he surely didn't need it now. Not that he'd accept advice from her about anything. They'd lost that kind of rapport long ago through no fault of Hunter's. She was solely responsible for that, along with everything else in her life that had deteriorated. No, Hunter wouldn't welcome her interference.

She stood at the east pasture fence overlooking a blanket of color. With spring just around the corner, Texas wildflowers were in full bloom. Splashes of blue and orange and yellow, colors that rivaled any painting. And in the distance, several colts frolicked like children while their mothers calmly cropped new grass. How could she bear leaving all this?

Movement at the barn door caught her eye. Kelly was leaving, loading her vet case and supplies into her SUV. Charlie, the old Lab, was at her heels, sticking as faithfully as if Kelly was still a child. Watching her, Lillian thought of Jocelyn and longed to hear from her, to see her. But if her relationship with Hunter was troubled, it was even worse with Jocelyn. Her daughter barely tolerated a phone call, let alone a visit. Could she be any farther away from Houston than at Key West, the very tip of the Florida peninsula? And if the physical distance was great, their emotional gulf was even deeper.

When Charlie barked, Kelly looked up and saw Lillian. She wasn't responsible for her son's decisions where women were concerned, Lillian reminded herself, and she hoped Kelly respected that and wouldn't mention her relationship with Hunter. Nevertheless, now she'd seen her, it would be impossible to avoid a chat.

As Lillian approached, Kelly closed the rear door of her SUV and slapped dust from her jeans and backside. "Hi, Aunt Lily. I saw your car and hoped you wouldn't get away before we had a chance to talk." She gave her a hug. "I guess Dad told you I was nasty and rude when he came out to the barn a while ago."

Lillian reached down to greet Charlie, rubbing his ears. "Hank mentioned that you seemed upset."

"Which is no excuse. He probably expects me to apologize before I leave."

Lillian smiled in sympathy. "Only if you mean it. But I wouldn't worry too much about it if I were you. Hank's like most men. When a woman's in a prickly mood, they generally prefer steering clear till the dust settles."

"Prickly, huh? I feel more like I've been run over by a

truck." She shoved her fingers into the front pockets of her jeans and gazed beyond Lillian to the colorful fields of the east pasture. "Hunter's out there somewhere on one of his solitary rides. I chased him down and we had words."

"Did you?" Lillian braced herself for the inevitable.

"Yeah." Her eyes still on the horizon, Kelly's lips trembled slightly. "He's having an affair, Aunt Lily."

Lillian felt a jolt of horror. Here was the confirmation of her fears. "Are you certain, Kelly? The two of you have been together for months now. He wouldn't just—" But she stopped at the look on Kelly's face.

"He would, Aunt Lily. Oh, he didn't admit anything outright, but he didn't deny that he'd met someone." Sensing her distress, Charlie pressed his nose against Kelly's thigh.

"That could happen to any of us, Kelly." The words were meant to reassure herself as well as Kelly. "We meet people of the opposite sex who interest us all the time, but that doesn't mean we toss aside commitments made in good faith."

"There was no commitment. Hunter was never ready for that," Kelly told her, stroking Charlie. "I knew it from the start, but I just didn't want to accept it."

Now it was Lillian's turn to study the hills in the distance. With a hand at her throat, she asked, "Did he tell you who it was?"

"He didn't have to. I know it's that artist, Erica Stewart. Buffy Goldman saw them at the symphony thing Saturday, which, I might add, Hunter never even mentioned a word to me about." Tears threatened and her voice thickened. "It just makes so much more sense that he'd be attracted to someone like that, Aunt Lily. He grew up watching your involvement in that arty scene, and even though he thinks he doesn't care about that stuff, he does.

Now he's met a woman who's tailor-made for him in a way I never could even pretend to be."

With a sick feeling in her stomach, Lillian turned back. In her skinny top and boot-cut jeans, Kelly looked about sixteen years old. Comparing her to Erica Stewart's dark, erotic beauty was like comparing a daisy and an orchid. But was there a competition yet? "I'm sure you're exaggerating this woman's influence, Kelly. It's probably just a passing fancy." She gently touched the younger woman's shoulder. "He'll get over it."

Kelly smiled sadly. "I don't think so."

Both turned then at the sound of a vehicle and watched as a white pickup approached, trailing a cloud of dust. Kelly suddenly straightened up, and using both hands, she quickly wiped the tears from her eyes. "Jeff Pickering," she murmured. "I forgot I asked him to drop by. I wanted his opinion on that colicky colt I've isolated in the barn."

It had been some time since Lillian had seen Jeff Pickering. She knew him from early childhood. His parents owned a summer home on an acreage that touched the western boundary of the McCabe-Colson property. He'd been Hunter's playmate when their summer visits coincided, which was often. Jeff and Hunter were the same age and inseparable then. Many times, Kelly had run into the house with crushed feelings because the two boys had shut her out from their play. Jeff, like Kelly, was a vet now. In fact, Lillian and Hank expected she would join Jeff in his practice when she decided to move back rather than setting up on her own. According to Hank, it had been Jeff's intention to offer her a partnership.

Lillian extended a hand as he approached. "Jeff, how nice to see you."

"Miz Lily." He kissed her cheek. "Same here."

"How are your folks? I haven't seen Mark or Helen in ages."

"They're fine. Leaving on a cruise next week." But he hardly spared Lillian a glance in replying. Instead, his gaze honed in on Kelly with a hunger that was so obvious it made Lillian blink. "Got your message, Kell," he said. "I would've been here sooner, but I was out on a call at the Farley place. They've got a problem with that bull Jim Farley bought up in Oklahoma last year." There was ruddy color on both cheeks, a dead giveaway of his feelings. If Kelly noticed, Lillian couldn't see it.

"I told him he didn't get enough background on those people before laying out that kind of money," Kelly said. She knocked her boot against a fence post to rid it of mud picked up on her rounds, then straightened and looked him in the eye. "I hope it wasn't on your recommendation that he bought it."

"No, he went off half-cocked on his own."

"As usual."

Lillian watched the interplay with fascination. She wondered how long Jeff had been in love with Kelly and whether he'd ever given her a clue to how he felt. He'd been very shy as a boy and maybe he'd never outgrown it, but he was as solid as a man could be. After hugging Lillian, it had been as plain as the star on a Texas flag that he'd wanted to greet Kelly with more than a laconic hello.

"I think I'll head back to the house," Lily told them. "If Hunter's here, Hank will probably appreciate help getting dinner since Theresa's gone."

"That sounds good to me," Kelly said. "Dad will love knowing he doesn't have to eat something I've cooked."

"Hunter's here?" Jeff's eyebrows snapped together in a frown.

"He came last night," Kelly said.

"To your place? Or here?"

She gave him an irritated look. "That's a personal question, Jeff."

He glanced at his feet, shoved his hands into his back pockets and eventually lifted his eyes, blue and blazing, to hers. "I've got a personal reason for asking, Kell. And you know it."

Lillian could see a storm brewing in Kelly's eyes. Clearing her throat, she lifted a hand. "I'd better get started on that dinner. You're welcome to join us, Jeff. But if I don't see you again, say hello to Helen and Mark for me."

Not wishing to get caught in a crossfire, she departed rapidly.

As Lillian was leaving the ranch, Morton was approaching the tee on the seventeenth hole at his club. His score so far was respectable, for he was no ace on the golf course. No one was if they couldn't put in the time necessary to shoot par. His handicap was a solid twelve. If he shot in the nineties, he usually finished the game feeling he'd acquitted himself well enough. What was important wasn't his score for eighteen holes, but whether the business he conducted on the course was successful. Sailing his yacht was the only thing he did without a particular business or professional goal in mind and today was no exception. Tom Jenson was tight with the governor, and with a little schmoozing, he'd be willing to add his weight to others Morton had lined up to recommend him for the ambassadorship.

He dropped his ball on the tee box, bent to tee it up, then positioned himself for the drive. It wasn't a lack of contacts that worried him about the nomination. It was his wife. Lillian was so damn fragile, had been for years. Funny thing was, it came in cycles and he never knew what triggered one of her episodes. To his disgust, every now and then she got a bug up her ass and started obsessing. And when it happened, there wasn't much he could do but wait her out. She always came around, but it was a goddamn headache putting up with her hysterics until she did.

He hit the ball with a solid smack and watched it arc high over the center of the fairway. A little short of his intent, he thought, squinting in the sun as it dropped, but again, respectable. He moved off to let Tom take his turn, while his thoughts returned to the problem at hand. This time, he had a bad feeling. With the nomination almost a sure thing, all it would take would be for Lillian to say something to the wrong person and he'd be up shit creek. Somebody like Hank Colson, for instance. That son of a bitch wouldn't hesitate to use any weapon he could come up with to bring Morton down. If she got desperate enough, she just might be capable of telling. He meant to have a talk with her and remind her of the consequences of doing something that idiotic.

He rammed his driver back into the bag and climbed into the cart while Jenson teed off. God, what he wouldn't give to divorce her and be done with it, but the hell of it was that he was inexorably tied to his wife. A divorce now would be as catastrophic to his plans as any misstep Lillian might make. There was only one surefire way to insure she never said anything, but there was no surefire way to make that happen without landing in even more crap than he was already in.

Jenson clambered up into the cart beside him looking pleased. "Twenty bucks says I'll take you on this one, Mort," he said.

Where the hell was Tom's ball? Morton cursed himself for letting his mind wander, then started the cart with a jerk and headed in the general vicinity of the fairway. A man planned his life, worked his ass off to reach a level some could only dream of achieving, and then all it took was a quick, vicious twist of fate and everything was turned on its head. One shitty decision made in a split second and he was down a road with no turning back. What he wouldn't give to live that moment over again. He spotted Tom's ball not ten feet from his own and swerved the cart toward it.

"You're on," he told Jenson.

Ten

"We'll be able to expand into catalog sales," Jason told Erica a couple of days after the auction as he gleefully shuffled through the rough sketches she'd done for the first few clients who'd placed orders. "And if you think the symphony gala proved to be a bonanza, wait until *Texas Today* comes out. Their circulation is huge, sugar. That's when we'll really be sitting pretty."

She was all for increasing sales, but going for the catalog market would mean sacrificing the one-of-a-kind originality of her jackets. Of course, even if she overcame her reluctance, it remained to be seen whether or not her designs proved popular enough, over the long haul, to go into any mass-marketing program. Confessing her reluctance, however, would deflate Jason's giddy mood. She found she didn't want to do that.

"Want to hear something delicious?"

She looked up to find him watching her with an excited gleam in his eye and guessed what he wanted to talk about. Jason was a born romantic, and lately he'd devoted himself to promoting what he viewed as her romance with Hunter. A complete lack of encouragement on her part did not discourage him. "What?" she asked, with some wariness.

"I've met someone."

She relaxed. Having him focused on his own love life meant he had less time to interfere in hers, even if her love life existed only in his mind. "Anybody I know?"

"Probably not. He's fairly new in Houston."

"What about Stephen?"

He waved a hand airily. "Stephen and I have an understanding, you know that. These things happen every now and then. You meet somebody, you click…" He shrugged, his expression a bit chagrined when Erica gave him a look. Jason might imagine his relationship with Stephen to be that open-ended, but she knew Stephen wasn't nearly so blasé when Jason got a crush on somebody new.

"Here's the best part," Jason said. "He's a junior partner at my father's law firm."

She put her sketch aside and turned to face him directly. "Your father's law firm."

He gave a wicked grin. "Wouldn't he croak if he knew?"

"Are you serious, Jace?"

"As a heart attack, sugar. It's Phillip Levin. I've seen him around at a couple of places where Stephen and I hang out sometimes and then-n-n—" he drew the word out tantalizingly "—we were introduced at the symphony gala. We've been together a couple of times since then."

"The firm knows?"

"That he's gay? God, no. He'd be banished to the file room in a heartbeat." He smiled, holding the sheaf of sketches against his chest. "We've been sneaking around. It's so much fun. I keep having this fantasy that my dad finds out and turns purple with apoplexy."

"And Phillip is comfortable with the risk he's taking?"

"We're cautious. To a point."

Jason fell in and out of love with the regularity of a rabbit, but it wasn't like him to dance so close to the flame of his father's prejudice, especially if it involved someone else. "Are you sure you know what you're doing, Jace?"

He shrugged. "When have I ever been sure about anything except my partnership with you?"

She drew her brows together in the beginning of a frown. "I'm going to remind you of this conversation when somebody lets the cat out of the bag and Phillip's job is in jeopardy and he blames you."

He reached over and snatched up the sketch she'd just finished. "Just keep cranking out these designs, sugar, and let me worry about my love life." He studied the sketch critically for a beat or two, then threw her a kiss. "Another winner. If you get any better at this, I'm going to feel real jealousy."

She rolled her eyes. "Go do something useful. I've got work to do."

On Wednesday of that week, Erica was at home working hard when Hunter showed up. Her heart gave a little jump when she saw him at her door. She stood for a moment and faced the fact that thoughts of him had been lurking in the back of her mind since Saturday night. It was unsettling. She hadn't been troubled by thoughts of a man in *that* way for years. She tucked a few strands of hair away, tugged her oversize sweatshirt down neatly and opened the door.

He grinned, looking big and male and all too appealing in a denim shirt and neat khakis. "It's lunchtime and I bet you forgot again," he said, holding up a take-out bag from a nearby deli.

She was never aware of the time when working. "I didn't forget…yet. I don't usually break for lunch at high noon." She didn't usually break for lunch, period. But she'd skipped breakfast and the aroma of whatever was in the bag was enticing.

"It's not kolaches, but it's almost as good." He stepped inside, coming a little too close. Then, before she saw it coming, he bent and kissed her. It was quick, over in a heartbeat. No hands, no touching, just the firm pressure of his lips on hers for a few heart-jolting seconds. But it was enough to rattle her. She didn't need the distraction of Hunter McCabe today, not with the workload facing her.

"Taco soup and spinach quesadillas," he said, handing it over.

Her mouth watering, she took the bag from him. "The food stays. You can't. But thanks, anyway."

He moved back a quarter of an inch with a look of mock disbelief. "You're kidding."

"About the food, no. But if I want to finish what's on my to-do list today, I can't be fooling around."

He assaulted her with another grin, this one slow and seductive. "Fooling around," he repeated softly. "As tempting as that sounds, all I had in mind was sharing lunch and a little information. But if I thought I could talk you into—"

She waved him to a stop. "You know what I—" She broke off, realized what he said. "What do you mean, information?"

Hips cocked, he propped one hand against the door frame, towering over her. "The topic is my mother's pin."

Her pulse jumped like a spooked rabbit. "The brooch? You asked her about it?"

He straightened up, sighing. "But since you need to work and don't have time—"

"Okay, okay. Twenty minutes." She grabbed a handful of denim shirt and dragged him across the threshold, laughing suddenly. There was something about Hunter that made her laugh, she admitted, something that made her forget she didn't usually take time for lunch. "You can tell me while we eat."

"Now you're talking," he said, and followed her into the kitchen.

He'd been outside working again, she noted, watching as he passed a hand over his windblown hair. His shoes looked dusty and he smelled of the outdoors. If he was an architect, when did he spend any time behind a drawing board? "Do you even have an office?" she asked.

He made a face. "I do, but mostly I feel cooped up when I'm there. I do a lot of design work out at the ranch, but when a project is in the construction phase, I have to hang close. I have a couple going right now, so I'm stuck in town."

She reached to open a cabinet. "I know what you mean. I'm torn between hanging out at the shop, which is where I like to be, and holing up here, which is where I can get the most work done." She moved to the breakfast nook with plates and glasses, feeling his gaze focused on her. Something about the way he watched her was unsettling. It made her breathless, aware of him all the way to her toes.

When she turned with their dishes in her hands, he took them and set the table as naturally as if they'd been in the habit of sharing meals together forever. "Let me guess," he said. "You're backed up with work as a result of the auction, right?"

"Right. I've taken so many orders that some of them probably won't be ready until next year's gala," she said dryly.

"Be careful what you wish for," he said, smiling.

It was his eyes and the way he watched her that made her so jittery, she decided. She had a feeling that all he needed to pounce and devour her was the tiniest sign from her. A part of her was tempted. A far more cautious part was appalled that she was even thinking it. "Water is all I have to drink. Is that okay?"

"It's fine." While she filled the glasses, he stood at the table and opened one of the to-go orders. "Have you always lived in this area near the Village?"

"No." She put napkins by each of their plates before adding, "But I've always lived in Houston."

"Me, too. My parents lived near Rice University when I was born. After my mother married Morton, they stayed in the house. As far as I know, he never even entertained a notion to move. The area was perfect for a man with Morton's ambitions. It took him fifteen years at CentrexO to snag the top job." It was the second time she'd sensed no love lost between Hunter and his stepfather. He must have seen the look on her face. "Enough of that," he said. "How about you? Where in Houston were you raised?"

"Not too far from where you lived," she told him.

He waited. "So, where?"

She took the food out of the sack. "Off Sunset."

Still studying her thoughtfully, he said, "Funny we never ran into each other, isn't it?"

"It's a huge city."

"Made up of closed neighborhoods, especially that neighborhood." He paused. "Unless you moved after your folks got a divorce."

"No, I stayed until I graduated. With my mother."

"Graduated high school?"

"Yes."

He crossed his arms, watching her. "Why do I sense that getting to know you will be an uphill struggle?"

"Do you want me to pop the soup into the microwave? It's probably lukewarm by now."

For a long moment, he said nothing, just looked at her. "Sure, sounds good."

She poured the soup into a glass bowl, set it in the microwave and hit the button for three minutes. When she turned back, he was holding up both hands. "Uncle," he said. "I give. You win."

She sighed. "I went to college at SMU, lived in the dorm the first year, then in an apartment with an assortment of roommates until I got my degree. When I returned to Houston, I had an apartment on San Felipe. Then I moved into a house. On—" She cleared away the sudden thickness in her throat. "On...Robinhood."

"Pricey neighborhood for somebody just out of college," he commented. "And your folks had moved away by then, I assume?"

"Yes." The microwave dinged and she wheeled around to open it. "This may be hot," she told him.

"Yeah." He waited while she poured the soup into two bowls, then politely held her chair. After taking his seat, he said, "Something's upset you. I'm sorry. I'll try not to hassle you with questions. I can see you don't like talking about yourself."

She stared into her soup, saying nothing. David had had a trust from his grandfather; otherwise, they'd never have been able to afford the house on Robinhood. Ignoring advice from almost everyone in her life at that time, she'd sold it within six months after his death. She simply couldn't bear being reminded of all she'd lost.

She looked up, startled, when he reached over and touched her hand. "No more questions until you give me some sign that you're willing." He settled back and picked up his napkin. "Did you ever figure out why you felt you'd seen my mother's pin before? That's an acceptable question, isn't it?"

"It is." Relieved to change the subject, she opened the to-go box with the quesadillas and arranged them neatly on her plate. "The answer's no. And I'm still a little embarrassed over making such a fuss in front of your mother and Mr. Trask."

"No need. And you didn't make a fuss. It looked to me as if your reaction surprised you as much as the rest of us. I actually thought you were going to faint."

"I almost did. No…" Her spoon suspended, she paused. "That's not quite the way I felt. It was something entirely different. As I told Jason, it was like being hurled back in time for a moment. The most puzzling part is how terrified I felt." She looked up at him. "Weird, huh?"

"Has anything like that ever happened to you before?"

"No, never." She gave a brief laugh. "It was a first, thank goodness."

He picked up a wedge of quesadilla and bit into it. After a moment, he said, "For what it's worth, I'm told the pin has been in my mother's family forever. It was a gift from her grandfather to his wife, an anniversary gift. That dates it to the turn of the last century, give or take a few years."

"Really?"

"Yeah. Which doesn't mean there couldn't be another one like it somewhere, although my mom insists it's an original piece."

"I'm sure it is. It was just a fluke that it set me off like that. I wish you hadn't even mentioned it to her. What must she think?"

"She thinks you're a strikingly beautiful woman."

She blinked, stricken with a rush of…something. "What?"

"Well, I'm the one who said you were beautiful." He wiped his mouth with a napkin, which almost, but not quite, hid his smile. "*Striking* was her word."

She was shaking her head and smiling now. "Hunter, *striking* is a word women use when they *don't* think someone is beautiful." She stood up, took his empty plate and bowl and dropped them into the sink. "This is a silly conversation. I need to get back to work and so do you."

He didn't stand but settled back, hooking an elbow on the back of the chair. "I wonder if there is something buried in your memory that was triggered when you saw the pin."

"Now you sound like Jason." She leaned against the sink, facing him. He'd already taken liberties she would never have allowed from anybody else, but she found that Hunter slipped through her defenses without making her feel threatened. Unsettled maybe. A little breathless, definitely. But not threatened. "He thinks it's some childhood trauma rising from long-buried ashes."

"And you nixed that?"

"Yes. I had a very normal childhood. There was the divorce, of course, and that's always hard for kids. I was no different. But I don't think my reaction had anything to do with that."

"No relationships that went bad?"

She moved to pick up the place mats from the table, pulled a drawer open and dropped them inside. "Why don't I write a bio and send you a copy?"

"Just this and my lips are zipped." He left his chair and moved around the table where she stood. "How is it that you aren't in a relationship? You're beautiful, you're talented, you're successful, you're independent and self-confident."

"Please…" She rolled her eyes.

"I mean it. Are the men you meet blind? Or is it that they're all gay?"

She sighed, looking away from him. For years, guarding her privacy had been a defense that helped her avoid intimacy. Other men had pressed her with the same questions and she'd found them intrusive, offensive even. Which made it relatively easy to deflect their curiosity. She sensed that Hunter's interest wasn't simply curiosity. And if it was seduction he had in mind, he was no different from all the others. But he had an interesting way of going about it. It almost disarmed her. She needed to keep in mind what she risked in letting down her guard.

Hunter lifted a hand and touched her hair. "There's no divorce in your past," he said, letting his fingers play with the curls near her ear. "You've told me that much. And no relationships gone sour. Has your work been your whole life? Haven't you needed something else?" His hand had settled at her throat, his fingers on her carotid.

Sex. That was what he meant. She wasn't so naive that she didn't know that. She suspected he'd be good in bed, too. And being a normal, healthy woman meant it would probably be good for her, as well. With her heartbeat speeding up, she caught his wrist, intending to push him away. She tried for a cool tone, knowing he probably felt her pulse throbbing. "You mean sex?"

"Not just sex." He bent and touched his lips to hers with gentle sensitivity. "But something just as necessary, Erica. Something emotional." He kissed her again, softly. "Something that feels good." Another butterfly-light kiss. "Something that makes you happy beyond the joy you find in your art."

She was now holding on to his wrist simply to keep herself upright. Did the man know the effect of those little kisses he bestowed so casually? Were his other women as beguiled as she was? Eyes closed, she savored the pleasure of it for another long moment, then murmured, "You have to go."

"In a minute." He moved in then, gathering her close as he took the kiss from sweet and gentle to deeply carnal. As his mouth covered hers and his tongue plunged, her thoughts scattered like so many birds startled into flight. Her hands went instinctively to his shoulders, where she should have pushed him away. Instead, they curled around his neck, unresisting when he brought her more fully against him. Spurred on by her response, he closed his hands on her hips and held her firmly against him, shocking her further by the evidence of his need.

With her mouth and her body yielding under his, the ability to think—to resist—seemed a million miles away. And the taste of him! Her tongue mated joyously with his, and when his mouth became less patient, racing over her face and eyes, her cheeks, her chin, she responded with all the fire that had been banked for nine years. Here was warmth and pleasure and sheer delight. Here was what had been taken from her. She moaned when his hand slipped under her sweatshirt and found her breast, unable to withhold the sound. He stroked and she shuddered. Her body came alive, flushed and singing. He tweaked her nipple and she lost herself in wild, mindless sensation.

And, inevitably, low, low in her belly, a slow and grinding ache was building. Oh, God, it felt so good. It had been so long. She whimpered as he pushed a leg between hers, guiding her to ride the pleasure, to milk it, to reach…to reach…

Suddenly, his hands and mouth were still. He pressed his lips against a throbbing pulse at her temple. "Let's take this to your bed, Erica."

His words were like a dash of cold water. What was she doing! Still, it was a moment before she wrenched back and pushed against him. Dazed and embarrassed now, she turned her face away, shaking her head. "I can't, I can't. I'm sorry."

He didn't move for a heartbeat. Then, drawing in a heavy breath, he said, "You mean that?"

"Yes, yes. I didn't mean this to happen," she said, unable to look at him. "I'm sorry. I don't know how I let it get so out of control so fast. I—"

He gave her a little shake. "Stop. There's nothing to apologize for. It takes two and we've been heading down this road since the moment we met. I want you. I have from day one. You have to know that. I sure haven't managed to hide it. Hell, I haven't wanted to. And if what happened just now is any clue, you want me, too. We're going to be great in bed together, sweetheart. You just tell me when you're ready."

"I'm never going to be ready!" she cried, tearing herself away. Turning, she buried her face in her hands.

"Why, for Christ's sake?" He moved up behind her, not touching. "What's so wrong about us taking the next natural step? I know you're not involved with anybody else and I—" He stopped abruptly and swore under his breath.

Her hands lowered and she looked at him. "And you are?"

"No. At least, not in a way that will be a problem."

"What does that mean, Hunter?"

Looking down, he put a hand on the back of his neck and rubbed it wearily. "I guess it's a good thing you stopped me before we—" He hesitated, as if needing different words. "There're some things I need to deal with in my personal life. I don't know why I've put it off. It's not like I didn't know you were going to be different from every woman I'd ever been interested in." He raised his eyes to hers. "I'm crazy about you, Erica. I've never felt this way before. And I didn't plan to try to get you in bed when I got here today. I swear I just wanted to see you. Have lunch with you. Talk to you. I want to get to know you." He smiled wryly into her eyes. "I still want all that, but one look at you and I want to jump your bones, too. I know you've done everything possible to show me that you don't feel the same way, but somehow, deep inside, I just can't accept it."

"Are you married?"

He gave a short laugh. "No. Never even come close. Never engaged, either. Not even tempted." His dark eyes locked with hers. "How about you?"

She drew in a deep breath. "Yes."

Stunned, he stared at her, then rubbed a hand over his mouth, obviously shaken. "Whoa, that's—I never thought—" He frowned. "Where is he?"

Turning away, she waved a hand to keep from saying the devastating word. "An accident. Nine years ago."

"You mean he's disabled? He's in a care facility of some kind?"

She closed her eyes briefly. "No, Hunter. It was a fatal accident."

"Jesus. He's…you're a widow?"

"Yes. He's dead. I'm a widow." She spoke in a flat tone, the words as dry as ashes in her mouth.

"Was it cancer? He had to be young."

"It was a hit-and-run."

"God, I'm sorry. I'm…I understand now. I wish you'd told me."

"You understand what?"

"That look in your eyes sometimes, the sadness." He laid a hand on her shoulder and gave it a warm squeeze. "It was one of the first things I noticed. I couldn't figure out what a woman like you had to be sad about. I finally put it down to your art. Someone with your talent might have a lot of emotional…stuff. I thought maybe it just came with the territory. But then I'd get glimpses of a lady with spunk, as when you locked your banker in the closet. Plus, once in a while, I think I see a sense of humor. Then there's your business. You've aced a difficult market with your shop. That takes guts and courage." He dropped his hand, resisting a more intimate touch, and stepped back. "One thing I do understand better now is your friendship with Jason. He's safe, isn't he?"

She looked up sharply. "Safe? You mean because he's gay?"

"If he's gay, yeah, he won't jump your bones, but—"

"But what? He's the dearest friend I have in the world. He encouraged me from the start when he had nothing to gain. Jason's been there for me. All I have to do is call and he comes. And careerwise, he's put my needs ahead of his own."

"Because, careerwise, you're a better bet, Erica," he said quietly. Before she could blast him again, he stopped her with a shake of his head. "I'm not trashing Jason. I can see what his friendship means to you. I like him myself. I also see how easy and affectionate you are with him, and when you're in the company of a man who might have a romantic interest in you, you throw up defenses. You may as well wear a sign saying, Stay Back. Don't Touch."

"It didn't seem to stop you," she said tartly.

"No," he said softly, "because I want you so much."

Refusing to reply to that, she brushed past him on her way to her front door. "You have to go now. And I'm sorry, but I won't be able to go to your ranch Sunday. It was a mistake to…to…"

"To begin trying to live as if you didn't die, too?"

She wheeled about, almost crashing into him. "Don't you dare talk to me like that! Don't you dare mention my life and how I live it to me ever again! You don't know anything about my life. You don't know a damn thing about me or…or D-David or…" Unable to go further, she turned back and reached for the doorknob. "And as for Jason, it's not true what you said. His art is wonderful. It's fresh and creative and…and…" Words failed her for a moment before she gathered her thoughts to forge on again. "If what you think is true, why would he push me to paint again? That would certainly not be in the best interest of our business, would it?"

He frowned at something she said. "Paint? As in art on a canvas? I thought those quilts and jackets were your art. You're saying you're an artist, too?"

"Not anymore."

"You gave that up when David died, too?" He paused a beat. "Along with what else, Erica?"

She jerked the door open to throw him out, but instead looked straight into the eyes of her mother and half sister coming up the porch steps. She almost screamed with frustration. Isabel Warren had a habit of simply dropping in when she came to Houston.

"Mother. I wasn't expecting you."

"I can see that," Isabel murmured. But if she was startled at having the door jerked open, she quickly recovered. Her interested gaze was now moving from her daughter's flushed face to the man beside her. Erica could only guess what she made of finding a man on the premises. She would certainly be intrigued by the air of hostility that simmered between them.

"It seems as if we're interrupting something, Steffie," she said to the twelve-year-old beside her. Stephanie's eyes almost popped with curiosity upon finding a man other than Jason with Erica. "We came to do some shopping for Stephanie," Isabel explained. "Spring break's just around the corner and we're going skiing. She's outgrown everything." Her eyes, not the smoky gray of Erica's, but a clear blue, moved again from Erica to Hunter. "Introduce us, dear."

"This is Hunter McCabe," Erica said. "Hunter, my mother, Isabel Warren."

"I can see the resemblance," Hunter said, turning on a charming smile. Effortlessly, or so it seemed to Erica. She was still upset, but apparently he could shrug off what happened between them without missing a beat. He reached out to shake her mother's hand. "My pleasure, Mrs. Warren."

"Oh, it's Isabel." With her hand still in his, she cocked her head to one side, studying him openly. "And don't let me interrupt. Please. Steffie and I thought we'd just say hi before getting started on our list of things to do. We stopped by the shop and Jason told us you were working at home."

"You aren't interrupting," Erica said with a steely smile. She glanced at Stephanie, who was also looking at Hunter with wide-eyed curiosity. "This is my little sister, Stephanie. Steffie, Hunter McCabe."

"Hi," Stephanie said, flashing him a smile heavily laced with braces. "Is that your Porsche?"

"Last time I checked."

"Cool."

He grinned. "You're partial to Porsches?"

"Are you serious? Isn't everybody?"

"I'll take you for a spin sometime."

Her blue eyes lit up. "Hey, way cool! How about now?"

"*Sometime* is not *now*," Erica said, cutting Hunter a deadly look. "Hunter was just leaving. He has work to do."

"I told Mom we should call first," Stephanie said. "I always tell her that, but she never listens."

"Because we don't want to give her a chance to make some excuse." The look she gave Hunter was classic what's-a-mother-to-do? "She works too hard. And now that she's coming into her own with her art, the family just has to grab a minute with her when we can. But, as you say, dear, that time's not now." With a hand on Stephanie's shoulder, she nudged her down the porch steps. "Hunter, there's no need for you to rush off on our account. We'll just pop on over to the Galleria and get started, then check back later. Don't worry, I'll phone first."

That would be a new twist, Erica thought. Her mother always defended her impromptu visits with a reminder that it would be odd if she drove all the way in from Austin without at least stopping in. Erica had often thought one way to curtail her surprise visits was if she were to find Erica in bed with a man…which had almost happened today, she reminded herself. Until today, it had never been a possibility.

"I'll show you my stuff after, Erica." Stephanie skipped a little to keep up with her mother. "And don't forget, you promised me a jacket for my birthday."

"I won't forget."

"Nice meeting you, Hunter," Isabel called as they reached the car.

"Yes, ma'am. Me, too."

As Isabel opened the door of her Lexus, she paused to look at them over the roof. "I almost forgot. John's meeting us for dinner tonight, Erica. He's bringing the twins. We're staying the night with the Morrisons. Why don't you join us? We haven't seen you since Christmas."

"I can't, Mother. I have a ton of work to do."

"You can bring Hunter, if you like," she said persuasively. "We'd love to have you both."

"I'm sorry. Maybe next time."

Isabel gave a little sigh. "Well, if you really can't…"

"Mom, chill, will you?" Stephanie said, reaching from

the passenger seat to tug her mother inside the car. "She's got *company,* can't you see?"

Erica watched in silence a minute later as the Lexus disappeared down the tree-lined street. Turning back, she found Hunter studying her with a look in his dark eyes that set her teeth on edge. "What?" she demanded.

"So, along with a life and painting, you also cut yourself off from your family."

She stepped out onto the porch and crossed her arms. "I know you've got something better to do than to stand here and waste time, Hunter."

"Who're the twins she mentioned?"

"After my mother remarried, Stephanie was born and then twin boys, Luke and Jack."

He stayed where he was for a long moment, studying her. "I'm trying to get a fix on who you are. Your mother and that little girl seem like genuinely nice people, people who care about you and who want to be in your life. Your mother jumped to the wrong conclusion on finding me here, of course, but judging from her reaction, I think she was tickled to discover that you still like sex."

Erica leveled her finger at the porch steps. "Will you please leave!"

"In a minute." He shoved his fingers through his hair. "I'm probably digging a hole here deep enough to bury myself, but I'm hoping you'll cut me some slack. This is a new ball game for me. What I told you about never feeling this way about a woman is true." He looked away and frowned. "You're probably thinking who the hell am I to judge how you've managed to cope after losing your husband, especially the way it happened. Except for my dad, who died when I was two, the only people I've ever lost are my grandparents, who went peacefully, for the most part." His gaze swung back to her. "But I still have a thousand questions about you, lady, and I know I don't have the right…at least, not right now."

"Just go, Hunter." In spite of her best efforts, her voice broke.

"One last thing and I'm outta here, I swear." He paused. "I'm not dumb enough to think I could take David's place. I wouldn't even try. But how long can you stay closed off to what's normal, Erica? Surely it's time to let go of the past. He wouldn't want you to act as if you were buried with him, would he?" He grimaced, as if he knew he'd stepped over a line.

"Damn, I guess that came out sounding insensitive and I'm sorry. But something special is happening between you and me whether you want to admit it or not. We were a heartbeat away from finding out just how special a minute ago. And you were with me all the way. I want you to think about that."

She was silent. Stubbornly silent.

He stepped past her then, coming close enough to trigger an odd little tingle. Close enough to remind her of what had almost happened. At the bottom of the steps, he halted, looking back at her. "And while you're thinking, here's a promise. Just because I've never been down this road doesn't mean I can't get it right. I can and I will. I'm not letting something this good slip away without a fight."

It was not regret she felt, she told herself fiercely, as she watched him drive away. She had a life. He was wrong about that. And it was a good one. He said himself he couldn't imagine what she felt, so he had no right to keep poking around—prying—into her secrets. Stirring up feelings that could only remind her. Undermining defenses that once were all she'd had to keep her sane. And she hadn't cut herself off from her family, she'd just…backed away a little. Being around Stephanie and the twins and her father's children just seemed to emphasize all she'd lost. It hurt less if she didn't see them, so she didn't, except rarely. Was that so weird? And as for sex, that had been forced into the same closed box with other painful memories. But she wasn't dead. She'd been tempted. Who wouldn't? He was a charmer, all male and oozing sex appeal. But giving in meant opening that box and risking all that came with it. The life she had now was fulfilling, it was meaningful, orderly. It was just the way she wanted it. She didn't need anything else.

She just had to keep that in mind.

Eleven

By the end of that day, Hunter was in a foul mood. And it wasn't because he left Erica's house with a hard-on that wouldn't quit, although that might be a factor. Except for those few incredible minutes when he thought he might be headed to bed with her, the day had been hexed with one problem after another. He'd returned to a disaster at one of his projects, which had taken most of the afternoon to resolve. That made him late showing up for a meeting with lawyers to finalize the details of the new lease agreement Hank had his heart set on. Dealing with lawyers and greedy people made him grouchy. Instead of wrapping it up for the day, he'd been forced to return to his office to work out a sticky change order on a project guaranteed to eat into profits on the job, which was three-quarters done. It was midnight before he finally climbed into the Porsche to head home to his condo.

The worry that Erica might refuse to let him into her life made him more than grouchy. He didn't know how it had happened in so short a time, but having her in his life had become very important. Vital. To make that happen, he needed her to get beyond whatever was holding her back from enjoying what he knew they could have together. But he was going to have to be patient. He hated that. He wasn't a patient man. She was almost paranoid when pushed for tidbits of her past. But why? What was it about her past—her marriage—that was so awful, or so painful that she couldn't even talk about it? Or maybe it was the opposite, he thought, pulling into the high-rise garage. But if it was so wonderful, why wouldn't she want to chance the possibility of finding the same thing again? Or something close.

The other thing bothering him was Kelly. He'd been stewing over that too long. He should have been up front about Erica from the get-go and now felt guilty and low-down because he hadn't. The minute she mentioned hearing it from some busybody is when he should have spoken up. He wasn't used to feeling guilty or dishonorable, because he didn't usually behave badly. And because he had, it added another level to his bad mood. His only excuse was that he'd never been down this road before. He met Erica and boom! Kelly flew out of his mind as if she'd never been there in the first place. He now knew she'd never been more than a good friend.

He punched the elevator to his floor and stared moodily at his feet while it rose. First thing when he got inside, he wanted a stiff whiskey. He'd passed on dinner with Hank after they left the lawyer's office, thinking the conversation might get around to his intentions about Kelly. It was likely she'd confided her suspicions about Erica to her dad, and the last thing he needed was a lecture from an outraged father. The elevator pinged. If Hank mentioned it, he thought, stepping out into the hallway, he'd just have to make him understand that his feelings for Kelly weren't the kind to build a marriage on.

His condominium was on the sixth floor. It was expensive, stylishly decorated and not unlike many others in the upscale condo developments in Houston. He had never felt as comfortable in it as when he was at his ranch, but it served the purpose. As he unlocked the door, he thought of Erica's house, so different from his high-rise. She'd restored it—or someone had. It should have been cozy and warm. Instead, it had a cool, almost sterile feel to it. Not so surprising now in light of what he'd learned about her. She lived a sterile, buttoned-up life.

He pushed the door open and was instantly on guard. The interior was dark. Two lamps timed to come on at dusk were off. He stood motionless, considering whether or not to back out and call security. If he'd been burglarized, there was a chance the thief was still inside. He realized then that there was a fire in the fireplace casting a shadowy glow. Odd. What kind of intruder would light a fire?

Closing the door, he walked inside, stopping at the bar that overlooked the expansive great room. The flames crackling cozily in the fireplace gave enough illumination to make out a figure on the sofa. She was stretched full-length on the cushions, a wineglass balanced on her tummy. For a wild and crazy moment, he thought that Erica might have forgiven him, had somehow managed to find his condo and was waiting for him. But that fantasy lasted only as long as it took to move closer and see her face.

"Kelly. What the hell are you doing here?"

She didn't answer, barely even glanced at him. Balancing the wineglass, she raised herself up slowly, then leaned over and carefully set it on an end table. That done, she settled back in the corner of the sofa, drew up her knees and locked her arms around them. "I have a key. Did you forget?"

He had, he realized. It had been the logical thing to do

at the time, a convenience he hadn't minded. It wasn't often she stayed overnight, and after a few times he'd been unable to meet her as planned when she came into Houston, she'd asked for it. "You've never used it without calling me first. And why are you sitting in the dark?" He crossed the room, intending to switch on a lamp.

"No, leave it. Please, Hunter."

With the reflection of the firelight on her face, he could see that she'd had more than a few drinks. "How much wine have you had?"

She gave a short laugh. "Not enough."

"What's going on, Kelly?" He stood at the foot of the sofa.

"I need to talk to you and this was the only way. It might be a long time before you come out to the ranch again. There's stuff keeping you here now."

"Nothing will ever keep me from going to the ranch, Kelly. Not for long, anyway. You should know that."

"But now, when you come, you take to the hills as soon as you can decently get away from Dad and Theresa. You avoid me altogether, Hunter. Don't deny it." She reached over and picked up her wineglass again. "So, like I said, this was the only way."

He stood for a moment or two debating the wisdom of talking to her while she was half lit. But knowing Kelly, if she was determined, there was probably no way to avoid it. With the bit in her teeth, she could be as stubborn as a mule. Resigned, he eased down onto the edge of an oversize ottoman. "So, how long have you been here?"

She held up the wineglass, pointing with a finger at the bottle on the bar. "Long enough to make a good dent in that wine. It's a good vintage. I took the liberty of choosing one of the best from your wine rack. I told myself I deserved it."

"You'll get no argument from me on that, but…" He stood up and turned on a lamp, then took the bottle from the bar and poured what remained down the sink. "No more for you tonight if we're going to talk. And I hope you aren't planning to drive back tonight. You're—"

"Let's cut to the chase, Hunter. You're seeing someone else."

He took a deep breath. "I'm not seeing someone else, Kell, but I have met someone and I have feelings for her. I'm sorry I didn't tell you as soon as I realized it was turning into something important. I'm not proud that I didn't speak up right away. I should have. And you have every right to cuss me out…or worse." He spread his arms in surrender. "So take your best shot."

Halfway through his speech, she set her glass aside. Now she stood up and walked to the fireplace. "It's Erica Stewart, isn't it?" she asked without turning around.

"I—yes." There was little to gain in denying it. Deep down, he was glad to have it out in the open. "I only met her a few weeks ago, and like I said, she's far from feeling the same way about me. We haven't even had a formal date. So it's not as if I'm involved in a serious affair. I would have said something to you before that happened."

She looked around at him. "Would you? When, I wonder. If two people are in a relationship, they owe it to each other to be up front," she told him. "You didn't do that, Hunter. That's what hurts."

"There was nothing to be up front about," he said. "I didn't go looking to cheat, Kelly."

"Maybe not, but that's what it feels like from my side."

"I'm sorry. But I tried to explain the way I felt before, Kell. I was never certain from the start that our relationship was the right kind to build a future on. You may have been certain of your feelings, but I never was. And I was careful not to make any declarations that would give you the wrong impression."

"You think I didn't notice that you never said I love you?" There was a small hitch in her voice as she spoke. "I used to think it was just a guy thing with you. That you actually did love me, but for some reason, you shied away from actually saying it."

"It wasn't that way at all. I have feelings for you, but they're just not the right ones for marriage."

"They were the right ones for sex, though. I didn't notice you rejecting that."

Shit. This was harder than he'd expected. "You're a warm and passionate person, Kell. What we had was good. But that doesn't change that you deserve a man who has deeper feelings, somebody who'll want more than what we had." She deserved someone who was as crazy for her as he was for Erica, but he could hardly say that. "There'll be someone like that, Kell."

With her fingers in a tortured knot, she took a deep breath. "Is it because I can't have children?"

"No," he said, in quick denial. "Jesus, Kelly. You know I wouldn't—"

"A lot of men would," she said.

"Well, not me," he said flatly. "And it'll hold true when you meet the right man, trust me on that."

Kelly had been fourteen years old when it happened. They were riding together one hot summer day. A snake slithered out from an outcropping of rock, spooking her horse. He'd shied and she'd slipped from the saddle, trapping her left foot in a stirrup. Hunter's heart had been in his throat as he chased the runaway horse dragging her across a field dotted with scrub trees. He saw the jagged stump and watched helplessly as it ripped her abdomen open. She'd been unconscious when he reached her and bleeding profusely. Later, in the hospital, he'd been with Hank when the doctor said her injuries would prevent her ever being able to conceive.

She smiled softly, sadly. "I guess it's really over for us, isn't it?"

"Only in that one way," he said, wishing he was anywhere else but here. "We're almost family and we'll still be friends. Nothing will ever change that."

She lifted her chin then and squared her shoulders. "I hope she's good enough for you," she told him, scrubbing at her damp cheeks with the heels of both hands. "I should beat the shit out of you for two-timing me, but Hank would disinherit me." She glanced around, found her jacket on the floor beside the dining table and picked it up. "He's never believed we were right for each other. He's tried I don't know how many times to tell me so, but what does he know? He's been in love with your mother for about thirty years and look how that's worked out."

"I'd feel better if you beat the shit out of me," Hunter said, beginning to relax. "And if you're thinking of putting that jacket on and starting back home, forget it. That bottle was three-quarters gone and so're you."

"I'm not an idiot, so relax, I'm not driving. I don't even have my car." The words were barely out before the doorbell rang.

"It's midnight," he said, heading for the door. "Who in hell can that be?"

Kelly retrieved her wineglass and emptied it in one final swallow. "Best guess, it'll be my chauffer," she said.

Hunter looked through the peephole. Jeff Pickering. He gave Kelly a quick, puzzled glance before opening the door. "Jeff. Kinda late for a visit, isn't it?"

"I'm looking for Kelly. Where is she?" As Pickering spoke, his gaze swept the interior of the condominium.

Spotting her standing in front of the fireplace, he shouldered past Hunter and headed across the room. "Well, are you satisfied now? Are you ready to go home?" He reached to take her by the arm, but she sidestepped him.

"Didn't anybody ever tell you it's rude to say I told you so?"

He looked at her, his blue eyes bloodshot but unwavering. "I didn't hear myself say that."

"It's written all over you. I let you talk me into driving tonight because…well, just because. But that doesn't give you the right to come storming in here and acting like… like some uptight guardian. I'm p-perf—" She hiccuped "—perfectly capable of handling this situation like an adult. I *am* an adult, if you haven't noticed."

He planted his hands on his hips. "Have you been drinking?"

"Look who's talking." She eyed his disheveled hair and his shirt, half in, half out of his pants. "You look like you've been pulled through a knothole backward."

"I've been waiting for you!" he shouted. "Worrying about you, like an idiot. What's with you and Hunter cozied up by a fire? It's sixty-five fuckin' degrees outside. This is Houston, not the Yukon." He shot Hunter a killing glance before facing Kelly again. "And you were supposed to call me."

She rolled her eyes. "Why is it everybody treats me like a teenager? Yes, Jeff, I have been drinking. Although it's a laugh that you and Hunter have turned into the drinking police. You forget I've seen you both falling down skunk-drunk. Besides, damn it, I have a right. In case you haven't noticed, my l-life is unraveling." She hiccuped again. "My plans have turned to shit, I'm depressed and I don't need a lecture."

"It was a stupid plan in the first place," Jeff shot back.

"You should have come into my practice when you came home instead of setting up on your own. That was *my* plan."

Not to be outdone, Kelly stuck her chin out, hands on her hips. "Did it occur to you that I might want to prove to myself I could do it on my own, Jeff?"

"Then you're the only one who needed proof," he told her. "It beats me—"

"Hey!" Hunter put two fingers to his lips and whistled. "Time, you two." Midway through their shouting match, he'd walked over and turned the gas off in the fireplace. The room was heating up fast enough without adding to it. "What the hell's going on? You sound like two kids in a sandbox."

Fists stiff at his sides, Jeff glared at Hunter. "Back off, Hunt. This is personal between Kelly and me."

Hunter put up both hands. "Not a problem if that's the way the wind blows. But since it is personal, it seems to me you might want to discuss it somewhere else. Somewhere private."

"She's been crying," Jeff accused.

"Now *that* would be personal between Kelly and me," Hunter pointed out.

"Oh, for Pete's sake!" Kelly caught Jeff by the arm and hauled him to the door. "You're making a jerk of yourself, Jeff. Let's go before Hunter throws you out. And before you start in lecturing me on the evils of drinking, you might want to sober up a little yourself."

"I've got an extra bedroom and the couch is comfortable," Hunter said, beginning to be amused. He'd never suspected Jeff had a thing for Kelly. It was a surprise, but then Jeff had always been a quiet one. Solid as a rock, he might be the perfect balance for Kelly's volatile personality.

"We don't need it," Jeff said, catching Kelly's wrist in his big hand. "I have a room at the Marriott."

"Kelly?" Hunter searched her face.

"It's okay." Without freeing herself from Jeff's possessive grip, Kelly rose on her tiptoes and kissed Hunter on the cheek. "I hope she's good enough for you," she told him again.

It was after they disappeared in the elevator that Hunter realized the day hadn't been a dead loss after all.

Twelve

Lillian stood at the elevator a full two minutes before finally reaching over and pressing the button to go up. She'd visited Hunter's office a grand total of three times in the four years he'd been there. Once for the grand opening, then for a Christmas party and a third time to pick up plans for the renovation of a building that had been left to the museum, for which Hunter had donated his services. The rift that had widened between them over the years had affected every facet of their relationship and she'd felt uncomfortable dropping in uninvited.

Today, invited or not, she was here.

His secretary was a young brunette, pencil-thin, with pretty blue eyes. The nameplate on her desk read "Jennifer Adkins." She smiled at Lillian in polite inquiry. "May I help you?"

"I'm Lillian Trask, Hunter's mother."

Jennifer's smile lit with genuine welcome as she rose to her feet. "Of course. What a nice surprise, Mrs. Trask."

"Thank you. It is a surprise as I don't have an appointment," she said. "Still, I hoped to catch Hunter in his office. Would you check and see if he can spare a few minutes?"

Jennifer was already out from behind her desk. "For you, I'm sure he can." She disappeared through a door and, in less than a minute, reappeared with Hunter on her heels. Smiling but perplexed, he crossed the small area and gave her a kiss on her cheek.

"Hi, Mom. What's up?"

"Can we go inside your office, please?"

His gaze narrowed, but with a touch to her waist, he ushered her away from the reception area and into his office. "How about a cup of coffee? It's pretty fresh, I think, but I wouldn't promise."

"No, I'll pass, thank you."

He gestured to a couch against one wall. "You'll be more comfortable over here." He bent, collecting a sheaf of papers and architectural plans strewn on the low table in front of the couch and placing them on the credenza behind his desk. "I just spent a couple of hours with a group of investors. Haven't had a chance to put this stuff back where it belongs."

She sat gingerly on the edge of the couch, as Hunter leaned a hip against his desk. "What's wrong, Mom? You look worried."

"You may toss me out when you hear why I've come." She locked her fingers together in her lap. "It's about Kelly."

He frowned. "What about her?"

"I was at the ranch Monday. I just happened to see Kelly in the barn and she was very upset to learn that you were having an affair."

He straightened, his smile disappearing. "She had no right to drag you into something that doesn't concern you. And I'm not having an affair."

"Then it's not true?" She felt a vast rush of relief.

"No, it's not."

"You're not involved with Erica Stewart?"

For a moment, he simply looked at her. She flushed under his scrutiny and quickly rose to her feet. "You don't have to answer that. I'm sorry. Of course, it's none of my business."

"Mom, what is going on? You haven't given a thought to my love life since I was in my teens."

"I certainly have, but until today I had the good sense not to mention it to you."

"Does Kelly know you're here?"

She put a hand to her head. She'd known Hunter was bound to hate this. "No, of course not." Wishing that she'd heeded her better judgment and stayed away, she faced him with as much dignity as she could muster. "It was understood that you and Kelly would…would eventually marry, Hunter. When she told me she suspected you were having an affair, I was almost as disappointed as she was."

"I'm not responsible for what people assumed, Mom. And I don't think you'll find Kelly going into a deep depression," he said dryly.

"But the two of you are perfect for each other. You have so much in common, Hunter. You have similar backgrounds, you like the same things, horses, the hill country, the ranch. Stop and think." She knew she was pushing, but there was so much at stake. "The ranch will one day belong to the two of you. Those are the things that make for a solid relationship."

With a hint of a smile, he relaxed a little and settled back on the edge of his desk. "Aren't you forgetting something?"

"What?" She gave him a blank look.

"I don't love Kelly."

She closed her eyes, shaking her head. She wouldn't—couldn't—accept that. "Of course you do."

"And she doesn't love me."

Now she stared with astonishment. "What can you be thinking? She's been in love with you since she was fifteen years old. Why else would she start—" She stopped before getting herself in even more trouble. "Why would she get involved otherwise, Hunter? She's not the kind of person to do that casually. She was planning a life with you. I just want you to stop and think before tossing it all away. As a mother, don't I have the right to say that?"

He pushed away from the desk, crossed to her and took her hand. "Here, Mom. Let's sit down." Hesitating only a moment, she did as he asked. When he was facing her, still holding her hand, he said, "You know that old saying, 'Nobody knows what goes on behind closed doors?' Well, with all due respect, you don't know about Kelly and me. Sure, I love her. But it's not the marrying kind of love."

"How do you know that?" she said, her voice rising. "With Kelly you'd have a better foundation than most."

"As good as you had with my dad?"

She dropped her eyes to her lap, unable to counter that. Releasing her, he stood up and clamped a hand on the back of his neck. "You're right that Kelly and I have a whole slew of things in common, Mom, but I've known from the start that something was missing." He gave her a slight smile. "Maybe I sensed what you and my dad shared, even if I was too young to understand it. And maybe Kelly was linked somehow in my mind with that fantasy. Whatever—and this is hindsight—I was wrong not to speak up before. Kelly and I have now talked this out. We're still friends. Nothing will change that. I can't turn the clock back, but trust me on this, Mom. Nothing is going to change what we feel into something it's not."

"Because you're involved with that artist, with Erica Stewart, aren't you?"

"It's because of Erica that I knew something was missing with Kelly and me. But why do you say 'that artist' as if you dislike her?" He was frowning.

She found it hard to meet his eyes. "How can I dislike her? I don't know her." Another lie, God forgive her.

"So since you don't know her, I'm curious to know why you disapprove of her?"

"I didn't say I disapprove of her. And it's not precisely true that I don't know her. I know of her by virtue of my connections at the Art Institute. She's very reclusive, Hunter. Hardly anyone knows anything about her. Except for Jason, who's her business partner, she has only a few friends. Is that someone you want to get involved with? I wish you'd reconsider."

"Then I have to remind you again, with all due respect, that I choose my friends, without consulting anybody, even you, Mom. I don't know what's behind this attempt to influence me against Erica. She's not a social butterfly, you're right about that, but I think with her family background, she could probably hobnob with the best. On the other hand, she's certainly not falling into my arms. In fact, I'm having a helluva time getting to first base with her. That should comfort you."

Lillian had moved to the huge glass window overlooking Houston's skyline. "She seemed agreeable enough to participate in the symphony gala," she said.

Hunter's eyes narrowed, picking up something in her tone. "According to Jason, somebody on the committee called and asked her. She didn't initiate anything."

"She never has to initiate anything," Lillian said bitterly. "The article in the *Chronicle,* the upcoming spread in *Texas Today,* the traffic to her shop in the Village, all of it was—" She stopped suddenly, appalled at herself.

"Wait. Wait a minute. You're saying what, exactly?" The look on his face was frightening. "Are you saying Erica has a patron, as in someone who boosts her career and her shop?"

"I spoke out of turn," Lillian said, looking around in panic for her handbag. Spotting it on a chair, she scooped it up and walked quickly to the door.

Hunter followed her, his eyes burning into hers. "Is she sleeping with someone?"

"I'm sorry, I have to run."

"Not yet." He put out a hand to stop her opening the door. "There's a name for what you're implying."

"I shouldn't have said anything. I was upset. I didn't mean it, Hunter. Please, I want to go now."

He heard her denials, but he wasn't convinced. "From the start, I've sensed something odd in the way you react whenever I mention Erica's name. She claims she doesn't know you and you say the same. Yet you freeze up when you see her label on your birthday gift. She nearly faints when she sees your antique pin. And yet you tell me it's a family heirloom. Erica couldn't possibly have seen it. Anywhere." He stopped, struck by a new thought. "Unless you're lying to me, Mom. Or she is."

"No."

"Or both of you."

"You have to let me go now, Hunter," she said, infusing the demand with a shaky dignity. She was so pale that even her lips were colorless, but she looked him in the eye. "I'm chairperson of a committee that meets in twenty minutes. I can't be late."

He held her gaze without replying until she looked away. "Lillian Trask late? We can't have that, can we?" he said softly. With cool courtesy, he opened the door for her. "Jennifer will show you out."

Thirteen

Erica stepped back and surveyed the emerging images on the canvas. She hadn't planned the painting, but in the end she hadn't been able to ignore blips and flashes of form and shape that made her fingers itch to pick up a brush. So, instead of working on the new designs she'd promised Jason, she'd started painting. Now, hours later, here was the result—another disturbing, vaguely impressionistic rendering similar to the thing that she'd shoved in the back of her closet a few days ago. Until now, she'd longed to be able to paint again, but not these macabre images from a source she didn't understand. It was eerie.

She froze suddenly at the sound of footsteps. She'd locked the door…hadn't she? But someone was inside, heading her way. She spun toward the door in panic, dropping her brush and palette. But before she had a chance to think where to run, Hunter appeared in the doorway.

She stared at him, her heart beating like a wild thing. "How did you get in here?"

He held up a key. "I guess you didn't hear me. I rang the doorbell and—"

Shaking like a leaf, she put her hand on her chest. He

moved to her side, frowning. "Maybe you'd better sit down."

But fear was fading fast as outrage took over. She reached out and snatched the key. "Where did you get this?"

"Jason gave it to me. He called and sent me over to check on you. You were supposed to meet him with some new designs hours ago."

"He called you?" She was still trembling, waiting for her heartbeat to slow. She wrapped her arms around herself to hide it.

"Because he couldn't reach you." His gaze narrowed. "Damn, I gave you a real fright, didn't I? I'm sorry. I thought—I don't know what I thought, but your car was outside and banging on the door and ringing your bell didn't raise you, so since I had the key…"

She'd been too focused on blindly transferring images to canvas to hear anything. Once, such concentration had been routine and she blessed whatever fate had returned it, even as the result troubled her. She didn't like being so zoned out that anybody could walk right in without her ever hearing anything. "Jason shouldn't have bothered you," she said, stepping in front of the easel to shield her work. "He knows I'll get the designs to him when they're done."

"It was you he was worried about, not the designs. He's been trying your land line and your cell for hours. I'm here because he couldn't leave the shop."

Her gaze fell at the stern look in his eyes. She was forced to admit she'd been thoughtless. It didn't surprise her that Jason had been concerned. He was a worrywart. But sending Hunter over with her key was a sneaky way of throwing them together. He'd been nagging her for days to call him.

"He could have closed the shop for a few minutes to check on me himself," she said. "This was totally unnecessary. You shouldn't have bothered."

He shrugged. "It's no bother. I was glad to do it." It seemed to interest him that she hovered in front of the easel. Moving closer, he peered around her to get a look. "I thought you weren't into painting anymore."

His interest disarmed her and she turned to study the painting herself. "I wasn't until just lately. But Jason's right, I should have been working."

"You're lucky there's somebody who cares enough to check on you," he said, but his gaze was still fixed on the picture. "He was worried." He turned to look at her then. "And so was I."

She bent to pick up her scattered palette and brushes. "I'm sorry. He shouldn't have dragged you away from your work. I hope you haven't lost too much time." It would snow in Houston before she told Jason anything else, she vowed.

"Jason didn't drag me into anything. If I'd been too busy, I would have told him so." He watched her for a moment as if weighing what he was about to say. "Besides, it gave me an excuse to see you again. I'm still hoping to change your mind about coming out to the ranch with me."

"Doesn't it get sticky trying to manage more than one relationship at a time?" It was a bitchy thing to say, but it was out before she thought. He would think his involvement with another woman mattered to her.

"There is no other relationship," he told her. "I was seeing a woman, someone I've known a long time. We talked the same night I left your place. We agreed it's over and we're still friends."

"There's no need to explain. Your private life doesn't concern me." She reached for a cloth and turpentine to deal with the paint spilled from her pallet on the floor, but before she could bend down to start wiping, he caught her arm.

"Wait, hear me out, please." With a firm grip on her wrist, he paused, as if carefully considering his words. "I wish I could pretty this up, but no matter how I say it, it sounds lame. Kelly's someone I've known all my life. She's a vet. We had—we have a lot in common—the ranch, a love of horses. We have that kind of connection," he explained, turning her wrist up and studying it. "To tell the truth, we sort of drifted into a relationship." For a second, she thought he was going to lift her wrist for a kiss. Her heart stumbled, then tripped into double time. She quickly withdrew it.

If he noticed, he gave no sign. "Our parents are close," he told her. "They were once in business together. All those factors were in place and it seemed a match made in heaven. Our folks thought so. Friends, too. But somehow we never got around to making a serious commitment."

"A lot of people have made do with a lot less."

"I know. But I swear I knew something was missing from the start." His gaze moved from her picture to look into her eyes. "And after I met you, I knew what it was."

She let out a long breath and reminded herself not to be charmed by a man who'd probably left a string of broken-hearted women long enough to stretch across Texas. "I'm not looking to have an affair with you, Hunter. If you've ended a relationship thinking you'll talk me into it, think again. That's your fantasy, not mine. My designs and the shop are the reality of my life and my future. I don't need anything more."

He didn't reply for a minute. She braced to resist him, thinking he probably had a dozen pitches to cajole a reluctant female. She only knew she didn't intend to be one of them.

"A future should have more than what you see, but I'll save that argument for another day," he said, surprising her. "Just tell me you'll go with me to the ranch Sunday as we planned."

She cocked her head and gave him a quizzical look. "Did you hear anything I just said?"

"I heard it all, sweetheart." He reached out and swiped at a smudge of paint on her cheek. "You don't want an affair, you're sworn off getting involved and you're too levelheaded to believe in fantasies. So, we'll take a picnic lunch and talk horses. Questions about your past are off-limits."

She smiled in spite of herself. "Let me hear you swear to that on your horse's life."

He raised his right hand. "Consider it sworn."

An affair with Hunter was out of the question, but the last time they'd been together, he'd hit a nerve with his challenge that she think about what she might have in her life if she let go of the past. A visit to his ranch and a horseback ride wouldn't lead to anything unless she was foolish enough to allow it. It might even be fun.

"Okay," she told him. "And I guess you're still planning to get an early start."

He grinned. "Six o'clock. And please don't get caught up in one of your painting marathons. Looks like you tend to lose track of time when you get a paintbrush in your hand." His gaze wandered once more to the painting. "Now that we're friends again, would it be out of line to ask what it is?"

Still holding the cloth, she stood with him studying it. "I'm not sure…"

Picking up something in her tone, he gave her a quick glance. "I don't know much about impressionist art—that's the style, isn't it?" When she nodded, he went on.

"Don't be offended, but it looks pretty grim. It could be the cover for a horror novel. I mean, it's sort of menacing. Is that what you meant to convey?"

"I'm not sure what I meant to convey. It's nothing like what I've painted in the past. I've never done anything so—" She trailed off, still puzzled to explain it herself.

"What?" He still watched her. "You've never done anything so…"

"Anything so…raw. So dark. But I haven't painted in nine years. I honestly thought I'd lost the ability to paint. Then, a few weeks ago, I was working late and suddenly I saw this picture…well, not exactly a picture, just images, little camera clicks of…something. I went over to the easel. Jason always insisted I could paint again someday, so he'd set everything up for the moment when I did. That was so long ago that I almost forgot the easel was there."

"Jason, your trusty friend for all reasons."

She gave him a speaking look. "Yes. Exactly."

"Don't worry," he said, lifting both hands, palms out. "I'm not into judging Jason today."

"Good. Anyway," she said after a moment, "on that particular night, I felt almost as if I was in a trance as I picked up a sketching pencil and started. This may sound odd, but it was as if someone else was guiding my hand. When I was done and I stood back to look at it, it terrified me."

"Why? What was it?"

"Nothing I could readily identify, but it terrified me. Something about it really freaked me out. It was similar to this one, very dark and littered with obscure images." She hugged herself as a chill ran down her spine.

"Where is it now? Did you destroy it?"

"No." She moved her shoulders restlessly. "I shoved it in the back of my closet. I couldn't wait to get it out of my sight. It was…so…weird." She looked away for a minute, thinking. "It was like when I saw your mother's brooch, that same peculiar feeling, except there was no brooch. What I painted was not even close, but it was meant to symbolize something, I'm sure of that. Looking at it gave me the same sickening feeling I had when I saw your mother's jewelry." She winced with dismay. "I'm sorry, I didn't mean that the way it came out. Your mother's jewelry was beautiful. It just—"

"Symbolized something that freaked you out."

She gave a wry shrug. "Yes. Didn't I say it sounded strange?"

"Maybe you should reconsider Jason's theory." When she looked puzzled, he went on. "Maybe there's something in your subconscious trying to surface. I'm not much into that kind of mumbo jumbo, but—" He glanced at the painting again. "If I were into that stuff, I'd say whatever's pushing you to paint those images might be trying to tell you something."

"Such as?"

"That's for you to figure out."

"Well, I just can't accept that."

"Why not?"

"It's too…weird. I'm not a weird person. You said it yourself. I'm levelheaded and practical. My feet are firmly on the ground. And I don't paint at the direction of some 'otherworld whatever' inhabiting my body and taking over my brain. At least, I never have," she added ruefully.

"It would be your inner world, your subconscious. And don't tell me you have no subconscious. It's there, even though it might be bottled up."

He said it with a teasing smile. She disagreed, of course, but didn't argue. Her gaze strayed again to the painting, and once more, she tried to make sense of it. "I always thought if I was finally able to paint again it would be a wonderful thing," she murmured. "Instead, it's turning out to be something…weird."

"There's that word again." His smile was not without sympathy. She was suddenly amazed at how easily she'd rambled on about something intensely personal. She realized that in talking to Hunter, she was coming dangerously close to letting him into a place she'd kept closed from others for a long time. "Look at it this way," he told her. "If you haven't painted for a long time, at least that part of you is alive and functioning again."

"On the other hand, I'm turning out work that's making me crazy," she said dryly.

"Maybe that's okay for now. Maybe you should just go with your instincts and see what happens."

Turning away from the painting, she reached for a cloth, moistened it with a cleansing agent and began scrubbing her hands. "I don't know why I'm bothering to have this conversation when I've got so much work to do," she said briskly. "And so do you."

He backed away, grinning. "Okay, subject tabled…for the time being."

After he was gone, she moved to her drawing board but found it hard to concentrate on new jacket designs when her mind and eyes kept going back to the painting and what it could mean. Maybe in time…

"Just go with your instincts and see what happens."

She truly didn't have much choice, she thought, unless she sacrificed the opportunity to paint altogether. And she wasn't willing to do that ever again.

Lillian stood at a window watching thin, icy sheets of rain lash the street as night moved in. The weather cell hanging over the city had produced a long, wet, dreary day, turning meteorologists into liars. Clearing by midafternoon, they'd predicted. So much for that. She glanced at the antique grandfather clock just striking the cocktail hour and longed for a cigarette. With no letup on a rainy day, she sometimes slipped into the sunroom to smoke where French doors made it possible to close off the rest of the house. But with Morton pacing the den and talking on his cell phone, she couldn't chance slipping away. He'd mentioned before taking the call that he wanted to talk to her. Maybe he'd been notified where he was to be posted as an ambassador. She felt not a scrap of enthusiasm, even if it turned out to be Paris.

"Well, Taiwan's out."

She turned with a baffled look. "What?"

"Taiwan." He punched a few numbers and put the phone to his ear, listening to messages. Another two minutes passed. Then, closing the phone with a snap, he walked to the bar and took a crystal tumbler from a glass shelf, removed the cap from a bottle of single malt Scotch and poured himself a drink. "I thought I might have nailed the appointment, but now it looks as though they're considering something in the Middle East."

She felt a spurt of dismay as visions of women, cloaked and veiled, rose in her mind. "Did he mention where, exactly?"

"Not really. If it turns out to be somewhere I hate, I'll take a shot at heading them off before it gets too far along." He moved to the window and stood beside her for a moment watching the rain. "I'd hoped for a place less controversial, but this isn't exactly a surprise. I can guess what's driving the discussion. CentrexO has done a lot of oil business in the Middle East."

"My God, Morton, that whole area is so unstable."

"Yeah, but it's highly visible and, because of that, it

might be the most advantageous assignment in the long run. I have plenty of connections there."

Yes, but it would be terribly confining to an American woman.

"That's a problem we can discuss later. Right now, there's something else on my mind." He tossed off the rest of his drink abruptly. "I woke up last night and realized you weren't beside me. It was after three, Lillian. Where were you?"

"I've been having some insomnia." Sleeplessness was the least of the problems plaguing her lately, but it was the only one she was willing to discuss with Morton. "My gynecologist says it's a common symptom once you give up taking hormones. She's suggesting some homeopathic remedies, but so far I haven't noticed it helping much."

Morton gave a dismissive grunt. He'd never been sympathetic about her struggle with the ups and downs of menopause. To her relief, he didn't press her further, but asked, "Did you reach Jocelyn?"

He'd been pressing her about Jocelyn for several days and she'd avoided telling him she'd heard nothing in spite of a dozen attempts. "Not yet, but you know how she is when she becomes involved in a new project. Maybe she's finally finding her niche in journalism."

"I checked into that outfit in Key West, Lillian. Brace yourself. It will not be a stepping-stone to the *New York Times*. When I called, all I got was a runaround from the guy who answered the phone. I want you to keep trying her cell. You can remind her that if she wants her regular allowance deposited next month, she damn well better call. That'll bring her around."

Lillian wasn't so certain. Morton had threatened to stop her allowance before without bringing her around. As her father, he had more control over Jocelyn than he'd ever had with Hunter. Not that it was ever very effective. She'd been a headstrong, troubled teenager, and at twenty-five, she was still prone to making reckless, sometimes desperately foolish decisions. Because of that, it was worrisome to Lillian that she wasn't able to reach her. All she got lately was her voice mail. She was going to ask Hunter to fly to Key West and check on her if she didn't hear something soon. It wouldn't be the first time she'd appealed to him to rescue his sister when Lillian became concerned about her.

"So what's the latest with Hunter and Kelly?"

She looked at Morton blankly. "I'm sorry…"

"Hunter and Kelly," he repeated. "Is that over or will you and Colson be able to hustle them to the altar after all?"

"It's over, Morton."

"No shit." Chuckling, he poured himself another drink. "You and Colson must have cried a river over that."

She sighed. "Hank and I had nothing to do with the relationship between Hunter and Kelly. It came about naturally because they were so ideally suited." She walked to a sofa and adjusted a cushion, plumping it up before settling it precisely in place. "Many marriages are based on a lot less. Hunter could've done much worse than to marry Kelly."

"Such as getting into the pants of that artist?"

She winced inwardly but kept her reaction to herself. "Kelly believes he's having an affair," she said. "And in spite of his denial, I think he's very interested in Erica. I'm afraid it's only a matter of time before he talks her around." She moved to a side table and fiddled with an arrangement of fresh flowers. "I have never known him to show so much interest in a woman before, Morton. I'm truly worried."

"Why? He's probably interested in fucking her, not marrying her. What difference does it make who he fucks?"

"Please. You know I've asked you not to use that word."

"She's a looker, too," he said, ignoring her. "Hell, you can't fault him for having the hots for a woman like that."

"There's more to his interest in this woman than sheer lust," she told him. "We've talked. I know what I'm saying."

"Who's talked, you and the artist or you and Hunter?"

"I certainly haven't spoken to Erica, you know that. I talked with Hunter. After Kelly told me he broke up with her, I wanted to know if his reason had anything to do with Erica Stewart. It did. He admitted it. I knew one day he'd fall for someone in a big way. It's only natural. Men are marrying later and later these days, but human nature hasn't changed. Even the most cautious fall in love eventually. It just took Hunter a while to get there. Now that he's met Erica, she's the one."

"Or you're convinced he thinks she's the one."

"No, Morton. She's the one. I don't know whether he realizes it himself or not yet, but he's in love with her." Thunder rumbled in the distance and she moved back to the window. "It is so bizarre that, of all the women in the world, she's the one he falls for."

"Well, I now know why you're floating around the house in the middle of the night, sleepless and paranoid. Get hold of yourself. You go through these spells every now and then, torturing yourself over shit that's ancient history. It's self-destructive, Lillian. You can't do anything about it, anyway. Hell, he's been rejecting advice coming from you or me since puberty."

"She insists she recognizes my brooch."

With his drink halfway to his mouth, he paused. "What?"

"Erica. My brooch. She almost fainted when she saw it that night at the gala. That concerns me, Morton. You know why." She was pacing now, her gaze on the floor. "I know what you say makes sense…that we're powerless to do anything to stop him, but I don't think I can bear it if Hunter's interest in her becomes truly serious."

"You can and you will." He faced her, speaking with real menace in his tone. "This is why I wanted to talk to you, Lillian. We are at a very delicate stage in my appointment. I don't want you screwing it up. Whatever happens with Hunter and that woman—with Hunter and any woman, for Christ's sake—it's nothing to do with you. With us. So back off, let him marry the bitch, for all we care. Just you keep your distance and don't, under any circumstances, say anything that will start him sniffing around in shit that could unravel our whole lives."

Tears had flooded her eyes long before he was done. With a hand clamped over her mouth, she stared at him in absolute misery. "Oh, Morton, if only—"

"Goddamn it!" He slammed the glass down, showering the table with petals from the arrangement. It cut her off as abruptly as if he'd struck her. "If only what? If only it hadn't happened? If only we could turn back the clock? If only we hadn't—" He stopped, pulled himself together and took a deep breath. "You listen to me and hear me well, Lillian. Put this back in the past where it belongs. Stay out of whatever's going on with Hunter and Erica Stewart. Focus yourself on acting and looking the perfect wife of a U.S. ambassador. I'm not just blowing smoke here, Lillian. I want this appointment and I don't want you screwing it up. If you do, I'll take you down with me. And you know I can do it."

Fourteen

To Erica's surprise, she'd come awake that morning to a sense of anticipation long before her alarm went off. Her doorbell had chimed at six on the dot. Hunter, bearing kolaches, coffee and an infectious grin, had been unable to suppress a restless yen to get to the ranch. He'd talked her out of taking time for breakfast, saying they could eat the kolaches in the car once they were under way. But instead of heading directly to the interstate, he wove through her neighborhood and eventually turned onto Shepherd.

It was when he turned next onto Kirby that she realized he had some destination in mind other than his ranch. "This is definitely a roundabout way to get to I-10," she said as they zipped by early bikers at Hermann Park. "Where are we going?"

"Hank called on my cell phone a few minutes before I reached your place. He asked me to swing by my mother's house to pick up some legal documents he needs that are stored in her safe. I know it's a pain, but he's up to his neck in a deal to lease additional land adjacent to what we already own at the ranch and he tends to be obsessive whenever he takes on a project."

"It's okay. As you say, it's Sunday. We're not on a schedule." She dug into her purse for her sunglasses. It was a beautiful day and she found herself looking forward to being in the hill country and on horseback again.

"And if you're wondering why my mother would hold legal documents that Hank needs, it's because he and my dad are the original owners of the ranch. When my dad was killed, his share came to me. Since I was only two years old, Mom held the documents and they're still in her safe. Now there's some kind of glitch that a surveyor found, and before Hank can finalize that lease he's so hot to have, it'll have to be squared away." He glanced over at her and grinned. "I guess that's more information than you wanted, huh?"

"It explains your attachment to the ranch," she said, slipping the sunglasses onto her face.

"Yeah, I guess. We'll just zip on over, pick up the papers and then get on the road. I'll make it fast."

"Will she be up at this hour?"

"Hank said he called to let her know I was coming, so I assume so. Morton's in Washington. He's been in and out of D.C. for several weeks now." As he approached a red light, he signaled for a right turn. "I think he's got something big cooking."

Erica tensed as he turned. This was a neighborhood she knew well. "Where exactly does your mother live?"

"Just a few blocks from here." He made another turn and her heart began to pound. He glanced over at her. "The neighborhood's looking familiar, right?"

"Yes." She turned her gaze to the passenger window as he drove past the street where she'd grown up. A few minutes later, he turned into a driveway and stopped before an ornate wrought-iron gate. The house itself was set back from the street on a luxuriously landscaped lot shaded by ancient oaks. Elegant and spacious, it had been built in the heyday of oil barons and looked much like its neighbors on the street.

"Hopefully, Mom will have those papers ready," Hunter said as he released the catch of his seat belt. "We won't need to go inside the gate if you don't mind waiting in the car while I get the papers. The front door is accessible from the street."

"I don't mind. Give your mother my regards."

"Yeah." He hesitated a beat or two before uncoiling his long legs and climbing out. Then, leaning down, he said, "I'm leaving the engine running. There's a selection of CDs if you get bored, but this shouldn't take more than a few minutes."

"I'll be fine."

Sensing something, he hesitated, but then he backed away, closed the door and with a soft knock on the roof of the Porsche, he turned and jogged off. Deliberately focusing her attention inside the car, Erica began sorting through his collection of CDs. She found Sarah Brightman's newest CD and popped it into the slot, then breathed deeply, giving herself up to the sweetness of the singer's voice. Blocking thoughts of the last time she'd been in this neighborhood. Shutting off memories. Closing off the pain in her heart.

She wasn't sure how long she'd been in that zoned-out state, only that she was intensely relieved when Hunter returned and slipped into the driver's seat.

"Sorry about that," he said, putting the Porsche in reverse gear. As he turned to back out, he glanced at her and instantly frowned. "Are you okay?"

She reached for the volume and turned it down. "I'm fine." The smile she gave him felt wrong on her face, but she kept it in place. "Just enjoying the music. She has a wonderful voice, doesn't she? It was quite a feat, moving from her operatic style in *Phantom of the Opera* to this. Don't you think so?" She fixed her gaze on the jacket of the CD. "Imagine having that kind of talent."

It was nervous chatter, a blatant attempt to divert him, and Hunter let her get away with it. He had no comment about Brightman's talent or the stark whiteness of Erica's face. After a beat or two, he released the brake and drove away from his mother's house. And Erica was profoundly relieved.

They made the drive from Houston to Hunter's ranch in a couple of hours, so that by nine in the morning, they were mounted and riding somewhere near the south property line. The beauty of the day was holding. Mild and sunny with just a hint of a breeze, it was just about perfect for what Hunter planned. It was when they crested a hill near a stream that Erica was treated to a sight that took her breath away. Pulling up on the reins, she sat back in the saddle drinking in a riot of color—bluebonnets, orange Indian paintbrush and pink primroses—wildflowers for which Texas was famous. Her fingers itched to begin painting.

"This is so beautiful," she told him. "Now I understand why you resent being cooped up in an office in Houston."

Hunter sat, resting both hands on the pommel, watching her and not the scenery. "Makes you want to set up your easel, huh?"

She smiled, wondering if her fingers had been twitching. "The thought came to mind, I admit."

"It can be arranged."

She turned to look at him. "Maybe…someday."

"I'll take that as a promise that you'll come again."

No promises, but she was enjoying being outside and

on horseback again. And, she had to admit, she enjoyed being with Hunter. She'd recovered from the unsettling re-action she'd had waiting for him in front of his mother's house. The neighborhood held nothing but bitter memo-ries for her and for nine years she'd avoided it. She couldn't get away fast enough.

"You were right, I still know how to ride a horse," she told him as they turned the horses toward a destination he had in mind for a picnic. "And it's fun. Lady is a darling. I'm glad I came."

"She doesn't get enough exercise, so taking her out today is doing us a favor." He pushed his hat back a bit to look over at her. "I thought for a minute you were about to change your mind after we stopped at my mother's house. I didn't realize just being in the neighborhood might distress you. I should have gone there first and then picked you up. I'm sorry."

"It's okay. It's hard to be sad in these surroundings. Being on horseback again is great, too. You must miss rid-ing when you're forced to stay in Houston."

"I do. In fact, most of the horses don't get enough ex-ercise now. One of these days, we'll bring your little sis-ter with us…um, Stephanie, right?"

"Right," she said faintly.

"Treat her to a spin in the Porsche, as promised, and a riding lesson. How old did you say the twins were?"

"How old?" Her mind was spinning at the way he was invading her life.

"Yeah, your twin brothers," he explained with amused patience. "The ones you told me about…the ones your mother mentioned!"

"Half brothers. Jack and Luke," she told him. "They're nine."

"Perfect age to get a kick out of learning to ride…un-less they know how already?"

"No. Ah…I don't think so." The truth was, she didn't know. Feeling uncomfortable and the sudden need to pull away from more intimacy, she urged Lady into a gallop. The horse responded with delight at being given her head, and with Hunter thundering behind her they raced across the colorful field. Moments later she was forced to rein in on the crest of a hill. Spread before her was an orchard. Although the limbs were naked, the trees had a pale green sheen as tender buds emerged.

"Hank's hobby," Hunter explained. "Several years ago he got the idea to plant pecan trees after someone invited him to a symposium at Texas A&M. He started with just a few varieties at first. Now, several thousand trees later, he's a recognized expert in the field. Actually, he's at some kind of grower's meeting in Austin this weekend, otherwise he would have been out on the porch to greet us today."

"So you don't have cattle on your ranch?"

"No, just a few horses and one aging chocolate Lab." He pulled Jasper up and caught the bridle of her horse. "Are you hungry?"

She was, she discovered. He'd promised a picnic but had not packed anything to eat that she could see. "Do you have some squished sandwiches in your saddlebags?"

"No, but I have a stash somewhere beyond that water well. We can stake out the horses there, water them and find a place to set up." Indicating the direction, he urged Jasper forward with a nudge of his knee. "Cisco should have dropped off a basket a while ago, and I promise you will find no squished sandwiches. Theresa will have packed fried chicken and all the trimmings."

The trimmings included potato salad, crisp dill pickles, cherry tomatoes, a loaf of French bread—still warm—and a bottle of chilled chardonnay. Erica looked on in amazement as Hunter took everything out of a wicker basket and arranged it on a blanket.

"If you had told me we'd be having a feast like this," she told him, polishing off a drumstick, "I would have worn my running shoes and jogged back to the ranch house. I have never tasted anything so delicious. What's for dessert?"

"More wine. Here, have some." He uncorked the bottle and refilled her wineglass. By the time he'd unpacked the food, she'd been unsurprised to see his "stash" included stemware and real silver.

"Thank you. Dessert would be overkill, I guess." Refusing to let her thoughts take her anywhere that would spoil the simple pleasure of the moment, she leaned back against a boulder and gazed up to enjoy the sight of birds gliding on wind currents. "Are those eagles?" she asked.

Hunter stretched out full-length and propped himself up on one elbow watching her. "I wish I could say they were eagles, or even hawks, since people seem to view them with awe. But to tell the truth, they're buzzards."

She smiled. "You're right, buzzards don't compare with their regal cousins, do they?"

"Except in flight."

"Uh-huh." Erica sipped more chardonnay and sighed drowsily.

"There's a lot of wildlife here, but we're not likely to see much in broad daylight, although the appearance of an eagle isn't unusual. And hawks are plentiful." His voice, as he spoke, was a deep, gentle rumble. "It's even more enjoyable watching them if you lie down. Here," he suggested, patting a place some distance between them, "use these extra napkins for a pillow and stretch out." Then he lay back, tilted his hat over his face and appeared to go to sleep.

Maybe it was the wine. Or maybe it was because it was a perfect spring day and the scenery so beautiful that she felt thankful to be alive to appreciate it, and consequently her defenses were down. Maybe it was that her tummy was full and she'd had a little too much wine. Whatever the reason, she set her wine aside and cautiously, quietly, stretched out beside him. She was careful not to touch him and lay for a few minutes just gazing up at the huge birds circling high above some wounded prey located by their remarkable sensors. It was just before she slept that she heard the wild cry of an eagle.

Next thing, she was dreaming. In it, she stood before an easel painting. She felt so good, lighthearted, glad to be alive. It was a familiar feeling, one she'd taken for granted when painting had once been her sole passion. She gloried in it as shape and form and color flowed effortlessly from her brush onto the canvas. But oddly she couldn't see what it was. Even though she smelled the paint and felt the brush in her hand, it was almost as if the artist was another person and she stood at her shoulder watching…watching…

And then the painting materialized and she felt a chilling rush of dread. Instantly, she fought to resist it. The near-awake part of her knew this was a dream but, like a reel of film set in motion with no off switch, the dream played on. And then, somehow, she was outdoors, desperate to escape. Terrified, she moved on legs that were slow and sluggish. She struggled to make her way through dense fog, able to see only vague shapes until suddenly a wrought-iron gate materialized out of the mist. The design was ornate, but she could see that it was a formidable metal barrier. She approached with her heart beating in terror, desperately aware that she needed to get inside. Whatever was behind that gate, she knew she was meant to see. With her heart in her throat, she gripped the cold bars, knowing what was meant for her to see was terrible. Unspeakable.

"Shh, shh, it's okay, Erica. You're dreaming."

"Oh God, oh God, oh God, no, don't..." she sobbed. "Please, please..."

"What is it, sweetheart? Tell me."

"My baby, oh, God, my baby. Don't let them take my baby!" Her voice rose to a wail. "Please, please, don't take my baby."

"Wake up, sweetheart. It's only a dream."

She fought the dark veil enveloping her. But her hands were trapped, imprisoned. Strong arms bound her.

"It's okay, Erica. You're okay, sweetheart."

She came to herself to find Hunter holding her. It was his voice in her ear speaking reassurance. But the horror was still with her, consuming her. Shuddering, she gave in to a spate of abject weeping. Deep, gut-wrenching sobs seemed ripped from the very bottom of her soul. "Oh, God, no, no, no, no," she wailed. "Why? Oh, why? Please, no, I can't...I can't..."

His lips were at her temple, his hands stroking her back as she wept in utter despair. "It's all right, sweetheart. Whatever happened, it's over now."

"No, never...it'll never be over. She's gone, she's gone. Oh, God, I can't bear it. Danielle, Dani, Dani, Dani..." Her voice rose in a wail of anguish.

Hunter held her, rubbing her back as she wept, his face revealing shock and confusion. "You want to tell me about it?"

In a few more moments she was fully awake, but shaken as always by the power of the dream. "I r-really can't," she told him, taking the napkin he offered. Pressing it to her face, she lay for a moment until she'd quieted enough to speak without gasping. "I'm sorry," she whispered.

"There is nothing to be sorry for." His lips were pressed against her temple as if tasting her pain, and she lacked the strength, or the will, to pull away. "You can't control what you dream," he told her gently.

"Nightmare," she managed to say, thankfully feeling some of the terror finally subsiding.

"And a bad one."

It was, after all, not real, she told herself—at least, not now. But there was still pain and it would never subside. "I'm usually alone when this happens," she said, wiping her nose while his hand continued moving gently up and down her spine. "You must think I'm...so...weird."

With her head tucked beneath his chin, she felt him move in denial, felt his arms tighten about her. "There's that word again. Tell you what. Let's agree to banish it once and for all. I don't think you're weird. I know you well enough now to tell you're anything but. I don't know what happened, but whatever it was, it still gives you nightmares." He hesitated, kissing her hair. "Who is Danielle?"

She was silent so long that he thought she wouldn't answer. Finally, in a whisper, she replied, "My baby."

Shock made him start. Jesus. Had she lost a child along with her husband in that accident? Her next words confirmed it.

"It wasn't just David who died," she said, now resting her cheek on his chest. "I—I lost my b-baby, too." Her voice broke and she was weeping again, this time softly, in quiet, heartrending despair.

Stunned, he tried to imagine surviving that kind of loss. Her husband, her baby—her whole world—all wiped out in a matter of seconds. "Ah, sweetheart, I'm so sorry." When her sobs had subsided somewhat, he was frowning thoughtfully as he asked, "This was the hit-and-run accident?"

She nodded, dabbing at her eyes with the napkin. Then, when he said nothing more, she guessed he was honoring his promise not to plague her with questions. Oddly, now that he knew the worst, she found herself willing to tell it all. She pulled away and sat with her arms circling her knees.

"It happened very late one afternoon when I took my b-baby for a walk," she said in a voice thick with tears. "David had to work that day, Saturday. He wanted to make partner and he put in a lot of hours, even on the weekends." She paused and looked as one of the horses stamped and blew out a soft whinny, but what she saw was another day, one with no sunshine and a sky that was not blue and beautiful, but darkening as night settled in.

It would have been dark in another ten minutes that day and the bugs would start. Mosquitoes were a menace in Houston's warm, humid climate. Erica always applied repellant to exposed areas of Danielle's skin as babies were so vulnerable to the pesky things, but she did so reluctantly. If only Dani would agree to wearing a hat, at least her little head would be protected, but no. She tugged the baseball cap off within seconds of Erica putting it on.

There wasn't much activity in the neighborhood as she pushed the stroller through an intersection. The routines that defined people's lives changed on weekends. After a few minutes, she turned onto the main street leading back into her subdivision and picked up her pace smartly. It had been nine months since Dani was born and she wanted to shed another ten pounds, so she'd stretched their daily outing to two miles and was puffing now, out of breath. Strolling at a leisurely pace did not burn enough calories.

To face oncoming traffic, she crossed to the left side of the street and kept well to the edge of the curb for safety's sake. With night falling, the occasional driver might not remember to turn on headlights. She'd waited for David until the last minute before readying Danielle to go outside today. Apparently, he hadn't been able to get away, as he'd promised. Although it was Saturday, he'd been forced to schedule two important depositions to accommodate hostile witnesses who were unwilling to take time off from their jobs during the week. With the trial date creeping ever closer, he'd had no choice. But it meant sacrificing half their weekend time together. The law firm was not sympathetic to young not-yet-partners who refused weekend work. With Erica electing to be a stay-at-home mom after the baby came, their income was significantly reduced. So David felt the pressure to make partner on a fast track. It was a given that he would. He had everything it took to succeed.

Just then, she heard him call out. Squinting a little in the fast-falling twilight, she saw him jogging toward her and her mood was instantly brighter. He'd managed to get away after all. He wore aged cutoffs and the ratty sweatshirt he'd had since law school, the one with the sleeves cut off that had a small Rice University emblem above his heart. His shoes were the old Nikes she'd threatened to toss out after giving him new ones for his birthday last month. A creature of habit, David. But it still made her heart smile, just to look at him.

"Daddy's here, Dani," she said, and laughed as the baby recognized who it was heading their way. She began bouncing up and down in her stroller and waving her little arms in an exuberant appeal to be picked up. "Say hi to Daddy, sweetie."

As she watched David jogging across the street, she heard a car somewhere behind her making the turn onto the street. She hesitated, thinking to get up onto the sidewalk, but it was an aging neighborhood and the sidewalk was riddled with cracks from tree roots and damage from South Texas's relentless heat and frequent rain. Strolling at any pace was nearly impossible.

But at just that moment, Danielle squealed with delight and pitched her sippy cup at David, who'd reached them now, breathing hard and grinning. The cup went rolling toward the drainage basin and, without thinking, Erica dived for it. David, laughing, reached for Danielle, lifted her up out of the stroller and held her high above his head. More squeals and baby laughter. Erica was smiling as she rescued the sippy cup. When she straightened, Danielle and David were both bathed in golden light from the headlights of the approaching car.

"It was too close," Erica told Hunter with a frown, seeing it all again. "The car was coming straight at David and Danielle. They weren't looking," she murmured.

She turned to look at Hunter, but he could see that her mind and her eyes were filled with the moment when she realized her world was in desperate, dangerous jeopardy. "I was horrified. I put out a hand," she told Hunter, giving an incredulous little laugh that broke in the middle. "As if I could hold back the monster bearing down on them. But, of course, I couldn't. The car swerved and I caught a glimpse…"

She paused, her forehead furrowing as if to capture some fleeting memory just beyond her grasp. After a moment when she spoke, her voice had gone flat and distant. "They were both killed instantly."

He couldn't bring himself to say anything for a minute, but now he remembered the accident—a young family struck down while out for an evening stroll with their baby—then the driver of the car sped away, leaving them dying on the street.

"Jesus. I never—" He stopped, stunned that Erica was the tragic young woman who'd been all over the media.

"You never what?" she asked, looking up at him.

"I remember it, Erica, but I never connected it to you." He was frowning, thinking back. "I must have read your name. The media sure made certain we got all the details." He said *media* as if it had a bad odor. "It had all the elements of a real-life tragedy. I guess the surprise would have been if they hadn't played it up." He reached for his wine and tossed back what was left of it in one gulp.

After a second, he picked up where he left off. "I was living temporarily with my mother and Morton in that neighborhood at the time. I'd just bought a condo and it was being renovated. The police, the neighbors, everyone pulled out all the stops to identify whoever it was who'd done it. Everyone wanted to nail him, force him to face up to what he did."

"The police assumed it was a case of drunk driving, but they had no way of knowing for sure."

"But it seemed the only reasonable explanation. Death didn't happen often in that neighborhood." He set his glass aside. "Maybe in other less-affluent sections of Houston, but not there. And certainly not so heinous a crime as a hit-and-run."

"Vile and depraved behavior isn't restricted to inner-city slums," she said bitterly.

He struggled to find something to say that wouldn't fall short considering the magnitude of her loss. "I'm so sorry," he said again, unable to think of anything better.

Erica gave a mute shrug, her gaze fixed on the horses.

"It's hard to imagine what you went through," he told her. "In fact, I don't know how you made it."

"I did…somehow. And people were very kind." She plucked listlessly at a blade of grass. "But the truth is that, for a long time afterward, I was simply in a fog, which included the memory of the accident. Which is probably a good thing. Back then, all I recall is wanting to die myself. And when I wasn't wishing I was dead, I was feeling anger so intense that I drove away most anyone who tried to approach me."

"Your mom," he guessed.

"Seeing her meant being around Stephanie, who was still a toddler and, to me, a reminder of Danielle…." She frowned, remembering, and finally admitted, "Seeing her was hard."

"But Jason managed to get through to you."

"Only after months of trying. I don't know why he didn't give up. I was hardly good company. I wasn't any kind of company at all. I couldn't paint. I couldn't be with people. I couldn't…I couldn't just pick up the pieces and pretend I was alive when I wasn't. I was dead. I died with Danielle and David."

"No, only a part of you died, sweetheart," he countered gently. "But that hasn't kept you from trying hard to bury the rest of yourself."

With her chin resting on her knees, she turned and looked at him. "I did what I had to do to survive."

Without any personal tragedy that could remotely compare to hers, he had no reply to that. "So you weren't hurt in the accident?" he asked, trying but unable to recall the follow-up media. "Physically, I mean."

"I had a head injury that put me in a coma. I woke up after four days."

He imagined her coming awake in a hospital, in pain, then being told that the two people she loved most in the world were gone. It was hard not to reach for her, gather her close and promise she'd never have to know that kind of pain again. "You mentioned not recalling much of what happened at the time," he said, after clearing his throat. "How much memory loss do you have?"

"It's hard to describe," she told him. "After seeing the car with its headlights bearing down on us, I have scraps of…I don't know…impressions, images." She frowned and seemed to be looking inward. "It's vague, nothing I can actually define, but sometimes…"

After a few beats, he prompted, "Sometimes…"

"As I said, it's vague." After a moment, she tossed the blade of grass and brushed her hands together. "It's probably just something that comes from reliving the accident a thousand times. Or the nightmare."

"You have the nightmare often?"

"Not often, but enough. Less now than in the beginning. Sometimes I'll go for months before something triggers it." She glanced at the horses and beyond to the pecan orchard, then her gaze wandered up to the huge scavengers still circling overhead. "I never know what brings it on, otherwise, I'd avoid it. It's happened twice recently, for some reason."

"Is it always the same?"

"Basically, yes…well, for the most part, it is. But today there was a new twist. I was painting, but I was two people, one who knew what was taking shape on the canvas and another who didn't. And then the dream took its usual pattern. I'm alone, I'm moving sluggishly toward something. But I never reach a point where I know what it is, or recognize anything useful, like what I might have been painting on that canvas, or where exactly I'm going as I walk, or who was driving that car or—"

"Nothing about the size of the car?" he interrupted. "Was it an SUV, a passenger car, a pickup?"

"The police asked that, of course. It was big. At least, I think it was big. Maybe because it was coming straight at us, it just seemed huge. I suppose it could have been a pickup.…" She paused, frowning, then shook her head. "I just don't know."

"Go back to what you see in your dream. Vague images, you said. Such as…"

She squinted into the distance. "You know how you get these little flashes of memory sometimes, but they slip away before you can form them into an image? I can't quite get a fix on what it is, an idea, or an object, or…"

"A person?"

"I wish." She contemplated a tiny white flower in the grass before reaching over to touch it with her forefinger. "For the first few months after it happened I fantasized about meeting the driver and recognizing him instantly. In my fantasy, I confronted him and railed at him, saying all the things you would say to a man who did something so depraved. To run over people like that and then cut and run—" She scrambled to her feet suddenly. "I don't want to get started on that," she said, standing with her back to him.

"Then you think it was a man?"

"I think of him as a man, but I don't really know. It could have been a woman, I guess."

Hunter, now on his feet, moved to stand at her shoulder. "I wonder if those paintings you're feeling compelled to create now could have anything to do with the accident," he said.

"I don't know…."

He could see that she didn't reject the idea outright. Maybe she'd been thinking along those lines herself. "You said they terrified you."

"But they weren't anything of substance," she said, frowning. "They weren't anything you could make sense of, just abstract…stuff. Dark and grim, a lot of color depicting…I don't know, violence, I guess."

He wanted to touch her, but he dared not. She was too fragile right now. "Wouldn't you say that describes the accident, at least in your mind?"

"I guess."

"Have you thought of having some kind of therapy to work through whatever you've blocked out?"

"Such as grief counseling, hypnosis, Sodium Pentothal?" Her tone was sharp, but after a moment she seemed to settle and added more quietly, "Yoga? I tried them all." She drew an unsteady breath and wrapped her arms around herself. "I needed a miracle and they were all fresh out."

Tentatively, he touched her hair, then rested a hand on her shoulder, keeping his touch light and reassuring. "It's easy to see why you turned to your art."

"But not with the remotest idea of marketing anything. David's insurance was more money than I would ever need. It felt somehow obscene taking it in return for the lives of my husband and baby. So, yes, I suppose you could say I concentrated on the pattern of a quilt or the design of a jacket as a way to live a day at a time."

"Have you thought such fierce concentration might have kept those disturbing images at bay when maybe you could have nailed something down that would help the police identify the killer?" He knew the moment he said it that he'd gone too far.

She spun around, breaking his touch on her shoulder. "Don't you think I would have moved heaven and earth if there was the slightest possibility of that? I burned, Hunter, I literally *burned* to make him pay for what he did." Her face was flushed and her eyes flashed with righteous rage. "He ran into three people and just drove away. That was a low act, a vile act. A person who'd do that needs to be locked up. Society needs to be protected from—"

"I'm sorry." Hunter caught her arms and held her fast. "I swear to God I didn't mean that as a criticism. I wouldn't presume to judge anything you did or didn't do at a time like that."

The fight suddenly died out of her. "There's nothing buried in my memory," she said in a forlorn voice, wishing with all her might that there was…even if it was only a scrap of a clue. "I've spent nine years trying to dredge up something—anything—but there's nothing!"

Her misery was his undoing. He pulled her to him, wrapped his arms around her and held her close against his heart. "Let's put this away for a while," he told her gently. "We've mucked around in enough grim stuff for one day, don't you think?"

"Yes." He felt her sigh and relax against his chest. "Lord, yes."

She was just where he'd wanted her to be for weeks, and as emotion swelled in his chest, he wondered how he'd be able to give her the time she needed before declaring himself. With her head nestled beneath his chin, he rubbed her back the way he would have soothed a hurt child. "If there's anything you need to remember, it'll come in its own time, sweetheart."

"That's what I've told myself for the past nine years," she said in a doleful tone.

He combed his fingers through her hair, then bent to inhale the scent of it. Her scent. Struggling not to rush, he ran his lips down the side of her throat. She tipped her head to one side and he nipped the skin lightly. "Um, do you know how good you taste?"

"After riding for hours in the sun? Not so good, I bet." She almost sounded like herself again.

"Wrong." He found a spot beneath her ear and used his tongue in a way that sent a burst of delicious sensation to her toes. With her hands anchored at his waist, she made a small sound, but it wasn't resistance.

"I can't believe I'm doing this," she said as her limbs turned to water.

"We're doing it because it was meant to be," he told her. With his hands now roaming over her back, he tipped her face up and looked into her eyes. "That's what I've been trying to tell you since day one." Without giving her time to argue, he dropped his mouth to meet hers. It was a tender kiss, flavored with wine and the moment, now she'd shared her story. The kiss was open and gentle to begin with, a substitute for the inadequacy of words when there was no way, other than this, that he could express the sympathy he felt for all she'd lost. He let the feeling build, savoring the softness, the warmth and taste of her. Then, when their tongues touched, he pulled her hips to his and the kiss became something much more.

Emotion that he'd kept on a tight leash burst in his chest, spreading out and down to his sex. Unable to help himself, his mouth opened wide in a deep, lush exploration of hers while their tongues mated joyously. With her arms linked around his neck, pressing herself close, he knew she was with him now. Thought of control slipped away from him then. His hands began to move urgently, pulling her shirt free of her jeans. He worked at buttons, fumbled at the clasp on her bra and finally found her breasts. With a sound deep in his chest, he took the nipple into his mouth while cupping both breasts in his hands. When he bit her gently, she gasped at the pleasure of it and he knew he had to have her now.

He broke the kiss to run his lips over her face, her throat, back up to her mouth. "I want to lie with you on this blanket," he told her in a rough tone. "I want to strip you naked and touch you and kiss you everywhere. I want to be inside you now, Erica. Now."

Overhead, a flock of blackbirds suddenly flew out of the top of a tree, cawing loudly. Lifting his head, he saw a pickup truck in the distance headed their way, trailing a plume of dust in its wake. Cisco, he thought, coming to retrieve the picnic things, as instructed. He groaned, pressed his face to her throat. "But this is not where we need to be the first time we make love," he said, nuzzling a spot beneath her ear. "Maybe another time this'll be great." He managed a soft, low sound, a travesty of a laugh. "Yeah, definitely, it'll be great, but not today." His blood roaring and his body screaming, he gave her a quick, hard kiss on her mouth and stepped back.

"Not today," she repeated in a dazed tone. It took a minute, but she finally stepped away from him, still flushed and shaky. Using both hands, she smoothed her hair, then straightened her shirt, buttoned it up, dusted the seat of her pants. That done, she said, "I'll repack the basket while you get the horses." She set about collecting and tossing items into the basket.

Hunter hesitated, watching her. She worked with hands that were a little unsteady, not looking at him. It would be easier to find a safe path through a mine field than to try talking to her, he decided. But how he'd love to be a mind reader and know what she was thinking. Stunned, probably, over what had nearly happened. Did she feel sorry? Guilty? She'd spent nine years denying any need for sex. How did she feel about responding the way she had to a man other than her dead husband? But that was something she would have to work out on her own. He, on the other hand, had caught a glimpse of the future they could have together, and he was elated. Whether she wanted to admit it or not, this afternoon marked a change in their relationship. Hunter knew who she was now. And he knew he was in love with her.

Fifteen

On the way back to the barn, Hunter left Erica with her thoughts, for which she was thankful. Other than her grief counselor, she had never been able to talk so openly to anyone. Any attempt and the words had stuck in her throat, strangled before coming out. Talking about it felt too much like reliving the horrible moment. That is, until today with Hunter when it had brought blessed relief, like throwing the doors and windows open to sunshine and fresh air in a house that had been closed and locked for a long time. Which probably explained why she'd found herself on the point of having sex after nine years. Outdoors. In broad daylight. So much for thinking that nothing of any consequence could happen if she spent some time at his ranch.

It must have been the dream, she decided. She was always shaky and vulnerable after the dream and today it had been especially traumatic, not really a dream, but a nightmare. She looked down at her hands, almost feeling the chill of the iron bars on her palms. And then, a mental image crystallized. Her breath caught in shock. She turned impulsively to Hunter, her face alight with discovery.

"I remember now!" she cried, and was almost unseated

as Lady reacted skittishly, bumping into the big Appaloosa and dancing nervously. With a startled oath, Hunter made a grab for the mare's bridle as Erica clung to the reins.

"Whoa, Lady," he said in a low tone, holding on to the bridle while the mare calmed. "Easy, girl, easy."

Erica reached down and patted the horse's neck, soothing her in a low-pitched voice. She gave Hunter a contrite look. "I'm sorry, but I forgot for a minute that I was on a horse."

"You gave her a start, calling out like that when you haven't spoken a word for the past twenty minutes." He held on to the mare's bridle as they cantered across a cattle guard and released it only when they were on the road leading to the ranch compound. "What was it you remembered?"

"My dream. Remember I said something kept floating around in my memory, then slipping away before I could get it? It was the gate to your mother's property, Hunter. It was in my dream. The exact gate. The unique pattern of the wrought iron. The bars. Everything. I was standing at that very gate, but I couldn't get inside."

"You've dreamed the same dream many times?"

"Yes. I mean, no, not exactly. Oh, I'm always walking and searching in the dream, but this time I came to a gate, which has never happened before. And it was the gate at your mother's house." She was almost giddy at finally identifying something that made sense.

"You're talking about the gate you first saw this morning, the gate I parked the car in front of while I went inside the house?"

She took his remark as skepticism and it dampened her excitement a little. "Well, when you put it like that, it doesn't seem to mean anything," she said hesitantly. "But I was meant to get inside that gate, Hunter. Something's inside that I need to see."

Hunter thought for a moment before saying, "It sounds as if you're coming around to Jason's theory."

"That I have memory about something and it's trying to surface?" Both animals, scenting home, had perked up. She dropped back to allow Hunter and the stallion ahead, then urged the mare forward. "I think it's true. And it would make sense as to why the dream, or whatever you call it, has persisted all these years." Still seated on the mare, she turned to look at him. "Maybe I did see the driver, Hunter. Or at least, maybe I saw something or—"

Arriving at the barn Erica pulled on the reins, signaling Lady to stop, then without waiting for Hunter to give her a hand, dismounted. Her thoughts still grappled with the mystery. "But what? Who? What is it that's trying to get through to me?"

"You're the only person who knows the answer to that." He caught the bridle and led both horses into the dim interior of the barn. Lady, after a gentle slap on her rump, went docilely into the first stall. "But, as you say, you've been living with it for nine years without nailing it," he said, securing the door. "You may be a little closer after today, although I don't see how that particular gate could mean anything. Since you once lived nearby you could have seen it as you drove past, but why you'd feel terrified is harder to explain."

"You think I'm making a big something out of nothing, don't you?"

He led Jasper into a stall, went inside with the horse and set about unbuckling the cinch. "What I think doesn't matter," he said a few minutes later, carrying the saddle. "I'm sticking with my theory that it'll all come out in its own time."

He was probably right, she thought, but it would be hard to wait patiently until another clue was offered up in a dream. Still, she'd lived this long with a totally blank memory. "I need to take care of Lady," she said.

"In a minute." Hunter hefted the saddle up onto a shelf, then turned to face her. "I'll say it again, let's put this on a back burner for a while, okay?"

"I don't think I have much choice," she said, then caught her breath as he tilted her face up. "What—"

He closed his mouth over hers and she didn't think once of resisting. She sank right into the kiss along with Hunter, slipping her arms up around his neck and tucking her body into his as if the fit was so natural and familiar that she'd been doing this for years.

It was Hunter who drew back, propping her chin up with both thumbs so he could look right in her eyes. "Speaking of memory, it's been an hour since I had a taste of you," he told her, nipping at her lips. "I just felt the need to refresh it."

"You're impossible," she said, unable to repress a smile.

"I thought you might be obsessing over what we didn't get around to doing after our picnic," he said. "I just wanted to remind you what we have to look forward to."

Pushing against his arms, she managed to put an indignant look on her face. "I have been thinking about that, you're so right."

"Uh-huh." He dipped his head to take a little nip of her ear.

She controlled a shiver. "Do you realize what would have happened if Cisco hadn't appeared when he did?"

"Yeah, and I was tempted to fire him for his really rotten timing."

She could take offense or she could laugh. It was no contest. She chuckled as he nibbled on her neck. He was so much fun. And he was so darn sexy. "I didn't bargain for this when I agreed to—" She lost the thought as he fastened his mouth on hers again. It was just so…delicious, the hot, impatient way he kissed. It was as if he focused every skill he'd ever mastered in the art of kissing on her. And where it might lead now, in the relative privacy of the barn, she had no trouble imagining. Except that suddenly they had company.

Someone—a female—cleared her throat and said, "Am I interrupting?"

Hunter swore and sent a dark scowl in the direction of the barn door where a woman stood watching them, silhouetted against the bright sunlight. Erica instantly assumed this was the woman Hunter had recently broken off with. She could see little of her face, but she appeared to be petite with a delicate build. She wore a man-style white shirt, skintight jeans and Western boots. Her tiny waist was accentuated by a leather belt with an engraved silver buckle. On her head, cocked at a jaunty angle, was a cowboy hat.

Hunter set Erica aside and moved toward the visitor. "Jocelyn? What are you doing here? I thought you were in Key West."

Erica glanced around looking for an escape route, but the only exit was blocked. "I'll just take care of Lady," she said, thinking to give them some privacy by going into the stall where the mare stood waiting placidly.

"Cisco and Earl will take care of Lady," Hunter said, stopping her. With his eyes still on Jocelyn, he reached back and captured Erica's hand. "Come and meet my sister, Jocelyn."

Sister? She didn't know he had a sister. Erica allowed him to pull her to his side as Jocelyn, thumbs stuck in her pockets, sauntered over to them. Once she was out of the glare of the sun, a purple bruise was clearly visible on her cheek.

"Jesus, what happened to you?" Dropping Erica's hand,

Hunter made a startled move to touch Jocelyn's face and get a better look, but she shied away. In avoiding him, her hat came off and fell on the ground.

"It's nothing serious," she said, scooping the hat up and dusting if off. "You should see the other guy."

"My sister is quick with the wisecracks," Hunter said to Erica, but his eyes were fixed sharply on Jocelyn's face. "Let me guess. Your editor turned out to be a son of a bitch."

She lifted one shoulder. "I sure know how to pick 'em," she said, but Erica caught a glint of tears in her eyes before the hat was clamped back on her head. Still, it was defiance on her face as she tucked the flat of her hands into her back pockets. "And before you start in with the lecture, I've already spent the very long trip from Key West chewing out my own ass, so save it, Hunt. I made a mistake, but what's new?"

"You drove all the way from Key West?" he asked in disbelief.

She shrugged. "I couldn't very well leave my car, could I? What would Daddy say if I abandoned a sixty-thousand-dollar Mercedes? And I damn sure don't intend to go back."

"Have you told them you're back?"

"Who, Mommy and Daddy?" Again, she shrugged. "I thought I'd let you tell them…in a day or two. I should be presentable by then."

For a few beats, Hunter said nothing, just studied her face with its angry bruise in baffled silence. Then he remembered Erica and nudged her forward. "This is a friend, Erica Stewart," he said in a tight voice.

Erica's name wiped the impudence from Jocelyn's face in the space of a heartbeat. Going deathly pale, her jaw dropped and she stared at Erica in wide-eyed astonishment.

A second later, looking dumbfounded, she turned back to Hunter. "You aren't serious, right? This is your idea of some kind of sick joke?"

Shocked at her words, Hunter reacted sternly. "What the hell does that mean? Explain yourself. Now."

More than ever, Erica wanted to escape. She couldn't remember ever seeing Jocelyn before, but by the woman's horrified reaction to her name, Erica was no stranger to her. "Why don't I give the two of you some privacy?" she said, intending to edge around them and exit before there was bloodshed. Hunter was that furious.

He caught her wrist, stopping her. "No, wait." Holding Erica fast, he looked suspiciously at Jocelyn. "Do you two know each other?"

Jocelyn ignored him, her gaze fixed on Erica. "What are you doing here? What's going on?"

"I'm sorry, have we met?" Erica said, mystified as well as uncomfortable.

Jocelyn hesitated, but her gaze didn't waver. She was still focused intently on Erica, struggling to put together a puzzle with pieces that clearly didn't fit. She looked again at Hunter, who still waited angrily for an explanation. After a moment or two more, she gave a short laugh and made a visible effort to lighten up. "I guess I have you mixed up with someone else," she said to Erica. "Sorry."

There was something about the way she kept staring that put the lie to her words, but Erica was relieved to pretend otherwise. "I have a shop in the Village," Erica said. "Maybe you saw me there."

"Yeah, it's possible," she said, but she still looked doubtful. She turned back to Hunter. "The two of you are…involved? I mean, that's the way it looked to me a minute ago."

After that rocky start, Hunter was in no mood to satisfy

her curiosity. "Maybe you should quit while you're ahead, Jocelyn."

She opened her mouth to give him a flippant reply but, for some reason, didn't. "Yeah, I guess that was rude. Put it down to sleep deprivation." Forgetting the bruise, she started to rub both hands over her face, then winced on touching her cheekbone. "I haven't had a lot of sleep in the last three days. That always makes me crazy."

"It was crazy to take off to Key West with some yo-yo you met in a Miami bar," Hunter said gruffly.

"I gave myself that lecture already, remember?"

"Go up to the house, Jocelyn," he ordered. "I'll be up there as soon as I locate Cisco to tend to the horses. We need to talk."

"There's nothing to talk about, Hunt. I went to Key West, I screwed up. Now I'm home again." Her chin went up, but her mouth was not quite steady. "Story of my life."

She spun around about to leave, but at the door she stopped and looked back at him. "What happened with Kelly? I thought you two were headed for the altar." She flicked a glance at Erica. "Does she know about this?"

"You're pushing again, Jocelyn." Hunter's face was a grim mask.

Kelly must be the woman he'd been sleeping with, Erica thought. And another ten minutes under those pecan trees and *she* would be the woman he was sleeping with. She was suddenly overcome with weariness. The long day had been an emotional roller coaster. She'd allowed herself to get carried away by the charm of the man and his ranch. She'd wrung herself dry weeping over the past. She'd been the victim of insufferable rudeness by his sister and now she just wanted to go home.

She waited until Jocelyn was well out of earshot. "I'd

like to start back to Houston soon," she told Hunter. "Will that be a problem?"

"Now that Jocelyn has turned up? Maybe." He took a moment to measure his words. "I need to talk to her, Erica. You saw her face. I don't know if she's running from someone. I'm not sure she should be alone." He raked a hand over his hair, looking harassed. "Can we talk about it after I see what's up with Jocelyn? And by the way, I apologize for the way she spoke to you."

"Forget it. I understand." She headed for the door.

"If you do, maybe you can explain it to me." Falling into step beside her, he walked with her toward the gate. "Jocelyn can be…difficult, but she isn't usually downright rude. On top of that, I'm still trying to figure out why she reacted as if she'd seen a ghost when she heard your name."

"It could be stress," Erica said, willing to let it go, for now. "Breaking away from an abusive relationship is bound to be stressful. And if I drove for three days, under any circumstances, I'd probably have a meltdown, too."

"I'll cut her some slack over breaking off with that jerk, but she'll have to come up with a better reason than stress for offending you," he threatened darkly.

"I wasn't offended," she replied. "I was simply puzzled. I don't know your sister." And with that, she pushed through the gate and left him standing there.

Frowning, he watched her go. Erica might not know Jocelyn, but Jocelyn sure acted as if she knew Erica. The possibility that Erica was linked somehow, some way, to his family was too bizarre. Wasn't it? But bits and pieces were coming together in a way that made it seem possible. From the start, his mother had seemed cool to his interest in Erica. And cool to receiving a gift of one of her designs. Next came the odd scene at the gala when they were introduced. Still, he hadn't picked up on outright disapproval until his mother's vague insinuations at his office and her frantic backtracking when he pushed for details. Jocelyn's shock on finding him with Erica simply added another level of suspicion. There had to be something going on.

Heading back into the barn to check on the horses, he was in deep thought. Was there some mystery that involved all three women? But how, since they claimed they'd never met? Aside from the fact that Erica's career was in art and his mother was active in the art community, they didn't seem to have much in common…except the fact that they'd all once lived in fairly close proximity. But that had been nine years ago. Jocelyn would have been only sixteen years old then. What could have happened nine years ago to link them?

When he got back to the ranch house, he found no sign of Jocelyn, but Erica was in the kitchen removing something from the oven. It was so completely unexpected that he was struck dumb for a moment. "What are you doing?"

"Following instructions," she said as she placed the piping-hot dish on a trivet. "There was a note from someone named Theresa—your housekeeper, I presume. She left this casserole in case you decided to eat here instead of returning to Houston. Since with Jocelyn's arrival that looks to be the plan, I heated it up while you were tending the horses. There's French bread and a salad, too."

She looked so good in his kitchen, as if she belonged there. He'd expected her to be waiting on the front porch, impatient to be on her way to Houston. Instead, he'd walked into a fantasy. "Speaking of Jocelyn, where is she?" he managed to ask.

"I think I heard her having a shower when I came in from the barn, but I haven't seen her." Without looking at him, she took a large bowl out of the refrigerator. "I know you're worried about her, so if I were you, I'd check to see if she's all right."

"You should have waited," he said, as she reached into overhead cabinets for glasses. "I didn't mean to put you to work in the kitchen."

"Oh? What was your plan for dinner?"

She had him there. Phoning out for pizza wasn't an option since there was no delivery to the ranch. "I guess I didn't have a plan."

"Then it's a good thing Theresa did. Besides, it gave me something to do." He watched her take a towel out of a drawer and then close it with a twist of her hips. It was, for some reason, an outrageously sexy little move. "If you have a bottle of red wine, it'll go nicely with this casserole," she said. "It appears to be something heavenly, lasagna, I think. But first, I really wish you'd check on Jocelyn."

He nodded. "Yeah, I'll do that. And I'll be back in a minute with the wine."

Erica checked the bread in the oven and found it needed another few minutes. She looked over the table and decided she'd done what was necessary, so she walked to the window and stood gazing out. It was a scene worthy of any artist. Mentally, she set up a canvas and began planning a landscape. It was something that, as an artist, she did almost instinctively. She couldn't remember a time when she hadn't looked at the world with an eye to painting it.

She'd overreacted in the barn when she realized she might be forced to stay at the ranch overnight. Of course she could stay. There was nothing so pressing that the world would end if she wasn't back in Houston before morning. Hunter was to be commended for being concerned about Jocelyn. It appeared he had good reason. Judging by that nasty bruise on her cheek, she might be in some danger if she were being pursued by the man who'd done it.

The timer on the oven drew her away from the window. It worried her that she was being drawn into Hunter's world at too fast a pace. In spite of her vow to keep him at arm's length, it was proving harder than she expected. Every time she turned around, there was something else pulling her toward him. She didn't want to fall in love with Hunter.

He was back just as she took the bread out of the oven. "What's wrong?" she asked, seeing the look on his face.

"She's asleep," he said, rubbing his jaw with chagrin. "I knocked on her bedroom door and got no answer. I didn't know whether she was okay or not, so I went in." He cleared a place for the bread on the countertop.

"And was she okay?"

"Sleeping dead to the world. I tried to wake her up to ask a few questions. Was she followed when she left Key West? Does she think he might show up here?" He looked worried as his gaze shifted to the window. "But there'll be no talking to her tonight. I think she's exhausted."

"She probably needs sleep more than anything," Erica said. "She looked pretty used up to me, too."

"Yeah, but since Hank or Theresa won't be back until sometime tomorrow, there's the problem of getting you back to Houston."

"It's a problem only if I insist on returning and I don't."

"Are you sure?"

She set the bread on the table. "Don't worry about it, Hunter. Stuff happens. The shape your sister's in, she shouldn't be alone. Jason can feed my cat if I stay overnight. I'll call him after we have dinner."

"Thanks. I appreciate that. Still…" He moved his shoulders in a way that told her how unhappy he was with how the day had ended. She knew he'd wanted it to be perfect.

She touched his arm. "It's okay, Hunter. Truly."

He gave her hand a squeeze and lifted it to his mouth to kiss. "Well, at least the day started off well, didn't it? I'll make it up to you, I promise."

"What? You'll do the dishes?"

He laughed and they sat down to eat.

Two hours later, Erica was in the guest bedroom wondering what she was going to use for a nightgown. A discreet search had revealed every toiletry anyone might need, including a bathrobe conveniently hung on the back of the door. The room was used by Lillian Trask when she stayed overnight, but opening the chest of drawers and rummaging around in someone else's lingerie was not an option. What did it matter, anyway? There was no one to see if she slept in the nude.

She took her time in the shower, deliberately shying away from dwelling on the more disturbing events of the day, which had been relatively easy at dinner. Once they sat down, Hunter had devoted himself to entertaining her. Because he mentioned Hank Colson so often, she was sorry to have missed an opportunity to meet the older man.

Dinner over, he'd shown her around the house. It was so clearly a man's domain, she'd observed with amusement. Anything that could be made of leather, metal, glass or deer antlers was. For a moment, she had imagined adding a few softening touches, rugs with color, interesting pottery, paintings on the walls that weren't of a Western theme. Still, seeing it all through Hunter's loving eyes was a treat. He was lucky to have such a place to escape to, she thought as she soaped up with a fragrant body wash. It didn't hurt that there was someone to cook and clean, as well as company in the person of Hank Colson to give it the feel of a real home. In fact, she suspected that that was exactly how Hunter thought of it. His condo in Houston was simply a place to hang his hat.

But in spite of trying to keep disquieting thoughts in a box, she found it wasn't possible. Jocelyn's appearance had taken some of the shine off the day. What had been behind her bizarre reaction when they were introduced? Why this feeling that Jocelyn knew her when they'd never met? Why was the woman shocked to find Hunter and Erica together? More than that, she'd seemed almost…horrified. Why?

With questions spinning in her head, she stepped out of the shower and went through the routine of toweling off, gave her hair a quick blow-dry and applied scented moisturizer to her skin. Was she making something out of nothing? She did have an active imagination and the day had been emotionally stressful. And if there was anything, how was she to go about following up? She certainly didn't see Jocelyn answering questions. Giving herself a mental shake, she slipped on the bathrobe and left the bathroom just in time to hear a soft knock on the door. She hesitated, knowing it would be Hunter, then walked over to open it.

He stood at the threshold, his formidable size made more so by being backlit by a lamp on the hall table. In his hand was something that looked like a T-shirt. "I thought you might need something to sleep in," he said, his dark eyes shadowed and unreadable.

After another slight hesitation, she stepped back and let him in. When she turned and saw him standing in the middle of the room, she felt an instant rush of heat and she nervously tightened the sash of her robe. A room that had seemed spacious and roomy now appeared to have shrunk right before her eyes.

"It's a T-shirt," he said, offering it to her. "It's clean and it'll be too big, but it gets chilly at night. I guessed you wouldn't be comfortable using someone else's clothes, even though you're welcome to anything you see."

"Thank you. This robe is beautiful, but it's not meant to be slept in."

He gave the room a quick survey. "Did you find everything you need?"

"Yes. Whoever chose the guest things has exquisite taste."

Silence descended as they faced each other. It was odd, she thought, being in a bedroom with a man again. She tried to bring a picture of David to mind, but failed. For a second, panic fluttered. Her memories of David were more than…memory. They were comfort, security. They'd carried her through many a lonely night.

"My mother."

She looked at him blankly. "What?"

"My mother is the one with the exquisite taste."

His dark eyes gleamed in the low light of the lamp, traveling slowly from the top of her head to her toes. Warmth spread over her skin, as if his hand, not his gaze, stroked her.

He took a step toward her. "I don't think I remembered to thank you for making dinner."

Her limbs were suddenly afflicted with a heavy, liquid lassitude. "It was already made," she murmured. "You should thank Theresa."

"I will," he said, moving in. "But not the way I want to thank you."

She saw it coming and had a fleeting thought of where they were and what he had in mind. A part of her feared the feelings he stirred in her, and a different part of her craved more. If she didn't want this, now was the time to stop him. But she didn't object when he took the T-shirt from her hands and tossed it aside. Then he was cupping her shoulders and his mouth descending to hers.

He was going at it slow and easy, she thought, giving her time to tell him no. Maybe she would…should. In a minute. Because his lips were now touching hers, brushing lightly, as if tasting a delicacy he'd wanted for a long time. But he failed to deepen the caress into a real kiss. Instead, his lips skimmed lazily over her cheek, to the soft indention beneath her ear, then back to her mouth.

"I like the idea of you sleeping in my shirt," he said, his mouth hovering over hers.

A little dazed, she clung to his arms with both hands. "I—thank you for thinking of it."

"Better yet, if you'd sleep in my bed, you wouldn't need anything."

Her heart skittered at the raw sensuality in his voice. But before she found words to tactfully retreat, he was kissing her for real. Suddenly deep and urgently gentle at the same time, he made love to her mouth. He persuaded with his tongue, with hands that swept over her shoulders and down her arms, before finding the curve of her bottom. With the flavor of wine and the fire of desire mingling in her mind, she slipped her arms around his waist and her head fell back, welcoming the onslaught. He pushed a knee against the part of her that was at once soft and moist and throbbing and she gave a tiny, half-strangled sound. Desire flared, urging the give-and-take that would bring on pleasure she hadn't felt in so long, so long….

She was suddenly disoriented as he swept her up into his arms and turned to the bed. "Let's do this right, sweetheart," he said. Laying her down on the rose-patterned comforter, he braced one knee on the bed and reached for the sash of her robe. "I've been thinking about this since the first day I saw you."

"Wait. Slow down, Hunter." She put up a hand to stop him, but he was already cupping her breast.

"Damn," he said softly, swiping the nipple with his thumb. "It's going too fast, isn't it? I'll slow down. We've got all night, sweetheart."

Closing her eyes, she swallowed hard. "No, we don't. I want you to stop."

He looked at her in disbelief. "You want to stop? Now?"

"Yes. Yes, I do."

He literally growled in frustration, but she pushed him aside and managed to sit up, closing the robe. She felt a pang of sympathy for him, but not enough to make her change her mind. She could guess how he felt. Her own body vibrated with thwarted desire, too. The prospect of an orgasm wasn't something she resisted lightly, especially considering she'd lived a nunlike existence for years.

Standing now, she tightened the sash and crossed her arms over her chest. "I'm sorry, I'm just not ready for this, Hunter."

He still sat on the side of the bed. "Honey, if you were any more ready, this bed would be on fire."

"Which only means that I'm human. I can be sexually aroused." She pushed her hair away from her face. "I meant that I'm not ready for…for this kind of thing. I told you that in the beginning."

She paused, giving him a chance to reply, but he simply eyed her with a brooding stare. After an awkward minute, she added, "And if you thought that my staying here overnight meant I had changed my mind, I'm sorry. It was never my plan to spend the night here, remember?"

"Okay, okay." He got up from the bed, waving a hand. "But I'm confused here. There's no way you can convince me you weren't just as ready as I was to make love just now. We're mature, consenting adults. Neither one of us is in a relationship with anyone else. Nobody will be hurt if we do what both of us want, what both of us need. I'd like to hear why you're holding out like this."

"I'd just rather not get involved in a relationship," she said stiffly. Which was not a real reason, she thought, moving to the dresser to avoid looking at him. She wasn't sure she could put into words a real reason.

"Do you mean for the present," he asked. "Or is it in your plan to resume a normal life someday? Like maybe in another nine years or so?"

She spun about. "I have a normal life. If you mean a person isn't normal unless they're having sex on a regular basis, then maybe I'm not normal."

"Is it normal to live in denial for nine years, Erica?" he asked grimly. "At least be honest with yourself. You've avoided anything that comes even close to making you feel real emotion again because it's safe, it's guaranteed to prevent the kind of pain you know all about, but what kind of life is it?"

"It's the life I choose."

He paced away from her, frustrated that she didn't see it. "You're not the kind of person to have sex just because it feels good. When you do decide that's what you want, it'll mean you're ready to risk all that comes with loving someone. The question is, will you ever get there?"

"Are we turning this into a counseling session?" She didn't quite manage a sarcastic tone.

"You told me you did that already." He stopped in front of her. "But now that I know about David and your baby girl, at least I understand what's going on."

She turned her face away. "Fine. We both know where we stand."

He put a finger beneath her chin and forced her to look at him. "I jumped the gun tonight and I apologize. The next time we get this far along, it'll be because you know where it's leading to and you're good to go with it."

To her consternation, she felt tears well up in her eyes. "I'm sorry," she whispered. "I didn't mean it to get as far as it did, but—"

"But it just felt so good, huh?"

She nodded mutely.

He reached out and stroked her cheek. "I love you, Erica. I've never said that to a woman before."

Her heart began to pound with something very like fear. Why would it be fearful to know she was loved?

Now his warm palm curled around her nape. "I want us to be together, so I'll wait until you believe what we can have together is worth the risk."

The very idea had more panic burgeoning up in her throat. She never intended to love that way again. She couldn't. What they were feeling right now was simply strong physical attraction, she told herself. And why not? Hunter was an all-round nice guy. And very attractive. And sexy. Maybe the sexiest man she'd ever met. And, like she told him, she was a normal, healthy woman, but she wasn't willing to jeopardize her hard-won serenity for an affair.

"I can almost see the wheels grinding," he teased, smiling. "So, I'll leave you to work it out, baby." Then he leaned down to kiss her, stopping a heartbeat before it happened. "Uh-oh, better not." Instead, he tapped her nose lightly with a finger and turned to leave. At the door, he glanced back and winked at her. "Be sure and let me know what you decide."

Sixteen

Hunter caught Jocelyn as she left the bathroom the next morning. She was fresh out of the shower and hadn't yet applied makeup. The bruise on her cheek was fading, but it was still an ugly reminder of the kind of life she was leading. "Got a minute, Sissy?"

She looked surprised to see him. "I thought you'd gone back to Houston," she said, averting her face. "And don't call me Sissy. It makes me feel about six years old."

"Sorry. Force of habit," he replied, giving her a quick smile. "You were zonked when I looked in on you last night, but I didn't want to leave before making sure you were okay."

"I'm okay. So now you can leave."

He sighed. He wanted a few details about her hasty departure from Key West, plus he wanted her to explain her reaction when she heard Erica's name. In her present mood, getting her to talk wouldn't be easy. "You're not worried that your boyfriend might follow you here?"

"He's not my boyfriend anymore and he doesn't even know about this place. So, I'm okay. Like I said, you can leave now."

He drew a deep breath. "Let's go to your room to talk." He glanced down the hall where the door to his mother's bedroom was closed. There had been no sound from Erica, but he wasn't taking any chance that she might hear them. He didn't want a repeat of Jocelyn's rudeness the night before. "And before you refuse, I'm telling you I don't intend to leave until I get some answers. So the sooner we have this conversation, the sooner I'll be on my way."

She flounced past him, nose in the air. He followed and closed the door when they were both inside. She went directly to the bedside table to get a cigarette, but before she could put it to her lips, he took it from her and shoved it back into the pack. "No smoking in this house, Sissy. You know that. When we're done, you can go outside and light up."

She glared at him. "Now you're treating me like a six-year-old." When he simply looked at her, she flopped down on the bed and wrapped her arms around her knees. "Go ahead. Get it over with."

"What exactly was the job all about in Key West? I'm assuming the bit about Sanchez being the publisher of a respectable publication was bullshit."

"I don't remember telling anybody that I was going to work at anything respectable," she said, studying her nails. "It's not my style, is it?"

"Let's just say we were all hoping. You definitely allowed Mom to assume that things were going well."

She laughed without a trace of humor. "I could hardly tell her what it really was now, could I? Besides, it didn't fool you for a minute, did it?"

"I was willing to wait and see. You've got a degree in business. And there was an outside chance that Sanchez was on the level. It was possible you might have landed in a good situation."

"Yeah, well, it didn't happen that way."

"Can I get a straight answer here, Jocelyn? Do you think Sanchez might come looking for you?"

She gave a resigned sigh and finally seemed to consider it seriously. "I can't swear to it, but it would surprise me. He's got a neat little shop up and running, and with me cutting out on him, he'll have to double up on a lot of the layout stuff. He's making a lot of money, so I don't see him abandoning that to come after a woman who—in his estimation—gives him nothing mostly but grief."

"Seems to me you're the one getting grief," Hunter said, flicking a glance at her cheek.

She brushed her fingers over the bruise. "This old thing? Sugar, this was one of our disagreements that didn't go the distance. I finally got sick and tired of him turning that vile temper of his on me. I didn't know a thing about his line of work when I got there, and I had it nailed when I left. Along with his layout artist, I became his accountant, if you can believe that. Looking back, I think once he knew about that freakin' degree, which I was dumb enough to tell him about the first time we met, he saw me as a cheap date."

His eyebrows rose. "You were doing his books?"

She shrugged. "What can I say? It was a match made in heaven."

"And he thought slapping you around would persuade you to stay?" Hunter didn't think the whole situation could get any more bizarre.

"No, he thought slapping me around would force me to keep my mouth shut about the way he liked to cook the books, and how he made most of his income."

"And what was that?"

"Internet porn."

Hunter struggled to keep his reaction from showing on his face.

She shot him a defiant look. "Not the kiddy stuff, so you only have to feel marginally disgusted over this particular screwup from me. I'm not proud that I didn't walk off the minute I realized what a creep he really was."

Hunter wondered whether she finally realized what a creep he was when she learned he was trading in Internet porn, or the first time he used his fists to make a point. But he crossed his arms over his chest and said nothing.

"I actually believed he was in the publishing business and it was icing on the cake that it was in Key West," Jocelyn said, getting a depressed look on her face. "I'd always wanted to go there. To live there would be really neat. Or so I thought." She made a grimace, plucking at lint on the bedspread. "The only regret I have about the whole thing is leaving Key West. Something about the place really spoke to me, Hunt."

He guessed what it was. Jocelyn had chafed under their mother's strict code of decorum and Morton's bullying from her earliest teen years. In Key West, an artist's mecca, she could give full rein to the free spirit within her in a way she'd never known while under her parents' thumbs.

"If you didn't leave when he first roughed you up, and you didn't leave when you found out what his Internet operation was about, when did the relationship sour enough that you finally left?"

"He became convinced that I was skimming money and cooking the books to hide it. But he was crazy. I wasn't, but he wouldn't believe me." She got up from the bed and moved to the window. "He liked drugs, mostly cocaine. But he wouldn't hesitate to experiment with other crazy shit. The problem with that, other than the obvious, is that a person gets screwed up and they get paranoid about stuff. He'd take money from the accounts himself. Or he'd skim off money before it ever got on the books. But he didn't always remember blowing it off, so to speak. So he thought I was skimming."

Hunter was shaking his head. "It couldn't have been much fun."

Her gaze followed Cisco penning up two frolicking colts in the paddock. "I wanted to leave him and the drugs and the dirty business he was running, but I wanted to stay in Key West. I wanted to find a way. I'd made yet another bad decision and I wanted to fix it myself, not run to you or Hank."

As she watched the colts run toward their mothers, Hunter noticed that she hadn't even considered running to her mother, or Morton.

"We'd have an argument and I'd pack up. Then he'd apologize and I'd unpack." She turned and looked at him from over her shoulder. "The day he gave me this bruise, he didn't just hit me." She pulled the collar of the robe away from her neck to reveal purple marks circling her throat. "He almost killed me with his bare hands."

"Don't tell me, let me guess. You didn't call the cops. You threw your things in your car and left."

"Pretty much," she admitted. "And I was so scared that I could hardly keep the car straight on the road for looking in the rearview mirror to see if he was following me."

Hunter blew out a tired sigh. "Do you think his business is illegal?"

"What's illegal on the Internet nowadays?" She closed up her robe and kept one hand on her throat. "To tell the truth, I don't know. I wouldn't think he could stand close scrutiny from the law, but it's a moot point as far as I'm concerned. I'm out of there and he doesn't know where I am."

"And you're sure about that?"

"He doesn't know the ranch exists. He couldn't, since

I never gave him my real name. He knows only that I was raised in Houston. Fortunately, since the name on my credit cards and stuff is still Jocelyn Murdock, there's no way he can trace me." She made a face. "That's about the only good thing to come from marrying Leo."

He let that pass. He'd said plenty before she married Leo Murdock, but as usual she'd been hell-bent to do what she wanted in spite of the fact that Leo had loser written all over him. "There's a job for you in my office if you need it," he told her. "All you have to do is say the word, Sissy."

She was facing him now, taking no offense at the affectionate name. She shook her head. "Why doesn't anybody get it that I'm not cut out for the business world? I only got that degree because Dad would have stopped my allowance if I'd refused. I'd be miserable in some high-rise in Houston, Hunt, even if you designed it. So no, thanks." Her jeans lay in a heap on the floor. She bent over and picked them up. "On that long trip back to Texas, I didn't think much about what I was going to do once I got here. I just wanted to get here." She gave a short laugh. "Maybe Cisco and Earl need a helper. I like horses and dogs and I'm good with them." Her mouth twisted. "That may be the only thing I'm good at."

"Speaking of Cisco and Earl," he said as he moved across to the door, "I've given them a heads up. Any stranger getting within a mile of the ranch is likely to get a nasty surprise. Just in case Sanchez does decide to come after you."

She folded the jeans and turned to put them inside a dresser drawer. "He won't. I was spooked that night, otherwise, I'd have realized I wasn't worth the effort it would take for him to chase me down. Why would he? He can find somebody else to keep his books and God knows there were plenty of women ready to sleep with him."

He couldn't see her face, but he suspected there were tears in her eyes. For a minute, he watched her transferring clothes from her suitcase to the drawer. "There was something else I wanted to ask you, Sissy." She didn't look up. "You appeared more than surprised when you heard Erica's name. I want to know why you had that reaction."

"It surprised me to find you making out with somebody besides Kelly."

"I don't think you were just surprised. You turned pale. You looked stunned." He moved to try to see her face, but she went to the closet and opened it. "Are you going to stand there and tell me you've never met her?"

"Did she say we'd met?"

"No. She seemed as puzzled over your reaction as I was."

"Accept it, Hunter. We've never met."

"And you won't explain why you were shocked to see me with her?"

"I did explain. I expected Kelly." She moved back to her suitcase and grabbed up another armload. "She wasn't Kelly."

He gave up with a sigh of impatience and turned to leave. "You need to call Mom and let her know you're okay."

"I thought we decided last night that you'd do that for me."

"She'll want to hear your voice, Sissy."

"I'll call in a day or so. I just want a little time to get myself together." She closed the suitcase with a snap. "Does Mom know about your girlfriend?"

"They've met."

She seemed about to say more, but instead she bent and shoved the suitcase under the bed. "Tell Theresa I'd love some of her pecan pancakes, will you?"

"I'll tell her."

* * *

Hunter pulled away from the ranch house an hour later. Erica rolled down her window and waved to Theresa, who stood on the porch seeing them off. The housekeeper had served up a breakfast that was fit for royalty. Erica wondered if Hunter and Hank Colson, who still had not returned from his business trip, realized what a treasure they had in Theresa.

"Are you sure it's okay to leave Jocelyn?" she asked, buckling up. His sister, it turned out, had come to the kitchen early and had taken her breakfast to the barn to eat. There was no trace of her now and Erica wondered if it was personal. She'd been more than surprised to find Erica with Hunter in the barn. "I could have called Jason to come and get me," she said. "Monday's usually a slow day. We would have been back to Houston and open again by noon."

"Cisco and Earl are on alert for any strangers getting within a mile of here and Hank will be back by noon. Frankly, I need to get back to Houston," Hunter said. "Work awaits, plus my mother should know Jocelyn's back and you heard me promise I'd tell her."

That would be a tricky conversation, Erica thought. How was he going to tell Lillian Trask that Jocelyn's lover cum employer was in the publishing business all right, but it was Internet pornography?

"I don't know how she always manages to get mixed up with the dregs of humanity," Hunter said, looking concerned and baffled. "She has a degree in business, if you can believe that. She could have an interesting career, but on the rare occasions when she decides to get a real job, she never sticks around long enough to make it count." He frowned, contemplating the mystery of it. "It's as if she deliberately sabotages herself by getting mixed up with some yo-yo and it never has a happy ending. It beats me why—"

He stopped, wiped a hand over his mouth as if to silence himself. "Sorry. I didn't mean to bore you with all that."

Erica preferred talking about his sister to having the conversation centered on herself. With just a few words last night, he'd managed to destroy her peace of mind. "Has she been involved with other men who've abused her physically?"

"Who knows?" He paused, eyes narrowed. "After hearing what she said this morning, I'm not sure how honest she's been about her personal life."

"We all have our secrets," Erica murmured.

"I guess. She claims this guy won't try to find her, but if he was mixed up in something illegal and she has knowledge of it, I wouldn't be so sure." He pulled into the passing lane to go around an eighteen-wheeler. "In spite of the fact that she really liked Key West and wanted to stay there, I notice she came straight to the ranch where she knew she'd be safe."

"She had nowhere else to go, Hunter," Erica said softly.

He looked at her. "That's very generous of you, considering how rude she was."

"She wishes I was Kelly."

"Well, I don't."

She smiled, then it faded as she added, "And you believe this guy she's running from doesn't know about the ranch?"

"That's what she believes." He frowned, looking doubtful. "Anyway, with Cisco and Earl on the lookout and Hank coming back in a couple of hours, she's in good shape for the moment. Also, Theresa's almost as good as a bodyguard."

"Jocelyn might benefit from some counseling. Was that ever a consideration?"

"Yeah." He glanced over at her. "Like you, she's been there and done that, but it doesn't seem to have helped her avoid bad choices."

They rode in silence for a while. She'd expected him to be furious with her last night. Most men would, at the least, have been righteously outraged on being brought almost to the point of no return and then rejected. Some would have stormed around and made a lot of noise. Or sulked. Some might even have pushed her a lot further, been a lot more intimidating. Her financial adviser certainly had, and with no encouragement on her part. But not Hunter. He'd been frustrated, but he'd been so reasonable that she was the one left feeling guilty. As if she hadn't played fair.

He reached over and touched her arm. "Hey," he said softly.

Warily, she turned to look at him. Because her own thoughts had strayed into territory she wanted to avoid, she hoped he was still thinking about his sister. "What?" she asked.

"I'm done talking about my sister."

She felt a rush of relief...until he added, "This is about you."

She shifted in her seat, studying his face, but he was watching a rusting pickup just ahead overloaded with building materials. "What about me?"

"The more I thought about the accident last night, the more I remembered. I recall having to detour on my way to Mom's place because the police had the street cordoned off. She'd been to a wedding, I think, she and Morton, but they looked like they'd been to a funeral. That's how it affected most folks in the neighborhood." He fell silent, remembering, then added in a puzzled tone, "Something so evil…it's upsetting to know there are people among us who'd do that."

"I keep thinking that one day we'll know who did it," Erica said wistfully. But she'd waited nine years for the truth to come out…and she was still waiting.

"Maybe someday we will." They were in the city now and, as always, traffic was thick and sluggish. He reached for her hand and gave it a squeeze before bringing it to his lips for a kiss. "I'd be willing to bet money that that's what your dreams and those strange paintings you're doing now are all about."

The spot he'd kissed tingled and Erica closed her fingers around it, as if to capture the feeling. As for finding answers in her dreams or in the images she was painting now, she couldn't believe it could be that simple after all these years.

"That's why you've got to keep on painting." His thumb moved on her wrist.

"And dreaming?" She was smiling now.

"Only if you're in bed with me."

By the time Hunter reached his mother's house that day, he wasn't certain which item on his list to start with. His mother needed to know Jocelyn was back in Texas and safe…for the moment, but he'd do his best not to give a hint of the unease he felt over her last hair-raising caper. He still wasn't totally convinced that Sanchez wouldn't chase her down, but no need to worry his mother with that. As for the questions he'd put to his sister about Erica, Hunter knew she was lying. Sooner or later, he'd find out to what extent and why she was lying. Be interesting to hear what his mother had to say about that.

He parked at the curb in front of the Trasks' house, hoping he wouldn't be unlucky enough to catch Morton at home. After he pressed the doorbell, his gaze wandered to the ornate gate that had cropped up in Erica's dream. Was it a coincidence or did the neighborhood have some significance? There were several similar gates on this street alone.

It was Lillian herself, not her housekeeper, who opened the door.

"Hi, Mom. Have you got a few minutes? We need to talk."

She put a hand up to her throat. "Is it Jocelyn?"

"She's at the ranch. She's okay." He stepped inside, closing the door behind him. "Is Morton here?"

"No." After a moment, she turned and led the way to the sunroom in the rear of the house. He guessed she wanted their conversation held in the only place in the house where she smoked. Sure enough, she paused at a table and removed a cigarette from a pack almost hidden beneath the drooping fronds of a fern. "I've been trying to reach her for days. Are you sure she's all right?" she asked after lighting up.

"She is, Mom. She's been on the road. That's probably why you haven't been able to reach her." He'd leave it to Jocelyn to explain why she couldn't have answered a call from her mother on her cell phone. He'd also leave it to Jocelyn to share the sordid details of her affair. If his mother knew the worst, she'd be too distraught to think about anything else. "She broke it off with the editor, guy by the name of Sanchez."

"Tony Sanchez," Lillian said.

"Do you know anything about him?" Maybe his mother was more aware of the situation than he realized.

"Nothing except his name. She was very unforthcoming with details about him, but so excited about becoming a journalist. I was afraid it wouldn't last."

"Yeah. I think her career in journalism is cut short for the time being. Sanchez is a shady character, she admits that. But I'll let her tell you all about it. She knows you're worried and she wanted me to tell you she's okay. She says she just needs some time at the ranch. She's…upset because the job—and the man—didn't work out."

Lillian turned away, contemplating the exquisitely landscaped grounds beyond the patio. She brought the cigarette to her lips and drew on it deeply. "It's where we all go to lick our wounds, isn't it?"

Hunter's eyes narrowed. Was that a chance remark or did she suspect Jocelyn was being abused by Sanchez? He could not see her expression to decide.

Still looking out, she asked, "Is she…too thin? Does she look as if she's well, physically, I mean?"

"She looks about the way you'd expect someone to look who's ended a relationship that was never too positive to begin with."

"What does that mean, Hunter?"

"Well…tired, I guess. A little strung out. But a few days at the ranch with Theresa bullying her to eat right and rest up will put her back on her feet. She'll be fine."

Lillian nodded. "At least she's home now. I'll call Morton." Distracted, she moved toward the phone. "He's been worried."

"You can call him after I leave, Mom." "Worry" would be a mild description of Morton's reaction if he knew the details of Jocelyn's latest escapade, Hunter thought. He was paranoid about his public image. If the press somehow got wind of Jocelyn's connection to a porn peddler in Key West, he would be forced to do major damage control.

He took a seat on one of the wicker chairs and watched his mother carefully when he said, "Jocelyn wasn't the only visitor at the ranch yesterday. Erica was there."

He saw her go rigid hearing Erica's name. She took a quick drag on the cigarette. "We had a great time," Hunter said. "Spent the best part of the day on horseback."

Lillian was pale when she turned to look at him. "And Jocelyn saw her?"

"That's the other thing I wanted to talk to you about, Mom. Yeah, she saw her, and her reaction was a lot like yours right now."

Lillian managed to look mystified. "What in the world does that mean?"

"I don't know, Mom. I was hoping you'd tell me." He watched her turn her gaze to the landscaped grounds again. "When I introduced them it was plain that she was shocked. In fact, she asked me if the two of us being there together was some kind of sick joke."

Lillian stubbed out her cigarette with a shaky hand. "Jocelyn is sometimes a bit tactless."

"She recognized Erica, but she denied it. I caught her early this morning and tried to get an explanation. I didn't want to risk Erica overhearing, although she seems willing to cut Sissy some slack in spite of her rudeness last night. Frankly, I'm beginning to wonder whether my family is a tad dysfunctional."

With her arms crossed tight at her waist, Lillian turned to face him. "Does that include me, since I know you don't consider Morton family?"

"You have to admit, your reaction was as odd as Jocelyn's when I introduced Erica at the gala."

"As I recall, I'm not the one who nearly fainted."

"Erica's reaction wasn't because she recognized you, Mom. She thought she recognized your jewelry. Aren't you curious as to why? Or do you already know? What's this all about? I'd like to know why Jocelyn freaked out, why you came to my office and tried to talk me out of seeing

Erica again, and why I get a feeling that I'm the only person in this crazy charade who doesn't know what the hell is going on."

"I told you I've never met Erica Stewart. I don't know what else I can say."

"And she tells me she's never met you." He was getting the same story from all three women. Frustrated, he got up and went to stand at the French doors looking out. "If you claim you've never met, why were you so set against it when you realized I was dating Erica?"

"I've apologized for that, Hunter. I'm simply disappointed that you dropped Kelly after giving her—and everyone else—the idea that the two of you would share a future." With her chin angled, she said in a chilly tone, "As your mother, I believe I have a right to express disappointment."

"What about your insinuation that Erica has slept her way to success in her career?"

"I beg your pardon," she said, instantly defensive. "I never said that. I never insinuated any such thing."

"Okay, maybe I misunderstood." He watched her fumble for her cigarettes and light up again. He knew he was browbeating her and he hated it, but how else was he going to get answers? "But didn't you say she'd been helped along in her success? That she couldn't take full credit for being given the opportunity to participate in the symphony gala or for being featured in *Texas Today?* You mentioned the spread in the newspaper, too. Is somebody doing all this for Erica behind the scenes and expecting nothing in return?"

"Maybe you should ask her that."

He shifted away from the doors in frustration. "I'm asking you, Mom. You're the one who planted the idea in my head. Now you owe it to me to tell me where your suspicions are coming from. I'm in love with Erica. I want to marry her."

A small anguished sound came from Lillian. "Have you asked her? Is she in love with you?"

"No." With his thoughts elsewhere, he failed to notice how appalled she looked. "I'm working on it, but it may take a while. She's had a lot of sadness." He paused to gather his thoughts. "She lost her husband and baby in a hit-and-run accident. It was a long time ago, nine years, but anybody can see she's still—" He stopped, glanced at his mother. "You might remember it. I did, because I was living here while that first condo I bought was being renovated. It happened just a couple of streets over."

"Yes, I remember," she murmured, dead pale. "It was terrible."

"Yeah, really. She was hurt, too. In a coma for several days, so she doesn't remember much about it."

"They say trauma victims can lose whole blocks of memory." Her voice was unsteady.

"Or maybe because it was so terrible, she wouldn't let herself remember it…until now."

Something flickered over Lillian's face, but she quickly hid it. "Until now?"

"Yeah. She's beginning to recall bits and pieces, mostly in dreams. And lately she's regained her ability to paint, which wouldn't be significant except that she wasn't able to paint at all after losing her husband and baby." Again, with his thoughts on Erica, he failed to note Lillian's expression. "I never put much stock in that kind of stuff, but I was there when she woke up from one of those dreams— actually it was a nightmare—and it was all about the accident. The images were so vivid that she was almost hysterical. You should have seen her." He shook his head, glad that moment was behind him. Fixed on the memory, his gaze was on his feet, not his mother. "What's odd about the stuff she's painting is that she doesn't plan it. She just feels compelled to paint and it is what it is when it's done. We think it comes from those suppressed memories...or her subconscious, whatever you want to call it."

"We?" she inquired faintly.

"Jason had the idea first, but Erica wouldn't listen. Now she's beginning to think maybe it could be." He stopped, his hand clamped behind his neck. Caught up in the puzzle of Erica's past, he realized he'd let himself drift away from his purpose. "Damn, I didn't mean to get sidetracked. It's just that I don't think Erica's been able to get on with her life, and it's possible she won't until she resolves this." He gave a wry smile. "Which means she won't be falling in love with me—or anybody—at least, not anytime soon. So you can rest easy there. For the present."

Lily stood before the fern and picked at a few brown ends. "You're caught up in this woman's life, Hunter, but I don't see how this relates to me."

"Maybe it doesn't. But I've had a strong feeling lately that there's some connection between my family—that is, you and Jocelyn—and Erica. So, before you even start with the protests, I admit it's unlikely. Still, it's there. The only link I can think of is that Erica and her husband lived in the same neighborhood as all of us, but it was nine years ago. If you know of a connection, I'd like to hear it."

"Just because people live in a neighborhood doesn't necessarily mean they ever meet." Her hands, tending the plant, went still. "I remember the accident. It was...horrendous. A tragedy. Everyone was...was just...just appalled that it happened."

"Were you aware of any speculation by the neighbors as to who might have done something like this?"

"No." Outside, a bird called, drawing her gaze up. "The

neighbors couldn't imagine anyone being capable of something like that."

He waited to see if she would volunteer anything else, but somehow she seemed to have drifted miles away. "Your gate appeared in Erica's dream yesterday," he said.

She turned. "What?"

"The iron gate outside," he explained, watching her closely. "She dreamed that she stood before it but couldn't get inside. She said she felt absolutely certain she was meant to see something that lay beyond that gate."

For a moment, she simply stared at him. "And that's why you've developed these suspicions about me?" she demanded on a note of incredulity. "Because of some…some dream of Erica's? Do you realize how absurd that is, Hunter?"

"Yeah, I do. Absurd, unlikely, far-fetched, it's all that. But I had to ask, Mom. I can't get it out of my head that Erica isn't a stranger to you."

"Well, try!" she said, finally giving way to full anger. "You come in here with wild-eyed suspicions based on nothing more than the bizarre dreams of some woman who's captured your fancy, and when I don't give you the answers you want, you won't leave it. You just keep on and on."

"Mom—"

She waved him silent. "You've always had an active imagination, Hunter, but you've crossed a line with these interrogations trying to link me to your latest girlfriend. I would appreciate it if you'd have a little respect. And the next time you decide to drop in, do not mention that woman's name to me." She was a picture of wounded pride and outrage.

"Mom, I just—"

She took an abrupt step back before he could touch her.

"Please. I wish you'd go now, Hunter. Tell Jocelyn her father will be calling whether she wishes to talk or not." With that, she turned and left him.

By the time she reached her bedroom, she was shaking, cold to her bones. She had always known that someday the elaborate web of deceit that she and Morton had spun would come back to haunt them. But to have it rear up in this way, for Hunter to be the instrument of her destruction seemed a punishment conjured up by the devil himself. But, she thought as she sank to her knees on the floor, she'd made a pact with the devil, hadn't she? And now he was here to make her pay.

The day had crawled by with no response from Morton to Lillian's frantic messages. He assumed, of course, that she knew the rules—his secretary was instructed to block any unscheduled callers—and that included his wife. He expected her to abide by them. Lillian had long ago accepted the insult implicit in that, but she'd tried to impress upon his secretary how urgently necessary it was to speak to Morton. Consequently, by the time he got home that evening, she'd had two very stiff martinis and was working on her third. Usually, she waited for him—no matter the hour—but she was feeling the numbing effects of gin and had prudently climbed the stairs while she was still able.

He was clearly irritated when he entered their bedroom. "What were all those messages about today, Lillian?" He loosened the knot of his tie and jerked it off. "How many times do I have to tell you that I don't like to be bombarded with phone calls in the heart of my day? It's distracting." With his fingers working at the buttons of his shirt, he moved toward the closet. "By the time you coerced Giselle into interrupting my meeting—a very important meeting, I might add—it became downright embarrassing. If I'd had a free moment, I would have called. When did that dawn on you?"

"After the fourth brush-off, Morton."

Although deep in the bowels of his closet, something in her tone brought him out to look at her. "Have you been drinking?" he asked, narrow-eyed.

"Yes, I have." She held up the martini glass that had been in her hand when he'd walked in the door. If he'd looked at her, he would have seen it. Which proved, she thought wearily, that she was nearly invisible to her husband. "This is my third, I think. But it's possible I've lost count."

She had his attention now. Moving toward her, he slowly pulled at the tails of his white shirt. "You look like hell. What's going on?"

Morton was a handsome man, she thought vaguely. He didn't have a lot of time for his wife, but he was able to find an hour a day to go to the gym. Of course, it was right there in the CentrexO complex, so it was convenient. Paid off, too, she decided, her gaze roaming over his well-developed pecs and flat tummy. The problem was, she felt nothing looking at him except to wish it was Hank in the bedroom with her and not her husband.

"What's the matter with you, Lillian? I asked you a question."

"I heard you." She opened the drawer of her nightstand and took out a pack of cigarettes. Taking her time, she lit up and felt perverse satisfaction in seeing the flare of surprise in his eyes. He'd banned smoking in the bedroom, so she was in flagrant violation of the rules. "Life as we know it is over, Morton," she said through a haze of smoke.

He stared at her. "Jesus, Lillian, you're drunk."

"Not drunk enough, dear." But a look at the fury in his face and her alcohol-induced defiance dissolved. Her eyes filled and her lips began to tremble. "When you hear what's happened, you'll probably want to get drunk with me, Morton."

"Oh, for God's sake!" Cursing angrily, he strode across the room and wrenched the martini out of her hand, then stalked to the bathroom and dashed it, olive and all, into the toilet. On his way out, he furiously tossed the glass into a pretty ceramic bowl. Lillian made an incoherent sound as shards of Baccarat crystal flew.

"And put out that goddamned cigarette!" he ordered. "Maybe then I can get some sense out of you."

Moving jerkily, she turned away and stubbed the cigarette out in a tiny ashtray. Without looking at him, she drew in a deep, unsteady breath. "Hunter was here this morning. He drove in directly from the ranch. I'm not sure if he spent the full weekend there, or just Sunday. I know he stayed overnight."

Morton waited, radiating impatience. "So?" he said, prompting her. "That's hardly a news flash. He spends every spare minute there. What's the big deal?"

"He came to tell me that Jocelyn was there, too." Judging from his expression, Lillian realized he was surprised.

"Is she okay?" he asked. "Have you seen her?"

Is she okay? Lillian closed her eyes in some relief that he'd asked. At least he had some interest in his daughter's well-being. There had been times in the past when she worried that he'd washed his hands—and his heart—of Jocelyn with all her problems. "Hunter says she's okay. And no, I haven't seen her. She—" She hesitated and felt her throat go tight with tears again. "She left the job under suspicious circumstances, I believe. Hunter didn't have details...or if he did, he chose not to share them with me. She's asked us not to call or come to the ranch. She wants some time alone."

"Licking her wounds," he said without sympathy.

Lillian said nothing. Weren't those her very own words when she heard where Jocelyn was?

Morton headed back to the closet, shrugging out of his shirt on the way. "What did you expect me to do about this, Lillian? Jocelyn's running true to form. She makes an irresponsible decision to hightail it to Key West with some jerk without having a clue to his character, and after a few months she's back home expecting sympathy, a free bed and a fresh check. A month from now she'll hike off somewhere else and do it all over again." Muttering with disgust, he balled up the shirt and tossed it into a hamper. "Face it, she's never going to grow up. The only positive I see in this is that she chooses to run to the ranch and Hunter instead of holing up here. Last thing I need is to explain a neurotic daughter to John Frazier, or any other of the president's spies who might be lurking around waiting to see me step into shit and kill my appointment." He disappeared into the closet.

"Erica Stewart was there."

He was out in a heartbeat, scowling at her. "Where, the ranch?"

"Yes." Lillian sat abruptly on the side of the bed, swallowing hard. Acid burned the back of her throat and she prayed she'd be able to hold it down. "She spent the night there, Morton. Hunter is serious about her. He wants to marry her."

"Shit."

"Jocelyn apparently hadn't a clue she was there, otherwise, I know she would have stayed away."

"What happened?"

"Can't you guess? Jocelyn was shocked to her toes. Hunter said she tried to pretend it was because she was surprised to see Erica and not Kelly. But he wasn't fooled." She watched Morton pacing now. "That's why he was here this morning. He had a list of questions, and he wasn't in a mood to be put off."

He stopped in front of her. "What kind of questions?"

She sighed. "The obvious. Why was Jocelyn shocked to see Erica there? Why was she…sickened at the thought of Hunter and Erica being together?" With her stomach threatening to rebel, Lillian pressed it with an unsteady hand. "He wanted to know why he had this feeling that there was some kind of connection between his family— Jocelyn and I—and Erica." Blinded by tears, she fumbled in the drawer for a tissue.

"Why would he think something like that?"

She wiped her eyes. "He believes Erica knows something about the accident, but that she's suppressed the memory for all these years. Morton, she's beginning to regain some of that memory." The mix of fear and gin was lethal. She could feel herself beginning to shake and longed to rush to the toilet. "That's why she nearly fainted when she saw my brooch. And the gate—" She gazed in distraction at the grounds outside the bedroom window. "She said there was something behind the gate that she was meant to see. And she's painting abstract art without knowing what it means. She hasn't picked up a paintbrush in nine years and now she's painting pictures, and Hunter thinks they're going to be keys to unlocking…whatever." Her voice rose on a note of hysteria. Devastated and desperate, she looked up at him. "What are we going to do, Morton?"

"Hold on a minute." He paused, trying to sort through the rush of words. "What's this about a gate? You're not making any sense, Lillian. What gate?"

She locked her arms around herself. "She dreamed about our gate, the privacy gate that blocks our driveway."

"So what? We don't have a monopoly on gate design,

for God's sake. Not that one, anyway. I could find ten like it within an hour right in this neighborhood." Irritably, he went to his armoire and took out a golf shirt. "As for painting abstract pictures, the woman's an artist, Lillian. That's what she does, she paints."

"Why did she almost faint when she saw my brooch?"

His head emerged from the collar of the shirt as he pulled it on. Shoving his arms through the sleeves, he tugged the tails down and neatly tucked it into the waistband of his pants. "You've got me there. I don't know what the damned brooch has to do with anything, but I do know this…." He stopped and pointed a finger at her face. "I want you to remember what's at stake here. I don't want you freaking out. If Hunter asks you anything else, you know nothing, you hear me?"

"What about Jocelyn?" she whispered.

"You let me worry about Jocelyn. I'll drive out there tomorrow, as inconvenient as it is for me." He shoved his wallet into his back pocket and swept up his car keys. "I guess I'm wasting my time telling you to get a grip. I can see it's too late for that. But stay away from the booze. I mean it, Lillian." He glanced at his watch, his thoughts moving on to the next item on his agenda. "I've got a tee time in twenty minutes, otherwise I'd cancel and go to the ranch now, but Frazier might think something's up and start nosing around. One snoop nosing around is enough." At the door, he looked back with an expression of distaste · on his face. "When I say get a grip, that includes not running to the ranch to cry on Hank Colson's shoulder. Stay away from him."

An hour later, Morton stood watching as John Frazier sank a fifteen-foot putt at the second green. He made all the right noises in an effort to appear relaxed as though he was enjoying the game as they strolled back to the cart, but his brain teemed with a boatload of possibilities that could wreck his life, none of them relating to golf. Not only did he have to worry about Lillian's tendency to go off the deep end, but now he'd have to keep Jocelyn on a tight leash, too. Hell, he could handle the women in his family. The one wild card was Hunter and his sudden urge to play detective.

He stowed his putter in the bag and climbed into the cart beside Frazier, who had just confirmed that the appointment was as solid as the president's administration. Staring straight ahead as he took off, Morton cursed. Two million women in Houston and Hunter finds Erica Stewart. Well, it figured, goddamn it. He'd been nothing but a pain in the ass almost from the day of the wedding. Even as a little kid, there was no getting close enough to him to win him over. He seemed to suspect everything Morton did, for no reason, so that by the time he was an adolescent, it was open warfare between them. He'd have thought Lillian would have supported him disciplining the little shit, but she was worse than useless. She worried that Hunter would move out and go live at the ranch with that son of a bitch Colson. Hunter had an ally there and he knew it. Took advantage of it. For his part, Morton never gave a fuck if he did leave.

Morton stopped the cart abruptly, staying put while Frazier carefully chose a driver. That goddamn ranch and everything it meant had been a thorn in his side from day one. If he'd had his way, he would have forced Lillian to sell out. The property was worth a small fortune. But the estate was set up with Colson as trustee. Like Hunter, Colson had taken a suspicious dislike of Morton from the start. The bastard had a wife back then, but he'd fancied Lillian and she'd fancied him. He'd never worried about the two of them getting it on. Both were so moralistic that they'd never cheat.

He watched Frazier tee up and drive a beaut right down the middle, but he was too caught up in his thoughts to make much of it. Nine years. Nine goddamned years and Hunter hooks up with the one woman who could ruin everything. Hefting his driver, he strode to the tee. He'd worked too hard for success to sit by and have it undone by some frigging twist of fate. But this was a circumstance he'd anticipated years ago and the solution he'd worked out then was still the only way today. Of course, the devil was in the details, but that was not a problem. He was a detail man.

Seventeen

Erica tore the paper wrapping from a bolt of bronze satin, gave it a halfhearted glance and shoved it aside. She must have had something in mind when she ordered it, but she hadn't a clue what it was at the moment. She slipped her shoes off and moved to the window of the tiny office and watched Jason work his magic with a customer. Thankfully, he'd refrained from dragging her into conversation with the woman. She would not even be at the shop except that a shipment had arrived and only she could check that it was exactly what she'd ordered.

Jason ushered the customer to the door and walked straight back to the office. "Okay, tell Daddy all about it, sugar. That's the third customer you've snubbed today. I'm running out of excuses trying to do damage control here." With his hands on his hips, his gaze was so intent that she knew he was in one of his get-to-the-bottom-of-the-problem moods. "What's going on?"

"I haven't snubbed anyone, Jason. I just don't gush over customers the way you do."

"That customer bought two very expensive quilts, honeybunch. It's time to gush when I make a forty-five-hundred-dollar sale. And I didn't hear an answer."

"I didn't hear a question."

Rolling his eyes, he turned about, walked through the shop to the door, flipped the Closed sign and twisted the lock. "It's only thirty minutes short of closing time," he said, glancing at his watch. "I'm meeting Phillip, but he'll wait. And the question was, what's going on? You've been in la-la land for the past week. I'm good at math. It was one week ago that you spent the weekend with Hunter at the ranch. I'd be a lot happier over this if you looked like a woman who'd been laid, but you don't."

"I wish you'd stop obsessing over my love life, Jason. And there's nothing going on." She flipped aimlessly through her sketch pad, wondering why she'd ordered a hideous peacock print. "I'm just at one of those low periods. If I was an author, I'd have writer's block. I can't seem to come up with anything worthwhile. We've taken a lot of orders, but I can't seem to focus. It's scary. I'm worried."

"I think you're focused, all right, but it's on something other than the label." He flung himself into a chair. "Admit it, Erica. You're in love. You finally woke up and reentered the human race. And speaking of Hunter, where is he? How is it you spent a weekend with him and he hasn't been around?" He gave her a suspicious look. "Have you pissed him off? Did you do what you're best at when a man gets the hots for you?"

"I haven't seen Hunter since Monday morning when he drove me back from his ranch. This time, I'm not the one who's backing off."

"Has he called?" he asked, frowning.

"No."

"You've been dumped?" For once, she'd surprised him.

She inspected a spool of black fringe, then dropped it back in its box. "Is that so incredible?"

"Yeah, it is. I would have bet the shop that he was falling for you in a big way, sugar." His mouth twisted wryly. It wasn't often that his famed astuteness failed. But then he went narrow-eyed as a thought struck. "Did he try to get you in bed and you refused?"

She turned away with a frosty look. "That's not what this is about, Jason."

"That's it! Damn it, Erica, you've got to take the plunge—pardon the pun—sooner or later. You'll see. Once you begin acting like a real live woman again, you'll like it. You'll wonder why you waited so long."

"It isn't about sex, Jace. It would be simple if it was." She sat down, tucking her bare feet beneath her. "We talked about David. I told him about the baby."

He was up off the chair and at her feet in a heartbeat. "Oh, shit, sugar. I'm sorry." On his haunches, he took both her hands in his. "If you tell me that turned him off, I'll kill him for you…even if it means going over to one of those testosterone-city sites where he hangs out with all those construction hunks."

She laughed and made him turn her hands loose. "No, he was very…touched when I told him. He couldn't have been more sympathetic, even when I had the nightmare, which must have been enough to freak out anybody. He—"

"Nightmare? You mean you spent the night with him and didn't have sex? God, he's so gorgeous. How could you resist?"

"We were outside, Jason," she said patiently. "His housekeeper packed a picnic lunch with the most delicious stuff, including wine. He spread a blanket and we ate. It was really nice. Then, I don't know how it happened, but

I fell asleep and the next thing I knew, I was having the dream. Only this time, I was at a gate." Pausing, she saw it again, coal-black bars, impenetrable iron. "Jason, it was the gate at his mother's house. It was locked, but I had this truly urgent need to get inside because there was something beyond that gate that I was meant to see." She saw that he was listening avidly. "Isn't that weird?"

"Only if you've never been to his mother's house to know about the gate."

"Well, that's just it. We were there that morning. Hunter needed to get something from the house. We parked in front of the gate and I waited while he went inside. So, it doesn't mean anything, does it?"

"You sound as if you think it does mean something."

She'd been thinking about nothing else ever since. Try as she might, she could not accept that she'd dreamed about that gate simply because she'd sat in front of it for a few minutes that day. The urgency she felt was too real. "I know you won't believe this, but I do think it means something." She sighed at the implausibility of it. "I just don't have a clue what it could be."

Jason had picked up her sketchbook and was idly turning pages. "Do you know these people," he asked. "Hunter's parents?"

"No, until that night when he introduced us at the symphony gala, they were complete strangers. Except for Mr. Trask, of course, whose picture is in the paper occasionally. But I just don't think that's it. It's something about his mother." She decided not to mention Jocelyn and her shocked reaction to finding Erica with Hunter. His sister's personal problems were best left within the family. But Jocelyn was another link to Hunter's family, even though an obscure one, she was sure of that. Her gaze strayed to her sketch pad where Jason was studying a drawing of Lillian

Trask's brooch. She'd somehow sketched it from memory in meticulous detail. How she'd done that, she hadn't a clue.

Shifting her gaze to Jason, Erica said, "So, maybe it was all a little too much emotion for our precious Hunter. Maybe that's why he hasn't called."

Taking the sketch pad with him, Jason sat back down. "Is your heart broken?"

"I would have to be in love with him for that to happen."

"Yeah." With the pad held to his chest, he crossed his legs and settled back. "So, is your heart broken?" he repeated.

"I am not in love with Hunter, Jason."

"Maybe not yet, but I have hopes." Just then they heard a movement at the door and they both yelped in surprise as Hunter appeared at the door of the tiny office. Before she had a chance to overcome her astonishment, he walked straight to Erica and kissed her, hard. Then he turned and scowled at Jason. "And you…this is twice I've walked into the shop through the back door. There are plenty of transients roaming around this neighborhood, especially in the delivery zone. Anybody could walk in here while you're busy with customers, and Erica would be the victim, Jason. An unlocked rear door is a thief's wet dream."

Midway through the lecture, Jason had risen to his feet, not to dispute Hunter, but to glare at Erica. "I told you to be sure and lock that door, Erica! You're preaching to the choir lecturing me, Hunter," he said, still scowling at her. "I've told her a million times to be more careful, but it's like dripping water on solid rock trying to tell her anything."

"Wait. Both of you." Erica was on her feet now, sans shoes, trying not to be bowled over by Hunter's sudden appearance and the effect of that brief kiss. "I thought I locked the door. There was a second delivery because the UPS guy discovered he'd overlooked a package. I got busy opening stuff after he left. I actually don't really remember if I locked up." When she was skewered by glares from both men, she put her hands on her hips and glared at her partner. "Jason, you know that lock is tricky."

"Which is why you have to jiggle it," Jason said, dropping the sketch pad on the chair on his way to the door. "She'll have to be drawn and quartered, Hunter…or worse," he said with a wicked smirk. "If you need whips and chains…or leather, just let me know. Meanwhile, I've gotta go. I'll double-check the locks on my way out."

"He's such a kidder," Erica said with disgust. But Hunter missed the remark. Instead, he stood stock-still, studying the drawing of his mother's brooch.

"What is this?" he asked, holding the sketch pad.

"It's your mother's brooch, of course," she said. "I was doing sketches to be embroidered on a jacket and it sort of took shape on its own. I didn't plan it."

"You managed to reproduce it exactly," he said, shifting his gaze to her. "How did you do that?"

"The same way I'm doing those weird paintings. They're coming from somewhere, but I haven't a clue how to explain it."

He leaned against the drafting table, frowning. "You must have seen it somewhere before and my mother swears it's an original piece. So where do you think you saw it?"

"Other than on your mother's jacket at the gala?" She gave a mystified shrug. "Your guess is as good as mine, Hunter."

He was still troubled, caught up in his own thoughts. "There has to be a connection. One or two coincidences might be believable, but we've got a whole string going. When you add Jocelyn's reaction when she saw you, it's too much." Idly, he paged through more of her sketches before handing the pad back to her. "Are you sure you haven't crossed paths with either one of them before?"

"Yes, I'm sure. Trust me, I've racked my brain trying to find a logical explanation and I still come up with nothing. But give me time," she quipped. "Maybe the mystery will be cleared up in one of those bizarre paintings I'm turning out."

He glanced blankly at the sketch pad. "You're doing a lot of them now?"

"More than I should." Noticing his interest in her sketches, she added, "Nothing in there. I'm painting at home. Ordinarily, I work in the evenings on the ton of special orders Jason has lined up. Instead, I find myself going straight for my easel and painting like mad." She smiled at him. "I know it sounds crazy, but I'm so happy to be able to paint again that I don't even care that I'm neglecting business."

"Maybe painting should be your business."

"It's a little late to change careers." Not looking at Hunter now, she rummaged around in a search for her shoes. She was bent over thinking they were buried under a mound of wrapping paper when Hunter caught her arm and pulled her around. He had her shoes in his hand, dangling them just out of her reach. "Looking for these?"

She heaved an impatient sigh as he handed them over with a grin. "I don't know why I do that!"

His grin turned into a slower, more seductive weapon. Moving in, he trailed his knuckles down her cheek. "Your skin is so soft that the idea of whips and chains is truly obscene."

A thrill of excitement went through her. When he walked in on her and Jason, a part of her had been tempted to throw herself into his arms. But now, with her heart doing a dangerous tap dance, a part of her urged caution, afraid that he would guess her thoughts.

"By the way, how is your sister?" Feigning nonchalance, she sat to put her shoes on, but he took them from her and went down on one knee.

"Ornery as ever." He took her bare foot in his hand, his thumb stroking the sensitive arch. It was all she could do to contain a delicious shiver. Her pulse skittered and her breath caught in her throat. "Between my sister, my mother and my work, I haven't had a minute to myself since I left you at your door Monday."

"I've been working, too," she said. Her shoes were on now, but he stayed where he was, his warm hands gliding up beneath her jeans to cup her calves and squeeze gently.

He lifted his eyes to hers, jolting her with just a look. "I missed you," he said.

"I missed you, too," she heard herself say, and marveled at how far she'd come in the few weeks she'd known him. Was Jason right? Had she fallen in love with Hunter? She certainly hadn't intended anything like that to happen...ever again. The possibility of opening herself up to that kind of pain was a frightening thought. But she couldn't deny how much it mattered that he was here.

He stood up, pulling her to her feet. "The hell of it is, I can't stay," he told her, slipping his arms around her. In a voice close to her ear, he said, "I've got a dinner date with a client. It'll last until midnight, then I've got to drive back to the ranch."

"It's okay." It wasn't easy to keep her voice steady while he nibbled down the side of her neck. "I need to work, too. I haven't been concentrating very well lately and orders are piling up." Closing her eyes, she anchored herself with both hands at his waist.

"What's the problem that you haven't been concentrating?"

His lips had settled on bare skin at the curve of her shoulder, so she tilted her head to capture the warmth. "Just…a lot of things."

He bit her then, a gentle nip on her earlobe that made her draw in a quick breath. "Am I one of them?"

"I think so." Certainly, no man had ever made her feel like this. Or else it had been so long that she'd forgotten. But how could she forget anything that felt so wonderful?

He tipped her head back so that he could look into her eyes. "Good. That makes two of us." Behind her head, he lifted an arm and looked at his watch. "I want to kiss you, but if I do, I won't stop there and then I'll be late. Besides, I don't want Jason walking in and commenting on my technique."

She smiled. "Jason's gone for the day. And don't worry, he will have made sure the front door is locked."

"Good." His gaze moved back to her face, roaming greedily from her eyes to one tiny gold stud in her ear, before settling again on her mouth. The heat in his gaze was almost as mesmerizing as a kiss. And in spite of what he said, Erica held her breath in anticipation. She could almost taste him, the musky, male, uniquely Hunter taste of him. And then, on a mad impulse, she was doing just that.

Her arms went around him, closing the whisper of space that separated them, and her mouth was on his, wild and reckless. Caught by surprise, Hunter staggered back. Then, finding his balance, he closed his arms about her and fell into the conflagration as instantly as flame follows an explosion.

Her lips were hot and insatiable, her body vibrating with need. It was more than he reckoned on, an unexpected, absolutely mind-blowing surprise. And in his exultation, he forgot everything but the taste and feel of her, the wonder of her abandonment. If, for weeks, he'd managed somehow to control his own lust, thinking to give her time to adjust to the idea of having him in her life, it was beyond him to resist now. With her hands fisted in his hair and her body like molten lava against his, he thought only of taking her. And with that thought, he went for the fastening of her jeans, then stripped them and her bikinis off. That might have been the moment when she could have stopped him, but she didn't.

Shifting his stance, he swept fabric and paper off the top of her desk with one hand, caught her beneath her bottom and lifted her, just enough to settle her on the desk. That done, he parted her legs to allow him access and found her hot and soft and ready. She made a sound—surprise or excitement—he couldn't tell which as he went for her mouth again, devouring it while his hands devoured her. She clung to him, moaning, as he stroked her intimately.

"Oh, oh, oh…that's…oh…"

With his mouth on her throat, he knew she was blind and deaf to everything except the excruciating tension of impending climax. He felt her straining to the breaking point and finding a scrap of control, he fought his own elemental need to be inside her, to ruthlessly drive himself into her and feel the ferocious joy of his own release.

And then she shattered. She came apart in his hands with a sharp, piercing cry. For a second, he was transfixed by the sight of her flushed and vibrating, lost in wild and mindless sensation. Teeth clamped, he forced himself to slow down, to take time to savor the moment. But his need was too much.

"Now. I want you now." His voice, sex-roughened, was somewhere near her ear as he fumbled with his jeans, tore them open and positioned himself. Still high on the pleasure of her release, she was boneless in his hands, totally yielding. Cupping her buttocks, he drove himself into her in a single, deep thrust.

For a heartbeat, he felt only a rush of triumph. Of fierce elation that he now had what he'd wanted for weeks. Then intense pleasure consumed him and the world and all thought fell away. Hard and heavy with need, he drove repeatedly into her, caught in that mindless state when his world was out of control. Until suddenly he was at the edge. Too soon, too soon, he thought, burying his face in her hair. He wanted desperately to prolong it, to make it last. But there was no holding it back. With a shout, he fell headlong into the glorious abyss.

Erica resisted the shrill sound of a passing police unit, wanting nothing of the outside world to intrude in the delicious afterglow. It had just been so long. And she was so wonderfully satisfied. Why had she resisted this? It didn't mean that she was giving her life over. She could enjoy having Hunter as a lover without setting herself up for the emotional pain that comes with marriage. And Lord, he was a forceful, impassioned lover. She was tingling with the proof of it. But she'd guessed that about him. She smiled, thinking he hadn't managed to remove his shirt or his pants and felt a pang of regret that she hadn't been able to see him naked. Actually, neither of them had removed enough clothes. He'd stripped her jeans and bikinis down, but not all the way. Oh, well, next time. With another cat-like smile, she shivered at the thought of the next time.

Hunter stirred, made a sound that was a muffled curse and prepared to pull away. Apparently, there would be no afterglow for him, either. With a sigh, she guessed the state of mindlessness that had hold of him was gone, too. She suspected the last place he would have chosen for them to make love was on a desk in her office...especially the first time. She didn't quite know how it had happened that way, either, but she certainly had no complaints.

Without meeting her eyes, he carefully withdrew from her and zipped up. Delving in his back pocket, he came up with a handkerchief and pushed it into her hands. "Here, you'll need this. Where's the bathroom? I'll get you something...a paper towel or...something. Water."

"No, I'm okay." She zipped her jeans and tugged the tails of her T-shirt down, putting herself in some sort of order.

"I'm sorry, Erica." He dragged a hand through his hair, looking anywhere but at her. "I don't know what happened...how it got away from me like that. I just lost control." His gaze bounced to hers and away again as he managed a strangled laugh. "This is a first for me. I don't usually jump the bones of a woman like that. Mostly, I have the decency to find a bed and get her consent."

It was interesting to see Hunter confounded. It had to be a new experience as he was one of the most self-confident men she'd ever met. It made his chagrin sort of endearing. "I did consent, Hunter," she told him gently. "If you recall, I started it, even though you told me you had an appointment. I should be apologizing to you."

He looked directly at her then. "Only if you want me to feel even worse."

She smiled. "It wasn't good for you?"

He turned away, unable to accept gentle teasing from her when he was bent on beating himself up. "Ah, Jesus, this is a helluva note. You're not supposed to be nice when I've just acted like a Neanderthal. You should remind me that I'm not a randy teenager. I'm supposed to be about twenty years beyond that."

"In a way it's a compliment to me, isn't it...sort of?"

She came up behind him and slipped her arms around his waist. "You still haven't answered me yet. Wasn't it good?"

He turned his head, then pivoted all the way around and caught her up in a fierce embrace. "If it got any better, I'd have to be scraped off the ceiling." With the scent of her hair filling his senses, he pressed his face to her throat. "You know I've wanted to make love to you from the start. God, I've gotten used to cold showers lately. You don't want to know how many. Or the times I've come awake in the middle of the night aching. But, damn, I wanted it to be in the right setting."

"Outside at the ranch on a blanket?"

He chuckled, beginning to get a grip. "I jumped the gun there, too," he said wryly. "Put it down to the power of your attraction. I get a little taste of you and I go crazy." His humor faded. "Seriously, I know it's been a long time for you and you've got a lot of…issues. I planned to wait until you were ready."

"I must have been ready." Erica rested her head against his chest. "And it would be silly to complain as I obviously wasn't doing anything to stop you. So, maybe we both acted a little out of character."

He kissed her temple. "The bad news is I've still got to meet that client, who's probably wondering where I am." He angled back to look at her. "But it doesn't mean I'm going to be satisfied from now on with grabbing a few minutes to see you. Don't you have to go to Austin for the awards dinner soon? I'm talking about the *Texas Today* thing."

"Yes, Jason and I are—"

He gave her a little shake. "Jason is not going to be your date that night, lady. I know he'll be there, but if he wants company, let him get his own date. So, when is it? You'll be staying overnight, won't you?"

"It's this Saturday, only three days away. And I'll probably have to stay overnight. There's a reception before the event, then the awards dinner, which I've been warned can last well into the evening."

"How many guests can you invite?"

She shrugged. "They sent me several tickets, about six, I think."

"You're inviting your mom and dad, aren't you?"

"Well…"

"They'll want to be there, sweetheart." With his arms loose about her, he did the math. "That's four, since they'll both have their spouses. Jason and me…that's six. And how about we leave early Saturday morning? We can do Austin."

"I've seen Austin. Every respectable Texan has," she said dryly.

"Okay, we'll do each other." He kissed a spot on her neck and she lost the urge to argue that she, and not Hunter, should plan the evening. Later, she promised herself. "And we'll do it right," he added, as he meandered his way over to her lips. Taking his time, he bestowed several lush, drugging kisses. And when he finally let her go, she was flushed and breathless and disinclined to argue with him about anything.

Eighteen

Contrary to Morton's orders and Jocelyn's druthers, Lillian went to the ranch. She would have gone the very next day after talking to Hunter, but she had to wait until she was certain Morton had made good on his threat to drive up and talk to Jocelyn. Of course, there wasn't much she would be able to add to anything Morton might say to her. For one thing, she'd long ago lost any credibility with her daughter. No, the real reason she was going to the ranch was her desperate need to see Hank and be comforted by his utterly undemanding acceptance of her and who she was.

He was standing on the porch watching her as she drove the last half mile up to the house. How he knew when she would show up was a mystery to Lillian, but he always did. It never failed that he sensed her need to see him and there was never a moment when she felt anything but most welcome. Before she was out of the car, he was at her side.

"Hello, darlin'." With a smile, he took her hand and brought it to his lips. It was a courtly greeting, affectionate, in no way beyond the bounds of respectability. But it almost reduced Lillian to tears. She felt a desperate longing to be able—to be free!—to step into his arms and be surrounded by the strength and sheer goodness of him. "I knew you'd be here soon what with Jocelyn finally turning up."

"Yes."

"She's out riding with Kelly just now," he said, falling into step beside her. "The two of them left this morning at daybreak. Should be back soon, definitely for lunch. Riding makes you hungry."

"It does."

He put a hand on her waist as they climbed the porch steps. "To tell the truth, I'm glad the girls aren't here just now. I won't have to share you…for a while."

It was an echo of her own feelings, as well. Which was probably selfish of her, she thought, but she'd feel guilty later. At the moment, she planned to savor what little time she could having Hank all to herself. She'd vowed not to burden him with her fears about Hunter and Erica, or her worry about Jocelyn, but she felt him studying her narrowly. He always could see right through her, as if her feelings were written on her forehead.

"Hank." Lips unsteady, she swallowed hard. "I had to come. I—"

Instead of going inside, she moved quickly to the porch railing and stood looking out over the east pasture. The wildflowers were fading now. In the distance, the hills were taking on the bright green of spring. "It's so beautiful here," she murmured.

"You've got a few things on your plate at the moment, eh, darlin'?"

She managed a meager laugh. "If you only knew."

"So tell me, Lily. We go back a long way. There can't be much you could say that would shock me, not after all these years."

Oh, yes, my darling. I could indeed shock you. How she wished she could share the dark fear in her heart, but it was hers alone to bear. So she settled for what they could discuss. "Hunter is serious about Erica Stewart, did you know that?"

"I must say it doesn't come as a complete shock." He offered a smile. "I got that from Theresa. She had a chance to study the two of them together last weekend. First thing she told me when I got in from that pecan growers meeting was that he'd met his Waterloo at last. The way he looked at that girl said it all." He paused, studying Lillian's face. "That is, that's Theresa's take on it."

"I have Hunter's take on it. He's in love with her and he wants to marry her."

He reached over and caught her chin, gently turning her face around so that he could see directly into her eyes. "And that's his right, isn't it, Lily, darlin'? Didn't you want him to find someone to love eventually? You surely want him to have children, don't you? You'd dote on Hunter's babies the way you doted on him and his sister. You want that, don't you, Lily?"

Unable to meet his gaze, she closed her eyes as a tear streaked down her cheek. He had no idea how those words pierced her heart like a hot knife. "But not her, Hank," she whispered brokenly. "I wanted Kelly to be the mother of my grandchildren."

He frowned. "This is so unlike you, Lily. Erica Stewart is everything you should want for Hunter. She's talented, creative, a beautiful woman if that newspaper article did her justice. Above all that, Hunter doesn't love Kelly. Hell, she doesn't love him. If she did, she wouldn't have been able to take his rejection almost as casually as if she missed being able to acquire a horse she particularly liked. The two of them were just biding time with each other, darlin'. You've got to let it go."

"I know." She sniffed and took the handkerchief he put in her hands. "I'm silly. I'm selfish. I'm a disgrace to motherhood."

"Yeah, you're bad to the bone, all right." He took her hand and urged her toward the door. "Come on inside. Let's have some of that lemonade Theresa made before she took off to look at that new grandbaby of hers. If you're half as silly over Hunter's—whenever it happens—as she is over hers, you'll look back and wonder what in the world was going on in your mind to make you think otherwise."

The house was as familiar and inviting as ever. She paused inside the door and let the memories come, washing over her like cool, clear water and easing some of the turmoil inside her. After a moment or two, she followed Hank to the den, where she took a seat on a corner of the leather couch and tucked her legs beneath her. "How long did Morton stay yesterday?" she asked. "He was here, wasn't he?"

"Yeah. He showed up ready to roll with his lecture for Jocelyn. He didn't pull any punches in letting her know he was disappointed in her, and that there wouldn't be another check deposited into her account until she demonstrated a change of attitude, and showed him she was putting out feelers for a real job."

Lillian held a cushion tight against her middle. It had happened just as she'd feared it would. "He said all that in front of you?"

"No, the two of them went outside to the porch, but I could tell by the way Jocelyn bowed up like a cat facing off a big dog. It was later after he left that she told me what he said."

"Was she crying?"

"Doesn't he always make her cry, darlin'?"

Hank stood behind her, so she was unable to see his face. But when she felt his touch on her shoulder, she lifted her hand and covered his. It was like touching gnarled wood, strong and weather-roughened. Life-roughened. He wasn't someone who'd spent his adult life working with his hands, but somehow he seemed to be that kind of man.

In fact, Hank had been every bit as successful in the air-cargo business he'd started with her husband years ago as Morton was at CentrexO. However, when Marguerite was battling cancer, he had decided to sell out. Just announced out of the blue that he was giving it up. They'd then moved to the ranch. After she died, he stayed. Lillian stared wistfully at her toes, knowing that kind of love had been lost to her long ago when Bart's plane had crashed.

"How could he be so heartless, Hank?"

"Jocelyn's his one and only. To his way of thinking, what she does is a reflection of his own success or failure. He can't bask in Hunter's success. Truth to tell, it's just the opposite. Hunter is Bart's offspring, not Mort's."

"Scolding and lecturing has never worked with Jocelyn. When will he see that?"

His palm was warm on her shoulder. Reassuring. "I wouldn't count on him ever seeing that, hon." He moved to the bar where a tall pitcher and glasses sat on a tray. "Which reminds me. What's the latest on his appointment?" He poured lemonade and brought it to her.

"He says it's firm. Everything's on course. He's just waiting to be told the location, and he claims he hasn't a clue where that is." She sipped the tart-sweet lemonade and said thoughtfully, "I wonder if he mentioned it to Jocelyn."

With his big arms crossed over his chest, Hank leaned against the bar with a look of disgust. "Didn't the two of you talk at all when he got home last night? With both of you so concerned about Jocelyn, you'd think there would be some conversation since he was so hell-bent on getting over here to lay down the law."

"He didn't come home last night. He went directly from here to Galveston. He's hosting a group of influential types from Washington on his yacht. His reason for wanting to talk to Jocelyn yesterday wasn't because he missed her and wanted to see her, even though it's six months since her last visit here. No, what he wanted was to warn her not to do anything to screw up his precious appointment."

"Then, if he's gone, why don't you stay a day or two?"

"What?" With the glass suspended in midair, she paused. "Stay here? I can't do that, Hank."

"Lily, he's gone for the rest of the week and probably the weekend. Jocelyn needs you right now. And if you're worried about how it would look, having her here makes it completely respectable."

"She doesn't want me around, Hank." Her eyes filled. "She has you and Theresa for any nurturing she needs. She prefers both of you over me. She's probably going to be upset when she finds I'm here today. She told Hunter to tell me not to come, that she was fine and she'd be getting in touch. She hasn't, of course." With her fingers pressed against her mouth, she managed not to cry. "I just have to see her. But you wait, she won't like it."

"Kids don't always know what they want, Lily."

"She's twenty-five years old, hardly a child."

"Maybe so, but she needs you right now."

She picked up something in his tone and her eyes narrowed. "What are you saying? You told me she was fine. Hunter said the same. I think Morton would have called me if he'd suspected anything. So—"

She stopped at sounds from the porch. Voices. As they headed inside, she heard Kelly speaking, the words quick and intense. Jocelyn's hesitant response came out husky and low. But she couldn't make out what they said. She quickly set her glass on the end table and stood up as they entered the room.

Neither spotted her at first. But both glanced over in surprise when she gasped at the sight of the bruise on Jocelyn's cheek. With her hair pulled back and caught in a clip at her nape, the discoloration on her face was shockingly visible. "Jocelyn! What happened?" She moved instinctively toward her daughter. "Did you take a fall riding? Are you hurt?" When she reached out to get a better look, Jocelyn recoiled, turning so that Lillian got only a quick glimpse before she pulled the clip from her hair. Thick and shoulder-length, it was a dark, heavy curtain falling forward and concealing her bruised cheek.

With a note of resignation, Jocelyn asked, "What are you doing here, Mother?"

As Lillian feared, her daughter was not happy to see her. "I've been worried. I wanted to see for myself that you were all right. Obviously, you're not."

She spread her arms out wide. "See for yourself, I'm fine."

"How did you get that bruise?" Lillian asked.

Jocelyn sighed. "It's a long story. Trust me, you don't want to know."

"Of course I want to know. If you didn't fall off a horse, what happened?" Lillian glanced at Kelly, thinking she might offer a little help, but she was pointedly examining her nails.

"Your mother asked you a question, Jocelyn." Hank spoke with quiet authority.

Lillian gestured to Hank without looking at him. "Could I have a few minutes with Jocelyn, please? We won't be long."

"I'm okay, Mother," Jocelyn said with heavy patience.

"Hank…Kelly. Please…" With her gaze still fixed on her daughter, Lillian waited until they were alone. She watched with some relief as Jocelyn stalked to the other side of the room. She was not happy, but at least she didn't walk out with Kelly and Hank.

"I'll leave soon after we talk if you still want me to, but I'm your mother. It's normal to be concerned when you leave a job under questionable circumstances, especially when you were so enthusiastic about it in the beginning. Now, without warning, you show up bruised and battered." Her gaze traveled from Jocelyn's head to her toes. Aside from the marks on her face, she was far too thin. The too-large shirt and skinny jeans made her look fragile, ready to shatter at a touch. "Well, any mother would be concerned." After a pause, she added, "How did you explain your appearance to your father?"

Jocelyn heaved another dramatic sigh. "I told him I fell down the stairs carrying my suitcase as I was leaving my apartment in Key West." She turned and looked directly at Lillian. "The truth is my editor was unhappy when I quit suddenly. Slapping me around was nothing to what could happen if I decided to rat him out about his 'business.'" She made quote marks with her fingers.

"He attacked you? He assaulted you?" Appalled, Lillian put a hand to her heart.

"Didn't I say you'd freak out if I told you?"

"Did you call the police? Did you have him arrested?"

"Mother…did you hear me? He was making certain I would keep my mouth shut."

Lillian shuddered with revulsion. Thank God she'd had the sense to get away from there. "What exactly is his business?" she asked. "Or do I not want to hear that, either?"

"Internet porn." Jocelyn tilted her chin, expecting shock and disgust.

Internet porn. Lillian was repelled but unsurprised. From the start, she'd had misgivings about the job in Key West and Tony Sanchez in particular. Now, hearing her worries confirmed, she felt nothing much but disgust. She hadn't suspected pornography, but she'd feared something was not right. What was far worse was the notion that Jocelyn might have been physically abused regularly. But even if it were true, there was little chance that she would admit it to Lillian. "Were you aware of the nature of his business when you went with him to Key West?" she asked.

"No." Still daring her mother to show her disgust, she added, "I felt like an idiot when I finally figured it out." She shifted her gaze to the window then, fixing on the fading wildflowers in the distance for a moment before turning back to look at Lillian. "None of this should surprise you, Mother. You're used to me screwing up, anyway, aren't you?"

More bravado. "Does this person know where you are now?"

"I've told Hunter all this, Mother. He'll fill you in."

"I don't want to hear this secondhand, Jocelyn. Tell me."

"He knows I'm from Houston, but I've never mentioned the ranch. He never even knew me as Jocelyn Trask." She shrugged, her mouth twisting with cynicism. "It turned out to be a good thing that my divorce from Leo was so fresh. I used my married name." The sound that came from her then wasn't quite a laugh, but something tinged with bitterness and pain. "That's about the only good thing I can say about being married to Leo."

"You did the right thing by leaving, Jocelyn. We'll just

put this behind us, and after a few weeks here at the ranch, you'll feel able to start searching for a job. That's what you need, sweetheart. Something challenging and worthwhile to focus on."

"Yeah, that's what I need." With a suspicious brightness in her eyes, she squared her shoulders and moved to the table where Lillian's purse lay. "You have any cigarettes on you?"

"I thought you'd managed to quit smoking."

"Uh-uh." Shaking her head, she helped herself to the purse, opened it and found Lillian's freshly opened pack. "Too much stress to tackle that while yet another attempt to reinvent myself is going down the tubes," she said, after lighting up. "And speaking of stress, imagine my surprise when I got here and discovered Hunter and Erica Stewart together in the barn all kissy-face." She blew out a cloud of smoke. "I mean, talk about shock and awe, color me that."

"He wants to marry her, Jocelyn."

"Get out."

"It's true."

"Whoa, what does Daddy say about that?"

"Nothing much, at least as regards to a match between Hunter and Erica. But in spite of his attitude, I think he sees the situation as something that has potential to complicate his life. Until now, he's been able to put the past behind him and he's pushed me to do the same thing. Since I don't compartmentalize as well as he does," she said bitterly, "he's given me a stern lecture about overreacting."

"Meaning, don't do anything that'll screw up his precious presidential appointment." She sucked angrily on her cigarette.

"He told you about that?"

"He warned me, too, Mom. He wants to be a U.S. ambassador, even it's to some godforsaken third-world country." She laughed shortly. "Imagine what he'd do if somehow Tony Sanchez were to show up here and my latest folly became news."

"Don't joke about that, Jocelyn. He has his heart set on this appointment."

"And what about your heart?" She looked at her mother in disbelief. "You're telling me you're happy about leaving Houston? You're okay with being away from Hunter for who knows how long? You won't miss your real passion, which is not Daddy, but your philanthropy to art students?"

"I don't see I have much choice."

"Why doesn't he just hit you, use the same abusive tactics as the Tony Sanchezes of the world?" It was a rhetorical question, tossed off as Jocelyn paced and smoked. "It wouldn't hurt as much as his goddamned high-handed, arrogant, controlling, do-as-I-say method of marriage management."

"A political ambassadorship is supposed to be a prestigious thing, Jocelyn."

"Only if both of you are pleased about it." She stopped, looking intently into her mother's eyes. "Why don't you divorce him, Mom?"

Lillian shook her head sadly. "You know why."

Jocelyn, silenced, drew deeply on her cigarette. "We could always…" She paused, ground out the cigarette on the fireplace hearth and tossed the butt. "Nah, it's too late for that, isn't it?"

"Yes."

"Do you really think Hunter's serious about wanting to marry her?"

"Without a doubt. He told me so." With the pack of cigarettes now in her hand, Lillian removed one slowly. "And that's not all. He's convinced there's a connection between our family and Erica. He's determined to search until he figures out what it is. He has strong incentive, Jocelyn. He thinks she needs to put all this to rest before she'll be able to make a commitment to a new relationship."

Jocelyn swore softly. "But how can he figure it out? The police never came up with anything. It's been what…ten years?"

"Nine."

"So what does he have to go on?"

"Erica's art and her dreams. If you can believe that."

She looked confused. "What?"

"It seems she suffered memory loss as a result of the trauma, but lately she's been compelled to paint abstract scenes that Hunter is convinced relate to the accident. She's also dreaming about it. Hunter feels it's only a matter of time until she identifies something that will be solid enough to give the police a lead."

"Shit." Jocelyn sat down abruptly. After a stunned moment, she gave a bitter half laugh. "Well. Life's a bitch, and then you die."

Later that day, at home in her studio, Erica was studying combinations of fabric and trim when her telephone rang. Glancing over, she debated whether or not to let it go to voice mail. But if it was Hunter… No, she needed to work. She'd slacked off enough lately. Orders had piled up until Jason threatened to lock her in her studio and not let her out until she at least made a dent in the backlog. She would see Hunter soon enough when they drove to Austin on Saturday for the *Texas Today* awards ceremony. Until then, she needed to work nonstop.

No doubt about it, Hunter was a distraction. And then, yesterday! She pictured herself making love with him on that desk! Until then, she had been able to keep thoughts of him at a safe distance. Until then, she'd been willing to enjoy him, even to cautiously explore something more than friendship with him and then draw the line. The problem was that she'd been unprepared for his powerful appeal beyond sex. He wasn't just a man on the make who was attracted to her sexually, although that was heady stuff. He was solid and hardworking and honorable and caring—of his mother, his troubled sister, his aging partner. Of her. He had been so kind and understanding when she told him about her baby. It was hard to resist a man like that.

She found herself smiling, thinking of his stubborn determination to figure out what her dreams and bizarre paintings meant. Jason had been speculating about her repressed memory for ages, but Hunter would do more than speculate. Not that he'd said anything…she just knew it and it added the spice of anticipation to what was already a fascinating change in her life. An exciting change and Hunter was the reason.

The telephone was still ringing. Unable to resist, she picked up just before voice mail kicked in.

"Hello?"

"Hello."

His voice, low and husky, made her heart jump. "Isn't this odd?" she said softly. "I knew it would be you."

"How did you know that?"

She could hear a smile and found herself smiling back. "Everyone who knows me has strict orders from Jason not to call until he gives the all clear that I'll have two major orders ready for clients to view tomorrow morning."

"And are the orders ready?"

"Almost."

"So that means you can take a break."

She glanced at the table strewn with fabric that represented more hours yet of work. "Where are you, Hunter? I thought you had to be in Dallas today."

"I do. I am. I suffered through a three-hour lunch and now I'm following the client to a site he's negotiating to purchase outside of Conroe. At least I'm heading in the right direction. So where are you now?" he asked. "What are you doing?"

She smiled. "What if I said I was in deep concentration and you interrupted what might have been the creation of a stunning Erica Stewart?"

"But are your shoes on?" he teased.

She glanced down at her bare toes. "What does that have to do with anything?"

"Just that I've only seen your naked feet. I want to see all of you naked."

She felt a rush of sensation and, for a heartbeat or two, couldn't think of a thing to say to that. It was so close to her own thoughts. "Me, too," she finally said in a burst of honesty.

"Jesus, Erica." The sound he made was pain and laughter mixed. "Are you trying to kill me?"

"I'm sorry."

"Let's leave early Saturday morning," he told her in a tone rife with frustration. "I want the whole day with you again, like we had at the ranch. But most of all, I want a night with you. I've made reservations at the hotel. I wish we didn't have to do the reception and the dinner. I don't want to share you with anyone."

"Hunter..."

"I know, I know." Another brief sound, this one self-deprecating and wry. "I'm coming on too strong, right?"

"I'm not sharing a room with you. I've made my own reservations."

"I'm way ahead of you. I guessed that and I requested adjoining rooms. I just didn't want us separated by five or six floors. Did you get around to asking your parents?"

"All my guest tickets are taken," she told him dryly. She hadn't needed to contact her mother. Isabel had called assuming she'd be welcome and she'd taken the liberty of calling her ex-husband, who was coming with his wife. "If you wished for an intimate evening, forget it."

"I have to share you with Jason, anyway…for a while."

"Yes, and be nice about it. He's as deserving of this honor as I am."

"It's Twenty Women to Watch, Erica." There was definitely a chuckle in his voice.

"You know what I mean. And he's not staying over, so I asked him to feed my cat while I'm gone. I told him it'll be simpler if he just sleeps here, which he'll probably do. Willie hates being left on his own. He goes on a tear if he's by himself too long."

"You spoil all the men in your life."

"Willie's a cat!" she sputtered while laughing. "And Jason—"

"Yeah, I know. I'm not complaining. I can't wait to get in line."

She stood with the phone in her hand after disconnecting with a smile on her face that wouldn't quit. It had been a long time since she'd indulged in the sexy give-and-take that happened between two people who were attracted to each other. It could be an exhilarating ride, an emotional roller coaster. She'd forgotten how much fun it could be, but she'd have to put the brakes on Hunter's tendency to run things. Having sex once didn't mean she was turning her sovereignty over to him.

Drifting back to the table, she picked up a piece of creamy satin amid the jumble of color and fabric and held it against her cheek, her face thoughtful. She was going to have to guard against falling in love with Hunter. That would be a complicating factor of immense proportion. Just because he made her smile—okay, he didn't just make her smile, he made her happy, he made her body sing, he made her feel alive again. None of that meant he was safe. She knew the danger in thinking joy was a permanent given. Though once, sadly, she had believed just that.

She and David had been in college when they fell in love. The decision to marry had been made in breezy confidence that the future held endless possibilities and they were fearless facing it. And it had happened exactly as they expected, complete with successes in David's career and critical recognition of her art. Danielle's birth had simply added another dimension to their joy. Joy, she now knew, could end in a heartbeat. Possibilities could be snatched away in the blink of an eye.

Careful, Erica.

There was danger in letting herself forget that.

Nineteen

"Thanks to all for coming, and again, congratulations to the Twenty Women to Watch in this great state!"

Applause greeted the words from the emcee and Erica breathed a sigh of relief. Hunter waited a respectable minute before rising from his chair and turning to assist her to her feet. She needed no urging. Though grateful for the honor of being one of such a prestigious list, she was glad the ceremony was over. One look around her, however, and she was reminded that the evening wasn't over.

Erica didn't know how he'd managed it, but somehow Hunter had arranged for everybody who was anybody in her life to be on hand for the awards dinner. The list had grown from six to twelve. It would have been thirteen, but Phillip, as Jason's guest, had backed out at the last minute.

"I thought the guest list was limited," she said in a low voice to Hunter as soon as she caught a lull in the conversation.

His mouth tilted in a half smile. "I have friends in high places."

She gave him a sidelong look. "Such as?"

"My mother." Spotting somebody he knew across the

room, he smiled and lifted a hand. "She made a couple of calls when I told her we needed a few more tickets."

A few? Not only had her parents and both stepparents come, but her stepsiblings, as well—all five of them. "I must remember to send her a thank-you note."

He squeezed her knee undercover of the table. "That would be nice."

Isabel and John Warren, her stepfather, had appeared at the cocktail reception. Hunter explained that her father, Ashton Hall and his wife, Katherine, would miss the reception, regretfully, but they'd be at the dinner, possibly late, but they'd be there.

"An unavoidable conflict," Hunter told her. "Your little sister, Anastasia, has a gymnastics recital. They'll head over here as soon as it's over."

She simply stared in bemusement. She hadn't seen six-year-old Anastasia or her brother, Trey—Ashton, III—who was eight, since Christmas and then just for an afternoon when gifts were opened. It was always awkward having to work out the logistics of holidays. After losing David and Danielle, she'd mostly avoided holidays with her family altogether. She simply couldn't pretend to be happy.

"He looks like you," Hunter had observed, when Trey and his sister arrived with Ashton and Katherine.

"He looks like Danielle," she said, watching him gamely try to catch the attention of the twins, Luke and Jack.

Hunter had instantly leaned over and kissed her temple. "Then she must have been a beautiful baby."

"She was." The hole in her heart was still there, but the pain wasn't as crushing, she realized with a pang of…what, guilt? When, she wondered, had that happened?

"It's hard to keep them all straight," she said now as everybody began drifting toward the exit.

Hunter caught her chin in his hand, forcing her to look at him. "I don't believe that. You know perfectly well who they are. And they all look at you with big eyes. The kids, your parents and your stepparents. You're special to them, sweetheart."

Was that true? She was touched at the thought. And a little ashamed that it had been Hunter who'd pushed to include everyone in this event. Had her grief kept her from appreciating what family remained after David and Danielle were gone?

"When can I have a hug?"

Ashton Hall crossed to her side. Hunter would have recognized him as Erica's dad anywhere. It wasn't just his dark coloring and gray eyes, so like hers, but something in the shape of his face, the same stubborn chin, the way he looked directly at you. Erica was simply a feminine version of Ashton Hall. He watched her being caught up in a bear hug and envied her a father who openly displayed his affection.

"Hi, Dad. I'm glad you were able to make it."

"Well, of course I made it, sweetie." Still cupping her shoulders with his big hands, he smiled down at her. "I apologize for being late. Annie had a gymnastics recital, but fortunately it was over in time for us to jump in the car and drive here as fast as we could without missing too much of the ceremony. I'm so proud of you, baby."

"Thanks, Dad."

He turned to Hunter. "I understand it was you who made it possible to include the kids, Hunter." He glanced over to where Erica's stepsiblings had merged as naturally as if they saw each other daily. "We don't often have a chance to be together like this. Actually, we never get together like this. Thanks for making it happen. Maybe you can see to it that Erica's willing, and we'll do it a lot more often now."

"My pleasure. Erica has a great family."

"I won't argue that." Keeping her close with an arm around her shoulder, he smiled down at her fondly. "We don't see enough of her. Maybe you can persuade her to find more time for us, her mother and me both. Do what it takes to drag her away from that shop now and then. She works too hard."

"It's because I work hard that we're here tonight, Dad," she said dryly. "If I sat around on my duff, nobody would ever have heard of the Erica Stewart label."

He glanced at Hunter with a gleam in his eye. "Called my bluff on that one, didn't she?"

"She's a sharp cookie, all right," Hunter said.

Erica rolled her eyes, still caught in her father's embrace. "My dad's one to talk," she said to Hunter. "He's a corporate lawyer. I remember the long hours he worked when I was little. I hardly ever saw him."

"My loss, sweetie. But not anymore. Ask Katherine." Ashton glanced beyond her where his wife was talking to Isabel. "Children are a gift. It took a tragedy close to home to teach me that. After I remarried and Trey was born, I vowed to be a real father." His arm tightened around her and his tone was husky as he said, "I'm so glad to see you smiling again, darling."

His words caught her completely off guard. "I'm doing okay, Dad."

He looked at her intently, as if checking on the truth of her words, then he let her go and shifted his gaze to Hunter. "I understand you have a ranch in the hill country. Do you get to spend much time there?"

"Not nearly enough," Hunter said, smiling. "I'd live there if I didn't have that pesky day job."

"I hear you." Ashton chuckled with understanding. "You run a few cattle?"

"No, no cattle, but we stable a few horses. My partner grows pecans, but that's his hobby, not mine."

"Horses, eh?" He glanced at Erica as he rubbed his chin thoughtfully. "Now, if you really want to win my little girl's heart—"

"Dad!" Erica admonished him with a look.

"As I was saying, Erica had a horse from about the time she was big enough to climb aboard one. You want to take her out to that ranch and remind her to put something besides work in her life."

With his arms crossed, Hunter studied Erica as if the thought of taking her to the ranch had never occurred to him. "I'll sure keep that in mind, Ashton."

"Ash. Call me Ash." He stuck out his hand. "It's been a real pleasure meeting you, Hunter. If you're in Austin, give me a call. You do any fishing?"

"From time to time. I don't have a boat, but I like to wet a line."

"The boat's not a problem. I've got a nice little skiff. Keep it docked at our place on the lake at Somerville. You want to see some fine catches, you spend a day with me on my boat. You can bring your own gear, of course, but I'm pretty well outfitted with anything you might prefer. Just bring yourself." He glanced at Erica. "Katherine and the kids would love to spend a weekend with Erica."

"A weekend?" Erica said weakly.

"Actually, Somerville's not too far from my ranch," Hunter said.

"I think Katherine's trying to catch your eye, Dad," she said pointedly.

Ashton glanced toward his wife, where Jason had joined her and Isabel in an animated conversation. "Just one more thing, Hunter. If you give Erica her head too much, she's like a spirited mare. She'll take the bit in her teeth and run."

"Dad!" she repeated in exasperation.

He ignored Erica. "Take my advice," he went on with a wicked gleam in his eye. "Let her know who's the boss from the start. She might chafe a little at first, but she'll come around. Oops, Katherine's ready. Gotta go. Bye, sweetie." He chucked his daughter once under her chin and kissed her cheek, leaving her standing with her mouth open.

"I like your dad."

"I guessed that," Erica said dryly.

"Yeah, he's a great guy." He reached around her and punched the up button on the elevator, then stood waiting with his hands shoved in his pockets. "He loves you and he's proud of you. Best of all, he isn't shy about showing it. You're lucky. When I was a kid, I used to fantasize how good it would be to have a real dad. I was two when he died, so I didn't have any memories of him. My mother married Morton when I was six, but I never warmed up to him."

"Was that because Hank was your first choice for a stepdad?"

"Not really. Or not at first. Hank was a married man with a family of his own." The elevator doors slid open and he ushered her inside. "We saw a lot of him, out of necessity, because he was running the air-cargo business after my father died. They each held equal shares in the business and they were best friends. Beyond that, even though I was only six, I think I sensed an obligation on Hank's part to look out for my mother. I think he knew my father would have stepped up to the plate if the situation had been reversed."

"Why is it you couldn't warm up to Morton?" She pictured six-year-old Hunter having a dad at long last after his mother remarried and being somehow disappointed when Morton failed to measure up.

"He didn't love me, I was sure of that. He married my mother for a host of reasons, the least of which was that he might have fallen in love with her. I'll give him the benefit of the doubt on that. She would have been easy to fall in love with. She was a beautiful woman. It didn't hurt, you can bet, that she was very wealthy, came from a family with powerful political connections and he was an ambitious guy with an eye to the main chance."

"On the surface your mother seems to have a life to be envied."

"Trust me, it's only on the surface." He gazed thoughtfully at the elevator control panel. "I've never been able to understand why she's stayed with him all these years."

"You said he was unloving to you. Was he cruel, as well?"

"No, but he was controlling and overly strict. For the kind of kid I was—headstrong, opinionated, spoiled—I suppose I would have been a challenge to any man who married my mother. But none of that explains why she didn't leave him years ago. He's just as tyrannical toward her as he always was toward me."

"Jocelyn," she guessed. "Your mother had one fatherless child. It's easy to imagine her wanting to avoid having another. Maybe she stayed for Jocelyn's sake."

"I don't know why. He was as heavy-handed with Jocelyn as he was with me. Her teen years were even worse than mine. I'm almost eleven years older, but I don't recall her giving anybody much trouble until she was about halfway through high school. And boy, when she did rebel, it wasn't a pretty sight. The only person who doesn't rebel after living under his thumb is my mother. Go figure," he added with feeling.

Then, as the elevator doors slid open, smothering an oath, he seemed to come out of his reverie. "Sheesh, enough about my family. I don't know how I got started," he said, watching as she unsnapped her small bag to look for the key to her room.

"One family's not much different from another," she said, stopping at her door. "We all have skeletons in the closet."

"Yeah? Name one in your closet."

She'd turned before inserting the key, delaying the moment when she would leave him at the door to go inside. Now, with her back against the jamb, she thought about it.

Hunter, meanwhile, rested his hand high on the wall beside her head. As always, when she wanted to make a good impression, she'd tried to tame her wild, curly hair, this time by pulling it straight back and clipping it at her nape. But little wisps had escaped at her ears and temples. Making a moue with her lips, she blew at a strand that had settled close to her eye. It was an enticing little gesture, unconsciously seductive. He caught the scent of something flowery mixed with the scent of her body and it was a powerful aphrodisiac. How, he wondered, was he going to persuade her to let him inside that room with her?

"One night," Erica said, "my great-grandmother caught my great-grandfather messing around, and when he got home, she was waiting for him with a shotgun. Fortunately, she missed."

He laughed. "That's your skeleton."

"She could have killed him," Erica said, deadpan.

"This was right here in Texas?" His free hand was at her throat, inspecting a tiny diamond cross she wore on a chain.

"Six generations back."

Now his hand had slipped to the clip in her hair. "I don't know what else you expect from a self-respecting Texas woman, under the circumstances."

"Show a little common sense? She could have destroyed five generations."

"Now, that—" he leaned in close, just barely touching his mouth to hers "—would have been really bad. Yeah, that's an awful skeleton."

With the kiss as light as a butterfly on her lips, her breath caught in her throat. There was really no reason to say stop right now. She'd expected a good-night kiss. But he suddenly stepped back, taking the key from her lifeless fingers. He slipped it in the slot and pushed the door open.

"You know what," he said, using the key to caress her cheek. "I was going to suggest a little celebration. I ordered champagne delivered to your room while we were at the awards ceremony. But I've changed my mind."

With her back pressed to the jamb, she stared at him, uncomprehending. "Okay…"

"I don't want any champagne, Erica. I—"

"Here they are! I told you they'd be right here, Mom, and I was right!" Stephanie's shriek was as effective at killing a mood as a bucket of ice water. With an agonized groan, Hunter turned to meet the little girl, dashing from the elevator. The rest of the Warren family, John, Isabel and the twins, followed at a more normal pace.

Isabel met Hunter's gaze ruefully. "Isn't this a coincidence? We're all on the same floor of the hotel."

Steffie stood looking up at Hunter worshipfully. "Are you still going to take me for a ride in your Porsche?"

"Well—"

"Hah! I knew it was bogus," one of the twins said with wicked glee.

Stung, Steffie rounded on him angrily. "You didn't let him finish, Jack! He was gonna say later, probably at his ranch, huh, Hunter?"

"When it snows you-know-where," his twin crowed.

"Luke!" John Warren barked. "Watch your language."

"But I didn't say anything bad," Luke said, looking insulted.

Warren ignored him, then with a stern glare that included all three, he said, "Listen up, all of you. If you want to watch that movie, as promised, you'll head down the hall to our room right now and wait at the door for your mother and me. And don't argue."

"But it'll just take a minute to—"

"Stephanie Lynn," Isabel warned, "I believe you heard your father."

"Oh, okay…" Feathers drooping, Steffie turned with lagging footsteps to go with her brothers, both of whom smirked with satisfaction.

Hunter, fighting a smile, said to Warren, "Could I say a word before they're banished?"

All three kids turned around instantly, bright-eyed and expectant. "Yeah, Dad, let him, please…." Steffie begged.

Without a word, Warren waved a hand as if to say, "Whatever."

"I promised Steffie a ride in the Porsche," Hunter said, "and I'll make good on my promise. How about all three of you coming out to the ranch for a visit? Find a weekend convenient for your parents and I'll see that everyone gets a turn in the Porsche."

"Thank you, Hunter," Steffie said with delight, before turning and sticking out her tongue at her siblings.

"And," Hunter added, "when you visit the ranch, there are a couple of horses just right for you. If you don't know how to ride, there's plenty other stuff to do. Or I can give you your first lessons."

"Wow, do you mean it?" Luke said.

"Yaaay! You hear that, Dad?" Jack said. "Is it okay?"

"It's okay," Warren said, and watched with a smile as the kids scampered down the hall. After they turned the corner, he looked at Hunter. "I guess you know you've got three fans for life after that," he said wryly. "And when they're all together, it's a challenge to keep them in line. I hope you have a horsewhip in the barn. You'll probably need it."

Erica laughed.

"John, for heaven's sake," Isabel chided, giving her husband a look. "Hunter might think you're serious."

"Hell, I am." But he smiled and winked at Hunter. "And don't say I didn't warn you. Congratulations, Erica," he said, turning to his stepdaughter and kissing her cheek. "You make us all proud."

"You do indeed, darling," Isabel said, catching both her hands. "It was wonderful seeing you getting the kind of recognition you deserve. And what made it extra special was having the whole family sharing it."

"Thanks, Mom," Erica said, from a tight throat. It had been a long time since she'd felt so much a part of her family. It had been so painful being around their children after losing her own child. But tonight hadn't been painful at all. With Hunter at her side, she'd enjoyed every minute. She was a little leery about exploring what that meant.

"We'll be getting an early start tomorrow morning," Isabel said, rubbing at a smudge of her lipstick on Erica's cheek. "So we'll say goodbye now. Hunter, thanks again for putting the evening together. Usually, Jason is the one we rely on to drag Erica to any family function, but it's all too rare. I suspect you're harder to bully than Jason." She gave him a grateful hug.

"Time to go, Isabel," Warren said. Catching her elbow, he turned to steer her in the same direction the kids had taken.

"I'll walk with you," Hunter told them. "'Night, Erica." With a peck on her cheek, he fell into step beside the older couple. Thinking he must be kidding, she stood watching as all three reached the corner in the hall, turned and were out of sight. She waited, expecting Hunter to reappear, but after a full minute, she realized he wasn't returning. Let down and a little miffed, she turned slowly and went into her room.

Twenty minutes later, she had slipped out of her shoes, removed her earrings and pulled the clip from her hair. Halfheartedly, she ran her fingers through her curly mop, freeing it. That done, she stood looking at her reflection in a mirror and wondered at the dejection she felt. It was an incredible honor to be recognized by such a prestigious magazine, and she was touched by the many expressions of congratulations she'd received tonight. Her family was openly proud of her, too, and Jason was already anticipating the boost to the label when the feature in the magazine hit the stands. She should be feeling elated. Over the moon. Instead, she felt restless and out of sorts, as if something wonderfully anticipated had fallen flat. She drifted over to a table near the window where the bottle of champagne Hunter had ordered was chilled and ready to drink. With no appetite for it, she moved on. Champagne, like success, wasn't meant to be enjoyed alone.

She parted the heavy drapes at the window and studied Austin at night without much enthusiasm. What kind of good-night kiss was that peck on the cheek he'd given her? Her mother's kiss had been a lot more loving. It certainly wasn't the act of a man who claimed to be in love with her. Not that she wanted him to be in love with her. That was a complication she didn't need. But still, he'd walked away so casually that it was hard not to feel a bit of an anticlimax.

She glanced at the digital clock radio on the bedside table. After eleven, but not really all that late. Her gaze shifted to the connecting door and she admitted, a little sheepishly, that even though she'd specified separate rooms, she expected that he would try to persuade her to change her mind. Her mistake. Moving slowly, she went to the door on her side and, as silently as possible, unlocked it and pulled it open. The door on his side was still closed. She put her ear close and listened for any sound.

Nothing. Absolute silence.

She looked at the clock again. Either he'd gone to bed early or he wasn't in his room. Which meant that he was probably out somewhere. Choosing something else besides just the two of them celebrating. She was surprised at how much that hurt and the significance of it wasn't lost on her. Maybe she was falling in love with Hunter. Considering the way she felt, she couldn't deny the possibility and it scared her. Why else would it matter that he wasn't here with her to celebrate?

She jumped like a startled rabbit when the lock on his door was suddenly turned. Before she had a chance to act, he had it open, catching her standing there. She saw that he'd removed his jacket and tie. The first two buttons on his white shirt were open and he looked relaxed and confident. With his mouth tilted in a half smile, he looked very much like a man with a plan. She felt her cheeks go pink and her heart leap into double time.

"I thought you'd gone out," she said inanely.

"I did," he said, holding two champagne glasses in one hand. "I went down to the bar and got these."

She had to smile. "Oh."

"Yeah." He let his gaze roam over her face, her hair and on down to the pulse throbbing in her throat. "Damn. I'm disappointed."

"Why?"

He set the glasses on the table near the champagne, then caught her face between both hands so that they looked at each other, their smiles meshing. "You took that clip out of your hair and I wanted to do it."

She laughed shakily, her senses humming. Now that he was here, her dejection fell away as if it had never been. "When you didn't come back after that good-night peck on the cheek, I thought the evening was over."

"Are you kidding?" Moving his hand down to the small of her back, Hunter slowly ground his pelvis against hers. "That peck was for your parents' benefit. For us, the evening's just beginning. I've been planning it since the moment you sashayed out of this room in your sexy little black dress with your hair refusing to be tamed in that clip, and dispensing smiles to anybody and everybody at that blasted ceremony and expecting me to pretend it wasn't killing me to wait until now to get you all to myself." He buried his mouth in her hair, muffling a groan. "The whole evening was slow torture."

Drawing in a quivering breath, she wrapped both arms around his neck and pressed her face into his shoulder. "I'm sorry," she whispered, shamelessly savoring the feel of him, hard and urgent, against her softness.

He planted a hot kiss on the side of her neck. "I don't want to rush you this time," he told her, his lips skimming her cheeks, her nose, her eyes. "We'll have some champagne, we'll talk about the ceremony if you want. This is your special night. I want it to be perfect."

With his mouth at her temple and his breath hot in her ear, she had to smile. He was talking one thing, but his body and hands and mouth were saying another. "Are you sure about that?" She shifted a bit to look at him and he made a noise somewhere between a laugh and a groan, a sound that told her his control was hanging by a thread.

"Maybe not," he rasped, kissing his way down her throat to the cleavage bared in the deep V of her dress. She dropped a kiss on his hair as he reached behind her for the zipper. Her dress didn't require a bra, and when he pulled it from her shoulders, her breasts were suddenly free, heavy and tingling.

He paused, breathing hard, and looked at her. "You're so beautiful, you're perfect. I knew you would be." She tangled her fingers in his hair, drawing him down and sighing when his mouth covered the softness of one breast. With her head thrown back, she gave him free access, forgetting she'd had a baby and that the evidence was there, tiny purpling lines, marks of her pregnancy and the joy of motherhood. With his mouth warm and suckling, striking at some deep, erotic chord in her, she was soon swimming in a swirling pool of pleasure.

"The bed," he said, pulling back suddenly. "I promised you a bed next time." Still holding her fast, he swung her up into his arms and in three strides was across the room. He set her down, but only long enough to finish unzipping her dress and stripping it off her.

"Oh, Jesus," he breathed, admiring the wisp of a garter belt and sexy stockings she wore, but he took only a moment. Then he was pulling them off and tossing them aside, too. Next, with his pulse thundering in his ears, he stripped away her bikinis.

There was no time to savor the riches he'd uncovered. Erica was fumbling at his belt, finally managing to unbuckle it before tugging at the zipper on his pants.

"Hurry," he rasped, lavishing frantic openmouthed kisses over her taut breasts while he worked one of his shoes off, using the toe of the other. When finally they were both naked, he took one step backward, bringing him to the edge of the bed. Pulling her down with him, they fell together with Erica sprawled on top of him. For a second, he drank his fill of the sight of her. Dark, curly hair framed her face in wild disarray, her gray eyes glazed with passion, her lips were moist and swollen from his kisses. Hunter was enthralled.

"I can't wait much longer, sweetheart," he told her hoarsely.

"Don't wait, don't wait…"

Her plea destroyed what was left of his control. His hand swept down her body and slid between her thighs. They groaned in unison. She was soft and moist and ready for him.

"Now," he said, and with a cry muffled against her throat, he entered her. Sighing, Erica cupped his hard buttocks and arched her hips to draw him deeper still. Eyes locked, they remained still for a heartbeat, marking the moment.

"I love you," Hunter said, looking deep into her eyes.

For a split second, she was on the verge of echoing the words. She lifted a hand and gently touched his face. Smiling, she pulled him down slowly until his mouth met and melded with hers. Then, with a moan, Hunter began to move, chanting her name. It was a loving litany that made her soul sing, that dared her to deny what brought them to this moment. Emotion that could not be locked away rose in an unbridled tide and was suddenly released in a brilliant, splintering climax. In seconds, Hunter followed her over the edge.

This time, she was able to bask in the afterglow. There was a lot to be said for making love in a bed, she thought, as she lay sprawled beneath Hunter, who had shifted just enough to take some of his weight from her. She smiled up at the ceiling, feeling deliciously satisfied. Her fingers stroked over the skin at his neck, combing through his hair. He was damp, they both were. The scent of passion was all around, creating an intimacy like no other.

She stretched languidly and murmured at his ear, "Can we talk now?"

It took some effort, but he raised his head to look at her. There was a sleepy, equally satisfied air about him. "Tell me you're kidding."

She gave him a wide-eyed look. "Tonight you were the one who said we could talk if I wanted to, drink a little champagne and maybe even relive the highlights of my special evening."

Propped on one elbow now, he studied her intently for a minute. "I was hoping you would consider this as the highlight of the evening."

For a second, she simply enjoyed looking into his eyes. Then she chuckled and pulled him back down, snuggling up to him in a better fit. "Had you going there for a minute, didn't I?"

"Yeah, for a minute."

"Well, it was payback for giving me that peck of a kiss in front of my mother and John and then walking off and making me think you were on your way to Seventh Street to barhop…or something."

He was up on his elbow again, looking at her in disbelief. "You are kidding this time, right?"

"Well, if you'd been five minutes later, I'd have been in bed."

"And I'd have been overjoyed to find you there."

"And that connecting door would have been locked."

"Which reminds me…" He tucked her head beneath his chin and tightened his arms around her. "How come, if you were mad at me, was your side wide-open?"

"I was just checking that you hadn't had a heart attack or something."

He was still for a second, then with his arms tight about her, he rolled over, taking her with him. Resting on his arms, he fixed her with a steady gaze. "Does that mean you care?"

She went quiet and very still. His words rang in her mind. *I love you.* Her gaze dropped to his lips. For a minute, when she thought he might not be back tonight, her reaction had been that of a woman in love. Then, in the chaos of passion, she had felt something very akin to love. Had she fallen in love with him?

Suddenly, the musical ring of her cell phone came from across the room.

With a groan, Hunter dropped his head back and swore. "Do we have to answer that?"

"Possibly not," she said, scooting away with some relief. "But I need to check who it is. Most everyone who would call knows where I am tonight." On her feet now, she looked around for something to cover herself, but her dress lay in a heap on the other side of the room. The only thing in reach was Hunter's white shirt. With the phone still ringing, she quickly grabbed it up and put it on.

"It's Phillip Levin," she said, frowning at his name and number.

"Jason's friend?" Hunter moved across the room, magnificently naked and totally comfortable with it.

"Yes." Still frowning, she pushed the button. "Hello, Phillip?"

"Yeah, it's me, Erica. Sorry to interrupt. Did I wake you?"

"No, no, I—" She cleared her throat. "I was still awake."

"Erica, Jason's in Houston General Hospital."

"Hospital?" Her eyes flew to Hunter. "Oh, no. How? Did he have an accident? He's such a bad driver."

"It was no accident. He wasn't driving. Apparently,

when he unlocked the door, he surprised a thief. The guy attacked him, roughed him up with a baseball bat, I think. He's got a concussion."

"Oh, my God. Is he—I mean, how serious is it?"

"I'm not sure. Not being a relative, they won't tell me much. He wanted me to call you, not his parents."

"You said he surprised a thief? Was he at the shop?"

"Oh, didn't I say? He promised to feed your cat, so rather than get up early the next morning, he just decided to spend the night there. So he was at your place when it happened."

"My place? My house?" She stared in wordless shock at Hunter.

"What's going on?" he asked, frowning.

She silenced him by raising her hand. Phillip was talking again. "I know you planned to stay overnight in Austin," he went on, sounding regretful. "But since he didn't want his parents to know, there's no one else to call and I know how close you and Jason are…"

"Yes, I'll leave right away. Thank you for calling."

"It could have been you, Erica," Phillip said.

Twenty

Hunter flipped the lid of his cell phone before anchoring it at his belt. "The cops will meet us here at the hospital in a few minutes," he told Erica as she paced the floor of the waiting room. "Apparently, someone called 911 from your house after the assault, so they've been there and put up a crime-scene tape. They'll dust for fingerprints, but they prefer to do it after daylight."

"I can't believe this!" she cried. "Jason was attacked and nearly killed because I decided to coddle my spoiled-rotten cat when he would have been perfectly fine boarded out for one night. It's all my fault."

"It's not your fault and you don't know that he was nearly killed," Hunter told her as he poured two cups of coffee out of the courtesy pot in the waiting room. Like most hospitals at that hour, it was ghostly quiet except for the hum of a machine down the hall where a janitor polished floors. Besides Erica and Hunter, only three other people waited, all of whom dozed in the grievously designed chairs. At four o'clock in the morning, it was mostly hospital staff stirring.

He handed over the coffee. "If you're looking for somebody to blame, try the scumbag who broke into your house."

"Willie didn't even need babysitting," she said, sinking into a chair. Needing warmth more than coffee, she held the cup in both hands. "He would have been fine on his own for a day and a half. It's just that he hates being left at the vet." She sipped, made a face at the bitter taste and set it on the table beside her. "He's not like other cats."

"I seem to remember that Jason volunteered to take care of Willie. Besides, I got the idea that he wanted to come back to Houston because he had something planned with his new best friend." Hunter's arm came around her and she leaned gratefully into him. "Stop beating up on yourself, sweetheart. I, for one, am just thankful it wasn't you unlocking the door."

Later, she would probably think about that and the possibility of what might have been, but just now her thoughts were of Jason. "What is taking so long?" she cried suddenly. "When will they tell us something? And now that you mention Jason's new best friend, where is Phillip? I thought he'd be here. He should be here!"

They'd made the trip from Austin to Houston in less than three hours, arriving at the hospital before daybreak. Not being blood relations or a spouse, they'd been told nothing of Jason's injuries from the clerk at the admissions desk except that he had been admitted and was presently having a CAT scan. Phillip, who might have given them a few more details, had inexplicably made himself scarce.

Unable to sit, she again got up to pace. "I can't imagine why a thief chose my house. There isn't anything in it worth stealing. I have very little jewelry and I don't see how my designs could be used by anybody else. They're mostly commissioned pieces and nothing's complete. It's not as if he could sell anything."

"What if he wasn't after your valuables," Hunter said, voicing the thought that had been in the back of his mind ever since Phillip called. "What if it wasn't a few trinkets he was really after? What if he wanted you?"

She paused, looking out the window where a pale gray dawn was pushing at night shadows. Buildings were still dark hulks. Too early even for the birds. "I can't accept that. Whoever it was would have been watching me a while. Isn't that the way it happens?" She shook her head firmly. "No, I've lived in that neighborhood for almost nine years. I think I'd sense something like that."

Hunter let it go, but from his expression, he was reserving judgment. "Did Phillip say he was with Jason when it happened?"

"I assumed so, but now that I think about it, I'm not sure. I was so shocked I didn't get many details." At the sound of a ping down the hall, she turned as two men approached from the direction of the elevators.

"Looks like the cops are here," Hunter said beneath his breath.

"How can you tell?" she murmured, studying both men. "They aren't wearing uniforms."

"I can tell. And detectives don't wear uniforms."

To her artist's eye, the two men were intriguing opposites. One was lean and tall, with ebony skin and odd green eyes. His suit looked expensive and his white shirt was still as crisp as if he'd put it on minutes ago. His name tag read "Sullivan." His partner, whose name tag read "Hernandez," was plump with a blond comb-over, very fair complexion and blue eyes that were spaced a little too close together. He wore a suit that appeared to have been slept in. Both flashed badges, but it was Sullivan who spoke with formal courtesy.

"Ms. Stewart? Erica Stewart?"

"Yes, I'm Erica Stewart."

"I'm Detective Patrick Sullivan, Houston Police Department, and this is my partner, Detective Frank Hernandez. We're following up on the assault of Jason Rowland at your address."

"Good," she said. "I'm glad you're here."

Sullivan hesitated, looking at Hunter, who stepped around Erica and held out a hand. "Hunter McCabe. I was with Erica when she was told about the assault."

Sullivan shook his hand, studying him with a cop's straight-on stare before refocusing on Erica. "The 911 came in around midnight reporting a disturbance at your address, Ms. Stewart. A police unit and EMTs were dispatched. The victim was transported by ambulance to the hospital before we arrived at the scene, so we haven't questioned him yet. It would be helpful if you'd answer a few questions."

"Gladly. I was stunned when Phillip called to tell me what happened."

"Phillip?" This from Hernandez. "He got another name? Because the call we got came from your neighbor…ah, let's see—" He rifled a few pages in a tiny notepad. "That would be one…Edward Kane." He looked up at her. "You know Mr. Kane?"

"Yes, of course. Eddie Kane. He lives next door." She frowned. "Phillip didn't call 911?"

"Nothing here from anybody named Phillip," Hernandez said.

"That's odd. He called my cell phone and I just assumed—"

"Any chance Phillip and Jason got into a little tiff and Jason got the worst of it?" Hernandez asked.

"No! Jason and Phillip—" She stopped, deciding not to reveal what she knew of their relationship. "Whoever attacked Jason, it wasn't Phillip. He sounded very shaken when we talked."

"And Phillip's last name is…" Hernandez paused, looking at her. His ballpoint hovered over a clean page in his notepad.

"Levin."

"An address would be helpful, if you have it," Sullivan said gently.

"I don't have a clue," she said, "but I do have his cell phone number…if you'd like to have it."

"Peachy," said Hernandez.

She shot him a cool look before reaching for her cell phone. Scrolling, she paused as the number came up, then pointedly turned to Sullivan instead of Hernandez and repeated it. She watched him write it in a notepad identical to his partner's. "Have you learned anything about who might have done this?" she said.

"Not yet, ma'am. Were you in the habit of keeping valuables on the premises?"

"No. I have very little jewelry and I'm not very interested in electronics, so my TV and VCR are pretty dated and aren't worth much." She paused. "Since I haven't been to my house yet, I don't know what, if anything, was taken."

"It appears that the thief—if that was the motive for breaking into your house—was interrupted in the act," Sullivan said. "The place is quite a mess. Of course, it's hard to say how long he'd been inside. Not to frighten you, ma'am," he said in a reassuring tone, "but we have to consider the possibility that he was waiting for you. If so, when the door was unlocked and Mr. Rowland entered instead, it would have been a nasty surprise."

"Not as nasty as it would have been to me," she said with feeling.

Hunter spoke up. "How unusual is a robbery in Erica's neighborhood?"

Sullivan slipped his notebook inside the breast pocket of his jacket. "It happens, naturally, but not enough for the area to be considered a high-crime environment." He shifted his gaze to Erica. "Can you think of anything you have or that you're known to keep on the premises that might interest a thief?"

"No, not really. I have some art projects in a room that I use as a studio, but I work in fabric, so everything's fairly worthless in its present state. I don't keep cash around, either." Mystified, she spread both her hands. "I can't think of a thing."

"Do you have any rejected suitors who might find it hard to accept no for an answer?"

"No, absolutely not."

"Michael Carlton," Hunter said.

"Hunter!" She gave him a look of exasperation before turning back to Sullivan. "There's no one, Detective Sullivan."

Hernandez had not stowed his notepad. Holding it, pen again poised, he asked, "That would be Carlton, spelled…" He gave her a questioning look.

She spelled the name grudgingly.

"You want to give us a hint as to his address?" Another questioning look.

"His office is downtown," Hunter supplied helpfully. "Financial planning."

"Michael would never do anything…violent," she said. Then, catching Hunter's eye, added, "I mean, he wouldn't wait in a dark house and attack a person with a baseball bat."

Hernandez pounced. "How did you know it was a baseball bat?"

"I don't know it. I'm quoting Phillip," she said. She turned again to Detective Sullivan. "As soon as they let me see Jason, I'd like to go to my house. Will that be okay?"

"If you could hold off until we've dusted for finger-prints, it would be helpful," Sullivan said, his smile taking the sting from the order. "The tech people will probably be finished by midmorning. For purposes of excluding you and Jason as suspects, it will be necessary to take your prints, too."

"Fine. Just tell me what to do, where and when."

"Thank you, ma'am." He nodded to her, then Hunter, be-fore turning smartly and walking away. Without bothering with polite niceties, Hernandez shoved his notepad in a hip pocket and, forced to do double time to keep up with his partner, caught up finally, then both headed for the el-evators.

"Good cop, bad cop," Hunter said, watching them go.

"I always thought that idea was just a plot element in books or movies," Erica said. "Do you suppose their act gets more results than if Detective Hernandez actually put on a clean shirt and pressed his suit?"

Hunter chuckled and headed back to the coffee bar. She watched him pour himself another cup and refused one for herself. "I'm still trying to take it in, Hunter," she told him a few minutes later as they strolled in the hall, killing time. "I've always felt so safe in my neighborhood."

"Nobody's safe if an intruder is determined to get in-side." The look on Hunter's face boded ill for whoever the intruder turned out to be. "Having no alarm and flimsy locks makes it easy, especially if someone's been waiting for a chance to get at you." When she opened her mouth to argue, he added, "Okay, if not you, then the same thing applies if he was watching for a chance to burglarize your house. Whichever it is, the first thing we're doing before you spend another night at home is upgrading your locks and installing an alarm system."

"Jason's mentioned the same thing several times," she admitted. "He won't be happy that he's proved right this way."

She glanced at her watch as they passed the nurses' station. "And where the heck is Phillip, I'd like to know? He knew there would be nobody here for Jason, no parents, nobody, at least until you and I got here."

"It does seem odd that he's not around," Hunter said. "Or that he hasn't at least called."

"What if you and I were delayed somehow? Or didn't show up at all? He made sure I knew that Jason wanted me here. He had my cell number handy enough for that. So, why hasn't he checked to see that I made it? What if Jason took a turn for the worse and needed somebody? What kind of person is he?"

"One who doesn't like hospitals?" Hunter looked down at her. "My advice is to forget about Phillip for the moment. Could be there's a perfectly reasonable explanation that he isn't here. Let's wait—" He stopped. "Oh, good, here's the doctor, I think."

"Family of Jason Rowland…"

A man in hospital scrubs stood in the entrance waiting for a response from the seated occupants. Erica quickly headed across the floor toward him.

"Jason Rowland family?" he repeated as she approached with Hunter at her side.

"I'm not a relative, but Jason is my business partner and friend," she told him. "There's no one else here for him, so could you please tell me how he's doing? Is he conscious? How bad is it?"

"May I have your name, please?"

"Erica Stewart."

"I'm Dr. Moreno," he said, flashing a tired smile that included Hunter. Signaling that they should follow, he moved to an area of relative privacy away from others in the room. "He said you'd be out here and asked that you be given the results of the CAT scan, Ms. Stewart." He spoke in a low tone. "Jason's head injury wasn't as serious as it could have been. When he presented in the ER, it was a given that he was concussed, but we needed to be sure there was no internal bleeding and we found none. He was lucky. The attack could have caused severe damage, but he managed to fend off the assault."

"How do you know that?" Erica asked. "Is he talking?"

"He hasn't stopped talking," Dr. Moreno said dryly. "He has what we call defensive injuries. The hands and forearms were raised to ward off blows to the head and upper torso. Jason sustained some damage to his fingers. We've applied splints. He won't be writing longhand or manipulating the keys of his computer for a while, which seems to distress him more than his concussion. There are a few mean-looking bruises on his forearms, but no broken bones. He's a tough guy."

By now, Erica's hands were clasped together and lodged beneath her chin. "He's going to be all right?"

"It'll take more than a nasty assault with a baseball bat to put a guy like Jason totally out of commission," Moreno said with a smile. "We're going to keep him another day…just to be on the safe side. He'll have a killer headache, so he'll be better off here with the meds I'll prescribe than at home. He tells me he lives alone."

"Do you have any idea what was used in the assault? Was the intruder armed?" Until now, Hunter had listened in silence.

"Well now, you're into territory that is better answered by the police, who I understand, are questioning him now,"

Moreno said. "I'll tell Jason you'll be in to see him as soon
as he's settled. Someone at the nurses' station will notify
you. Shouldn't be too long."

"Thank you, Doctor." Erica extended her hand and managed a smile. It could have been so much worse. She shuddered to think what would have happened if she'd been
alone. The prospect was terrifying. She moved closer to
Hunter, who slipped an arm around her. With her face
turned into his chest, she would think later about how right
it felt that he was with her.

"I mean, I didn't have a clue when I unlocked that door."
Jason punched at his pillow, doubled it under one arm and
propped himself up. With his head bandaged, both eyes
blackened and fingers on both hands splinted, he looked
like something from a horror movie. "Somehow, I don't
know, I sensed something, movement…whatever, and a
good thing I did, 'cause I saw him just as that damn baseball bat came at me. It was only a split second, but he didn't
get to land a solid blow with the first swing. Not that it
didn't hurt like hell." He reached up, touching his bandaged head gingerly. "If he'd connected the way he meant
to, it would probably have beaned me one straight out of
the ballpark to the promised land."

"Thank God for small favors," Erica said fervently. She
handed over a small cup of apple juice with a straw stuck
in it. "Drink this, Jace. You need energy. I bet they haven't
given you anything since you got here."

"What I need is some more of that stuff they shoot you
up with for pain," Jason said, but he sucked obediently at
the apple juice. "I've got a headache you wouldn't believe." After a moment, he looked up. "Where's Phillip?"

"We haven't seen him. He called my cell phone to tell
us what had happened and then he just vanished." She

shrugged, baffled. "He wasn't around when we got here, and he hasn't checked in."

"Was he with you when you went inside Erica's house?" Hunter asked.

"He waited in the car. I changed my mind about staying over. I knew I wouldn't get back to the house the next morning until late and Willie would be hungry. I planned to fill his bowl and give him fresh water, then we'd be on our way." He settled back, allowing Erica to adjust his pillows. "He isn't taking any chances on anybody at the practice finding out who he really is."

"Such as your dad," Erica guessed.

Jace grimaced. "Yeah. I knew it would put Phillip in a real tight spot if he had to call my dad, so I told him to call you."

Hunter was looking confused. "How's that? Why would it put him in a tight spot to notify your family that you've been the victim of an assault?"

"Phillip, who has yet to admit that he's gay, is a junior partner in the same law firm as my dad. Trust me, it won't be an advantage to Phillip to admit he's not straight. I knew there would be cops asking questions, and if my parents were here, they'd eventually figure out that Phillip was with me when it happened. No way to stay in the closet after that," Jason said.

Erica touched his hand. "I'm sorry, Jace."

He managed a smile. "Shit happens."

"Please let me call your parents now," she begged. "You don't want them hearing this on TV, do you?"

He shrugged. "I guess it doesn't matter now, with Phillip dogging out. Call them if you want, but only after you leave, please. I don't want to talk to my dad on the phone. If he gives a damn, let him come to the hospital."

"He will, you'll see, Jace."

"Yeah?" He looked at her. "I don't think I'll hold my breath waiting for him."

"Can you tell us anything about the guy who attacked you?" Hunter said. "Did he say anything? Did you get any sense of why he was there? Was he looking to burglarize Erica's house, or do you think he was waiting for her?"

"No, no and no and your guess is as good as mine." Brow wrinkled, Jason thought back. "This is just a gut feeling, but I think he was surprised that I opened that door and not Erica. He hesitated just a split second before swinging that bat, which makes me think he expected her and he had to resort to plan B when his victim turned out to be me."

With his splinted hand, Jason reached for Erica and brought her fingers to his cheek. "It hurt like hell when he was swinging that bat at me, but thank God it was me and not you, sugar." His gaze shifted to Hunter. "Whoever the sleaze is that did this, you've gotta find him, Hunter. If Erica was his intended victim, we need to figure out why. I don't need to tell you that she won't be safe until we do."

"Don't even think of staying alone in that house for the next few days," Hunter said as they left the hospital. "Jason's right. Until we figure out who it was who did this, or at least come up with a motive for the break-in, we can't take a chance that he won't be back."

"I'll have the locks changed and a new alarm system installed," she told him. "But I can't put my life on hold indefinitely. Besides, where would I go? My mother lives in Dallas and my father in Austin. They have families. I suppose I could move in with Jason. He definitely wouldn't mind."

"You'll stay at my place," he told her. "The complex is gated and there is security in the parking garage." Seeing protest gathering on her face, he took her arm and ushered her toward the elevator. "We can argue about it later. Right now, let's make a run by your house and see if you spot anything to clue us in."

"Did I ever tell you I don't like taking orders?"

He chuckled as they stopped in front of the elevators. Reaching over, he pushed the down button and then kissed her hard on the mouth. "That makes two of us. It'll make living together real interesting."

In another part of town, Lillian sat at the breakfast table sipping coffee with the Sunday paper open in front of her and fought her craving for a cigarette. Morton had called to let her know that he was still in Galveston on his yacht, but planned to dock before dark. It would be hours after docking before the yacht would be shipshape. He told her not to expect him before midnight. His courtesy in calling was unusual. As of late, he forgot more often than not to keep her apprised of his comings and goings.

She pulled out the *Zest* magazine and a few minutes later spotted a small article about the awards ceremony sponsored by *Texas Today* honoring their annual list of successful career women in the state. She quickly scanned the column and, sure enough, there was a quote from Erica Stewart, graciously thanking her business partner, her family and the magazine. Lillian's craving for a cigarette intensified. Pushing the paper aside, she rose from the table, taking her coffee with her, and headed for the sunroom.

After lighting up, she was restless and bored. She could do Sunday brunch with a couple of her friends. Gossip had somehow gotten around about Morton's appointment and curiosity among her friends was rampant. But her friends' hints to fill them in were getting more and more pointed lately and she didn't feel up to coping with that today. Even in her social circle, a presidential appointment was impressive.

She drew deeply on her cigarette. What she really wanted was to drive to the ranch. But it wasn't possible to make the trip and get back before Morton returned. Lately, he'd ordered her to stay away from the ranch. His arrogance chafed, made more hurtful since it meant she could not see Jocelyn. It was a futile hope that Jocelyn might want to see her.

Nothing interesting on television, either, she decided as she smoked and watched a few minutes of a Sunday-morning news telecast. She grimaced with distaste as the anchor recited a litany of shootings and stabbings. The weekend, it seemed, brought an unsavory element crawling out of the woodwork to wreak havoc. She wondered if Morton's appointment would land them in a place any less hazardous than Houston.

She was stubbing out her cigarette when she heard Erica's name. Frowning, she moved closer to the TV as the anchor—a woman—gave details of a break-in at the artist's home in the early-morning hours. "Stewart's star has been on the rise lately," the anchor read. "Her art and her thriving Village boutique are hot. The artist was out of town at the time participating in an awards ceremony where she has been named by prestigious magazine *Texas Today* as one of the state's Twenty Women to Watch. Stewart's business partner, Jason Rowland, surprised an intruder when he entered her house to feed her cat. He was severely injured with a weapon thought to be a baseball bat.

"Rowland managed to fend off the attack," the anchor continued, "and is hospitalized in fair condition. The intruder fled on foot. He's described as male, about six feet tall, of average build. If you have any information that might be helpful to police, please call the hotline number listed on the screen."

Lillian sank slowly to the couch in the sunroom, pale with shock. Her heart was beating wildly. Guilt rose up to overwhelm her for her recent ungenerous thoughts about Erica. She didn't want Hunter falling in love with Erica, but she certainly wished her no harm. Picking up the remote, she clicked it to kill the sound on the television and lit another cigarette. Troubled, she rose, drifted to the glass doors and stood looking out. Her mind teemed with possibilities. But for a strange twist of fate placing Jason Rowland at her house and not Erica, she could have been killed. Bob and Sheila Rowland were probably in a state of shock today. She would be if it had been Hunter.

With all her might, she resisted a thought that lurked in the back of her mind. She wished she knew more details. Hunter would know, of course. But even if she decided to call him, catching him today was unlikely. He'd mentioned going to Austin to be with Erica at the *Texas Today* thing. When she told Morton about it, he reacted with his usual indifference to anything about Erica. Should she call Hunter? But if he was still with Erica, he wouldn't be free to talk.

She was suddenly impatient for Morton to come home. He had no patience with her inability to put their role in this hideous mess in "proper" perspective, but he was also the only person who— No, no, she wouldn't go there. She drew deeply on her cigarette. The problem with calling Morton was that his idea of the proper perspective was light-years different from hers.

On the heels of her wish to talk to Morton came a sudden, overwhelming desire to see Hank. To be with him. To feel the warmth of his embrace. To bask in the sheer goodness of him. But, just as Hunter was inaccessible, so was

Hank. Oh, not because Morton decreed it. If she really wanted to go to the ranch, she would. Often had. But Hank already suspected that something was wrong in her life lately, something beyond what he knew had been wrong for a long time. If she appeared, he would take one look at her and have questions. And she would have no answers. No, she couldn't go to Hank. Or Hunter. And Morton would be as unsympathetic and impatient as ever. No, she really had no one. Basically, she was alone.

Twenty-One

Erica stood in the open doorway at her house and gazed at the desecration of her living room. A small table was overturned and the lamp that once sat on it was broken, pieces of it strewn over the floor. Beyond that, a chair lay on its side, one leg missing. The drapes on the window nearest the door were pulled from their moorings and hung drunkenly on their rod. A framed watercolor painted by her grandmother had fallen to the floor, the glass smashed.

"It's true," she murmured, trying to take it all in, "what they say about being the victim of an intruder at your home. You feel violated."

Hunter put a hand on her shoulder. "There are professional services to clean up when something like this happens. I'll get a name."

Yes, a good idea, she thought. The prospect of wading through the detritus left behind by the man who'd hurt Jason was sickening. She bent down to pick up her grandmother's watercolor, but recoiled when she realized that it lay in something sticky and wet. She stared at the red smear on her fingers. "Oh, God, is this blood?"

"The assault was pretty vicious. There would be blood."

"I didn't know—I mean, I guess I should have guessed that."

"Here, let's wash that." With his fingers closed on her wrist, Hunter pulled her toward the tiny powder room. "Let's make this inspection pretty brief, what do you say? Look around, try to get a feel for whether or not this was a botched burglary and then I'm taking you out of here." At the sink, he turned on the water and let it run over her hand. "I'd like it to be a botched burglary instead of…something else."

Erica dried her hand with the towel he handed over. "You seem convinced it wasn't a burglary."

"I'm not convinced, no. I just want to be convinced it wasn't the opposite. I want to know that he wasn't waiting for you."

"I don't think anything's missing," she said a few minutes later, leaving her studio. She had inspected her kitchen, her bedroom, the guest room, a second bath. Her jewelry box was open—she remembered leaving it that way—and nothing was taken.

Hunter wandered to the French doors that opened onto her tiny patio. "Here's where he got in," he said, examining the jimmied lock. "It would have been easy. This lock is a joke. I'll board it up before we leave." He pushed one of the doors open and took a brief look outside.

"Erica, come out here," he said after a brief silence. "And bring a bath towel, please." He waited until she appeared with the towel, then pointed.

"Oh! What—" Three paintings were stacked against the wall behind her barbecue grill, almost obscured by the grill's canvas covering.

"Could this be what he wanted? No, don't touch!" he ordered, catching her before she made contact. "I don't see any sign of the fingerprinting compound that's all over inside. Damn, could the cops have missed this?"

"They're the paintings I've been working on recently."

"Hand me the towel, would you?" Hunter said in a grim tone. "I need to take these inside without adding my prints to what's already here."

"I can't imagine why he thought these were worth stealing," she said, watching Hunter throw the towel over the canvases. "My name doesn't mean anything as an artist who paints pictures. I have a couple of quilts almost completed in my studio that would be worth a lot more than these things."

"Who knows you've started painting again?"

She followed him inside, frowning as she thought back. "It's not something I've talked about much. Jason, you. One of my seamstresses is a friend, Charlene. I've mentioned it to her. I guess that's about it."

"Would they tell anybody?"

"I didn't ask them not to, so, yes, I guess so." She cleared a place on the coffee table, still frowning. "Charlene might have said something to the other seamstress. Sometimes they work together. A lot of the quilting is handwork and they tend to chat while they work."

Hunter straightened up and fixed his gaze on the outside patio. "I told my mother."

Something in his tone struck her. She gave him a puzzled look. "Did you?"

"Hank knows, too. He could have mentioned it to Jocelyn, since she's staying at the ranch. And according to Hank, she's spending time with Kelly at her practice and I'm thinking your name has probably come up," he said, "the way women talk."

"Really."

"Yeah. So add Kelly to the list." He was scowling, still looking out, his mouth set in a grim line.

"I don't see what you're getting at, Hunter. Nobody we've named would steal anything."

"Yeah, you're probably right."

"They have no commercial value. They only exist because of the recent compulsion I've had lately to put images down on canvas. I know you and Jason think there's a connection between what I'm painting and the hit-and-run, but—"

The words died abruptly on her lips. Eyes going wide, she began shaking her head. "No, that's too big a leap. Nobody but Jason and you and I know that I painted those pieces with anything in mind except what I do as an artist. Nobody knows they come from some—" she hesitated "—some*thing* deep inside that comes over me when I'm thinking about the hit-and-run. I'd have to figure out what they mean before they could ever be a clue to the identity of the driver, wouldn't I?"

"Yeah." He looked at her then. "That's what worries me."

By the end of the day, Hunter had located a cleanup crew who promised to set Erica's house in order, remove all traces of blood, fingerprinting compound, broken glass and crippled furniture. But it would take a while. Rather than allow strangers to decide what was beyond repair, he'd rented a storage unit where her things would be safe until she felt ready to deal with it. It was a good excuse to keep her on his turf, too. A call to Detective Sullivan had resulted in a second visit from an embarrassed crime-scene team to dust the paintings they'd overlooked for fingerprints. After finding the paintings on the patio, he couldn't shake a feeling that Erica had been the real target.

"What's your plan for opening the shop tomorrow?" He watched her hang a few—very few—things in the closet of his guest room. If she'd had any other option rather than accepting his hospitality, she wouldn't be here. He knew that. And without having her spell it out, he knew she would be sleeping in the guest room, not in his bed. He was willing to take it one step at a time. It was enough just to have her here. For now.

"I'm not opening tomorrow," she said. "I want to be sure Jace is okay, and if all goes well and he's out of the hospital soon as the doctor said, I'll help him settle in at his apartment."

"I guess we can't rely on the faithless Phillip for that."

"I'm not even asking him. Fortunately, Stephen, who's a longtime friend, has a job with flexible hours, so he's promised to pop in and out until Jace is recovered from the concussion and those splints are removed from his fingers."

"Which means you'll need help at the shop." He followed her out of the bedroom. "Isn't there somebody you use in time of peak sales?" He didn't like the idea of her being at the shop alone, even in broad daylight. He'd called a locksmith to install more secure locks and a sophisticated alarm system in the shop, but nothing was truly secure if an intruder was bent on getting at his victim.

"I've already called a woman who works for us at Christmas and other times when Jason or I have a conflict. She's opening up for me on Tuesday." With a sigh, she sank onto the upholstered arm of a chair. "I still can't believe this has happened."

"You're exhausted. Things will look better after we have something to eat." Moving behind her, he began kneading the tension from her shoulders and smiled when she groaned with the pleasure of it. "We'll go somewhere that's quiet, have a leisurely meal, then head back here and crash."

"That won't be a problem," she said, dropping her head forward to give him better access. "We didn't get any sleep last night."

"Tell me." Leaning around her, he saw she was blushing. "I didn't mean—"

Cupping her chin, he tipped her face up and gave her an upside-down kiss. "I know you didn't." He pulled her to her feet. "C'mon, let's leave while we're still standing. We can finish this later."

The restaurant was near Hunter's condominium complex, small, quiet and exclusive. Fortunately, they didn't have to wait since he was instantly recognized by the maître 'd, and as soon as they were seated, he ordered a bottle of wine. By the time their food was placed in front of them, they were both feeling the effects of the wine and fatigue.

"I'd better watch out," Erica said, spearing a shrimp. "Another sip of wine and I may just slide off this chair."

"Then let's talk about something to keep us awake," Hunter said. "For instance, have you done any other paintings besides the three that were almost ripped off last night?"

She nodded. "Actually, I've done two. They're in the trunk of my car."

Hunter put down his fork. "Two?"

"Uh-huh." She smiled. "It appears that Erica's found her groove again...as they say."

"And they're in the trunk of your car."

"Well...yeah." Still smiling.

He frowned. "And the reason you've been carrying them around in the trunk of your car is..."

"I had this vague notion to show them to you and Jason." She picked up a small spreader knife and dipped it into a small pot of herbed butter. "Both of you seem convinced that I'm painting from some inner source, so I wanted you to look at them and...well, speculate." She realized he was scowling and stopped what she was doing.

"I wanted to know if it's just a figment of my imagination or if there is really something there."

"You think you're seeing something recognizable?"

She looked pained. "Who knows? It could be…as I said, a figment of my imagination. That's why I wanted to know what you thought. You and Jason."

"And they're stashed in the trunk of your car. When were you going to mention this?"

"A lot has been going on. I've been busy." She picked up her fork. "I'm not sure it's anything, whether it has any meaning or not. I've never been—"

"Erica? Erica Stewart…"

Both turned to see a petite woman two tables over smiling at them. They'd been so focused on each other that they hadn't noticed the party of four being seated. The woman, fiftyish, stylishly thin and smartly dressed, touched the arm of her companion, murmured something to the others and headed for their table.

"What a pleasant surprise seeing you. No, no, don't get up, dear," she said, gesturing to Hunter to stay seated. "I just couldn't miss a chance to say a word to Erica."

"How are you, Miranda?" Erica said. "Hunter, do you know Miranda Quinlan? She chaired the auction event at the symphony gala."

"Well, of course he knows me." Miranda patted his shoulder affectionately with a bejeweled hand. "His mother and I are the oldest of friends and he went to school with my Muffy." She turned back to Erica. "I'm so glad to see you, darling. After what happened at your house last night, you must be wondering what is the world coming to. I saw it on the early-morning newscast as Parker and I were having coffee. I was so shocked. I said to Parker, is anybody safe anymore?"

"It was very distressing," Erica said.

"And Jason getting the brunt of it," Miranda said, shaking her head and giving a little tsk-tsk. "How is he?"

"They're keeping him overnight, which, I think, is good news. I'll tell him you asked about him."

"Please do. Such a nasty surprise, opening the door to a thug. And all because he was nice enough to feed your cat for you. How thoughtful is that? Of course, he's always been such a thoughtful boy."

"He's a dear friend and I feel horrible that he was hurt," Erica said.

"Well, naturally." Miranda shifted her gaze to Hunter and smiled slyly. "I shouldn't be surprised to see you with Erica, dear." She wagged a playful finger at the two of them. "It may take me a minute, but I eventually put these things together. Wait'll I tell Muffy."

Erica chanced a look at Hunter, who winked at her. She gave him a stern frown in return before taking a deep breath and smiling brightly at Miranda. "So, do you come here often?"

Miranda chuckled and, without missing a beat, allowed the change of topic. "I told Lillian when she called and suggested your name for the symphony gala that I didn't know why we hadn't thought to include you before. Your art is simply charming, Erica. So fresh. So creative." Hunter, fiddling with his wineglass at this point, glanced up quickly.

"Lillian?" Erica repeated blankly.

"She's your biggest fan, or surely one of them. Why, Lillian must have sent a ton of people to your shop since it opened."

Erica carefully set her knife and fork down. "Mrs. Trask suggested my name for the gala?"

"She did indeed." Her large smile included both of them, but began to fade at the look on Erica's face. "Oh. Oh, dear." She pressed her fingers to her lips. "I hope I haven't let the cat out of the bag. Please tell me you're aware how Lillian has championed your career for years."

"Years," Erica repeated in a murmur.

"Yes, indeed. And lucky you, she has clout where it counts, Lillian does."

Eyes wide, Erica stared helplessly at the older woman. She opened her mouth for words, but nothing came out.

"What do you mean she's championed Erica's career?" Hunter demanded, grim-faced. "Are you saying—"

"Excuse me." Abruptly, Erica pushed her chair back and stood up.

"Erica—" Hunter, now on his feet, too, reached for her as she dashed past, but missed. He muttered a curse, dug in his pocket for bills and tossed them on the table. Then, without a glance at Miranda Quinlan, he followed Erica, leaving the older woman standing with her mouth open.

He caught up with her in the parking lot, where she was pacing the area between his car and the next, her arms tight around her middle. Head down, she scowled at her feet. Any hope he had that she didn't believe Miranda Quinlan died a quick death.

He approached her warily. "You shouldn't be out here alone, Erica."

She gave a blank look around, as if not realizing how she got where she was. "I'm okay."

"No, you're not okay. Until we know who got into your house and the reason he did it, you aren't safe in an area with no security." Since she was standing near the passenger side of his car, he quickly unlocked it and held the door open. "Come on, let's get out of here."

"I don't want to go with you."

He couldn't blame her, but still he felt as if she'd sliced into him with a knife. "You don't have your car. And have you forgotten, you can't stay in your house or Jason's? If you absolutely refuse to stay with me, a hotel is your next best bet, but I wish you wouldn't. We need to talk about this."

She looked directly at him then, and it was almost his undoing. Her eyes were filled with confusion and distress. "Is it true? Did it happen the way Miranda said?"

He raked a hand through his hair. "I don't know. You probably won't believe this, but I don't know what the hell she's talking about."

"How could you not know? She's your mother!"

"I don't know everything my mother does any more than you're aware of every little thing Isabel does."

"I would know if she was tinkering with someone's life. And I would demand to know why she'd do something like that. It's…it's creepy."

"If what Miranda Quinlan said is true, she has only done good things for you," he reminded her.

"I didn't ask for her help. I didn't want it! I don't want it!" She kicked out at one of the Porsche's tires. "And I plan to tell her so myself."

He would definitely have to give his mother a heads up. If Erica knocked on her door in the frame of mind she had right now, Lillian would be annihilated. "You have a right to demand an explanation."

"Thank you," she said sarcastically. She gripped the side of her head, tearing at her hair. "Ooh, I feel like such an idiot! I've been telling Jason forever that I had this feeling something or somebody was doing things behind the scenes. I should have—"

"Should have what? Gone around asking people if they knew the name of your sugar daddy? That would have sounded nice, wouldn't it?" He didn't tell her he'd been wrestling with that suspicion for weeks. "Then, the next time you were featured in the newspaper or recognized in some way for your work, what would people say?"

"What will they say now?" she demanded, glaring at him.

"Nothing…if you don't stir up a hornet's nest."

"You don't sound like someone who didn't know anything about this as you claim, Hunter. You sound like someone who's doing damage control. Or trying to cover your backside…or trying to protect your mother." She looked at him sadly. "The truth is I'll never know if you were aware of it all along."

"I guess you can't know that. And I guess taking me at my word isn't likely to happen." Unable to bear the condemnation in her eyes, he looked beyond her to the traffic passing on the street. "We haven't been together long enough that we can weather something like this. Still, my offer stands. My guest room is yours as long as you need it."

If she heard him, she gave no sign. Like him, she turned her gaze toward the street. "If it's true, you know what it means, don't you? It means I've been living a lie. All these…this recognition is meaningless. I didn't earn it. It was handed to me."

He brought his gaze back to her, drinking in the look of her. With her mouth tremulous with distress, he wanted more than anything to take her into his arms, to argue that her talent was a given, that her art was wonderful. That no amount of tinkering on her behalf by his mother or anyone else could have resulted in the level of success she'd reached. But in her state of mind, she wouldn't hear him. Wouldn't believe him.

"A parking lot is the wrong place to talk," he said. "And right now, while you're so upset, it's the wrong time. I'll see my mother tomorrow, first thing, count on it. I've got as many questions as you have, maybe more. After we sleep on it—"

"I'm not sleeping with you! Have you lost your mind?"

"That was a figure of speech, Erica. I know you're not going to let me within a mile of you now. I wouldn't try. You may not believe it, but I'm upset over this, too. I'm suggesting we let it go for tonight. Besides, I haven't had a look at those paintings, and whether you're mad at me or not, I want to see them."

He still held the door open. She looked at him, her eyes dark with a wealth of indecision. "I hate this," she said finally. "I hate finding myself in this position."

"But you'll go with me tonight?"

"Only for tonight. Because when Jason gets out of the hospital tomorrow, I'm moving in with him."

A reprieve. Hunter closed the door with a profound sense of relief and headed around to his side of the car. He'd dodged a bullet. Barely. Tomorrow was another day.

Time for Lillian had passed at a snail's pace that day. When the walls had closed in on her, she'd gone out for lunch. But one could sit at a table only so long. She supposed she could have called a friend, but she simply wasn't up to the deception. Her face would show the strain she felt and that would provoke questions. The rest of the afternoon she'd passed at the Galleria, window-shopping mostly. Then dinner. A bit of Brie with crackers and—to hell with Morton's edict—a pitcher of martinis. She was starting her third drink in the sunroom and watching a vintage movie on television when the phone rang. Without bothering to look at caller ID, she answered. "Hello?"

"Mom. Jocelyn."

"Jocelyn?" She started, nearly spilling some of her

drink. She set it carefully on the coffee table and fumbled for her cigarettes. "What is it? Where are you?"

"I'm at the ranch. Are you watching television?"

"Yes, a movie. It's old and I've seen it before, but—"

"The news, Mom." Jocelyn's tone rose with impatience. "I meant the ten-o'clock news. Wait'll you hear."

She looked around for the remote to reduce the volume. "Hold a moment while I—"

"Erica Stewart's house was burglarized. She wasn't there, somebody else was—this guy who was supposed to feed her cat while she was gone. Anyway, somebody had broken in and when her friend got inside, he was attacked with a baseball bat. He's in the hospital."

"Yes, yes, I know. I heard about it this morning." She clicked the mute button. "It was Jason Rowland, her partner. You remember him, don't you? Oh, maybe not as he's quite a few years older than you. Actually, he's Bob and Sheila—"

"Mother! I don't give a damn who he is. Have you stopped to think about this?"

In the act of lighting up, Lillian paused. She'd done nothing but think about it…all day long, but warily decided against telling Jocelyn that. "What is there to think about?" she asked in a careful voice.

"Is Dad there?"

"No, he's in Galveston. On the yacht."

"Okay…" A moment passed as she paused, considering. "So, when did he leave?"

"Wednesday. He's hosting a group of VIPs. He called this morning to tell me he would be docking late today."

"So if he wasn't in town last night, he couldn't be the bastard who was waiting in Erica's house armed with a baseball bat."

"Jocelyn!" Lillian put her cigarette in an ashtray and

groped for her martini. After swallowing a bracing mouthful, she said, "That's a terrible thing to say about your father. What if someone overheard you? Have you thought about that?"

"I'm out in the barn using my cell phone. Besides," she added bitterly, "even if Hank overheard, he would hardly be surprised. We both know what he thinks of Dad."

"He wouldn't think Morton would stoop to the level of a common thug, and I'm disappointed that you would mention such a thing."

"Yeah, well, I guess the apple doesn't fall far from the tree, does it?"

"Jocelyn, why are you talking like this?" Lillian's heart was pounding fearfully. Jocelyn had been through several distressing emotional episodes over the years. When she was in these downward spirals, she was capable of anything. Lillian frowned at the now-silent TV screen. Maybe she should get in her car and drive to the ranch. But on second thought, she rejected the notion. She was in no condition to drive. "Promise me you won't talk to anyone else like this, Jocelyn."

"Didn't you tell me that Hunter thinks Erica's memory might be returning?"

"He mentioned it, but I think it's extremely unlikely." She drew shakily on her cigarette. "If she were going to regain her memory, I think it would have happened before now."

"And you've researched loss of memory as a result of trauma, have you, Mom?" Jocelyn said, openly sarcastic.

"I know it's extremely rare."

"Where's Hunter?"

"What?"

"I said, where's Hunter? I tried calling his condo to ask if he knew what happened, but I didn't get an answer. Have you talked to him?"

Lillian closed her eyes in dismay. "Surely you aren't suggesting that Hunter had anything to do with this…this horrible thing?"

"Did I say that? I just thought since he's hot for Erica that he'd have details."

"No, I haven't talked to him. As far as I know, he was with her in Austin at the awards ceremony. I assume they're back, since she would have been notified that her home had been invaded."

"This sounds serious. Do you really think he wants to marry her?"

"He said as much. So, yes, I think he's serious. I know he is. We may as well brace ourselves. As soon as he can persuade her to fall in love with him, there will be a wedding. Count on it."

"What awards ceremony?"

"Pardon me?"

"You said they were together at an awards ceremony."

"Oh. She was named by *Texas Today*, as one of the state's Twenty Women to Watch."

"Wow."

"She's very talented. Very capable. Very focused."

"Sounds like a daughter-in-law to die for."

"Please, Jocelyn. That's not funny."

"And everything I'm not, huh, Mom."

Lillian sighed, pinching the bridge of her nose. "I didn't mean to imply—"

"Forget it." There was a sound as Jocelyn clicked her lighter and then exhaled. "As for persuading her to fall in love with him, she's there already. It's a done deal. I saw the way she looked at him when they were together here at the ranch. No surprise to me. She's no different from any single woman right here in Houston who'd kill to have Hunter fall in love with her. Looks like she's the lucky one."

"Any woman Hunter loved would be lucky."

"Because we know she's damn sure had her share of bad luck, right, Mom?"

"Jocelyn—"

Jocelyn's laugh was a bark devoid of humor. "This is almost too bizarre to be real, isn't it?"

Lillian stubbed out her cigarette. It was simply beyond her to go down this road tonight. "I think I hear your father, Jocelyn. Get some rest. You know you tend to overreact when you're stressed." She then lowered the phone, blurrily located the disconnect button and ended the call.

"I see a face. It appears to be a woman, but your technique makes it hard to be sure. It's as though I'm looking at her through water…or something." Hunter looked back at Erica. "Did I get it right?"

"You see what you see," she said, rubbing at her temples. "What about the other one?"

"Totally different. A bunch of images, but I get a sense of action…like a lot's going on here." He turned to see what she made of his remarks.

She shrugged. "Anything else?"

"There's something in the background, a shape or a pattern of some kind that seems familiar…somehow." Hunter took a couple of steps back to study it from a distance. Both paintings were propped on barstools. He took his time before saying what he thought. In the second painting, the effect was not only of action, but of violence. She'd painted an explosion of primary color—red and yellow, touches of blue and white, a lot of white as if to portray light. In the background, a slightly geometric shape seemed to emerge. She had painted it in hard, black slashes.

"I get the feeling I'm looking at the headlights of an oncoming car," he said after a while. If the paintings were an expression of her buried memory of the hit-and-run, his interpretation was almost too simplistic. He turned to Erica, who had slipped out of her shoes. "Is that what you see?"

"Anything else?"

He turned back, studying the shape in the background. "Something about this—" he touched it with a finger "—is familiar. Maybe it'll come to me if I study it a while."

"Okay." Erica moved to lift the first painting from its perch, holding it gingerly as the paint wasn't completely dry. At the door, she set it down, face out. "I'll leave it here overnight, but I'm taking them with me tomorrow."

"Was what I saw in line with what you intended when you painted it?"

"I'd rather not say yet. I wanted to hear your impression—and Jason's—first."

When she turned to get the other one, Hunter had it in his hands. He placed it beside the first and offered her a paper towel to wipe a few smudges from her fingers. His gaze lingered on her face as she went about meticulously removing all traces of paint. "What time do you plan to leave for the hospital in the morning?" he asked.

"Early." She looked around for a trash can. "I'll call first, but I expect Jace will be agitating to leave. You needn't bother with anything like coffee, if that's what you're thinking."

He took the paper towel from her. "It won't be a bother. I'm an early riser myself, so I'll be up."

"If you insist…but it's not necessary."

"I insist." Before she could do it, he bent down and picked up her shoes. "And I'll take the paintings down to your car. I'm assuming you want to show them to Jason as soon as the two of you get to his place."

"Yes. Thank you." She took her shoes from him and

scooped up her purse from the bar. "I'm going to bed now. I'm tired." Just before reaching the hall, she turned back. "I'll be taking all my things when I leave."

"Yeah. See you in the morning."

Lillian lied about hearing Morton. It was another two hours after Jocelyn's call before she heard his car pulling into the garage, well after midnight. She quickly squirted breath freshener in her mouth to mask the smell of nicotine, which he hated, capped and pocketed the small aerosol cylinder and made her way toward the kitchen. Although she craved more alcohol after talking to Jocelyn, she'd resisted temptation and had actually sobered up a bit after taking a long, cold shower and drinking several cups of coffee. She wouldn't sleep now, but that was hardly unusual.

He unlocked the door and stepped inside, looking refreshed and healthy and mildly surprised to find her waiting for him. "You still up?" he asked, shrugging out of his jacket. "Anything wrong?"

"Nothing's wrong, Morton. But you did say you were docking the yacht before dark, so I assumed you'd be home before now. I waited. It's been a long day."

"What? Has the City of Houston shut down? Were all the museums closed? The Galleria…God forbid. Were there no artists hanging out that you could mentor?" He tossed his jacket over the back of a tall stool at the breakfast bar. "Spare me the whining. There are a dozen things you can do to fill your time, Lillian."

"The one thing I might have enjoyed you've declared off-limits, Morton."

"The ranch? Yeah. And nothing's changing for the time being. You stay away from Hank Colson and that damn place." He headed for the refrigerator.

She sighed. "Our daughter is at the ranch, which is why I would have liked going there." She was thankful that the cold shower and hot coffee apparently masked the effect of the martinis.

"So what did you do all day? I should say, what have you done with yourself for the past five days?" At the refrigerator, he removed a bottle of beer. "I, for one, have been networking with people who will be useful when we get to Washington. The yacht is proving to be more of an asset than I expected…and I had considerable expectations from the start."

She watched him upend the bottle and take a long swallow. "So you've been out on the Gulf all this time?"

He lowered the bottle, giving her a straight look. "Where else would I be?"

She shrugged. "I was just thinking that you probably haven't had a chance to hear the news."

"The yacht isn't exactly a third-world country, Lillian," he said, his lip curling. "We have television via satellite. We have XM radio. And, if all else fails, we have ship-to-shore communication." He set his beer on the counter with a look of disgust. "Jesus, it's past midnight. What news is it you think I may have missed?"

She watched him move to the pantry. His weakness for junk food was almost as strong as her own addictions, but he was generally able to resist unless he was feeling a stress overload. "Erica Stewart's house was broken into last night," she said.

With his back to her he dug into a bag of Doritos, and she was unable to see his face. "Well, now, that's one major news flash that we didn't pick up at sea. And why is it significant?"

"I thought you'd be interested. It isn't as if she's a total stranger, Morton."

"Yeah, and she'll be a lot closer if your baby boy has his way."

"She wasn't at home."

He turned to look at her. "So…"

"She must have stayed overnight in Austin after the awards ceremony. She asked Jason Rowland to feed her cat, so it was Jason and not Erica who surprised the burglar. Or the intruder…whatever. He attacked Jason with a baseball bat."

"Ouch."

She stared at him. "Ouch? That's all you have to say?"

He made a dismissive gesture with his beer bottle. "By the way, I'm heading back to Galveston tomorrow and I want you to come with me. Tom Jenson's thinking of buying a condo on the beach and I told him he could look ours over, stay a day or two. He's bringing his wife. We'll have to do a little schmoozing."

"I don't know, Morton, I—"

"It's settled, Lillian," he told her. "Jenson can be useful if I need him regarding the appointment. Besides, you'll like having company for a couple of days."

She was too weary to argue. "About Jason, Morton," she said. "He's in the hospital. Bob and Sheila must be horribly upset. I tried calling them today, but I kept getting their answering machine. There wasn't much in the news about how seriously he was hurt."

He took another swig of beer. "A kid his age, they're tough, gay or straight."

She just shook her head at his callousness. "I do wish you wouldn't talk like that, Morton."

He made a gruff sound, stuffed another chip into his mouth and picked up his beer. "These things are stale," he said, heading across the kitchen to the trash compactor. "I wish you'd learn to toss the bag into the trash once it's opened. They're never any good in this humidity."

"A baseball bat in the hands of a strong person can be lethal."

"Kid was in the wrong place at the wrong time." He took another swallow. "No good deed goes unpunished, huh?"

She looked at him, wondering if anything touched him anymore except his precious appointment and his expensive yacht. "Do you remember me telling you that the awards ceremony was scheduled for Saturday and that Hunter was going?"

He shrugged. "Not really. Why would I?"

"Just this. If they'd come home and Hunter was with her, which is a good possibility since he claims he's in love with her and wants to marry her, we might be at the hospital tonight instead of Bob and Sheila. If Hunter had been the one to unlock her door, he would have been the one who was attacked."

"Do we have any cheese dip?"

Twenty-Two

In spite of her exhaustion, Erica couldn't asleep. Like a mouse on a treadmill, she kept going over and over the events of the past twenty-four hours. A day crammed with nasty surprises—her home desecrated, Jason hurt, Lillian Trask's interference in her life turning her success as an artist into the worst kind of fraud. Her whole world was shaken to its foundations. Did Hunter know? Had he deceived her, too? Somehow, that would be most hurtful of all.

She kept going over in her mind the times she might have guessed a particularly favorable review or prestigious recognition came not from a genuine appreciation of her art, but from her benefactor working behind the scenes. How could she have been so blind? Why hadn't she heeded her instincts? There had been times when she was so convinced of an unknown…something. And nothing Jason said could talk her out of it. It was no comfort to learn he was wrong and she was right. With these thoughts playing over and over in her head, it was hours before Erica finally slept.

The dream began abruptly, as if waiting for just this particular moment in her sleep-memory to pop open the lid of that closed box. Her defenses were weakened from the disturbing events of the day. She stirred restlessly, tangling the bedclothes as she fought to block the images. The street. She saw it with clarity. The neighborhood. She recognized it instantly. Her head moved back and forth on the pillow. No, she didn't want to go there. She whimpered with distress to find herself on the sidewalk watching David and Danielle silhouetted in the bright lights of the oncoming car.

She was suddenly cold with terror. She tried to move forward, thinking to warn them, but her body refused to obey. Her feet were mired in thickness, heavy and sluggish. Then the moment of impact and a scream wrenched from her soul. Oh, God, she could only watch in unspeakable horror as the joy in her life ended and the car sped past. And just before the glancing blow that caught her at her knee and tossed her high and clear, she looked inside. She saw a woman, a woman in black wearing a brooch high on her shoulder. A woman whose face she recognized. Lillian Trask.

When she came to herself, she was in Hunter's arms. One hand stroked her back, her shoulders, the other was clenched in her hair, pressing her face into his throat. "It's only a dream, sweetheart. Just hold on. It'll pass," he told her, his voice touching her ear. "It's just a dream."

She was shivering, cold to her bones. She burrowed into his warmth, desperate to dispel the images lingering in her mind. The car. The crash. The blood. The horror. The brooch. Lillian Trask's face.

Oh, God, his mother.

"I owe you for last night." Erica brought the mug—clasped in both hands—up to her lips and took a tiny taste.

"It must have given you a start, waking up to all that commotion. I apologize. Thank you."

"There's nothing to apologize or thank me for."

"I woke you up. I disturbed what could have been a peaceful night's sleep."

"More than thirty-six hours without sleep could trigger a nightmare."

She chanced a quick look at his face. "I don't remember when you left. I just…woke up this morning and you weren't there anymore."

A smile touched his lips. "Once you relaxed, I did, too. But around daylight I woke up. Figured you wouldn't be happy to find me in the sack with you."

"What could I have said after what happened?"

"Good morning? Let's make love?" The smile stretched to a grin.

She buried her nose in the mug. "Well, thanks, anyway."

"Forget it." He straddled a chair and draped his elbows over the back, cradling his coffee in both hands. "Have you ever thought that maybe you're more prone to having those nightmares when you're not a hundred percent?"

"Maybe." She stared into her coffee, barely able to recall coming to herself in his arms. But she remembered vividly that unsettling look at his mother's face and the horrible images that wouldn't quit, even with her eyes squeezed tight shut. She'd been like a wounded animal caught in a trap. It had seemed so right and natural to burrow into him, to seek his strength. His calm.

With her gaze fixed on his hands, she had a sudden dim recollection that he'd been naked. But there had been nothing sexual about him as he spoke reassuringly in her ear, talking her down from the terrible place she was in.

"Want to talk about it?"

"What?" She looked up blankly. "Oh, no. No, it's okay. I'm okay now."

"Whatever you say." He stood up. "I've taken the paintings to your car. If your suitcase is ready, I'll take it down now."

"It's ready. It's just inside the door of my…uh, your guest room." She poured what was left of her coffee in the sink and carefully rinsed the mug. She'd been badly shaken by what Miranda Quinlan had said last night, and when she went to bed her mind was made up to put some distance between herself and Hunter. Now that it was time to go, she found she wasn't quite so certain that she wasn't making a mistake. Tonight, if Jason was released from the hospital, she could stay with him as long as necessary, but the prospect wasn't as pleasing as it had been before she woke up from last night's nightmare safe in Hunter's arms. Still, it was the logical thing to do, she told herself, until everything was sorted out. She'd survived these nightmares by herself for nine years. She could keep on doing it indefinitely, she told herself.

Why then, she wondered, was she second-guessing her decision?

"Thank God you're here!" Fully dressed except for his shoes, Jason tossed aside the newspaper he was reading from his hospital bed and threw Erica a kiss. "Another hour in this place and they'd have to put me on the psycho floor. Have you ever tried to read a newspaper when your fingers were fat sausages?" He held them up for her inspection before swinging his legs to the side of the bed. Upright, he suddenly groaned and put a hand to his head. "Oops, we're a little groggy, I guess."

"You idiot! When you've got a concussion, you don't jump out of bed like a four-year-old." Erica moved to his side and peered closely at him. "How was your night? Did you get any sleep?"

"Have you ever tried to sleep in a hospital?" he said darkly. "They kept bugging me."

"They're supposed to check a person with a concussion frequently."

"Well, when they finally gave up, I slept like a baby." Now, spotting the smudges beneath her eyes, his look sharpened. "But it doesn't look like you did. Please tell me you were sleepless because you and Hunter were making mad, passionate love. Or then please explain why you look like somebody ran over your kitty cat."

"Willie's caused enough trouble, but he's still healthy… as far as I know. He's in Eddie Kane's care until I can get back in my house." Ignoring his reference to Hunter, she went to the closet and got his shoes. "Here, put these on if you want out of here."

"What happened?" Jason demanded, not to be put off. "Where's Hunter?"

"I could ask you the same thing. Where's Phillip?"

"Safely in his little cubicle at the firm, I guess." Jason sat down gingerly in a chair to put on his shoes. "He called to apologize for cutting out on me last night in my hour of need. He's thought it over and decided it's too risky to be seen with me. Can't chance running into my dad. Jeopardizes his position at the practice and all that." He stood up, giving her a lopsided grin. "I guess you could say I've been dumped."

"Oh, Jason, I'm sorry." She touched his shoulder, rubbed his back, then gave him a hug. "If he's that spineless, he's not good enough for you."

"Damn right. C'mon, let's get out of here." He grabbed a duffel bag and fell into step beside her. "Now it's your turn. Where's Hunter? I thought he'd be sticking close by for a day or two, at least until we find out what that jerk was doing waiting in your house."

"You're the one who needs a babysitter, not me. So I'm going home with you and I'm staying there until I'm satisfied you're okay." At the elevator, they stopped and waited to go down. "Helen Greene's prepared to work full-time until you're back and your hands are good as new."

"A week at the most," he said airily. "Just because I can't punch the buttons on the cash register doesn't mean I can't sell. Hey, the notoriety is probably good for business."

"We'll see. What about your parents? I thought they might be here this morning."

"They showed up last night…right after you left. Dad was—" he paused to find the right word "—okay. He seemed pretty shaken up to see me looking like a piñata after the party. I guess you can disapprove of everything about your kid, but it's something else entirely when his life is threatened." He glanced at her with a cheeky smile. "His words, not mine."

"Oh, Jace, that's so good to hear." She caught his arm, leaning into him with affection. "I told you he'd come around."

"He was glad I wasn't murdered, Erica," he told her dryly. "He's still uncomfortable with who I am."

"He'll get there. He will. You'll see."

Jason grunted skeptically as the elevator doors slid open. "I didn't get an answer to my question. Where's Hunter?"

Inside, she turned to him with a resigned sigh. "What does it matter where he is? I'm here, you're here. We can resume life as it used to be." She glanced at his bandaged head as the elevator whooshed them down seven floors. "As soon as you're a hundred percent."

"You had a fight."

"No, we did not have a fight. If you'll wait until we get into my car, I'll tell you all about it." She paused as the doors slid open and they walked out into the lobby. "I'll just say this. From the first day I met Hunter, I should have kept the old saying in mind that when something seems too good to be true, it usually is."

Hunter stood at the front door of his mother's house after pressing the doorbell for the third time. And still, no answer. Glancing at his watch, he saw that it was barely nine o'clock. He'd expected to find her at home at this early hour on a Monday. On an impulse, he left the stoop and jogged around to the garage to check on her car.

He spotted it through a side window, but Morton's Mercedes was gone. So wherever she went, she wasn't driving. If she'd taken off with Morton, they'd be traveling together. He turned back to gaze at the house thoughtfully. It wasn't often he really needed to talk to his mother, but he wanted answers that only Lillian could supply. His relationship with Erica was threatened and he felt an urgent need to put it right.

Loving a woman wasn't the rosy experience he'd imagined it to be when he'd been on the other side looking in. When he'd watched his friends fall in love over the years, he'd seen only their happiness and the way they'd willingly adjusted to accommodate the change from a single life to sharing everything—bathroom space to the dinner entrée at a restaurant. He had always assumed he'd do the same one day and be glad about it. He damn sure hadn't been prepared for the bumps in the road.

Erica had been prickly from the start. Wary. Cautious to a fault. Tragedy had made her so. He knew that and he'd accepted it, knew it would take time. But he'd assumed— arrogantly, it seemed now—that he'd win her over. It hurt like hell that she didn't take him at his word when he told her he knew nothing about the bombshell Miranda Quinlan lobbed at them last night.

Scowling, he headed away from the garage and on out toward the street where he was parked. What really worried him was finding yet one more bizarre link connecting his family to Erica. He pulled his phone from a clip on his belt and dialed his mother's cell number. What he had on his mind couldn't be discussed on a cell phone, but he meant to locate her, come hell or high water.

After the fourth ring, her voice mail kicked in and he swore. Where the devil was she? "Mom," he said abruptly into the phone. "Call me when you pick this up." Troubled and not a little worried, he headed back to his SUV. Try as he might, he couldn't shake a really bad feeling.

Had Hunter been a bit later at his mother's house, he might have met up with Erica, who made good on her threat to go directly to Lillian Trask and demand an explanation. Like Hunter, she hadn't wanted to deal with such a personal matter on the phone. She was a bit deflated to discover, when nobody answered the door, that she'd made the trip for nothing. Unfortunately, she couldn't hang around and wait to see if the woman might show up. She'd left Jason with Stephen, who'd taken a long lunch hour to pop in and see him. She had to get back.

"I'm not giving up," she told Jason later as they stood before the two paintings she brought in from her car. She had forgotten about them until Jason asked if she had painted anything lately. "I'm going to knock on that woman's door every day until I see her. I want to hear her explain why she took it upon herself to intrude in my life without doing me the courtesy of asking if I wanted her help."

"Can we do one thing at a time?" Jason asked, holding his head. "You're giving me a headache talking about Lillian Trask's audacity in boosting your career the way some artists only dream of. Then you shove these paintings in my face and stand over me waiting to hear what I think."

She sat down abruptly. "I'm sorry, Jace." Rubbing her forehead with thumb and forefinger, she tried to rein in her temper. "It's just so bizarre. What would make a person go to such extremes for somebody she doesn't even know? Until that gala, I had never met Lillian Trask."

Jason was listening with half an ear as he studied the first painting. "This one's a face, of course." He stood with his hands on his hips, head cocked. "A woman, I think. Although maybe not. It's hard to tell." He glanced at Erica. "Which is it?"

"It's feminine, I think. But I don't recall thinking that as it took shape."

"Your pesky little subconscious again," Jason said. "Which means you don't have anyone in particular in mind."

"Speaking of my subconscious…" she said as he continued to study the painting. "The oddest thing happened last night, Jason. I had another nightmare about the accident. That makes twice now I've actually seen images of the moment it happened." She clasped her arms around herself, recalling the horror. "But this time it was so vivid. The whole thing happened sort of like a movie in slow motion. That's the nearest I can come to describing it."

She got up and began pacing. "The images were so real, the neighborhood, the street—" She stopped, shaking her head. "I don't want to keep having these flashbacks, Jason. When will they end?"

"Have you considered that this could be a good thing?" he said. "I know it's hard, but before it's over you may be able to retrieve something that could lead to the bastard who did this."

"I'm not so sure. In fact, I'm pretty sure that the issue is so emotional that it's hard to trust anything I see. For instance, just before I woke up last night—in a panic, naturally—I thought I saw someone in the car."

"No shit!"

"Don't get so excited," she said wryly. "The face I saw was Hunter's mother. And, guess what? She was wearing that damn brooch. It really freaked me out. I think I was screaming. Actually, I know I was, since I'd just flashed back to the accident and had to watch it happen all over again. Anybody would scream." She shuddered. "Anyway, Hunter came into the bedroom, probably thinking I was being attacked. And this morning, he asked if I wanted to talk about the nightmare. It had been hours, but I could still see his mother's face as plain as I see yours right now."

"That is really weird."

"No, not really, if you think about it. I'd just learned all that stuff from Miranda Quinlan about his mother. I stewed over it for hours until I finally fell asleep, so when the nightmare came, she popped up."

"And the brooch? Why was she wearing that in your dream?"

She wasn't quite so certain about that detail. "I guess the most logical reason is that Mrs. Trask was wearing it when I first met her. Maybe the woman and the brooch go together somehow in my mind." She spread her hands doubtfully. "I don't know."

She looked up and found him shaking his head. "What?"

"I was just wondering what Hunter's reaction was when you told him."

"Are you kidding? I couldn't tell him I'd placed his

mother at the scene of the crime. Besides, the atmosphere was pretty strained this morning."

"Meaning you're hell-bent to blame him for something his mother did, even though I'm still having a hard time being mad at the woman."

"I just thought it was wise to back off a bit, Jason. I admit I was—am—attracted to Hunter, but we were just getting to know each other. Then finding out that for years his mother has been like a shadowy presence in my life is…well, it's creepy. I can't imagine why she'd do something like that. And keep it a secret."

"It'd be helpful to know why," Jason agreed. He was again studying the second painting, backing away to get a different perspective. "You still should give him a chance to explain before going off the deep end," he said, but he spoke in a vague tone as he refocused his attention. Moving toward the painting, he pointed to the edgy black shape in the background. "You know what this looks like to me?"

It took Erica a moment to refocus. "No, what?"

"At first I thought it might be a peace symbol," he said, shifting his gaze to her, "you know, like in the sixties? But now I think it's a hood ornament."

"Can you be more specific?"

"Yeah." He drew a circle in the air with one splinted finger. "It could be the little tripronged thing inside a circle. The Mercedes-Benz logo."

"That's what I thought, too."

"Which means the car was probably—voilà—a Mercedes." Warming to his discovery, he studied other areas in the painting for a moment longer. "It's really not very mysterious, once you think about it in context. You can't deny anymore that you're painting scenes from the hit-and-run, sugar. You're painting the moment that changed your life. All this violence is probably your memory of how everything went down." He glanced at her and saw that she was staring at the painting with a hand pressed to her mouth. He was instantly sympathetic. This was a subject so rife with pain that she rarely mentioned it. "I know it's horrible, but you apparently have decided that it's time now to face up to it."

"I faced it nine years ago, Jace," she said, feeling her throat tightening.

Smiling gently, he moved over to her. "No, you didn't. You coped. You kept on keeping on, because the alternative was to die with David and Danielle." He touched her hair. "But you didn't start to live again."

"You're saying I've been living in a state of denial for nine years."

"Not exactly denial, but more like someone on automatic pilot. Then Hunter comes along and you're suddenly back where most of us generally are—living without knowing what's next, or how to keep from getting hurt, or how to avoid pain. The problem with that is it's an impossibility. We're vulnerable and we have no control over it."

"So…" Erica managed a shaky smile. "Where did you get your degree, Dr. Rowland?"

Chuckling, he slipped an arm around her waist and hugged her. "That's my girl, blow it off. Say it ain't so. Keep denying that Hunter McCabe isn't the best thing that's happened to you in nine years."

"If something seems too good to be true, it probably is," she reminded him for the second time in one day.

"Let's talk a little about that." He went to the couch and sat down, then patted the place beside him. "Where the hell is he, by the way? What happened—besides the fact that some old crone at a restaurant spilled the beans?"

She sat, giving a sigh, and clasped her hands between her knees. "I don't know where he is—working, I suppose.

He claims he doesn't know anything about his mother's be-
hind-the-scenes maneuvering, but—"

"But you don't believe him?"

She frowned. "I'm not sure. She wasn't at home when
I tried to see her this morning, but I know he was probably able to get in touch with her. He claimed he was going
to demand an explanation. If he did as he intended, you'd
think he would call me."

"Maybe he hasn't been able to talk to her yet. He's not
the type to just blow something like this away, especially
after seeing your reaction to Miranda's bombshell." Jason
found a cushion and placed it in the corner of the couch.
Moving gingerly, he lay back against it. "But, correct me
if I'm wrong, it sounds to me as if you left him thinking
you were pissed not only at his mother, but at him, too.
What, besides your paintings, did you take when you left
his condo this morning?"

"Everything."

"Erica, Erica, Erica… And you're wondering why you
haven't heard from him? Why should he call you? To get
his ass chewed out again? To be punished for something
his mother did?"

"I don't think it's unreasonable to expect an explanation," she said coolly.

"We're covering old ground here. We've mentioned the
possibility that he hasn't been able to find her. What if she's
out of town?"

"He could call and tell me that."

"Which would bring both of you right back where you
were when you walked out prissy-faced this morning. Still
not knowing why Mommy treated you so miserably, showering you with opportunities that boosted your career to
the skies. Poor baby."

She stood up suddenly. "Okay, I'm an ungrateful witch!"

"No, just a silly one."

She laughed suddenly, giving him a wry look. "If you keep on, Jason, somebody might think you have a personal stake in my relationship with Hunter…if I still have one."

"I wouldn't stand a chance," he said, managing to look woeful. "He's head over heels in love with you, you silly goose. Now, the next thing we need to move this relationship along is for you to admit that you're head over heels in love with him, too."

Erica was back at the shop the next morning. She felt if she was open for business, at least that part of her life was back on track. With Stephen dropping in to keep tabs on Jason at home, and Helen Greene helping her on the floor with customers, life seemed somewhat normal. There were orders that only she could fill and that's what she concentrated on, except when she found her thoughts straying to Hunter and his mother's inexplicable meddling. She hadn't heard from him since her cool departure from his condo the day before, although Jason said he'd called to be sure that she was staying put and not thinking of moving back into her house. She didn't let on to Jason that she was a little miffed that Hunter hadn't wanted to speak directly to her.

Whether she talked directly to Hunter or not, she still intended to talk to his mother. Around midafternoon when there was a lull in business at the shop, she decided it was a good time to swing by and try to have a chat.

"I don't think I'll be gone more than an hour, Helen," she said, scooping up her handbag and heading for the rear exit.

"Take your time." Helen smiled and waved.

Head down, Erica was searching for her car keys when the door suddenly opened and Hunter stepped inside, looking as if he wanted to growl at her. She came to a startled halt, while her heart did a crazy flip.

"You left the back door unlocked again," he said, shooting her a glare. "Just because it's the middle of the afternoon doesn't mean you forget all security precautions."

"I didn't. It was probably Helen. She accepted a delivery and I guess she didn't check to see it was locked." She was talking fast, all too aware that she felt joyously pleased to see him. "You know it's tricky," she ended lamely.

He still glowered. "I called a man to fix that. If he didn't show up, you should have let me know."

"Well, I didn't." She threw up her hands. "Did you come here to pick a fight with me, Hunter? If so, it's not a good time."

"I just saw a couple of homeless types scrabbling around in the trash a few doors down. You need to be more careful."

"They're probably hungry. Jason and I sometimes buy them a sandwich at lunchtime," she told him. "They don't hurt anyone."

He rolled his eyes, then noticed the purse anchored at her shoulder. "Are you going somewhere?"

"Yes. I'm on my way to your mother's house."

"Forget it. She's not at home and I can't find her."

With a glance at Helen, she gestured to the door of her office and, without waiting to see if he followed, went inside. After she tossed her handbag on a chair, she turned to face him. "What do you mean, you can't find her? She's your mother. You must have an idea where she is."

"Apparently, she and Morton have gone somewhere. I figured they might be at their condo in Galveston, but there's no answer when I call. Could be they're on the yacht. But even when I finally track her down, I don't want to discuss this on the phone."

"Or is it that you just don't want me to talk to her?"

"You do what you have to," he told her in a grim voice. "I plan to tell her you're determined to speak to her face-to-face. As ticked off as you are, I'd hate for you to hit her cold. But whether you do or not, I intend to find out what is going on."

She contemplated that and then waved a hand as if to say *whatever.*

Hunter made a soft, half-strangled sound. "What am I doing? I haven't seen you for two days and it's driving me crazy. So I finally find a minute to get away, I leave a job site that's got more problems that any I've worked on in the past five years and first thing I do is chew you out over the security, then I waste the next five minutes in a pointless argument."

Inside, she glowed at the thought that she had been on his mind. Outwardly, she shrugged and leaned against her drafting table. "So, if you haven't talked to your mother, why did you want to see me?"

"For this." His hand shot out, catching her at the back of her neck, then he pulled her toward him and kissed her. Her eyes went wide before the first taste of his mouth. She caught her breath at the swift, intense rush of arousal. But the kiss was slow and lingering, not the hurried, urgent claim she expected…at least until she lifted her arms around his neck and fell into it with him.

He gave a low groan as she scooted into him, matching her softness to his strength, and then he deepened the kiss, turning the moment into a swirling kaleidoscope of pure sensation. Of bright, hot color. If she were painting this, she thought, savoring the taste and scent of him, the canvas would be alive with color, with vivid slashes of light and dark, with the highs and lows of shadow and depth. Of pleasure.

She felt a rise of deepest need. It left her limp and pliant in his hands, steeped in pure sensation. But they weren't alone. They were in the tiny office off the floor of her shop with customers milling about and Helen Greene very likely to walk in if she encountered a problem that required a consult with Erica.

Hunter seemed to reach the same conclusion at that moment. Breaking the kiss, slowly, slowly, he drew back while she kept her eyes closed, greedily holding on to the pleasure until the last second. His arms were wrapped tightly around her, so that she was surrounded by his warmth and weight and substance. And at that moment, it was exactly where she wanted to be.

When he spoke, his mouth was against her ear. "Are you coming home with me tonight?"

She released a sigh, knowing that was exactly what she wanted. "I can't. Jason needs help for another day or two."

With a groan, he rested his forehead against hers. "Can't Stephen stay with him?"

"He could, but it's something I need to do, Hunter. I feel bad enough that he was hurt doing a favor for me." Pulling back, she looked up at him. "Besides, now that I know about your mother, I have to get to the bottom of it."

He moved away and shoved his hands deep in his pockets. "Are we back to that?"

"Don't you see that it could be something that affects us in a way that we can't anticipate? There has to be a connection. Why else would she—" She stopped, shook her head. "Whatever it is, I have to know." Seeing no give in his face, she went on. "How would you feel to discover something like this? Your mother has been a major player in my life for…I don't know how long, maybe years, Hunter. Maybe in my shoes you could just blow it away, but I can't. I need to understand why she did it. I don't intend to forget it until we've talked…as you say, face-to-face."

"Then I guess that's the way it'll have to be." He looked at his watch. "I've got a hell of a problem on a job, so I need to get back."

"I have a ton of work to do, too."

He glanced toward the interior of the shop where Helen was chatting up a customer. "You won't hang around after closing time, will you?"

"No."

"Good." He opened the back door with a little more force than necessary. "Don't forget to lock up behind me."

"I won't." She realized she'd managed to irritate him even though what she said was perfectly logical.

Without another word, he went out and closed the door behind him…definitely with a little more force than necessary.

It was an hour later that the day took another downward turn. Helen rushed into Erica's office and announced she had to leave, right then. She'd received a phone call that her fourteen-year-old son had been taken to the hospital in an ambulance. "I'm so sorry, Erica," she said, pale and shaken. "He was playing basketball in the gym. They think he may have a broken ankle."

Erica got up from her drafting table. "Don't apologize. Just get your purse and run. Do you want me to drive you?" Helen looked too upset to get behind the wheel of a car.

"No, no. My husband's coming to pick me up. He was five minutes away when he called. I guess he didn't want me to have time to panic." She sent a distressed look at two departing customers. "I can't believe I'm having to abandon you this way. I'll be back tomorrow if I possibly can…depending on Kevin's condition." Her fingers twisted into a knot. "What will you do if I can't get away?"

"Don't worry about it." Erica took her elbow and guided her toward the door. "In fact, I think when you leave that I'll just close up shop. It's almost four o'clock and the floor's empty. It'll give me an opportunity to finish what I'm working on with no interruptions."

"Oh, it's Howard. He's here," Helen said, spotting a car pulling up at the curb. With a flutter of her hand and another distracted apology, she hurried out the door. A threat to her son had pushed all other considerations out of her mind.

As it should be, Erica thought.

After watching the car merge back into traffic, she flipped the Closed sign on the door, shot home the dead bolt and lowered the overhead lights in the shop. With no customers and no life on the floor and, yes, Jason's absence, she felt an almost eerie sense of isolation for a minute. She stood for a moment in the quiet stillness, surrounded by the commercial success of her art, wanting to feel satisfaction. Needing it. But the joy she once felt was now tarnished. Whatever Lillian Trask's motives, knowing she had an unseen benefactor diminished the pride she once felt in her work. She had to know why she had been singled out for special perks.

But, with the woman inaccessible, she wouldn't find any answers tonight. Giving herself a mental shake, she turned and headed back to her drafting table. She missed working in the solitude of her studio at home. When she was truly under the gun, she tended to avoid distractions—people, telephones, the doorbell. A thousand and one things could crop up in a day. She took another look around. Well, there was nothing to distract her now. She picked up a pencil.

It wasn't long—an hour or so—before she tossed the pencil down in disgust after almost filling the trash basket beside her with crumpled sketches. What she really wanted to do was to paint. Lately, her passion for painting had returned and it was hard to resist the compulsion once it came upon her. At one time, before David and Danielle had entered her life, art had been the heart and soul of her existence. Although most of her supplies were at her house, she had the bare necessities here, she thought, easing off the stool. She moved to the supplies closet where she'd tucked a couple of fresh canvases picked up on impulse last week. In her mind, she saw the first bold strokes of color. Her eyes lost focus as she visualized the composition of the painting. She stood for a moment, thinking it through. A glance at her wristwatch showed a good two, maybe three hours that she could work.

Twenty-Three

It was far longer than three hours later that Erica's concentration was broken by the sound of an ambulance shrieking past. She looked in surprise at the time. Almost eleven. She had no idea it was so late. Jason must be wondering what in the world had happened to her. The thought brought a frown. It was strange that he hadn't called to check on her.

She stepped back from her easel and rotated her shoulders to ease the tension while pressing both hands to the small of her back. She vaguely recalled taking a carton of yogurt out of the small refrigerator in the storeroom around six. That and a handful of macadamia nuts had kept her going when she would ordinarily have stopped and noticed the time. But they'd been productive hours, she thought, standing back to study the painting with satisfaction. Not quite finished yet, but getting there. Whether her success with her design and quilt art was legitimate or not, tonight she felt she'd turned out a painting that pleased her. Take that, Lillian Trask.

She was cleaning her brushes when the phone rang. Hoping it was Hunter, she eagerly picked up. "Hello?"

"Where are you?" Jason demanded in an accusing voice.

"At the shop, Jace. I know it's late, but I got caught up—"

"Is anybody there with you?"

"No, Helen had a family emergency and had to leave around three. Hunter came—"

"You're alone? Jesus! Are you nuts? Have you lost your freakin' mind? I know better than to ask, but are all the shops on that strip closed?"

"I presume so, but…" She shrugged. "I'm inside, Jason. I honestly didn't realize the time. But, guess what, I've begun a really strong painting…and it's nothing weird." Head cocked, she studied it from across the room. "It's good, I think."

He wasn't interested in listening. "Don't you even think of leaving, Erica. You stay put. I'm calling Hunter to pick you up. And you better hope to hell I can find him. Meanwhile, stay on the phone and go to the back door to make sure that screwy lock is secure. If you come back here telling me it's not, I may get in my car, fat fingers and all, and personally wring your neck."

"Calm down, Jace. I told you, I just got—"

"Caught up. I heard you, but that's no excuse if you're mugged on your way to your car. This isn't Mayberry, U.S.A., it's Houston. Where is it, by the way?"

"My car?" She paused. "Well—"

"No, do not tell me you're parked behind the shop in that alley."

"I won't tell you then," she muttered, moving toward the back door. She was certain that she'd checked the lock after Helen left. Almost certain. "I just realized the time," she told him as she reached for the doorknob. "Is Stephen there?"

"No, he left around seven, thinking you'd walk in any minute."

"I'm sorry, Jace." She jiggled the knob and found it secure. "The door's locked."

"He talked me into taking a pain pill and I zonked out. I only woke up a few minutes ago and realized you weren't here."

"Well, you needed the rest. And I'm sure I'll be fine. We've both worked late many times in the past. And please don't call Hunter."

"I'm calling him. Just sit tight, Erica, I mean it. We don't know who was waiting in your house Saturday night, and until we do, we take no chances. You hear me?"

"What if he's already gone to bed?"

"Then I wake him up. Stay put. I'll get back to you." With an abrupt click, he ended the call.

She lowered the phone and looked around with a wary eye. Until she'd realized the time, she had worked in total concentration without a hint of unease. Now, probably as a result of Jason's paranoia and Hunter's grim suspicions of whatever, she found herself feeling some apprehension. But there was really nothing to be nervous about, she told herself. Jason and Hunter were overreacting. The simplest explanation for what happened at her house Saturday night was that Jason had surprised a burglar. There was really no reason to assume anything else.

She went back into her office and began collecting her things. With Helen possibly unable to make it back tomorrow, it probably was best not to open the shop for business since she had to work. Back orders were piling up, and instead of indulging in an orgy of painting tonight, she should have forced herself to stay at the drafting board. That's exactly what she would do tomorrow, she vowed. Jason would not distract her. He, of all people, understood.

She was in the storeroom looking for a fresh sketch pad

when her cell phone rang. It took a few moments to locate it. Jason again. "Hello?"

"I can't reach him, but I left messages on his cell phone and at his business number."

"It's okay, Jace. I think you're overreacting, anyway. I'll be all packed up in another ten minutes and ready to leave. I'll just—"

"No, damn it! I'm calling a cab and coming over there."

She gave an exasperated huff. "That is not necessary. I've carried everything to the front of the shop. I'll hurry to my car out in the alley and move it around to the front where I'm visible to anybody driving by on the street. I'll load everything from there. I'll be fine, Jace."

"I don't like it, Erica. I've got a bad feeling."

"Take another pain pill. And stand by. I'll call you when I'm all loaded and ready to roll." She clicked to Disconnect and dropped the phone into her handbag. If she allowed it, he probably would get up out of a sick bed and call a taxi. She wasn't giving him the opportunity.

After fishing out her car keys, she dropped her handbag at the front door with the collection of supplies she needed to load into her car and headed back through the shop to the rear entrance. The dicey lock resisted her efforts to open it, making her think it was more impervious to an intruder than either Hunter or Jason assumed. A bad guy would have to be really determined. The lock mechanism finally gave and she stepped cautiously out into the dark alley.

The very dark alley. Thanks a lot, you two, she thought, sending a message to both men as she surveyed the shadowy nooks and crannies of the alley. She'd parked her car here many times since opening the shop and it was frequently after dark when she was ready to leave. But for the first time, she was a bit spooked.

* * *

Hunter was grumpy and frustrated. It had been a day filled with setbacks. A problem-plagued job had gobbled up a large chunk of time. He'd wasted another chunk trying to find his mother. Then, when he'd finally taken a few minutes to see Erica, he'd had a taste of real frustration. With the day a dead loss, Erica needing space and his mother still nowhere to be found, as a last resort, he headed to the ranch to see his sister. He suspected she figured somehow in the mystery of his family's connection to Erica, so he might as well have another try at prying information from her.

He didn't find Jocelyn, but he finally tracked Hank down at the barn, preparing a chemical mix to spray his trees, Hunter assumed. "She's working," Hank said, studying the label on a gallon jug. "She's taking to vet work like a duck to water. Even got a formal title, veterinarian assistant. Makes a lot of sense when you stop and think about it. She's always been a lot fonder of animals than people."

"Good. I'm happy for her." Feeling more frustration, Hunter looked at his watch. "When does she usually wrap it up?"

"Depends." Hank carefully poured a nasty-smelling chemical into a tank. "Sometimes, if they're backed up with patients, she doesn't show up until ten, eleven o'clock. No way to tell which it'll be tonight."

"I can't stay the night," Hunter said, watching him add water to the mix from a hose. "I need to get back to Houston. And I can't hang around waiting for her. What if I swing by Kelly's practice and try to catch her there?"

"Better make it Jeff Pickering's practice. That's where she works. Kelly can't afford an assistant. Hasn't got enough clientele. So Jeff takes 'em both on part-time, Kelly and Jocelyn." He shoved his hat to the back of his head. "Funny thing there. I think Jeff's about to talk Kelly into merging her practice with his. Business is booming around here lately, between gentlemen ranchers from Houston with their horses and other pedigreed pets, and regular folks who've relied on Jeff since he hung up his shingle. Got more business than he can handle. Rather than recruiting another vet, I think he's set to recruit Kelly. What d'you think about it?"

"Fine idea…if they don't kill each other first."

Hank chuckled. "That's a fact. Like a match to kindlin', those two. I'm hoping they'll do more together than doctor sick cattle and dogs."

"I got a hint of that when he showed up at my place ready to defend her honor." Hunter scratched his head, looking chagrined. "I have to tell you, I didn't have a clue that's the way the wind was blowing, Hank."

"Well, these things sometimes happen quick." He bent over and checked to see how the tank was filling up. "Not that it's been so quick on Jeff's part. I think he's had a partiality for Kelly since…hmm, I guess since y'all were in your teens. Once she came back home, she made her partiality for you plain, and seeing as he's a man of honor, he wasn't the type to make a move on a longtime friend."

Hunter squinted off in the distance. He'd just as soon have this conversation over with, but he felt he needed to make an effort to show Hank that his own intentions as far as Kelly was concerned were not dishonorable. Just unsettled. "Kelly and I would never have been right for each other, Hank."

Hank looked up at him. "You think I didn't know that from the start? I did. And so did Jeff. It was Kelly who had to find it out for herself. So put your mind at ease over the way it's worked out. I figured when you found the right woman, you wouldn't waste time trying to make up your mind. Which is how I knew it wasn't going to be with you and Kelly." He bent and gave the water a final check.

Relieved, Hunter didn't quite know what to say to that.

Finished now, Hank turned off the water and, seeing Hunter still seemed troubled, gave him a shrewd look. "What's up, Hunt? You're acting like a man with a problem."

Hunter lifted his hat and settled it back on his head. "Let me ask you something, Hank. Do you have any knowledge of a relationship between my mother and Erica Stewart?"

Hank frowned. "Relationship?"

"Yeah. Say, in the past. Something…in the past." He left it at that.

"No," Hank said, shaking his head, still frowning. "I know Lily admires her work. But I told you that when her birthday rolled around. What makes you ask?"

"Forget it. I'm probably imagining stuff that'll turn out to be…well, nothing."

"What are you imagining?"

Nothing he was willing to say out loud, especially to Hank. "Like I said, forget it."

"Is that why you want to talk to Jocelyn?"

"Yeah." At a familiar sound from the barn, he walked inside. Jasper had caught his scent and now whinnied softly from his stall. He stroked the horse's nose and got an affectionate nudge to his shoulder for his trouble. "Sorry, boy, no time for a ride tonight."

"I'm right about Ms. Stewart, aren't I? You're serious."

"I want to marry her." He knew he didn't have the look of a man in the throes of a rapturous love affair, but he was certain of his intentions.

"I figured as much." Hank nodded, smiling quietly. "I remember how that feels, son. And I wish you luck. Frankly, you look like you need it." Then, studying his feet, he let his smile fade before looking up at Hunter again. "I'm telling the truth when I say I don't know of anything connecting Lily and your artist, but I believe there's something. Last time she was here, she mentioned being more than a little troubled over you falling for Erica. Made no sense to me as the woman's an artist, seems very nice and is smart and pretty to boot. You'd turn out some incredible grandkids. I told her so. But when I pressed her, she wasn't talking."

Hunter met his eyes. "What the hell could it be, Hank?"

Hank was shaking his head. "I don't have a clue, son. But I think before you and your lady can settle in together the way I want to see you settle, you'd better find out. Clear it up. Whatever it is."

"Yeah, I mean to do just that."

There was no sign of Jocelyn when he arrived at the vet office. No one manned the check-in desk, but there were three people with ailing pets waiting to see a doctor. He stood uncertainly for a minute or two, then Kelly appeared, her face lighting up in a smile. He was relieved that she seemed genuinely glad to see him.

"Hi, stranger." Smiling, she came through a half-door partition and hugged him. "What brings you out to the boonies on a Tuesday night?"

"I heard Jeff's got a new veterinarian assistant and I might recognize her," he said, giving her ponytail an affectionate yank.

"You bet, and she's really catching on, Hunt. She's especially good with small animals, dogs, cats, bunnies. Which is good as I'm partial to large animals and so is Jeff."

"Speaking of Jeff, Hank tells me you're about to let him talk you into a partnership. I hope you drive a hard bargain."

"I have made no commitments about that," she said, although there was a gleam in her eye. Then, to his amazement, she blushed. "However, I do have this, which should make bargaining interesting." She held up her left hand and waggled her ring finger where a large diamond winked in the lights overhead.

"Well, I'll be damned." He grinned with real affection. "I didn't know Pickering could move that fast."

"Twelve years is not fast. That's how long he claims he's been waiting."

"He's been hot for you for twelve years?" It seemed Hank had nailed it right.

"Hey, you had your chance, McCabe." Jeff Pickering materialized from somewhere in the back with Jocelyn. He walked up to Kelly and slipped an arm around her waist. Staking his claim, Hunter thought with amusement.

Jeff reached out to shake hands. "I didn't know you urban cowboys knew the way to the country in the dark."

"Congratulations, dude." Still grinning, Hunter clasped his hand hard. "Last time I spent any time with you and Kelly, I thought I might have to call the law to break up a brawl. So when's the big day?"

"Two and a half months," Jeff said promptly. He looked down at Kelly with a face so full of…something, that Hunter blinked. Was that the way he looked at Erica? he wondered.

"It'd be sooner if I had my way," Jeff said, "but she's holding out for a lot of that girlie stuff, so I was outvoted."

Kelly gave him a punch on the arm. "Girlie stuff," she said with mock disgust, before appealing to Hunter. "Tell him that a church, a preacher, a cake and a party is what you do when you get married, Hunt. What's so strange about that?"

"Sounds right to me."

"Me, too…if it could happen without waiting two and a half months," Jeff shot back.

Hunter raised both hands, palms out. "Okay, I'm staying out of this."

Jocelyn, silent until now, made a time-out signal with her hands. "I have to do that a lot," she told Hunter, smiling. "Otherwise, we'd never get any work done around here."

"We've created a monster," Kelly said, pretending to hover close to Jeff. "Jocelyn fancies herself a referee."

"And you need one," Jocelyn said, before turning to Hunter. "Is this a social call or do you have a sick puppy in your car?"

"No sick puppy." With a glance at Jeff and Kelly, his lips twisted briefly in a wry smile. "I see you still have patients, but if it's not too much of an inconvenience, I'd like to talk to Jocelyn for a few minutes."

There was a short, blank silence. Then Kelly looked at her. "Jocelyn?"

"Okay, sure." Jocelyn moved toward a door off the waiting room. "We can talk in the break room."

"You want some coffee?" Jocelyn said a few moments later when they were alone. "I should warn you, it's pretty rank. I think Jeff makes it to his own recipe, which is so strong that nobody wants it, meaning he has it all to himself all day. Me, I prefer diet Coke and Kelly drinks bottled water, nothing but." She wrinkled her nose. "Health nut, Kelly. She'll probably live to be a hundred and me and Jeff will croak before age fifty."

"Why are you nervous, Jocelyn?"

Her laugh had a definite edge. "Me? What makes you say that?" She paused for a heartbeat. "Did you say you wanted some of this?" She picked up the decanter.

"No, thanks." He drew a deep breath and guessed nothing had changed since he'd last tried to pry information from her. "When did you last hear from Mom?"

She shrugged. "I don't know, days ago. Last Wednesday? Why?"

"I've been trying to reach her home or cell or the phone at the Galveston condo and she doesn't answer. I've left messages. I was hoping you might have heard from her."

"No, sorry." She turned away and opened the refrigerator. "Want a diet Coke?"

"No, thanks." He watched her fingers go to work on the tab. "Did you hear about someone breaking into Erica's house?"

She took a sip from the can. "Yeah, actually, I did. You know what, I guess it wasn't Wednesday that I last spoke to Mom, it was…let's see, Sunday night, I think. She was pretty shaken up over it."

"Why?" Hunter asked, deciding not to ask why she'd lied about talking to her mother. "Mom doesn't seem to care for Erica."

Jocelyn gave him a chastising look. "She's a good person. She'd care about anybody being victimized that way. What's the matter with you?"

"For one thing, she never misses a chance to talk Erica down to me. She doesn't approve of her, and for the life of me, I can't figure out why. With her interest in art and Erica's success in that line of work, she should be everything Mom would want in a daughter-in-law. Instead, from her attitude, you'd think I was getting involved with a slut."

"Oh, come on."

"Let me ask you this, Jocelyn." He watched her tense up and turn away to begin fiddling with a few dirty dishes in the sink. "Do you know of a connection between our mother and Erica? A personal connection."

Jocelyn turned the water on and reached for a sponge. "How would I know that? I'm not the one living near her, you are. If there was something, I think you'd know about it before me."

"That's exactly what I've been telling myself." He picked up a used coffee mug from the small round table and handed it to her, moving so that he could see her face. "Until I ran into Miranda Quinlan Sunday night."

With only a tiny pause, she began loading up the dishwasher. "Who's Miranda Quinlan?"

"Don't give me that. You know her. She's been a friend of Mom's for years and she's very active in the arts community."

"So?" Jocelyn busily searched for something in the cabinet.

"She told me that Mom has been a major booster of Erica's career for years. That she paved the way for Erica to participate in the symphony gala, that she refers her friends to Erica's shop to buy her art, that she had a hand in Erica's recognition by *Texas Today*."

She turned with a box of detergent in her hand. "Lucky Erica."

"Maybe." He watched her bend to fill the dishwasher with detergent. "Why would she go to such extraordinary lengths to help somebody she seems to dislike?"

Jocelyn closed the door with a solid clunk and looked directly into his face. "Because she's a good person?"

He waited, holding her gaze, hoping to see something. Anything. "Okay, Sissy, how about this one? That first day you showed up after leaving Key West, why did you look so shocked when I introduced Erica in the barn?"

She turned, grabbing at a sponge. "Now you're suggesting I'm the one with a personal connection to Erica?"

"I'm asking a simple question."

"Maybe you misread my reaction, Hunt," Jocelyn replied, turning on a blast of hot water. "Maybe it was exhaustion you saw on my face, not shock. After all, I'd been on the road for three days and I was definitely sleep deprived. I was also scared that crazy son of a bitch Sanchez might follow me, and it was pretty tough knowing I'd screwed up yet again and would have to face you and Mom and Dad and the rest of the whole freakin' western world. All of which I've already told you. Or, hey, maybe I looked shocked to find you in a clinch with somebody besides Kelly." She ruthlessly swabbed the sides of the now-empty sink. "Which turns out to be just fine as she and Jeff are madly in love and no harm done. Also something I bet you didn't think about when you dumped her for the gracious and talented Erica."

He wasn't going to get any straight answers here tonight, Hunter thought. The irony was that he ever thought he would. She knew something, and no amount of her stonewalling could hide that fact. But she wasn't telling. Which only added to his determination to figure out what it was. As he left the ranch a few minutes later, he vowed he would not let his mother off the hook so easily.

She was affected by Jason's anxiety after all, Erica decided as she stood in the open door of the shop and considered the prospect of walking the relatively short distance to her car. The alley was truly as dark as pitch. Which struck her as odd until she realized the security light was off, burned out no doubt due to neglect on her part—or Jason's. She glanced uneasily up and down the alley, promising herself to see that a new bulb was installed tomorrow. But that was of no help now. What she saw now was only shadows that deepened to black nothingness. It gave her an eerie feeling. Directly across from the shop entrance was a lush bank of oleander shrubs, but they, too, disappeared in the dark. It was disorienting. Weird.

Bracing herself with a deep breath, she stepped out onto the tarmac before losing her nerve altogether. With the reassuring feel of her car keys in her hand and her cell phone in her pocket, she pulled the door closed behind her, giving it a firm yank to be sure the temperamental lock caught. As her eyes adjusted somewhat to the pitch-blackness of the alley, the trash Dumpster materialized a few feet farther down. Then—a feeling of relief—her car beyond the Dumpster. But farther away than she wished.

She was halfway there when she thought she heard a faint sound in the vicinity of the Dumpster. My imagination, she thought. Probably a cat rummaging in the depths of the thing. A possum? Like cats, they were nocturnal creatures. Please, not a homeless person. It pained her to think some people were reduced to looking for food in a Dumpster. Whatever lurked there, she wished she didn't have to pass it to get to her car.

Just to hear a sound that was familiar and not scary, she jiggled her car keys and shifted them from one hand to the other. She did it a couple of times. Wasn't that what was recommended when you were camping out and suddenly faced with a grizzly? You made a lot of noise because bears were intimidated by noise. Feeling, for some reason, that she was being watched, she sent a furtive look over her shoulder. Imagination again, she told herself. Alone in a dark place in the middle of the night, odd things happen to a person's mind.

She'd just passed the Dumpster with her car still another twenty feet away when she heard a sound that she definitely did not imagine. Footsteps. Out of the corner of her eye, a figure materialized from behind the Dumpster. Shock gripped her for a second before fear and a rush of adrenaline slammed home and she realized how dumb it had been to walk out here alone.

Terrified, she made a dash to save herself. She took only a step then cried out in blind panic when she was caught by the collar of her jacket and spun about. She would have lost her balance by the sheer violence of the assault, but he kept her upright by gripping her hair.

"Shut up or I'll kill you," he snarled.

Terrified, she struggled, trying desperately to fight him off, but he was behind her, his fist twisting in her hair until she felt it would be torn from her scalp by the roots. The pain was searing, blinding, almost incapacitating. She tried kicking him, using her nails to claw at him, but held off balance as she was, her efforts were too puny.

Oh, God, what was happening? Was she going to be raped?

And then, to her horror, she felt a cord settling around her neck and biting viciously into soft flesh. She went wild. Arms and legs flailing, she kicked and scratched and twisted desperately, but with cruel strength, he jerked the cord tight and cut off breath and sound and, she knew, life.

Frantically, she clawed at his hands, but he was brutal, twisting the cord, grunting with the effort, cursing her attempts to get away. Cursing her, she realized. From some vague vacuum, she heard the vile names. Such rage, she thought, in bewilderment. And then, with tiny lights dancing behind her eyelids, she felt herself slipping away. Inside, she shrieked at the unfairness of it. Not now...not now, she begged in silent despair. She thought of Hunter and the life they would not share. She thought of the paintings she would never create. She thought of missed opportunities. She thought of her baby...and then she thought of nothing at all.

Twenty-Four

Hunter was within ten minutes of his condominium when he checked his cell phone and found he had a couple of missed calls. He'd left the phone in his car, he recalled, when he'd been in Kelly's office, and as late as it was, he hadn't thought to check it again. Scrolling, he saw both were from Jason. His eyebrows drew together in a frown as he punched a few buttons, entered his code and listened. As he retrieved his messages, his frown was darker than ever.

Goddamn it! She'd promised to leave the shop with Helen. What was it going to take to make her understand a few basic precautions? That location was not a place for any woman to be after hours. For the life of him, he couldn't figure out why the bad feeling that had been on him lately seemed to loom larger than ever.

Fumbling with the numbers, he quickly dialed Erica's cell phone and cursed when only her voice mail kicked in. Maybe she was already safe at home with Jason. He scrolled to find that number and dialed it.

When Jason answered, he sounded frantic. "Hunter, thank God. Did you get my messages? Is Erica with you?"

"No. I take it she hasn't made it home yet."

"No, and she doesn't answer at the shop. I talked to her about twenty minutes ago. I hate to be a worrywart, but that area isn't exactly the Galleria at this time of night."

"Why the hell is she there so late?" Already Hunter was looking for a place to reverse course and head for the shop.

"Painting. She was painting and lost track of time." Hunter made a swift U-turn, ignoring the squeal of brakes from an outraged driver. "Look, when you get there, her car is in the alley behind the shop. If you don't see her inside, head out back."

"Yeah. I'm going. I'll get back to you." Face grim, he entered the ramp to the freeway and floored the Porsche. Jason was a worrywart, all right and thank God for it. He just hoped his concern tonight was for nothing. That Erica wasn't answering her cell phone because she was puttering around with her paints, cleaning brushes or something.

A trip that should have taken twenty-five minutes was done in fifteen. As he turned onto her street, uneasiness turned to something else. His heart took a dive when he spotted the blue lights of a police unit, then his heart stopped when it pulled up to the curb outside Erica's shop. He swerved out of his lane illegally and braked behind the cop car with a screech of tires. Then he was out of his car and running.

Both cops gave him a startled look. "Hey, hold it, buddy!" One turned and stepped in front of him, blocking him before he reached the door of Erica's shop. "Where you think you're going?"

"The owner's inside. She's my…" *Wife.* In his heart, that's exactly what Erica was. With his heart hammering, he quickly revised. "I'm a friend of the owner. What happened? Why are you here?"

"Let me see some ID."

Almost growling with frustration, Hunter groped in his back pocket for his wallet, his eye on the cop's partner, who was already peering into the front window. Holding his ID with hands that shook, he waited while it was examined, straining to see over the cop's shoulder for a sign of life inside the shop. But he saw nothing.

He felt alarm turning to panic. "She's supposed to be working late," he said. "I need to check—"

"No, buddy, we're gonna check. You're gonna wait out here."

"Police!" his partner called, jiggling the shop's front door. "Open up!" He paused, cupping his eyes with both hands to try to get a better look inside. "I don't see anything, Pete."

"We need to check the alley," Hunter told them urgently. "Jason said that—"

"We got a call that a woman had been injured at this address. Is he—"

The words were barely out before Hunter was in a flat-out run and heading for the access way to the alley, three shops down. His heart hammered with a fear so intense that he barely noticed the stygian darkness of the area behind the shop. He was vaguely aware of the cops following.

"Over here!"

The voice came from the direction of the Dumpster. Hunter pulled up short, squinting into the darkness, trying to adjust his vision and pinpoint it. In seconds, the cops drew even with him, both huffing, beams from their flashlights flicking over objects in the alley as they ran. A police radio crackled unintelligible words. One of the cops responded.

"Here!" A man, crouching on the pavement, suddenly stood up and beckoned. "What took you so long?" he demanded in a peevish tone, throwing up an arm to ward off the light flashed in his face. "When I called I said she was hurt bad."

Drawing closer, Hunter recognized the homeless guy he'd seen earlier that day. That was his last coherent thought as his gaze fell on Erica sprawled at the vagrant's feet. Terror washed over him in a tidal wave.

"Erica. Oh God, oh God. No..." At her side in a split second, he fumbled to locate a pulse at her throat with a trembling hand. It took precious seconds as he tried to calm himself enough to check, but he thought he found it, weak but there. He said her name over and over as he searched for a wound, for blood, praying there would be none. Her face, caught in a beam of light from one of the cops' flashlights, was too pale. And she was so still, he thought frantically. Fiercely reining in blind panic, he rubbed her wrists and hands with both of his, his eyes fixed on her face. "You'll be okay, sweetheart. Just hold on."

He glanced up at the cop. "Call an ambulance," he ordered. "She needs to get to the hospital."

"It's done, sir." The attitude of both cops had turned dramatically. "The EMTs will be here soon, shouldn't take more than a few minutes."

He cursed the wait. He wanted to gather her up in his arms, hold her close, but he was afraid to move her. He realized then that she was trembling, and the little he knew about shock sent more terror slicing through him. Moving urgently, he began shedding his jacket, which was warm with his own body heat. He tucked it around her, pulling it up snugly to her chin.

It was then that he saw the marks on her throat. Ugly, brutal creases that cut deep into flesh and were now oozing blood. What was this? He'd expected a gunshot wound, possibly an assault with a knife. What—

"Looks like somebody tried to strangle her," Pete said, keeping his flashlight focused.

New terror struck. Fearing she couldn't breathe, Hunter bent low, putting his ear to her lips. Relief rushed through him as he felt the faint warmth. Then his heart leaped in his chest when she gave a soft moan. But he could do nothing for her but wait for the ambulance while time seemed to have stopped. He had never felt so helpless. Was this a taste of how she'd felt at the scene of the accident that had taken her husband and baby?

Again, more squawking from the radio and Pete's partner moved aside a few feet to respond. Again, to Hunter, the words were unintelligible, but he forgot about the cops as he realized Erica was stirring, trying to talk.

"Hun-ter…" Her voice was hoarse, barely audible.

"I'm here, sweetheart. Don't talk. We're taking you to a hospital."

"Hurts…throat…"

"I know. But you'll be okay. Trust me, you'll be okay."

"Scared…"

"Oh, yeah." He nodded, unable to make more of a reply than that but vowing to find whoever did this and see that he paid. It would be hard to trust the justice system to mete out what Hunter felt he deserved.

"Hunter…" she whispered. "I s-saw…"

He bent low, gently cupping her chin as she struggled to speak, brushing kisses on her cheek and nose and temple. "Don't try to talk. You can—"

"No… Have to tell…" Tears leaked from the corners of her eyes. Even as her mouth trembled and tremors coursed through her body, she sought his eyes and tried to smile.

"What is it, sweetheart?"

"I…saw…my baby."

Twenty-Five

Later, he would hardly recall the ride to the hospital. They tried to keep him out of the ambulance, but finally the two cops had taken pity on him. He took a seat as near her as the medics would allow. Insisted on holding her hand. He would have gathered her into his arms and held her all the way to the hospital if he could.

"It was attempted murder," he told Patrick Sullivan later as he paced in the ER waiting room. The two detectives had appeared within an hour of Erica arriving at the hospital. "It's obvious that was no random burglary at her house Saturday night. This guy would have killed her then, but it was Jason who came through the door and not Erica."

"The woman has the luck of the devil," Frank Hernandez said, helping himself to coffee. "Can you beat it, her friend takes a beating from a baseball bat meant for her and on the would-be killer's second try, a homeless guy saves the day."

Hunter gave him a withering look but didn't bother to comment. Erica was still in the ER and he was waiting for word on her condition. He'd called her parents and Jason, but it would be a while before any of them made it to the hospital.

Hernandez brushed at a few drops of coffee spilled on his tie. "Funny thing about the homeless. I've known them to be within spittin' distance of a crime going down and they act like they just don't see it. Don't want to get involved. Here we have a guy who rushes the perp, starts beating him with a yard rake—can you believe that?—and the perp's forced to give it up and run."

"He saved her life," Hunter said, still weak in the knees at knowing how easily it could have gone the other way. Chilled to his soul at the thought. If her attacker had been armed, he would have killed them both. Erica because she was his prime target and the homeless guy because he could identify him. "What's his name, by the way?"

"Alexander Graham Bell," Hernandez replied, deadpan.

Hunter gave him a blank look. "Are you serious?"

"As a heart attack," Hernandez said. "At least, that's who he said he was. But after a bit of conversation, he showed some ID from the VA hospital with another less-illustrious name."

"James Porter," Sullivan said, shooting his partner a quelling glance. "He's got some problems." He had his notebook out. "We'd like to ask a few questions, sir."

"Have you had a chance to question Mr. Porter?" Hunter asked.

"It doesn't look like he'll be too helpful. Pete Spencer and his partner, Ed Beck, were the two uniforms first on the scene. They did question him, thinking luckily we had an eyewitness. Even in the dark, he should have been able to give us some good information."

Hunter guessed he was in for a disappointment. "You say problems. Do you mean mental problems?"

"He's like a lot of the homeless in the city," Sullivan said, clicking his ballpoint. "We don't quite know what to do with people who have problems dealing with reality, and even if we did, they often aren't able to trust the system to help them."

"Yeah, if it ain't drugs or booze, it's schizophrenia," Hernandez said. "One day he's Peter Pan, the next he's the dude who invented the telephone. Tell him who he said the perp was, Patrick."

With a wry twist of his mouth, Sullivan rubbed the end of his pen along the side of his face. "Claims it was the governor."

Hunter sighed, shaking his head.

"Yep, the governor of our great state," Hernandez said, chuckling. "The big guy in Austin himself. And Beck says he stuck to his story no matter how they put the question to him. He wouldn't go to the station, either. Flatly refused. Said they knew where his office was if they wanted to discuss it with him in more detail."

"His office is a large cardboard container behind the Dumpster," Detective Sullivan replied.

"So what do we do now?" Hunter asked.

"Well, looks like we're back to square one. First of all, can you think of any reason someone might want to kill Ms. Stewart?"

"No."

"Is there anything in her life, any involvement with persons or organizations—that kind of thing—that would put her in jeopardy?"

"No."

"Could she have a stalker? She's beautiful, she's in the public eye, especially lately, so she's a prime target for a stalker."

Hunter went to the coffee bar to refill his cup. "Don't stalkers give their victims some hint of their obsession? Don't they get notes or letters or phone calls or something?"

"Usually, but not always."

"Erica has never mentioned anything like that," he told them. He thought how she was convinced that some outside force was boosting her career. When everyone else had put it down to her imagination, she'd been proved right. But there was a big difference between a benefactor and someone bent on doing her harm.

Hernandez was watching him, narrow-eyed. "What about it, Mr. McCabe?" he prodded. "You think of something?"

Hunter shook his head. "No." Until he talked to his mother, he couldn't see how her connection to Erica had any relevance to this situation. She certainly wouldn't have anything to do with an attempt on Erica's life.

"How long have you known Ms. Stewart?" The question came from Sullivan.

"Not a long time," he admitted. He'd been thinking about that on the drive from the ranch, a trip that seemed to have taken place in another time zone. He might not have known Erica six months ago, but he couldn't imagine life without her now. "I met her the week of my mother's birthday—in February—when I bought one of her designer jackets as a gift."

"So, you're not really in a position to give us much information about her, are you?" This from Hernandez.

Just then, the ER resident appeared at the door. Hunter quickly tossed his cup, coffee and all, in the trash. "Her business partner has known her since college. Maybe you can learn something from him." He turned and went to meet the doctor.

They let Hunter see her within minutes of putting her in a room. He paused at the door, bracing himself. She lay still, her dark hair a stark contrast with the snowy pillow.

She looked small and vulnerable, he thought as he moved slowly toward her, her face too pale and the hands at her side too still. It dawned on him that she was a person who moved quickly and spontaneously. To see her so lifeless threatened the control he swore he'd hang on to when they let him in. She had an IV inserted on her left hand dripping something into her, but no bandages. He moved closer, quietly. There was nothing to indicate her near-disastrous brush with a madman except the ugly, angry bruise circling her throat. He made a sound then, unable to help himself. She heard him, stirred, turned her head and found him standing there.

"Hunter." Her voice was a weak, broken excuse for what it should have been, her lips unsteady. She moved her hand and he took it, feeling a pang when it felt as fragile as a baby bird. He carefully brought it to his mouth for a kiss.

"How you doing, sweetheart?"

"Sore throat."

He swallowed a pang of sympathy, barely able make out what she said. "Yeah, I bet."

To his amazement, she managed a tremulous smile. "I had another nightmare and you weren't there."

He swallowed hard. "I'm sorry, baby. It won't ever happen again." If he had to sleep on the floor beside her for the next lifetime, that's the way it was going to be. No one was ever going to get close enough to hurt her.

"My own fault," she said, forcing words through a damaged larynx. "I should have left with Helen. Shouldn't have started that painting. Should have—"

"Hush." He put a finger on her lips. He couldn't stand hearing her blame herself when nothing she did or didn't do was going to stop the bastard who was bent on getting to her. If not tonight, he would have found a way another time. Keeping her safe now was the important thing. "Do you have any idea who it was, Erica?"

She sighed. "No. It was so dark…it was so quick. He was…" She swallowed, winced with the effort.

"Do you want some water?" he asked quickly.

"No…doesn't help." She drew a slow, deep breath and started again. "He was very strong." She hesitated, remembering the vicious strength in his hands. "He cursed me. It…it was as if he was…furious with me. As if I'd done…something and deserved…to be punished."

"Can you recall anything he said, his exact words?"

"Bitch. He called me a bitch." She frowned, thinking. "Said…I'd caused…enough…trouble."

"Anything else?"

"Just…filthy names." She closed her eyes.

Sick bastard, Hunter thought, watching as her breathing evened out. He guessed a sedative was kicking in. A good thing, he thought. Rest was what she needed, drugged enough so she couldn't dwell on what had nearly happened. He pressed a kiss to her hand again, fighting his own memories of the way she'd looked lying lifeless on the pavement in that dark alley.

"Don't talk any more right now. Just rest." He tucked her hand beneath the covers. "I've called Jason and your parents. Your mother will be here tomorrow morning."

Her eyes fluttered open, roused by something he said. "Did you talk to your mother?"

"Not yet. Let's not worry about that right now."

Her eyes closed again and she seemed to relax. "She was…in the car."

"Who?" He frowned. "My mother?"

"I saw her…but it was a…nightmare, wasn't it?"

It took him a moment to realize she was disoriented from the drugs. "Yeah, baby, it was a nightmare."

Her hand suddenly groped for his, gripped tight. "Don't leave me."

"Never."

Erica was fully awake at 7:00 a.m. the next morning, being poked and prodded by the nursing staff. They were apologetic, but they had a job to do—temp, blood pressure, a minute examination of her ravaged throat and gentle insistence that she try to swallow Jell-O. What flavor would she prefer? Hunter made the decision for her and got rid of them.

She'd been given some kind of sedative the night before to calm her down as much as to help her sleep, but it seemed her brain simply transferred the horror of the attack to her subconscious and out it came in a nightmare. Hunter had come to her rescue then, too. She remembered swimming up out of the dream feeling so terrified that she couldn't breathe. Memory came rushing back then and she felt the cord around her throat. She threw up her hands to claw at the constriction choking off air and life and breath. And the next thing she knew, Hunter was beside her in the bed, his arms around her, talking her down from the horror. Safe in his arms, she went back to sleep.

"Thank you again," she told him now. And when he gave her a puzzled look, she explained, "For helping me through yet another nightmare last night."

"You were entitled." It cut into him that she'd been so restless, even with the drugs they'd given her. It was when she'd cried out and sat up, nearly ripping the IV out of her hand, that he'd crawled into bed with her. "Bad...dreams," she'd told him in a croaky voice. He'd gathered her close and stayed there until dawn broke.

He peeled the seal off a cup of Jell-O and offered it to her. "After what happened to you, it would be odd if you didn't have a nightmare."

She had a quick, vivid flashback of being rushed from behind. "It was so horrible, Hunter," she said with a shudder, refusing the Jell-O. "I don't think I'll ever go outside alone in the dark again."

He set the cup on a table and picked up her hand. "Yes, you will. But you won't have to worry about being alone for a while. As soon as you're released, I'm taking you to the ranch. The doc says late this afternoon, when they're certain your throat is clear."

She turned her head, looking away. "We'll see."

"You need to be in a safe place, Erica."

With her free hand, she pushed a button that raised her up a bit. "What makes you think he won't find me there?"

"Even if he learns where you are, you're not going to be out of my sight except to go to the bathroom. He'll have to go through me to get to you. And that won't happen."

"What about your job? You can't drop everything just to babysit me. The ranch is two hours away from Houston."

"I spent a good part of the night thinking about that. I have a laptop, a cell phone and assistants who're totally familiar with each job. Today, while you're safe here in the hospital, I'll make arrangements. Then we're outta here and no way in hell he can get to you there."

"I can stay with my mother in Austin."

"In a house that's open to the world? When he might hurt three children in his attempt to get to you? Or your mother?"

With a sigh, she turned her face to the window. "He's afraid my memory is returning. That's why he's suddenly decided I'm a threat."

"It's the only reason I can think of." After a minute, he said, "Tell me this. What were you painting last night? Was it another piece of the puzzle?"

"No. One reason I lost track of time was that it was so

natural, like I used to feel when I was painting. Each stroke led to another and another until I'd created this piece that, when I stood back and looked at it, made me smile." She shifted her gaze back to him. "It was good, Hunter. And it felt good doing it."

He brought her hand up to his lips. "I'm glad, sweetheart."

She pulled her hand away gently. "Jason had some ideas about the other pictures," she told him.

"Tell me."

"He thinks the figure in the background is a Mercedes logo. And I think he's right."

"Which means the car was probably a Mercedes." He offered her the plastic spoon and the Jell-O again. "Here, try to swallow some of this. It's good for your throat."

She scooted up a little on her pillows. "Nothing's going to feel good on this throat," she said, but she took it, anyway. "It feels like I tried to swallow razor blades."

"How about the other painting?" Hunter said. "I thought I saw a face. Was I right?"

"I think so. I've felt all along that it's a woman's face." But she couldn't tell him or Jason that she now thought she knew whose face it was.

Hunter didn't leave until her mother arrived. When the cleaning crew came to make her bed and mop the floor, he went outside with Isabel. "I'm going to take her home with me, Hunter," she said firmly. "I know the police say they're going to find whoever did this, but until they do, she isn't safe in Houston."

He had hoped to put off the moment when he'd have to stand her down, but he wanted—needed—to be the one to protect Erica. In light of what he was beginning to suspect, he was grimly determined to do just that. "What about your children, Isabel? You can't put them in harm's way. I understand you're worried and scared. You want Erica where you can see her, but she'll be safer with me at the ranch. Her attacker is a ruthless animal and, I think, desperate. We can't take any chances."

Agitated, Isabel put a hand over her mouth. "Oh, this is so awful, Hunter."

"Yeah, it is. But, at the moment, Erica is safe. She's untouchable here in the hospital. And once I get her to the ranch, she'll be untouchable there. So, if you'll stay until I get back, we can get under way by midafternoon."

"Of course, but are you sure about this? I want to discuss it with John, but—"

"I'll use the same argument with her dad, Isabel. Just trust me. Please." He was relieved of further argument when Detectives Sullivan and Hernandez stepped out of the elevator. Sullivan, he noted, had changed clothes since they talked at 1:00 a.m., but Hernandez wore the same shabby suit, right down to the coffee-stained tie.

"Anything new?" he asked, greeting them before they reached the door to Erica's room.

"Not much. We were discouraged from questioning Ms. Stewart last night—doctor's orders," Sullivan said. "It's a top priority today."

Hernandez laughed. "Yeah, because Alexander Graham Bell has moved, lock, stock and cardboard box."

Hunter frowned. "You think he took off because the killer might come after him?"

"If I was in his shoes—God forbid—it's what I would do," Hernandez said. "This perp is one mean dude."

"How is Ms. Stewart this morning?" Sullivan asked politely.

"Expecting you. We guessed you'd probably be here early," he told them, then introduced Isabel, trusting that she would play the role of protective mother and see that they didn't upset or overwhelm Erica. "I'll be back in a couple of hours." With that, he left to make arrangements for Erica to go to the ranch and to find his own mother.

Hunter called the house first and, to his relief, Lillian answered.

"Where have you been, Mom? I've left messages since Monday. What's the point in having voice mail if you don't pick up your messages?"

"And good morning to you, too, Hunter."

"Sorry. I've got a lot on my mind."

"I'm sorry you couldn't reach me. I was with Morton and some friends on the yacht. It was a spur-of-the-moment thing, and in the rush of getting away, I forgot my cell phone. Why were you calling? Was it important?"

"I need to talk to you, Mom. But not on the phone. And yes, it's important. I'll be there in twenty minutes." He rang off before she had a chance to reply. An abrupt disconnect might be disrespectful, but he remembered his mother's reaction the last time they'd discussed Erica. He couldn't take a chance that she might refuse to let him in if she knew he was making another attempt at it. After last night, the stakes were a lot higher now.

Twenty-Six

"My word, Hunter, you look simply awful," Lillian said when she met him at the door a few minutes later. "Are you sleeping in your clothes now?"

He wondered what she'd say if she knew he'd done exactly that. Stepping inside, he looked beyond her. "Is Morton around?"

"No. And I don't mind telling you it's nice that he's back at the office. I probably shouldn't say this, but it is stressful being with him for several days at a stretch, which is the way it is when we're in Galveston at the condominium, or on that ghastly boat."

"*Ghastly* isn't how most people would describe a cruise on a sixty-foot yacht."

"Think about being seasick. *Ghastly* is definitely appropriate."

They'd drifted through the foyer and now stood at the entrance to the elegant living room. "Let's talk in the kitchen," he suggested. "I could use a cup of coffee."

"I gave Maria the day off," Lillian said, heading toward the kitchen. "Frankly, I wanted the day to myself after playing hostess to Morton's guests without letup for three days. Now, let's see…" She surveyed the contents of a cabinet. "I've several kinds of coffee. What would you like?"

"Whatever. Just coffee without a flavor. Please."

"Oh, then let's try this wonderful dark roast. Morton was in Costa Rica not too long ago and brought it back with him. I think he's hoping to become the ambassador there."

"Are you okay with that?"

"Would it matter?"

He frowned. "Is everything okay with you and Morton?"

She went to the sink and filled the decanter with water. "Nothing much changes with Morton and me," she said.

"Then he's pretty confident he'll get an appointment?"

"He claims so. He's certainly doing a lot of schmoozing to make it happen. That's why we were in Galveston. I told him that it appeared he'd lost interest in his day job, but of course that was an exaggeration. Still, he's keen to get that appointment." She shrugged, measuring coffee beans into a grinder. "How about you?"

He waited until the sound of the grinder ceased. "Busy," he told her.

"Hmm." She transferred the coffee to the machine, touched the on button and turned to face him. "I suppose you're spending a good deal of time with Erica," she said. "How is she coping after that disturbing incident?"

He was surprised that she mentioned Erica. "It was more than disturbing to her. Jason could have been killed and she feels responsible."

"That, of course, is silly. But I suspect she's the kind of person who considers the bonds of friendship as binding almost as marriage, especially since she's had a relationship with Jason Rowland for years."

As the coffeemaker hissed and burbled, he leaned

against the counter, crossing his feet at the ankles. "You're right. I couldn't have said it any better myself…and I've only known her a short time." He paused, and then asked flatly, "How long have you known her, Mom?"

"Is Erica the important reason you needed to talk to me?"

"Erica and I ran into Miranda Quinlan at a restaurant. She's a friend of yours, I believe."

"I wouldn't say we're friends, but I see her occasionally." Lillian busied herself taking down two cups, pulling napkins from a drawer, finding a tray. "It's Morton who's closer to the Quinlans. He plays golf with Charlie."

"Come on, Mom. I remember Miranda coming to our house when you were having one of your luncheons or bridge gatherings. Muffy Quinlan and I were in school together and you hosted a tea for her when she graduated."

"Heavens, that was years ago. I see Miranda only occasionally now."

"Occasionally enough that you felt confident in recommending Erica and her art to Miranda, who just happened to be chairing the committee for the symphony gala."

"My, you have been busy, haven't you?"

"And with your recommendation, it was a done deal."

The coffeemaker beeped. Lillian turned, lifted the decanter and poured two cups of coffee. "Why don't we take this to the sunroom," she suggested.

Without a word, Hunter picked up the tray and followed her, knowing if she wanted to go to the sunroom, she felt the need for a cigarette. She wasn't as unconcerned about talking about Erica as she managed to appear. Sure enough, she lit up as soon as they were settled, Hunter standing at the French doors and Lillian perched on the edge of the rattan couch.

"I'll just cut to the chase, Mom. Miranda dropped a

bombshell that night. She said you were directly responsible for Erica being tapped for the symphony gala. She said you were instrumental in the *Texas Today* thing. She said you steered your friends to Erica's shop every chance you got. In short, she said you've been a very active benefactor in Erica's career for years."

"Miranda talks too much."

"Is it true, Mom?"

"Some artists would appreciate a little boost occasionally."

Hunter saw no point arguing that she'd done more than a little and more often than occasionally. He wanted to get to the reason for her "occasional boosts." "Some artists might, but since you did all this without her knowledge…or consent, Erica considers it interference. She's upset and bewildered. Her confidence in herself and her art is shaken. Why did you do it, Mom? What possible reason could you have for helping someone who's a total stranger to you? Or is Erica Stewart a stranger to you?"

She got up from the couch to pace the floor. "You were always a persistent child," she told him, waving at a cloud of smoke. "So stubborn…like your father. Once that man got an idea, he was like a dog with a bone. You inherited that gene and I suppose it's an asset, but sometimes I wish you were less…determined." She stopped and fiddled with an arrangement of camellias floating in a bowl. "From the time you were a little boy, if you became interested in something or if you'd get an idea—no matter how far-out or bizarre it was—you'd throw yourself into it with a passion."

"Mom, we're not talking about me. This is about Erica."

She sighed and moved to the window. "Yes, she's your passion now. I knew how it would be if you ever fell in love and I was right. Determined. Obsessed. Utterly focused. It was too late from the moment you met her."

Would he ever get a straight answer from her? he wondered. "Too late for what?" he demanded in frustration.

"Too late to talk you out of it. Too late to keep you from going all the way with your obsession." She spoke with a hint of temper, but it fizzled almost instantly. Her expression turned pensive, almost sad. She watched a young Hispanic outside servicing the pool, but her thoughts seemed elsewhere. "Too late to go back and change…" It was a murmur, almost as if she spoke to herself, not Hunter.

She stopped, seemed to catch herself, and then with a quick drag on her cigarette, she turned back to him. "This is one time when your persistence is not going to get results, Hunter. I'm sorry. I really am, considering your personal interest now. But I've said all I intend to say about Erica."

He stood for a long moment studying her, trying to decide what other tactic he might use to break through the wall of her stubbornness. "She was upset when she saw your brooch, Mom. It took only a glance at it the night of the symphony and she recreated it in her sketchbook in flawless detail. I find that…odd. More than coincidence. Yet you claim she'd never seen it before."

"It's a unique piece," Lillian said. "She has the eye of an artist. Artists note details."

"You sound as if you know her," he said, more baffled than ever.

She shrugged…and smoked. And said nothing. "Would it matter to you that she was attacked last night? That someone tried to kill her?"

He saw instantly that it did matter. She had turned, was now staring at him in shock. "What are you saying?"

"Erica was attacked leaving her shop last night. She would have been murdered except that a homeless man she'd befriended was nearby and ran to help her."

"Oh, my God."

"Luckily, the attacker didn't have a gun. For some reason, he used wire or a thin rope or cord. Whatever it was, it wasn't left at the crime scene."

Lillian's hand went to her throat. "When was this?"

"Last night. I've just come from the hospital." He glanced down at himself. "You had it right when you said it looked as if I'd slept in my clothes. I stayed with Erica. She was terrified."

She nodded vaguely at that, then said, "I mean, what time did it happen?"

He frowned, wondering at the question. "After eleven, near midnight. Why?"

"Is she all right?" Lillian asked. "Was she badly hurt? Where is she now?"

"Still at the hospital. She's pretty shaken up, which is understandable. It was a horrifying thing to have happen."

"Yes, of course. Terrible. You think it was a man?"

"We're certain it was a man. Not many women would have that kind of strength." He found something odd in her reaction. Considering her dislike of Erica, polite sympathy was about all he'd expected from her, not this spate of questions for exact details. "She put up a good fight, but the only reason she survived was that he was interrupted."

"Interrupted," she murmured.

"Yeah. It was a close call. You should see the marks on her throat. Another few seconds and—" He stopped. "But luckily the homeless guy intervened, otherwise we'd be planning a funeral today."

Now her hands were pressed to her cheeks and she looked ready to pass out. He moved toward her with concern. "You should sit down, Mom. Do you feel faint? Are you okay?" When she didn't answer, he took her arm, and as he guided her back to the couch, he realized she was trembling. He squatted down in front of her and took both her hands, rubbing them briskly. "Sit right here for a minute. I'll get something…."

He walked quickly to the den and found brandy in Morton's well-stocked bar. As he poured it, he puzzled over the way she'd reacted. Her questions were normal enough, but something wasn't right, although he couldn't quite pinpoint it.

When he reached the sunroom, he found she had apparently recovered her composure enough to be on her feet. She was again standing at the windows. He offered the brandy and she took it, but she wasn't quite able to conceal the tremor of her hand as she raised it to her lips.

"I'm sorry," he said. "I shouldn't have been so graphic in telling what happened."

She waved that away without a word. "You say a homeless man intervened," she said, turning once more so that her back was to him. "The police must consider that a lucky break. He'll be able to identify him."

"It doesn't look like that'll happen," Hunter told her. "Apparently, he has trouble separating reality and fantasy. Like a lot of street people, he's mentally ill."

He watched as she stood silently at the window, holding the brandy with both unsteady hands. He waited, hoping that she might now explain her connection to Erica. But, once again, she seemed miles away, caught up in her own thoughts.

"Mom, it's not just because I'm curious that I'm bugging you about the mystery of your connection to Erica," he said, pressing on. "God knows, you made it plain from the start that you didn't like her and you didn't want me getting involved with her. At that time, I wanted to know why because I intend to marry her. Now someone wants to kill her and nobody has a clue why."

He paused, hoping she'd say something, but she stayed stonily silent, gazing at the glistening surface of the pool.

"Erica has lived an almost monastic life since losing her husband and baby nine years ago," Hunter said, doggedly continuing. "She has no enemies, no stalker, no one has threatened her. So, the only way to figure out who's trying to kill her is to follow what few threads there are that might turn up a clue. One of those threads is your interest in Erica's career. You can see that when you clam up on me, it makes me wonder what you're hiding."

She finished the brandy, turned, set the glass on a table and finally looked at him. "Why do you have to know every little thing, Hunter? Isn't it enough to know that I had nothing to do with the attempt on Erica's life? I'm as shocked and horrified as her own mother must be over this, so you'll have to focus your attention on another thread."

"Then how about this thread," he said, determined to rattle her. "Last night, a couple of hours after the attack when she was finally settling down in the hospital, she said something that I haven't been able to put out of my mind. It was when she thought she was dying at the hands of that madman. She said that she saw her baby's face."

"I really don't want to hear any more, Hunter." Lillian leaned over and stubbed out her cigarette.

"Humor me, there's more."

Lillian was pale but stoic, as if bracing for a body blow. "Here's the part that really floored me, Mom." He watched her closely. "Erica also saw your face in the car."

Her lips barely moved when she asked, "What car?"

"The car that struck her husband and baby and then left them dying at the scene."

There was a moment of stark silence. And then Lillian reached instinctively for her cigarettes. Hunter waited while, taking her time, she lit up, inhaled and moved again to the window. "She'd been given a sedative, I assume," she said.

"Yes. I believe her defenses were down as a result of the narcotic. For nine years, she's blocked the scraps of memory that might have helped the police track down whoever it was. So I told myself the same thing, that she was doped up. Had to be, because how else would she come up with a remark so bizarre?"

"Because the two of you are spending so much time obsessing over what you see as my interference in her career?" Lillian's arms were again locked tight about her middle, but she held his gaze steadily.

"Mom, is there anything you'd like to tell me? Because now is the time. I don't like the way my thoughts are going here."

"Do you honestly think I would be involved in an attempt to kill the woman you've fallen in love with?" Lillian asked baldly.

"You tell me, Mom."

"Please, Hunter. I want you to go now." Her lips trembled and he saw that she had tears in her eyes.

He was shaking his head. He couldn't let it go. "This is something so bad that I can't begin to get my head around it. But it makes a kind of crazy sense. If, God forbid, you were in that car and felt some responsibility for the death of Erica's husband and baby, you might try to make amends by helping her in her career. It would have to be done secretly. You couldn't let her know what you were doing. That would be admitting guilt."

"I wouldn't try to kill her!" she cried.

"No, but maybe Morton would."

She stared at him, white-faced. "I have nothing more to say, Hunter."

"My God." In spite of his suspicions, he was stunned.

He began pacing in agitation. "If what I'm thinking is true, I'm responsible for the attack in a way. I've been keeping you posted on Erica's returning memory, telling you that she's ever so close to seeing the killer. That she's painting stuff that will eventually tell the truth." He stopped, looking at her accusingly. "And you've been feeding it all to Morton, haven't you, Mom?"

"You have to go, Hunter!"

"Where is he? In his aerie in that tall building where he's king of all he surveys?"

"Please, Hunter…"

"Was he driving, Mom? Did he plow into them and just drive away?"

Holding on to the back of a tall chair, she shook her head, tears streaming.

"Have you kept his secret all these years?"

She gazed straight ahead, her lips clamped tight.

"You can help me bring him down if you'll just tell me what you know."

"No." It was a whimper.

"Not even to clear my suspicion that you might have been involved in the deaths of a man and a little baby? My own mother? That's vehicular homicide, Mom. My God, talk to me."

She turned and looked directly at him. "No," she said stonily, but there was despair in her eyes. "Please. I want you to go."

With no other choice, he turned and left.

Isabel rooted around in Erica's suitcase and finally came up with a pair of jeans and a red knit pullover. "How about these? The neckline on the shirt is low enough so that it won't irritate your throat." She passed both to Erica, who was dressing in the bathroom. "Do you need anything else?"

"No, I'm good. Lord, I almost fainted when I saw myself in this mirror. Why didn't someone tell me I was looking like Dracula's wife?"

"Because it would be a lie, sugar." Jason sat on the bed, studying her chart. "You're beautiful even in dishabille. You want to see Dracula's wife, look at me. I swear, these bruises will be on my face forever."

Erica came out of the bathroom. "No, they won't. They're fading fast. And thanks for bringing my suitcase. By the way, you didn't drive over here with those fingers still bandaged like that, did you?"

"I'm not driving and actually it was Phillip who brought me." He turned a page in her chart.

She raised an eyebrow. "Really?"

"Uh-huh. He claims he felt terrible about the way he'd skulked away after my attack and wanted to make amends. You can imagine my surprise when I opened the door and there he was, offering pizza and an apology."

Erica picked up the shirt she'd been wearing when they brought her to the hospital and began folding it. "Did you forgive him?"

"Not until he added that he'd admitted to my dad to being with me the night I was attacked. It remains to be seen whether he's still the golden boy at the firm." He replaced her chart in its cubbyhole on the wall. "But, as they say, some of the bloom is off the rose, if you know what I mean."

"No kidding?" She paused in the act of folding the capris she'd worn.

"He has this annoying habit of bouncing one knee when he's just sitting and watching TV. It can be irritating. And he pops too many breath mints. Also, he sort of hums under his breath when he's on edge. Which is a lot."

Erica nodded. "Uptight."

"Nervous Nellie."

Isabel had been listening with amused interest. "Phillip works at your father's law firm?"

"Phillip works for Jason's dad," Erica replied, smiling into Jason's eyes.

"I've decided they have a lot in common."

Isabel laughed, and then let her smile go. "I haven't had a chance to tell you how distressed I was that you were hurt, Jason. I just hope the police soon figure out who this person is before he does any more harm."

"I'm counting on Hunter to figure it out," Jason said, glancing at his watch. "He gave me strict instructions not to let you leave with your mother, Erica." He sent Isabel an apologetic look. "I'm sorry, Isabel, but if you stop and think about it, we can't be certain that you and your children wouldn't be in jeopardy if Erica were staying at your house. This guy has proved he's one bad dude."

"That's true, Mom," Erica said. "And I appreciate you offering."

"I realize Hunter's plan to take you to the ranch is wise. But I just can't help worrying about you, darling," Isabel said, gently stroking a hand over her hair. "You've been through so much."

Jason flung himself into the only chair in the room. "If we could just figure out what motivates this sleaze!"

Erica looked at these two people who truly loved her and felt so blessed. "Please try not to worry, both of you. Hunter's right. At the moment, I'm safer at the ranch than anywhere else. And I'm going to be careful," she said hoping to hide the worst of her fears—and her suspicions—from both her mother and Jason. She knew, deep in her heart, that she had figured out the mystery—or most of it. But at this point she hadn't figured out what to do with what she knew.

Twenty-Seven

In the twenty-six years that Lillian had been married to Morton, she had never dropped in to see him during office hours. As CEO, he was untouchable while engaged with the lofty demands of CentrexO. His position and his work arena were sacrosanct. And for all these years, she had honored his command. Today, all that would end.

Hunter had hardly been out of sight when she'd gone directly to her bedroom, packed a bag, changed into a pair of slacks and a cream silk shirt and, with hands that trembled, carefully repaired her makeup. She did not intend to show Morton a tear-streaked face. And within an hour, she was on her way to confront him.

Hunter's reference to an aerie was apt, she thought, but she barely paused to acknowledge Giselle before stepping past the astonished woman and abruptly opening the door that bore Morton's name. Had he been in a meeting, it would have been awkward. But she was determined.

He was not in a meeting, but he was on the phone. His chair was swiveled around so that he faced a wall of floor-to-ceiling windows that offered a stunning panoramic view of downtown Houston. She thought vaguely that it was probably understandable how Morton's ego had inflated in the years since he'd assumed his position at the helm of CentrexO. How could it not, with him living and working in such grand style? He turned then and looked at her in blank surprise. It was a moment before he ended the call, but his eyes—hard and cold—never left hers.

When he disconnected, he stood up with a look of extreme irritation. "Lillian. What is the meaning of this?"

"You'd better sit down, Morton. When you hear what I have to say, you may need the support of your chair."

He ignored that. Bracing himself with his hands on the desk, he leaned forward slightly, looking at her suspiciously. "Have you been drinking?"

"Actually, I have had a brandy, but only one. And it was over an hour ago when I came close to fainting. Trust me, I needed it."

He glanced beyond her at the closed door of his office. "How did you get in here? I have strict rules—"

"I pulled rank, Morton. I told the security guard who I was and that I wanted to see you. I can only assume he thought your instructions to keep all riffraff away from you didn't include me." She wanted a cigarette but decided against it. She planned to do this with no crutch. "As for the receptionist, I'm afraid she was taken by surprise. While she was still collecting herself, I zoomed past her and—" she spread her hands "—here I am."

"If you're not drunk, you must have taken some of those pills you've got stashed all over the house."

"No, Morton, I'm totally sober and thinking straight." She sighed, weakening a moment as she rubbed her forehead in despair. "This is a terrible, terrible day. Only one other in my life was worse, I think." She was shaking her head. "Hunter just left our house," she told him.

His face twisted with disgust. "Hunter again. I might

have guessed. What is it this time? Has he set a date to marry that artist? Or has he eloped with her? I guess you would consider it terrible, but frankly I don't see why it's such a big deal. How many times do I have to say to you, get over it, Lillian."

She let him talk, watching his face, studying the look in his eyes, but for the life of her, she couldn't see anything except his usual impatience with her and a complete absence of any remorse for the horrific thing they'd done. And for the widening ring of sickening consequences.

"Where were you between 11:00 p.m. and midnight last night, Morton?"

"What the hell are you talking about? We went to bed together last night. We had sex, but sounds like you were too far gone to remember it. I know you knocked back a lot of gin, but…Jesus, are you having blackouts now?"

"You thought I'd remember—and I do—because we so seldom touch each other that way anymore, do we, Morton?"

He seemed to relent a bit. "We'll remedy that now. We'll have more time for each other when we reach my assignment."

She moved to one tall window and, with a pang, immediately picked out one of Hunter's buildings. "You haven't answered my question."

"I thought I did." He gave in again to his temper. "And now I want to know why you're asking such a fucking stupid question."

"Hunter—"

"Hunter again! Goddamn it, just let me have it in plain words."

"Hunter came to see me this morning. He wanted an explanation about why I have done so much to assist Erica Stewart's career."

"What kind of cockamamie shit is this? You don't even know the woman."

"I don't have to know her to help her. I recommended her to the symphony gala committee chair, Miranda Quinlan, and she was in. I called a contact at *Texas Today* and sent Erica's résumé for consideration when they were working up the list of Twenty Women to Watch." She saw him looking at her in astonishment and felt a little spurt of triumph that she'd bested him, for once. "I used your name, Morton. Fortunately, it carries quite a lot of weight. I've steered dozens of women to her shop, too. And when I heard that the *Chronicle* was doing a feature on businesses in the Village, I called and used your name to suggest Erica's shop and her art as unique and worthy of recognition."

"Bullshit! I don't believe you."

She gave a mirthless chuckle. "Believe me. I did it and it was such a paltry effort at making amends. For nine years, I've made it my business to know where she was, what she was doing, how she was coming along. I couldn't be more pleased with her success if she was my own d-daughter." Her voice broke, but she lifted her chin and met his eyes defiantly. "So, I'll ask you again, Morton. I know you weren't in the house last night, because contrary to what you may think, drinking to excess doesn't necessarily lead to a good night's sleep. I was aware of you getting up and leaving. So, since you weren't at home, where were you?"

"Working. I'd been away from the office, off and on, for almost a week, if you recall. I couldn't sleep so I left and came here."

"I hope you can prove it."

"Why would I need to prove it?"

"Because someone tried to murder Erica last night." She

watched him closely and saw nothing on his face, not even a slight change of expression in his eyes. Nothing. What had she expected? That he'd confess? That, with everything at stake, he'd simply nod his head and say yes, you're right, I did it. Morton, she knew, had long ago learned to play his cards close to his chest.

"She was working late," she told him. "Someone waited until she went out into the alley behind her shop where her car was parked, overpowered her and tried to strangle her. It was a hideous, horrific act of unspeakable violence. Only a monster would do something like that."

Midway through her description of the attempt on Erica's life, Morton had taken a seat in his big chair, kicked back and clasped his hands behind his head as she talked. He seemed almost amused by her unusual display of courage. "So why are we discussing it?"

"Tell me you didn't do it, Morton," she pleaded. "Please tell me you aren't that depraved. That after twenty-six years as your wife, I'm not married to a…a monster."

He laughed cynically. "You personally have done very well for someone who's married to a monster, haven't you?"

"Did you try to kill her, Morton?"

"Artists are flakey. They're jealous of one another. Jealousy makes people do crazy things. I wouldn't be surprised if somebody tried to eliminate the competition. It happens."

She realized with a sinking heart that he wasn't going to deny it. "You tried it Saturday night, because Hunter believes her memory of the accident is returning. But that didn't work. It was Jason who opened the door and not Erica. I had a horrible suspicion…and so did Jocelyn, but neither of us could quite believe you would be so evil."

Suddenly, all vestige of laid-back nonchalance was gone. He sat up. "You've talked to Jocelyn about this?"

"Only about the incident with Jason. We could never bring ourselves to say it out loud, but yes, Jocelyn is suspicious. She'll be even more so when she finds out a second attempt has been made on Erica's life."

"It was a burglary attempt, Lillian. The house was empty. It was a crime of opportunity. There's no proof it was anything else."

"You said you were on the yacht, but I spoke to a crew member. He said you went ashore Saturday and returned sometime before daylight."

He was on his feet now, livid with rage. She had a moment of concern for the crew member, but it was Hunter he focused on. "And you discussed this with Hunter? Are you out of your fucking mind?"

"No, I didn't discuss it with Hunter. He's suspicious and he had a hundred questions, but I refused to tell him anything."

"He'll probably put it together," he muttered, pacing furiously. He shot her a killing glance. "If I know you, the truth was probably written all over your face. And now that he thinks he's got something, he'll probably be here next, the asshole. But he won't find me as accommodating as you were."

"What will he put together, Morton? Are you saying you did it?"

"I'm saying we've got a problem and there's only one way it can be taken care of. I can't very well hire a hit man, can I?" His tone was filled with disgust. "How would I do that without incriminating us all even more? I have to fix this myself."

"It can't be fixed, Morton," she cried. "Don't you see that? And certainly not the way you want to fix it. It's wrong. It's evil. How can you face yourself in a mirror?"

"Oh, shut up! Look, Lillian, I'm going to say this only

once and I want you to hear me well. Do not share your crazy suspicions with another living soul…and that includes Jocelyn and Hunter. Do not mention Erica Stewart's name to anyone, do you hear me? To anyone! If just a whisper of your ramblings ever got out, everything we've worked for will be destroyed in a heartbeat. Do you understand that?"

"Hunter is going to marry her, Morton." Her eyes were filled now. With her heart as heavy as lead in her chest, she asked, "What are you going to do, catch her at a vulnerable moment—perhaps the wedding—and try again?"

He waved that aside in disgust. "This is a goddamn fiasco. I should have divorced your ass years ago."

"I suppose we've both thought that many times over the years, haven't we?" She turned and headed for the door. She had to leave, to think what to do next. In his desperation, Morton was dangerous. She knew now he would stop at nothing, even murder. With her hand on the doorknob, she turned back. "I won't let you do it, Morton. That's what I came to say. I've kept quiet for nine years and I just can't bear it another minute."

His face went dark with fury. "What are you saying?"

"I'm going to stop you, Morton." She opened the door.

"Lillian, hold up! Wait a minute!" He rounded the desk in long strides, but she stood straight and looked him dead in the eye.

"If you follow me out of this office, I'll tell anybody who happens to be listening what I think you've done and you'll probably have a lot of trouble explaining it. As you've said to me for months now, just a hint of scandal will put an end to your dreams." She glanced into the astonished eyes of Giselle, but ignored her and faced him again. "I'm tired of living under your thumb, Morton. I'm tired of your arrogance, tired of your everlasting selfishness. I'm tired of being a doormat, of failing to speak up when it mattered. Most of all, I'm tired of living a lie."

She walked out past a gaping Giselle at a fast clip. Morton followed, struggling to maintain a composed demeanor in front of his assistant. When he paused at her desk, Lillian seized the opportunity to dart into the elevator. "I'll see my wife to her car, Giselle," he told her with only a slightly strained smile. "Cancel my appointments for the rest of the day, please."

"No," Lillian said sharply, giving Morton a warning look. "I'm perfectly capable of finding the lobby on my own."

Hanging on to his composure by a thread, Morton gave a look that promised retribution of the harshest kind. Still, with her threat to blurt out everything, he had no choice but to let her go.

After an eternity, the elevator doors closed. Let him try to spin his way out of this, she thought darkly. But Lord, what must his precious assistant think after witnessing the ugly scene? If she hadn't been so scared, she'd almost find it funny. With her heart pounding in her chest, she was weak-kneed when the elevator reached the lobby. Stepping out, she breathed deeply, trying to compose herself. Trying to think. Morton would be like a cornered animal, dangerous and predatory, so she couldn't go home.

There was only one place she could go now.

Stupid bitch. Pathetic lush obsessing over ancient history. Morton stormed into the house, taking the stairs two at a time, and kicked the bedroom door open, slamming it against the wall with a resounding crash. He took a wild-eyed look around, but he'd known in his gut he'd find the place empty. Lillian was headed for that goddamn ranch to cry on Colson's shoulder. To blab everything. By God, it pissed him off that he had to deal with that shit when his house was burning down.

He was enraged that her crazy-assed ranting and raving threatened to screw up everything. The way she was talking, if she got to Jocelyn, there's no telling what could happen. Standing in the sumptuous master suite marked with his wife's flair for style and gracious living, he took a minute to curse the fact that he was forced to live with two loony females. He didn't doubt he could bring both women around, but was that the best solution, all things considered? Jocelyn knew who made her cushy lifestyle possible and he didn't see her as willing to give it up. Lillian was the problem, now she'd got this wild bug up her ass. She'd lost her chance to stand on principle long ago and he wasn't willing to step aside and let her take them all down. Hell, no.

Bottom line, Hunter was the wild card here.

Driven by a keen instinct for survival, his brain worked furiously. He had to stop this train before it got to the station.

Erica sat beside Hunter in the car, her face turned to the side as she took in the roll and sweep of the hill country, still lush and bright green in early summer. Within a month, the hills would be sweltering in the relentless Texas sun. But for now, cattle grazed on tender grass while wisely drifting toward a sprawling live oak, where they congregated in its shade like a gaggle of people at a church social. Watching them, Erica mentally composed a painting, something whimsical and fun, she decided. God knows, there was precious little whimsy in her life at the moment.

She turned to look at Hunter, who had been unusually quiet as he drove. It troubled her that he'd put his work and his life on hold on her behalf. She was grateful, but she didn't intend to allow that kind of sacrifice to go on too long. Besides, when she revealed what she suspected, depending on his reaction, the choice might be taken out of her hands. She faced the road again, pondering the problem.

It wasn't only Hunter's reaction yet to be revealed, but her own. Oh, she'd fallen in love with Hunter, she had no doubt about that anymore. But she didn't see how she could get beyond the fact that his family was responsible for David and Danielle's death. How could she *live* with that? She moved her gaze to the horizon. She couldn't just ignore what she now knew. She needed closure—deserved it—but there would be a price to be paid. By Hunter's family. What would he think—what would he do—when he learned what she planned?

What would she do?

Ahead of them, a tractor pulled onto the road. Hunter showed no impatience at the inconvenience and slowed to a snail's pace as it chugged along. It made her think he was as caught up in his thoughts as she.

"When you drive up into the hill country like this," she said, "you can understand why people fantasize about having a place here. It's so peaceful. The energy that drives us while we're in the city seems kind of ridiculous."

"Tell me." He slowed more as the tractor pulled off the road. "I've often thought of running my business from the ranch. In fact, this could be an opportunity to try it. If it works, I'd like to cut my time in Houston in half."

"If that's what you want and it does work out, then at least something good will have come of this."

"Much good will come of this," he said, as if to convince her and maybe himself. After a moment, he looked over at her and frowned. "You've been quiet. Is your throat bothering you?"

She touched a tender spot. "Not too much. It looks worse than it is." She paused, taking a sip of water from a bottle. "Does Hank know that he's about to have house guests for who knows how long?"

"He does. I called when we stopped for gas and you went inside to buy water. It wouldn't matter if we called or not. He's used to me coming and going without any notice."

"And your sister is staying there, too?"

"Either there or with Kelly. Since they're working together, they'll be tight. At any rate, there's a separate cabin that'll sleep six, bunkhouse style. It's used mostly by the extra hands Hank hires to harvest his pecans. It's private, but I'd feel better if we stayed in the big house." He caught her hand and held it. "I know you've been through an ordeal and I don't want to add more stress, but I'll feel better if I can keep an eye on you. I don't expect anybody to breach ranch security, but I'm not willing to take any chances."

She withdrew her hand to pick up the water bottle. "I just don't want to inconvenience you or Hank too much."

"It would never be an inconvenience having you in my home," he told her.

He might have a very different view after today, she thought. He was silent then for so long that she turned to look at him. He was frowning, as if mulling over something he wanted to say. "What is it?" she asked.

He drew in a breath, hesitating. "There's something I need to tell you, Erica."

Later, Lillian wouldn't recall how she'd managed to exit the high-rise garage after leaving Morton's office, then find her way out of the business district as she searched for the on-ramp to the interstate. She had always known that Morton was both cruel and ruthless, but she was aghast that he'd go so far as to commit murder to keep their dark secret buried.

She was not much better than Morton, she thought bitterly as she headed for the ranch. If she'd done the right thing, none of this would have happened and her conscience would be clear. Almost. Instead, for nine years she had avoided facing her part in the tragedy that was now going to destroy them all. She'd thrown herself into her role as wife to Morton, she had involved herself in Houston's social scene and the arts, she had—God help her—tirelessly sought ways to assist Erica's career. In the end, what did it mean? Nothing, compared to the loss of a husband and baby.

And now Hunter knew.

Tears of despair blurred the long stretch of road in front of her. He would despise her. He had fallen in love with Erica. He was going to marry her. It was God's punishment.

Ten miles down the road to the ranch, she was so distraught that she didn't realize a large vehicle had moved up very close behind. Only when the driver leaned on his horn did she glance into the rearview mirror. Her eyes went wide. Now he was swerving into the left lane, coming up alongside her. When he failed to pass, she glanced over quickly and realized the driver had lowered the window. It was Morton! He'd followed her.

She wondered how he'd managed to catch up with her so quickly. Now he was gesturing, letting her know that he wanted her to pull over. She actually slowed down, then it dawned on her that the secondary road to the ranch was virtually deserted, even at midday. If she stopped, she wasn't sure what he would do. With her rebellion, everything he valued was in jeopardy. He would want to talk her out of it. And if he couldn't, what would he do? Force her? But how?

A chill ran over her as panic set in. She sped up, wincing as he lay on his horn. He was infuriated, wild that she was ignoring a direct order. But she was through knuckling under to Morton. Another glance in the mirror and she saw he had fallen behind. But, moments later he was again crowding close, almost touching her rear bumper.

Her grip tightened on the steering wheel as he slammed into her car from behind. He was going to try to force her off the road! She knew a moment of absolute terror as she fought to keep the car steady. The pavement was narrow. If she skidded onto the soft shoulders, she would lose control. She might survive a crash, but she knew she wouldn't survive whatever Morton had in mind. He fell behind, as if to give her a chance to pull over, and when she didn't, he slammed into the rear of her car again.

Terrified, she began to pray. She wanted to cry, but a tiny spark of something—courage? outrage?—stirred in her. She had been party to a horrendous crime, but she wanted to make amends. True, it was high time, but it was not too late…yet. If he destroyed her—and she knew somehow he would if he managed to get his hands on her—he would escape unscathed. What would be Jocelyn's fate once that happened?

Please don't let it happen.

Twenty-Eight

"Let's stop here," Hunter said, spotting the sign indicating a roadside rest stop. "I don't need to be driving when I tell you this." He exited and parked in the area designated for cars. Several huge live oaks offered shade and the illusion of tranquillity. Beyond the trees, a small lake sparkled in the late afternoon sun. Hunter paused beside one of the picnic tables, brushed off the bench and waited while Erica sat down. Straddling the bench, he faced her, then hesitated, as if getting his thoughts together.

"I talked to my mother this morning. She didn't deny doing all those things to boost your career, but no matter how I pushed, she wouldn't explain why she'd singled you out of all the artists she could have helped. She was pretty upset with me when I left."

"So you just let it go? You just gave up?"

"I almost wish I had," he said. "This is a bad time for my mother. I hope, when you hear, you'll—" He hesitated, letting his gaze roam over her face. "For years, I wondered why she didn't divorce Morton. At home, with nobody around but Jocelyn or me, he was disrespectful. He never missed a chance to bully her, to remind her of her place…which was insignificant. He was the big cheese. She was…window dressing.

"Of course, they appeared to be the perfect couple to the rest of the world." He made a short, contemptuous sound. "And he managed to convince everyone that they were perfect. You saw him at the symphony gala. He's good. But it's a joke. I wondered for years why a woman would put up with that. Just walk out, I told her. Divorce him." He looked sadly thoughtful. "She didn't welcome anybody—including me—giving her advice."

Erica sat silent, watching ducks paddling in the lake.

"My mother and I were once very close," he went on, his gaze on the lake. "It baffled me when she changed from a really warm and affectionate mom to a closed-up, neurotic shadow of the person she used to be." He shifted his gaze back to Erica. "I used to wonder what it was about Morton that made her prefer somebody who treated her like that."

He went quiet again as a family in a minivan pulled into the rest area. Both watched as a toddler was unbuckled from his car seat. "You're wondering what all this has to do with you and your art."

She was afraid she knew, but all she said was "Yes."

"I wish I didn't have to tell you how it all ties together, Erica." He shifted on the bench, locking an elbow around one knee. "I knew from my mother's reaction when I first mentioned your name that there was something about you, something that she feared. It was clear that she didn't like you when it would seem the two of you had so much in common. You're an artist, her passion is art. But she kept denying it when I wanted to know why. And all the while, a number of little things that seemed to link my family with you kept cropping up. Next thing I know, Jocelyn freaks out on seeing us together. I asked myself what in the heck was going on. And then you told me about David and Danielle."

She sat grim-faced, her gaze still fixed on the lake.

"I didn't immediately connect Jason's assault with all this, but when Miranda Quinlan revealed my mother's interest in your career and then somebody tried to kill you, it all came together."

She was watching the small family amble down to the lake at a pace the toddler could manage. "It was your mother in the car," she whispered, tears blurring her vision.

Looking desolate, he rubbed a hand over his face. "How long have you known?"

She touched the corners of her eyes. "I'm not sure. It's been like a painting with blank spaces that I keep returning to, filling in." She turned away from the sight of the family. "A little here, a bit there, and suddenly there's a whole picture."

"Yeah."

"I couldn't believe it at first," she said. "I didn't want to believe it. I'm glad you figured it out. I didn't want to be the one to tell you that your mother—"

"I don't think it was my mother," he said, interrupting her. "I think Morton's responsible and I think it was Morton who attacked you last night. I think he was the one who was waiting in your apartment and got Jason instead of you."

She considered it. "You said all this to your mother?"

He nodded. "Yes. And she acted outraged that I'd come up with something so terrible, but I could see she was just…devastated. The more I pushed, the more she stonewalled. She absolutely refused to admit anything. But it's the only thing that makes any sense, Erica."

"So you just left, leaving Morton to keep on trying to kill me?"

"No. I called Detective Sullivan and told him what I suspected. I could tell he had his doubts. He thought I was reaching to suggest Morton with his sterling reputation would actually try to kill anybody."

"It is hard to believe," she murmured. "Assuming he managed to get me, how would he get away with it?"

"I don't know. He's smart and crafty. He's survived in a corporate environment where it's easy to get eaten alive, and he has a dream job waiting for him as a U.S. ambassador. The only thing that could screw that up is your returning memory. As the only witness to the hit-and-run, once you tell what happened, everything's wiped out, his reputation, his marriage, his life. I told all that to Sullivan and he was still skeptical."

He shifted, straightening on the bench so that he faced her directly. "Here's what concerns me. If my mother has gone to Morton and told him what I said, he'll be desperate to eliminate the threat of exposure. That makes him dangerous. He's proved he'll do anything to save himself, including murder."

"If that's true, aren't you worried about your mother? She shares his secret."

"And Jocelyn. I think she knows, too."

Ah. The logical explanation for his sister's reaction when she arrived at the ranch and found them together, Erica thought. She stood up, giving a last swipe at tearstained cheeks. When she spoke, her voice was clear. "In that case, I think we should get back on the road. Once you've dropped me off at the ranch, you can decide what you need to do to protect your mother and your sister."

If he expected more concern on her part for his mother, she was sorry. She didn't feel much of anything for the woman except a deep, seething anger that had festered alongside her grief.

"Erica…"

Reluctantly, she turned and met his eyes.

"I love you."

She loved him, too. But she feared there would be nothing left for them after today. Without realizing it, she'd been the central character in a macabre charade of secrecy and lies for nine years, thanks to his mother and Morton Trask. Only when they'd been made to pay would she be able to put her life back together.

And so, when she didn't reply, he touched her elbow and together they walked back to the car.

Lillian was an emotional wreck when she reached the ranch. Ordinarily, she was cautious behind the wheel, but she drove the last half mile as if the devil himself was on her heels. Which she knew was a definite possibility. Hank, watching from the porch, was down the steps and on his way to meet her just as she brought the car to a sliding stop and flung open the door. She tumbled out and literally fell into his arms, trembling all over.

"What's wrong, Lily?" he asked, shocked at the look of her.

"It's Morton! Oh, my God, it's Morton." With both hands fisted in his shirtfront, she clung to him, casting a nervous glance behind her.

"Here, here, darlin'…" He took her by the arm and led her to the porch steps. "Let's get inside and you can tell me what this is all about."

She sent another panicked look at the road. "He could be coming any minute, Hank. My God, he's lost his mind. I shouldn't have told him what I was going to do. I should have known. God, I should have known."

He had her on the porch now, and with an arm around her waist pushed the door open and urged her inside. She was still trembling like a leaf. He would have ushered her on toward the den, but she stopped him, clutching at his arm.

"Lock it, Hank. He might be—" She stopped, closed her eyes and took a deep breath. "Would you please call down to the barn and tell Cisco and Earl not to let him on the property? I don't know if he'll follow me right now, but he'll be here sooner or later."

"Lily—"

"Please, Hank." With fingers pressed to her mouth, she was almost sobbing. "Just tell them."

Frowning fiercely, Hank moved to the telephone. "I'll do it, but go over to the couch and sit down. You look like you're ready to fall over."

"I couldn't sit down," she said, running a shaking hand over her hair. "Is Jocelyn here?"

"No, she's with Kelly at a horse auction in San Antonio. They probably won't be back until late tonight."

"Where's Theresa?"

"That grandbaby of hers is sickly. She's at the doctor with her daughter." He pointed to the couch. "Sit. You look ready to drop. Theresa made some gingerbread before she left and there's lemonade to go with it." With another sharp look at her face, he lifted the receiver. "When did you eat last?"

Lemonade and gingerbread. She almost laughed. She was being threatened by a madman and he was suggesting lemonade and gingerbread. "Morton just tried to run me off the pavement, Hank. He would have managed it if a man in a huge truck hadn't come upon us just then." Putting a hand to her throat, she drew in a steadying breath. "Morton was in the wrong lane and was forced off the road himself. That's the only reason I got away."

"Hold it while I dial up Earl on his cell phone." With a

steely look, Hank punched in the number and waited. When it was picked up, he issued orders for both his men to stop anybody entering the ranch. He hung up and turned back to Lillian. "Now, tell me what this is all about."

"My God, where to begin?" she muttered, wishing for a cigarette. She'd left her purse in the car, but she was still too scared to go out and get it. "I've left Morton. I went to his office today and told him. He was furious. I couldn't go home." She drew in an unsteady breath. "I didn't know what he'd do if we were alone. I know now he probably would have killed me. He would have made it look like a suicide or something accidental, of course," she said bitterly, "and considering the habits I've developed over the years, everyone would believe it."

"That's a mighty serious accusation, Lily."

She released a short, mirthless laugh. "When you see the back of my car, you'll see just how serious. It's a miracle—" She stopped, looked over at the bar. "I need a drink, Hank. Something stronger than lemonade. It's going to be hard telling you the despicable thing I've done."

He hesitated, then seeing how shattered she looked, he walked to the bar, located brandy, poured a generous amount into a snifter and handed it to her. All without a word.

"Thank you." Using both hands, she brought it to her lips, keeping a wary eye on the window. "Is your shotgun handy?" When she saw his expression, she added, "In case Morton gets past your men."

"He won't, Lily," he assured her with some impatience. "And why am I going to need to shoot your husband?"

"Because he's become a monster," she said, her eyes filling. "And except for the grace of God, he would be a murderer."

"You think he was trying to kill you by running you off

the road?" He looked mildly skeptical. "Chances of a fatal crash that way are pretty slim, Lily. He's got a mean temper. You two argued, you say. I can imagine when you ran off it got his dander up." He sounded calm and logical. "It was crazy and reckless to try to stop you on a public highway, but Morton can be crazy and reckless. You don't kill somebody that way."

She studied the contents of her glass, wondering how to begin. "Hunter came to see me this morning. He told me that Erica Stewart was in the hospital because last night someone tried to kill her."

"Sweet Jesus," he breathed. "Is she all right? How bad was she hurt?"

"I'm not sure. Hunter said a homeless man saved her life. Thankfully, he didn't just stand by and let it happen. But it was a close call."

"How does this concern you, Lily? And don't tell me you had anything to do with trying to kill her. You couldn't hurt a fly."

She set the glass carefully on the table in front of her. "No, it wasn't me. I couldn't…I wouldn't hurt Erica for anything in the world." She raised her eyes to Hank's. "But Morton would."

His face went slack with surprise.

"It's true. He went over to her office last night and waited for her to lock up. Then when she was going to her car, he caught her from behind and used a rope or a cord and tried to kill her."

She had finally succeeded in shocking him. "You know that for a fact?"

"He as good as admitted it."

"Why would he do something so crazy, for God's sake?"

"Because she can now identify the driver of the car

who struck her husband and baby nine years ago and left them dying on the street."

"It was Morton? He was the—"

Hank paused as the phone rang. With his men set to stop intruders, he was quick to pick up. "It's Earl," he told her. After listening briefly, he moved to the window, checking the road. Rushing to his side, Lillian could see nothing.

Hank covered the receiver. "Jocelyn's at the gate. I guess Earl took me at my word not to let anybody on the property." He turned back to the phone. "Let her in, Earl, but be sure nobody else is in the car with her."

"Is she by herself?" Lillian asked after he hung up.

"Yeah, but he said she seemed real upset."

A minute or so later, the two of them watched as the small convertible materialized out of a cloud of dust on the ranch road. After skidding to a stop behind her mother's Mercedes, Jocelyn flung the car door open and hit the ground running.

"Not only upset, but in a big hurry," Hank observed, narrow-eyed. "Does she know about Morton and the accident?"

"Yes," she murmured, trailing behind him as he headed for the front door to let her in. "And when she hears what I'm about to do, she'll be even more upset."

He looked down at her. "In that case, she can do Morton just as much damage as you. Have you thought about that, Lily?"

She wanted to deny that Morton posed a threat to his own daughter—desperate to deny it—but he'd long ago proved just how cold-blooded he was. Now, with everything at stake, she couldn't be sure what he would do to save himself.

Hank barely had time to throw the bolt on the door and open it before Jocelyn burst inside. She barely spared him a look before zeroing in on her mother. "Mom, I've been trying to call you! Why didn't you answer your phone?"

It was not the greeting Lillian expected. "It's in my purse," she replied. "I left it in my car. What's wrong? Why are you so upset?"

She pushed her hair from her face in agitation. "Dad called me. He was on a tear like you wouldn't believe. Talking crazy. I've never seen him like that."

"Morton? What do you mean? He called you? When? What did he say?" She peered anxiously beyond Jocelyn's shoulder. "Where is he?"

"I don't know." With a shake of her head, Jocelyn dismissed the questions. "I was at the clinic when he called. I didn't see him, but something really weird is going on. What did you do to set him off like that?"

"I came to my senses, that's what," Lillian said, wishing she'd thought to warn Jocelyn. But since everything had happened in such a rush, she'd barely had time to think. "Tell me what he said."

"For one thing, he tried to convince me you're having a mental breakdown. He said—" She stopped as Hank moved to close the door. "Mom, we need to go somewhere else to talk about this."

"We can talk in the den." Lillian turned to head in that direction. "I should have guessed he'd try to get to you and I'm sorry I didn't think to warn you. It's just—" She drew a calming breath. "I blame myself that I didn't think it through before telling him what I meant to do. But thank goodness, he was only talking to you on the phone. He's far more dangerous in person."

"We should talk somewhere else, Mom." Jocelyn spoke distinctly, shooting a look in Hank's direction.

"There's no need for that. Hank knows. Now, come in here. There's so much I need to—"

"You told him?" She planted herself in front of her mother in an accusing stance.

"I did. And it was a profound relief to tell somebody." In the den now, she turned and faced Jocelyn. "I've left Morton."

"What do you mean you've left him?" she demanded, her voice rising. "You can't leave him. You know why."

Hank had followed them into the den. Now, retrieving his hat from the rack, he moved toward the door to leave. "Why don't I let you two talk about this in private? I'll go out and move your cars to the side of the house, get 'em out away from the front steps. And I'll get your purse for you, Lily."

"You don't have to leave, Hank," she said.

"I'll be back in a little while. Do your talking. And Jocelyn—" he gave her a steady look "—calm down and hear your mother out."

As soon as they heard the front door close behind him, Jocelyn faced Lillian. "Mom, what are you doing? Have you really told him everything?"

"Not in so many details, but he knows everything that matters. We—Morton and I—are both guilty of a horrific crime. It was bad enough that that young man and a precious baby were killed, but driving away without stopping makes us guilty of something far worse. I'd like to blame it all on Morton, but it's time I face my own culpability. I could have done the right thing once we got home that day, but I didn't. And I've never been able to forgive myself that I didn't. Because of that, I've never been able to get beyond it. None of us have, Jocelyn."

"So, is it only Hank you've told?" Jocelyn's brain seemed to be working furiously.

"Yes." Moving slowly, looking as if she'd aged in the last few minutes, Lillian sat on the edge of the couch. "But Hunter has guessed."

"What?"

"He's been suspicious from the moment he introduced Erica to me. As of this morning, he finally put it all together." Hearing the sound as Hank started a car up, she turned her gaze to the window, but her thoughts were on that dreadful moment with Hunter. "I don't know how long it would have taken me to get up the courage to put an end to this sorry situation, but after he left—after the way he looked at me!—I realized that I couldn't go on another minute."

"Dad's right, you are going mental," Jocelyn said with a clear absence of sympathy. "You've got to get hold of yourself, Mom. It isn't just your life you're destroying here. What about Dad's appointment? This will screw that up big time."

Lillian laughed shortly. "Is that what he said? Try to talk some sense into your mother? Try to stop her from screwing up his plans for a cushy new life in politics? And how were you going to do that? By reminding me how lucky I am to be the wife of CentrexO's CEO? Or what a happy life I have when my son barely talks to me once a month, and my daughter won't come home even to escape an abusive affair? That's pathetic, but so like him." She gave Jocelyn a sad smile. "I'm sorry, but no. I'm seeing a lawyer tomorrow."

"To get a divorce?"

"No, darling. To tell what I've done. What Morton's done."

"No!" Jocelyn said angrily. "You said you'd never tell. Have you forgotten that? And you made me promise never to tell, either, ever. Now you're saying you've finally got up the nerve to leave Dad and you're just going to make a clean breast of everything, but when you do it, you'll screw up my life! No, damn it, Mom. You can't."

"Oh, Jocelyn, you don't know what he's done," Lillian said, shaking her head. "I'll bet he didn't tell you that, did he?"

"Tell me what? I don't need to know anything except that you're going to try to ease your conscience without thinking what it means to anybody else." Agitation had her pacing back and forth. "Dad said you were going to do this, but I didn't believe him. He said he tried to talk some sense into you today, but you had this wild and crazy idea about making amends to Erica. It's too late to make amends to Erica, Mom. What's done is done. Why can't you just let it stay buried where it belongs? Why do you have to drag it all out? Don't you know what Hunter's going to think? He already hates Dad, so he'll now despise us all." She stopped, almost growling in frustration. "Is that what you want?"

"Did Morton tell you how he tried to talk some sense into me today?"

"No, how?"

"He followed me after I left his office. He caught up with me on the road to the ranch and tried to make me stop. When I wouldn't, he tried to run me off the road." She paused, shuddering at the memory.

"He wasn't trying to hurt you, Mom. He just wanted to stop you doing something he knew would mess up all our lives."

"You wouldn't say that if you had seen his face. Fortunately, a truck came by just then and it was Morton who was run off the road. I came here as fast as I've ever driven in my life."

Jocelyn looked troubled. "I know Dad can be…well, really mean, but I can't believe he would go so far as to—"

"Jocelyn, stop and think. Both of us suspected Morton when we heard about Erica's friend being attacked at her house, didn't we?"

Jocelyn paused, studying her mother's face. "Are you saying it really was Dad who did that?"

"Yes, I think so."

"But you don't know for sure."

"I do, Jocelyn. Why do you think he was so furious with me?"

She frowned, considering. "Man, that is really...bad. If it's true. And no wonder he's trying to convince me that you're having a nervous breakdown or something."

"I'm thinking straight for the first time in years," Lillian said tersely. "He's so egotistical he thinks nobody will believe he's capable of depraved violence."

"Knowing Dad, it must have pissed him off that he went to all that trouble and almost killed the wrong person."

Lillian drew a deep breath, knowing what she had to say now would be much harder than anything they'd talked about so far. "Morton tried to remedy that Tuesday night," she said. "He attacked Erica and tried to strangle her with a cord. If a homeless person hadn't stopped him, he would have killed her. He's turned into a monster." She stared down at her hands. "Maybe he always was," she murmured.

"Mom, I can't believe he would—"

"He would and he did. We've known for years that he doesn't have a conscience, haven't we? We've seen it firsthand."

"Yeah, but–"

"Why is it neither of us are shocked? And when I begged him to say it wasn't true, that he wasn't so depraved, he laughed. He *laughed,* Jocelyn. The only thing that concerned him was convincing me to keep my mouth shut...as I have done all these years," she said bitterly.

Jocelyn sat down suddenly. "Mom, I'm trying to get my

head around this, but it's too much." Lillian saw that she was pale and it struck her to the heart that she had to be the one to reveal the depth of Morton's depravity. Jocelyn had been forced to deal with so much over the years.

"He must be stopped. Now that we know he tried to kill Erica, it would be naive to assume he won't try to keep us quiet, Jocelyn."

"Where is he now?"

Lillian shivered and sent a wary look toward the hills beyond the ranch house. While they talked, the sun had set and dark shadows were settling across the landscape. "That's what worries me, dear. Nobody knows."

Hank walked into the den a few minutes later holding a portable phone to his ear and Lillian's purse in the other hand. Jocelyn had retreated to her bedroom after hearing that her father was a would-be murderer, leaving Lillian to wonder and worry about the effect of knowing the ugly truth about Morton. Desperate for a cigarette, which she would have to smoke out on the porch, she took her purse from Hank. She gathered from his tone as he spoke on the phone that it wasn't a call from either of the ranch hands saying they'd spotted Morton.

"That was Hunter," he said after ringing off.

Her heart stumbled. "What did he say?"

"He's on his way to the ranch," Hank said. "He's just a few minutes out. Erica is with him."

She fumbled with the pack of cigarettes, longing to light up. "Oh, God, I don't know if I can face either one of them, Hank."

"I understand now why you were so upset over Hunter falling for Erica," he said, watching her peer fretfully at the road. "Made no sense to me before, since she seemed to be everything you'd want in a daughter-in-law."

"She is, Hank." She pressed her fingers to her lips. "She's perfect. But once she knows what I've done, what if she holds it against him? If I've destroyed his chance at happiness, I just don't know what I'll do."

"That's between the two of them, Lily. It's out of your hands. You have to let it be." He moved close to her, touching her hair tenderly. "How'd it go with Jocelyn?"

"About as you'd expect," she said. "She was shocked to know her father is capable of murder." She reached for the brandy she'd left on the coffee table, then paused without taking it. When she faced Erica, she didn't want to be drunk. "And now I have to confess to Hunter that what he suspects is true. I had a chance to do the right thing and, instead, I was a craven coward."

"We all make a wrong choice now and then, Lily."

"No, it was more than that," she told him, struggling to keep from falling apart. "It sounded so awful when he put it together." She blinked eyes bright with misery. "Can you imagine having your own son accuse you of being a party to vehicular homicide?"

"Lily…" He took her hands in his. "I'm so sorry you've been living with something like this. Why didn't you tell me?"

She looked at him. He was such a good man. With Hank, things were simply black and white. There was no struggle in choosing right over wrong. Bart had been a man like that. And how different her life would have been if she'd waited until Hank was free after Bart died, she thought sadly.

"I may lose both my children today, Hank, and I deserve it."

"You hush talking like that, you hear me?" His arm went around her waist and he pulled her close, kissing her temple. "You know I'll stick by you, no matter what, Lily-

girl. I've loved you for years and nothing you've done—
or could ever do—can change that. We'll get through this
somehow."

Her throat was tight, but she composed herself as she
caught the sound of a car. Hunter was here. She grabbed
the handkerchief Hank shoved at her, wiped her tears and
prayed for courage.

Twenty-Nine

It was almost dark when Hunter arrived at the gate to the ranch and found it closed and padlocked. Down the road some distance, he saw the headlights of a pickup traveling toward him at a fast clip. "That'll be Earl," he told Erica before getting out of the car. "We don't usually keep the gate locked, but considering everything, I'm glad to see it." After hearing from Hank about what happened to his mother, he was more convinced than ever that the ranch was the safest place for Erica. He didn't know how she'd react when he told her that his mother was here.

He waited until the pickup came to a stop, then walked to meet the hired hand at the gate. "Everything quiet so far, Earl?" he asked, after the padlock was sprung and the gate swung open.

"So far, Hunt." Earl shoved his battered Stetson to the back of his head. "Since Miz Lily got here after nearly being run off the road, me and Cisco is gonna keep a look-out to see whoever it was don't get on the property to have a go at her again."

Hunter cursed inwardly at his stepfather. "Sounds good, Earl."

"Hank and Miz Lily is both up at the ranch house now." He spat on the ground. "No sign of anybody except Miss Jocelyn since me and Cisco got the word."

Hunter nodded. "You'd recognize my stepfather if you were to see him, wouldn't you?"

"Mr. Trask? Sure. He don't come around much, but he's the kind of man you notice when he is around."

"Yeah. Well, if you do see him, keep him away from the ranch even if you have to use a shotgun to do it."

"Yes, sir. I'll do that."

Hunter was grim-faced when he got back in his car. After driving through the gate, he watched from his rear-view mirror as Earl padlocked it again. The two ranch hands were loyal and true, but they couldn't patrol every inch of the place, even in daylight. With darkness moving in fast, Morton would have ample opportunity to try to breach security.

"It looks as if we guessed right about Morton being desperate and dangerous," he told Erica as the ranch house came into view. "Now it seems he's just plain crazy. He followed my mother and somewhere between the interstate and the ranch he tried to run her off the road. I don't know what he would have done if he'd managed to get his hands on her. Hank has the place on lockdown now."

"Your mother is here?"

"Yes."

She was silent for a moment. "Is she okay?"

"She's upset and scared, according to Hank."

"With good reason, it seems. Did he mention Jocelyn?"

"Yeah, when Morton couldn't get to my mother, he called Jocelyn and she drove straight to the ranch. So she's safe…for the moment. But there are miles of fencing and a dozen ways he can get onto the property once it gets dark."

At the house, he parked and turned to look at Erica. "As soon as I get you safely inside, I need to contact the sheriff if Hank hasn't already done it."

As they climbed the porch steps, Erica wrapped her arms around her middle. Now that she was about to face his mother, she wasn't sure what she wanted to say…or when she might find the right time to say it. Hunter, sensing her apprehension, put a reassuring hand at the small of her back. Still, her tummy was in a knot as she went inside.

Lillian Trask stood in the den with her back to the huge fireplace. Her face was pale and strained as if she were nervous, too. Erica guessed the tall, somber-faced man standing beside her was Hank Colson. Jocelyn had apparently chosen to make herself scarce.

"Hello, Mom. Hank." Hunter drew Erica forward. "Hank, I don't think you've met Erica Stewart. Hank Colson, Erica."

"I'm pleased to meet you," Hank said with gentlemanly courtesy, taking her hand in his big one. He was a handsome man, white-haired and as rugged-looking as the Texas hills. His handshake was firm. "Welcome to McCabe-Colson."

"Thank you," she said.

"I wish we could've met under more pleasant circumstances," Hank said.

"Yes."

Lillian came away from the fireplace. "Hello, Erica," she said, stopping at Hank's side. "It's wonderful to see you looking so well. Hunter told me about your narrow escape. Are you sure you're well enough to leave the hospital?"

"Hello, Mrs. Trask. I'm all right. Shaken up, but…all right." Erica shook the older woman's hand with its stunning diamond ring and felt a slight tremor in the delicate fingers. Unlike the first and only other time they'd met, she took a moment to study Hunter's mother. She looked her age tonight, fragile and anxious. In spite of subtle cosmetic surgery, her eyes were a little too puffy.

"Please, call me Lillian," she requested. "Would you like something to drink? It's a dusty ride to the ranch."

"No, thank you."

The niceties over, Hunter turned to Hank. "Earl was at the gate to let us in. He and Cisco have taken their orders to heart about watching the property. They won't let anybody in…provided they're on hand to see anybody trying to get in. But it's like patrolling the Texas border, too much land for the available manpower, Hank. I'm thinking about going to the sheriff and asking for help."

Hank was shaking his head before Hunter had finished talking. "You can try, but he hasn't got enough men to do that kind of thing. He'll have somebody driving by pretty frequently, but that's about all he'll be able to do. Of course, if something was to happen, or if we actually spot Morton on the premises, he'll send somebody out, but that'll be after the fact. No, I'm afraid we're on our own trying to hold Morton off, Hunt. At least, for tonight. As for tomorrow—"

Lillian touched his arm. "Tomorrow, I'll be going to a lawyer," she said. "Once that's done, Morton will have to face the consequences. He won't be a threat to me or Jocelyn." Her gaze moved to Erica. "It was Morton who tried to hurt you, Erica. He won't have another chance after tomorrow."

"He didn't try to hurt me, Mrs. Trask, he tried to kill me."

Lillian looked stricken, as if she'd taken a body blow. "I'm so sorry," she whispered.

"So, if you know how dangerous he is, shouldn't you go to the police rather than to a lawyer?" Erica said.

With a hand at her throat, Lillian said to Hank and Hunter, "Erica and I need to speak privately."

"We do need to talk," Erica said, "but it needn't be privately."

"I'd prefer it," Lillian said, stiffly polite.

"Fine." Erica didn't particularly care whether or not there was an audience listening when she spoke her mind to Lillian Trask, but if the woman wanted to preserve some kind of illusion with Hunter and Hank Colson, Erica had no objection. Soon enough, it would all come out and the whole world would know.

"We can talk in my…in the guest bedroom." Putting out a hand, Lillian made a gesture toward the door, as gracious as if inviting Erica to enjoy a cup of tea and a friendly gossip with her. Without a word—and without a look at either of the two men—Erica went with her.

Once inside the bedroom where she'd slept the one and only time she'd been at the ranch, she saw no evidence of luggage and wondered if Hunter's mother planned to use this particular bedroom tonight. She'd worry about a bed for herself later. Regardless of Hunter's reassurance to the contrary, it was going to be very awkward staying in close proximity to the woman with the blood of David and Danielle on her hands, even for reasons of safety.

Lillian closed the door quietly and hesitated only a second or two as if marshalling strength for an ordeal. Turning, and with a tiny lift of her chin, she faced Erica. "If you'd like to sit, we can use the small sofa near the windows."

"It doesn't matter," Erica said. And it didn't. She just wanted to get on with it.

"We'll sit, then." Lillian moved across the floor, waited

politely until Erica was seated, then perched herself on the edge with her hands folded in her lap. "Did Hunter tell you what he suspects?"

"He didn't have to tell me. I've recovered enough memory to figure it out for myself. I know you were in the car. That's why the first look at your brooch was so traumatic at the gala. I must have seen it that night, possibly just a split-second look at it, but I recognized it. The car was a Mercedes. The emblem on the hood came to me in one of my paintings. I think once the police check, they'll find a Mercedes registered in the name of Trask."

"Yes," Lillian whispered shakily.

"I couldn't see the driver and I'm assuming it was your husband. I think Hunter inadvertently revealed to you and Mr. Trask that I was regaining some memory. I believe he then felt he had to get rid of me before that happened. He tried on Saturday night, but it was Jason who unlocked the door of my house and went inside, not me. And now you've confirmed that he tried again Tuesday night."

"You're right, of course. I didn't realize how far he'd go." She made a move toward Erica, but stopped herself before touching her. Drawing in a deep breath, she said, "First, before anything, I want to tell you how deeply sorry I am for your loss. To lose a child as you did—and your husband, too—must have been nearly unbearable. I know nothing I can ever say or do will change one iota of your pain, but I am so very deeply sorry." She cleared her throat, looking away.

Erica was in no mood to accept anything as paltry as an apology for the destruction of her family. What were words after what this woman had done, whatever her role in the aftermath? What were a few assists to a career in the face of what she'd lost?

When Erica remained silent, Lillian spoke again. "I

take full responsibility for the years that you've suffered not knowing who it was, not being able to have closure because no one was punished…if there is anything such as closure for a tragedy like this. And so, before you tell me just what you think of me and all this comes out, I'd like to tell you what happened."

"I know what happened," Erica said, dismissing the idea that the woman could begin to understand her pain. "My husband and baby were killed instantly when you ran over them. You didn't stop. You drove away without looking back."

"Yes, that's true. God forgive me, it's true." Lillian's fingers were now in a knot. "When it…happened, my husband…Morton…grabbed the wheel and put his foot on the accelerator, preventing us from stopping. He seemed to grasp the consequences of being involved in a fatal accident within an instant of it happening. He acted to save his reputation and his position at CentrexO," she said bitterly. "I'm not excusing my own failure to do the right thing. I should have picked up the phone when we got home and confessed everything. But he threatened to harm Jocelyn, his own daughter, if I did." She looked into Erica's eyes. "I believed him. I know now that I should have called his bluff, but I didn't."

In spite of everything, Erica was shocked. She knew Morton to be evil, but the picture Lillian painted went beyond evil. Still, she could have gone to the police for protection. She could have confided in Hunter. Or Hank. There were ways she could have done the right thing. "If you were driving, I can't see how that would have hurt his reputation."

"I wasn't driving," Lillian said, covering her eyes with her hand. "Jocelyn was."

Jocelyn. So that explained why seeing Erica was such

a shock. Even though she resisted it, Erica felt a reluctant sympathy for Lillian, the mother. Beneath the skin, there were similarities between them after all, she thought. Mothers do desperate things for their children. She'd been caught in a trap that, once sprung, would have put Jocelyn and possibly Hunter in jeopardy, since Erica could easily imagine Morton doing whatever it took to keep Lillian silent. She was dead wrong in leaving the scene of the crime, but with Morton's foot on the accelerator, Erica could see how she'd had no choice. In that moment. And then, when she arrived home, Morton with his threats had made certain she was left with no choice.

But to live under that burden for nine years?

Unable to sit another second, Erica rose. "Did you think helping boost my career would absolve you of guilt?" she asked curiously.

Lillian made a harsh sound. "Hardly. It cost me nothing and you'd paid the ultimate price. I would have done anything—anything!—to ease your pain. And you may believe this or not, but I was fiercely proud of your success. I admired the way you moved beyond what happened and made a life for yourself. It was so much richer and more rewarding than mine. Or Jocelyn's," she added bitterly. "Hunter must have told you how her life has been ruined."

"You mentioned going to a lawyer tomorrow. I should tell you that I will be going to the police," she told Lillian now. "I'm sorry for what that means to Jocelyn and Hunter."

"Yes, I expected that. In fact, I've already told Jocelyn that we must see a lawyer for the purpose of turning ourselves in. He will tell us how best to go about it."

Erica moved to the door. "In that case, I think we've said all that needs to be said."

"Please—" Lillian was on her feet now. "Before you leave, there is something else I'd like to say." Looking into Erica's eyes, she drew a shaky breath. "From the moment Hunter mentioned your name, I've known that he was…taken with you. You can imagine how I felt. I asked myself what were the chances." Tears glistened in her eyes, but she managed a fleeting, but wobbly smile. "More than anything in the world, I want Hunter to be happy. And if you can bring yourself to believe it, I want you to find happiness again, too. If there's a chance that you love my son, then I hope you won't let my sins prevent you from claiming what the two of you can have together."

Oh, Lord, the woman was making it hard to hate her. "It's too soon to tell, Mrs. Trask. Really. And there's a lot to overcome."

"I know."

Eager now to escape, Erica opened the door and almost collided with Jocelyn, who hovered just outside. "Oh. Jocelyn. Hello."

"I wasn't looking to eavesdrop," she said quickly, "but I couldn't help overhearing a little and it didn't seem a good time to interrupt." She shot a glance at her mother. "They told me you were in here and I didn't think it was fair of me to let Mom take whatever you had to say alone since I'm really the person you should hate. You did tell her I was driving, didn't you, Mom?"

"I did."

"I don't hate you, Jocelyn," Erica said. "You were… what, sixteen? I can't see a teenage girl standing up to someone like Morton Trask."

"Which means you blame my mother as much as Dad, don't you?"

Erica was tempted to deny that, but only for a heartbeat. There had been enough dishonesty. "Not quite. But I do think there's plenty of blame to go around. At this point, your mother and I have said enough about what should have been done and anything else is simply a waste of time and energy. I'm just glad that you're both ready to do the right thing now."

"Is it too late to say how sorry I am?"

Erica closed her eyes for a moment, wishing she didn't see the pure misery on Jocelyn's face, knowing she had to forgive these people. She'd somehow believed that once she knew who to blame, she would be filled with a righteous rage. For years, she'd longed to focus her hatred on someone, a name, a face. But Jocelyn's life had spiraled downward from the moment she was forced to drive away from the accident. And Lillian's marriage had deteriorated into a travesty of what it might have been. She couldn't hate these people.

She managed a sad smile. "It's never too late to say you're sorry."

Hunter was waiting for her when she walked back into the den. He rose with a look of concern on his face. "Is everything okay? I mean, I know it's not okay, but did my mother—"

"We talked. I guess you could say we cleared the air. I know how it happened now and…" She looked beyond him, her eyes clouded with new knowledge. "Jocelyn appeared as we were almost done. She was worried about her mother taking the brunt of my anger."

"You don't seem angry," he told her, studying her profile. "If I had to characterize it, I'd say you appeared more…righteously determined to see justice done."

"Well, it will be now, I suppose, provided Morton is picked up before he has a chance to somehow get away." She moved her gaze back to him. "Actually, Jocelyn was driving the car. Did you know that?"

He drew a sharp breath, then frowned. "No. She was only a kid. She was—"

"Sixteen. I remember when I first got my license and how I begged to drive every chance I got. That's probably how it came about that she was behind the wheel."

Hunter looked thoughtful. "If that's the way it happened, Morton could have gotten off with only losing his reputation and his position at CentrexO. Now he's really screwed himself. Instead of being charged with leaving the scene of a fatal accident, he'll be tried for attempted murder."

Erica rubbed a spot between her eyes. "In spite of your mother's plan to confess, Hunter, this doesn't change anything. I'm still going to the police."

"I know. I can't lie and say I don't wish it would all just go away. Even knowing the consequences for Jocelyn, it's obvious my mother intends to make a clean breast of everything. There may be more serious consequences for her, but she seems prepared to accept that. As for Jocelyn, since she was only sixteen, I'm guessing she'll be dealt with leniently. I'm just glad to finally know the truth."

"I'm sorry to put you through this," she said. "But it's something I have to do."

He saw the distress on her face. "I understand. We—you and I—can get beyond this, Erica."

Erica wasn't so sure about that, but she didn't want to talk about it tonight. "Where's Hank?" she asked, looking around.

He paused, not ready for a change of subject, but there was something in the way she looked. "Okay, we'll talk about this later. Hank's outside somewhere. Neither one of us is comfortable leaving only Cisco and Earl on guard tonight, and he insists on taking the first shift. One of us needs to stay here in the house in case Morton somehow manages to slip through. We'll swap out in a few hours, but neither of us plans to sleep tonight."

"You won't be coming to bed at all?"

"No, so you can have my bedroom all to yourself." He tipped her chin up and gave her a slow kiss. "And you can stop worrying about how to tell me you don't want to sleep with me."

Thirty

She didn't sleep, anyway. At least, not very much. At the end of the long night, she knew she would not be able to hang around waiting for Morton Trask to strike. She'd jerked awake at every small sound and by the time dawn was breaking, she was grouchy and more than ready to get up. If she'd been at home, she would have spent the hours painting. Or working up new designs. Or doing something useful. As it was, she didn't have her paints or her sketchbook or anything else to make the hours productive. She appreciated Hunter's efforts to keep her safe, but she couldn't live her life this way.

She caught the smell of coffee brewing with a sigh of relief. Finally, someone was stirring. Throwing off the covers, she got out of bed. After brushing her teeth and pulling on jeans and a T-shirt, she followed her nose down the hall toward the kitchen. She was halfway across the floor in the den when she realized Hank was stretched out on an ancient recliner sound asleep. Now that it was daylight, he must have felt it was safe to relax his vigil. Hunter, she assumed, would still be outside. Must be Theresa brewing coffee.

It was Hunter. He stood at the counter with the coffee-pot, getting ready to pour it for himself. "Hey," he said, searching her face. "You're up early."

"I couldn't lie there another minute." She glanced at the mug in his hand. "I hope there's enough of that to share."

"Plenty." He took a mug from the cabinet, filled it and handed it over. "Careful, it's hot."

She leaned against the counter and took a cautious taste, savoring the kick of the caffeine. From the window, she could see the first pale pink streaks of dawn above the line of trees. In a few minutes, the sun would appear on the horizon. Not being an early riser, Erica rarely saw the sunrise.

"I assume Morton never showed," she said, cupping the mug with both hands.

"No. The ranch was quiet as a cemetery. Now that it's daylight, I'll ride out and relieve Cisco and Earl. They need to grab a little sleep. Then after I see to the horses in the barn, I'll stay close to the house with you."

"What about sleep for you?" she asked. "You've been awake more than twenty-four hours."

"I'll be okay. And to be on the safe side, Hank's going to ride with my mother and Jocelyn to see a lawyer. As long as he's driving, I don't expect trouble. The way I see it, Morton missed his best chance to strike during the night. Since he didn't, I hope he's come to his senses and is on his way out of the country. It's the only rational option left to him now."

"Good, then I can go home. First thing when I get back to Houston, I'll go to the police. I think Detective Sullivan is the most likely person to hear what I have to say." She could see from the look on his face that he didn't like that.

Hunter set his mug aside carefully. "While I said that I hope Morton has come to his senses, it bothers me that he's just disappeared. Why don't we wait until Mom and Jocelyn have seen the lawyer? Once that's done, Morton is cooked. There'll be no point in trying to keep you from telling what you know."

Another day of doing nothing. She didn't think she could stand it. However, she suspected Hunter would stubbornly resist driving her back to Houston. For the first time, she realized it was dumb not to have driven her own car to the ranch. "Okay," she agreed reluctantly, "but I can't just sit around the house. How long before you head out to find Cisco and Earl? I want to go with you."

"And I'd like that." His lips slanted in a smile, but she could see an argument coming. With his free hand, he reached out and cupped her chin. "But it's too risky. Until we actually find Morton, I think you should stay indoors."

She twisted away from him. "You want me to just cower inside? For how long? What if they don't find him for days, weeks? No—" she shook her head stubbornly "—I'm not going to let him do this to me. What he's done has overshadowed my life for nine years. He's not getting another ten minutes. You're using one of the ranch pickups, right? I can ride with you. What could happen—"

"No, I'm not using one of the ranch pickups. Cisco and Earl have one each. I'm relieving them, remember? I'll be riding Jasper."

"Let them both return in one truck," she argued. "You take the other one."

"And what about Jasper? I can't just slap him on the rump and tell him to go back to the barn."

"You can, you just don't want to." She stood at the window with her arms crossed over her chest. "I won't sit in this house like a…a mouse and let Morton Trask—or you—dictate my life, Hunter."

"I'm just trying to keep you safe." He plowed a hand

through his hair, looking frustrated. "And until he's in custody, I don't want to give him a chance to get at you."

"If you don't let me go, I'll saddle Lady up and ride out myself. If I stay indoors another minute I just might go crazy myself."

"He's tried twice to get to you, Erica. And you saw how far he went to try to keep my mother quiet. Who knows what he would have done if he'd managed to get his hands on Jocelyn? This is not a man who's used to being defied. He always plays to win and he's not just desperate and dangerous now. I think this has pushed him over the edge."

"It's daylight now." She waved a hand at the landscape through the window. "The ranch is mostly pasture and pecan orchards. Where can he hide?"

He stood studying her, gauging the stubborn tilt of her chin. Then, with a shake of his head, he moved toward the door. "Okay, I don't like it, but it's one way to keep an eye on you, I guess. I really don't think Morton's stupid enough to show up here now. What's the point?"

"I agree with you," she said, falling into step beside him.

"Oh, yeah?" With a dry laugh, he caught her by the waist and hugged her. "I think I should probably write that down, because there probably won't be many times I'll hear those words when we argue."

He talked as if they had a future. She was still not so sure.

In the barn, while Hunter went to Jasper's stall, Erica greeted Lady, speaking in a soft voice and falling into the familiar ritual of saddling a horse. Actually, it felt good to be doing something physical. The ride would help take her mind off the evil that had stalked her for weeks. It was only after Hunter had boosted her into the saddle that she noticed he had a rifle attached to his saddle.

"Do you really expect to use that?" she asked.

"Can't be too careful. It would be stupid to find myself in a situation where I needed it and it's locked up in a gun case."

"I don't know anything about guns."

"If you live on a ranch, you need to know how to shoot. Jocelyn's a crack shot and you might not think it, but my mother is, too. A rifle is a handy thing to have when you come across a snake or a varmint having a go at the quail coop."

"Quail? You raise quail on the ranch?"

"Not commercially, but just enough to satisfy Hank's craving for the little birds." He grinned as he guided Jasper toward the paddock gate. "It's another one of his hobbies. Nothing he likes better than quail, and the way Theresa prepares it is as good as any five-star restaurant in Houston."

While he opened the gate, Erica sat astride Lady looking around, drinking in the rolling hills and the wide sweep of green pasture where grazing mares minded their offspring. She smiled as a young colt tried out a gallop on spindly legs. In the distance, a small pond glistened, its banks dotted with weeping willows. And beyond that, the ranch house looked inviting and homelike, as appealing as a picture postcard. Evil had no place in this tranquil setting, she thought. When she brought her gaze back to Hunter, she saw he was watching her, a half smile on his face.

"You like it?" he asked, pushing his hat back a little to look up at her.

"Who wouldn't?"

"It can be yours."

"What?" She looked down at him in confusion. And as she did so, she saw his smile morph into a frown and then his eyes go wide with alarm. She turned to see, but he lunged toward her, unseating her just as a sound whizzed past her ear. She fell to the ground unhurt, but shaken. It all happened in a split second, but it was enough for her to know the sound was gunfire.

"Get down!" Hunter shouted. Controlling a spooked Jasper with one hand, he groped for his rifle with the other while the horse danced skittishly. "Take cover at the water trough!"

She needed no urging to flatten herself on the ground, instinctively scooting a few feet on her belly toward the trough. Except for that, there was no cover within reach. As she ducked behind it, she heard the sound of another shot and the ping of a bullet striking metal. She blinked as water spurted out onto the ground close to her face.

Then Hunter's arm was around her, pushing her head into the curve of his shoulder. "Stay still," he ordered, breathing hard. He sighted the rifle and then squeezed off a shot. "Son of a bitch is somewhere in the trees near the house," he muttered. "I saw the glint of his rifle before that first shot, but I can't see him now."

"What can we do?" she asked, terrified.

"Hope to hell that Hank gets off a good shot before he gets a better position to shoot at us again."

"Hank is asleep. I saw him when I came through the den."

"He won't sleep through gunfire twenty yards from the house."

"It's Morton, isn't it?" She risked a look up at him.

"Yeah. Keep your head down, darlin'. He's crazy." Hunter sighted his rifle, scanning the grove for a sign of his stepfather. "But where in hell is he?" he muttered.

"Can we call for help?" she asked. "You have your cell phone."

"But could anybody get here in time?" He swore under his breath. "What does he think he's doing?"

"Killing the messenger?" She was shaking like a leaf, but if she was going to be shot at, Hunter was the person she most wanted at her side. "Thank God you thought to take your rifle."

"I just wish you had one, too."

She managed a laugh. "And what would I do with it? I've never had a gun in my hands in my life."

"This is Texas. We'll remedy that as soon after the wedding as possible."

Wedding? His stepfather had them in the crosshairs and he was talking about their wedding? And then the sound of another shot came from a different direction, much nearer the house. Even to her ears, it had a bolder, louder sound.

"Shotgun," Hunter grunted, scanning the area around the house. Erica guessed he'd been right that Hank wouldn't sleep through a gunfight. Then she felt him go rigid with shock as he located the shooter. "Oh, Jesus, it's my mother."

Lillian had walked out of the house and now stood in the center of the backyard. With her feet planted firmly apart, she held a shotgun trained in the direction of her husband. "Morton!" she called. "That was a warning shot. I have you in my sights. Put your gun down and come out now. Don't make me shoot you."

Erica heard an anguished sound from Hunter. His arm tightened around her. "What is she doing?" he groaned. "He'll kill her. I've got to—"

"No, Hunter. Please don't." Erica put a hand on his cheek and forced him to meet her eyes. "This is something between your mother and Morton. I don't know what she's thinking or what she has in mind, but there's no way Morton will let you help her without taking a shot at you. You said yourself that the man is no longer thinking rationally."

"It's not rational for my mother to stand out in the open daring him to shoot her." He sent a quick, agonized look toward the house. "Where in hell is Hank?"

"I don't know, but Lillian was aware of the danger when she stepped out there. I think she's made up her mind to put an end to all the secrecy and lies, and she's not going to let Morton kill anybody else."

"If I can get into the barn, I could get a bead on him from the hayloft," Hunter said. With her heart sinking, Erica realized he was prepared to risk getting shot before he'd hide out of harm's way while his mother stood Morton down. He could be killed. She closed her eyes, praying for something—anything—to stop this madness.

"Morton!" Lillian called again. "Did you hear me? If you don't heed what I say, I'm going to have to shoot. And don't doubt me. I will do it."

"Don't be a fool, Lillian," he shouted. "This is the only way."

"You can't kill everybody, Morton. Too many people know what we've done."

Erica felt Hunter tense up and knew he was going to ignore danger to himself to save his mother. "He's insane," he said to Erica. "I've got to try to get him or he'll kill us all. I'm worried about Hank. The only reason he's not out here is that he's hurt…or worse." Then, before she could stop him, he rolled to his feet and ran to the barn, firing rounds from the rifle in the direction he figured Morton was hiding.

With a tortured cry, Erica huddled behind the trough. Bullets flew—it seemed like hundreds—kicking up dust in the paddock, ripping through the metal water trough and ricocheting off anything solid. She breathed a thankful prayer as Hunter disappeared inside the barn, still on his feet. From where she was, she saw him climb up into the hayloft where hopefully he would be able to stop Morton before Lillian was harmed—or before she actually did the deed that would stop Morton forever.

But when the dust and noise of gunfire died down, there was an eerie silence that sent a prickle of dread down her spine. Easing to the side of the trough, Erica saw Lillian throw the shotgun aside and, with a keening cry, drop to the ground. Watching in horror, Erica thought the woman had been struck by a bullet and that Morton had killed her. And then her gaze was drawn to movement on the back porch of the house. It was Jocelyn moving without haste down the stairs, walking as if in a trance across the yard toward her mother. She, too, had a weapon and was carrying it cradled across her arm.

To Erica's inexperienced eye, it looked like a shotgun. She sent a frantic gaze toward the trees, fearing at any moment to hear a shot from Morton. She was beyond doubting the man would shoot his own daughter. There would be no point in silencing Lillian if Jocelyn was left to tell everything.

Next, she looked up at the hayloft, trying to spot Hunter. To her relief, he stood in the opening of the hayloft bathed in bright, early morning sun. Grim-faced, he held his rifle at his side looking over at his mother and Jocelyn.

For a moment, she was so shaken by the sheer violence of what she'd seen that she didn't even try to stand. She was still trying to take it all in. Finally, rising unsteadily, she saw that Jocelyn had dropped to her knees beside her mother. It was only when Lillian threw her arms around her daughter, sobbing brokenly, that Erica realized the older woman had not been shot in the melee. As both women rocked together on the ground, Jocelyn's face was calm, without any expression whatsoever. Watching them, Erica was confused, trying to figure out what had actually happened. She was on the point of heading across to them when Hunter caught her from behind and pulled her around to face him.

"Are you okay?"

She put both her hands to her cheeks, shaken to the core. "Yes, I'm—" *shocked, appalled, terrified.* She might have told him the truth, but she settled for "—I'm all right."

"Thank God," he said, and caught her up in a crushing embrace.

"Is Morton dead?" she asked, with her face buried in his chest.

"I don't know, but he's down and hurt bad for sure."

"But how—? Who—?"

"I'm not sure," he said grimly. "My mother and Jocelyn both shot at him."

"Oh, my God."

His arms tightened around her again briefly, but he gave a start over something he saw beyond her. "It's Hank," he said. She turned as the older man burst out of the house, banging the screen door against the wall and heading in a flat-out run to Lillian and Jocelyn. "I wonder where in hell he's been?" Hunter muttered.

"I don't know, but he doesn't look like a man who's hurt." Erica knew he'd been worried about Hank.

With his jaw set and his eyes dark with pain, Hunter moved Erica aside. "Will you call 911 on my cell phone while I go over there? We need to get the law out here as soon as possible. And an ambulance."

"Yes. Of course." She took the phone and dialed the emergency number with trembling fingers. As she waited for an answer, she watched him walk toward his family and Hank. It was only then that she saw the bloodstain on his sleeve.

Thirty-One

"It's nothing. It's just a scratch. Some alcohol and a Band-Aid and I'll be fine." Hunter reached for his shirt to put it back on, but Erica stopped him, tossing it over the back of a chair, out of his reach.

"A bullet wound is not just a scratch," she argued, searching through the first aid kit she'd found under the kitchen sink. Her own hands were still a little shaky, but she found what she was looking for, a small bottle of antiseptic. He might be able to shrug off a close brush with death, but it would take a long time before those horrifying minutes when bullets were flying and she feared for her life and his faded in her memory.

The sheriff and the EMTs had arrived within a few minutes of her 911 call. Lillian had met them with a calm composure that was amazing considering she'd just shot and possibly killed her husband. Then, before Hunter could stop her, she volunteered to the sheriff that she was solely responsible for the carnage at the ranch that morning. At his request, she agreed to make a statement. Hunter, Hank and Jocelyn had instantly nixed that. A plan was finally agreed on. Hank would drive Lillian and Jocelyn to the sheriff's office, but any statements would only be made in the presence of the lawyer as they'd originally planned. The sheriff, a longtime friend of Hank's, agreed.

"The EMTs said Morton was talking when they loaded him into the ambulance," Erica said, reaching for sterile gauze. "I don't know about you, but for your mother's sake—and Jocelyn's—I'm glad he's still alive. He's lucky."

"If you consider being paralyzed lucky," Hunter said, with a wary eye on the bottle in her hand. "But I guess it's better than being dead."

"Paralyzed?"

"One of the EMTs told me that he took a bullet in his spine." He braced himself as she swabbed antiseptic on his "scratch." "But you're right. I'm glad he isn't dead. I wouldn't want Mom and Jocelyn living with something like that, but I can't feel too much sympathy if he's paralyzed for the rest of his life. After what he tried to do to you, he deserves what he gets."

Erica busied herself cleaning his wound, thinking that after what she'd witnessed that morning there wasn't much thirst for revenge left in her. She'd survived, and so had Hunter, and that was what mattered. "I'm still murky on the details. Everything happened so fast when the shooting started."

"Even though Mom had locked Hank in the cellar, he saw everything from the cellar window. He said Jocelyn was standing behind the screen door in the kitchen the whole time with her rifle trained on Morton. She knew he had a bead on me and she guessed he didn't believe Mom's threats. He figured—wrongly—that she wouldn't shoot him and I don't think Jocelyn was sure Mom had the nerve the shoot, either. Then, when I made a break for the barn, Mom and Jocelyn both opened fire."

"His own daughter," she murmured.

"Yeah. Morton and Jocelyn both underestimated my mother's determination to stop him, no matter what she had to do."

"She knew better than anyone what he was capable of."

"I can think of one other person who knew." His gaze went to the bruise on her throat. Because it was within easy reach, he leaned forward and kissed it lightly. "Mom was in more danger than she realized after she went to his office yesterday and told him she was through. If she'd been alone with him—at home, for instance—she might not have gotten away from him alive."

"It's scary just thinking about it."

With his hands resting on her waist, Hunter watched her rip open a packet containing a sterile bandage. "I believe he would have killed her and Jocelyn today after he finished off the two of us. I'm sorry to say that I made it easy for him by taking you outside before I knew for sure that he was in custody. It was a risky thing to do. I knew it at the time and I still let you talk me into it."

"I was at fault for pushing you, Hunter. If you hadn't agreed to let me go with you, I would have done it, anyway, after you left. I was stir-crazy after being cooped up with nothing to do." He winced as she sprayed something from a tiny aerosol tube on the wound. "Ouch! That stings!"

She quickly taped the bandage in place. "Do you need a bullet to bite?" she asked, with a teasing smile.

He pulled her between his thighs and rested his forehead against her midriff. "I need a little TLC," he told her. "I'm still shaking over how close I came to losing you."

She knew the feeling. The moment he had dashed to the barn in a hail of bullets, she'd let go of her doubts about loving him. There might always be some distance between her and his family, but it wasn't enough to make her walk away from Hunter. She knew that now. In a rush of heartfelt relief that she hadn't lost him, either, she bent and kissed him.

Hunter, however, wasn't so easily pacified. He caught her face in his hands and turned the kiss into something more intense. There was a vulnerability about him now that hadn't been there before. The scales had fallen from his eyes when he had discovered his family's secrets. She had seen his shattered look as he realized what his mother and Jocelyn had done…and why. Traces of that look were still there, and it stunned her how much it mattered that she wanted to see it gone, vanished. Loving him, she wished it were otherwise. But David and Danielle deserved justice, too. They deserved to rest in peace. There was a price to be paid for that and, sadly, Hunter would have to share in the cost. They could have a future if only he could get beyond that.

She would have stepped back, but he held her in place, so she simply linked her arms around his neck and let him settle her on his lap. "Speaking of being stir-crazy," he said, nuzzling her neck, "Hank is the one who can speak to that. You could have knocked me over with a feather when he came flying out of the kitchen after the shooting stopped. I knew nothing short of a bullet would keep him from coming to the rescue and apparently my mother knew it, too."

With fingers sifting through his hair, she studied his face. "It's almost funny what she did."

Lillian, it turned out, hadn't slept much, either. She'd been sitting on the back porch steps quietly smoking when she spotted Morton carrying a rifle and heading into the grove of trees. A minute before that, she'd seen Hunter and Erica disappear into the barn. She realized instantly that from his vantage point in the grove Morton had a good view of both the house and barn. She slipped back inside, intending to get a shotgun from the cabinet in the den, but she found Hank was up and stirring. She knew he'd lay his life down to protect the people he loved, but she didn't intend to give him that chance. Coming up with some ruse, she'd managed to get him to follow her down to the cellar, then she'd slammed the door on him, which locked from the outside. With Hank safe, and assuming Jocelyn was still sleeping, she'd taken his shotgun and headed out, determined to keep Morton from killing again.

"She was protecting Hank, just as she believed she was protecting the rest of us," Hunter said. With a last lingering kiss, he set her aside and stood up to get his shirt. "I can only imagine what he was thinking as he watched the whole thing from that tiny, ground-level window in the cellar. There was no point in busting it open," he said after pulling his shirt over his head. "He was too big to crawl out of it."

"And it took him precious minutes to pry the door open with the crowbar. I guess your mother didn't have time to remove any tools that might prove helpful in breaking the door down," Erica added wryly.

"The only thing she didn't count on was Jocelyn," Hunter said.

"What do you think will happen to her?" Erica asked.

"Not very much," he said. "We can both testify that she and my mother were justified in shooting Morton this morning. If he hadn't been stopped, one of us would have been his victim. As for the other, the hit-and-run—" He stopped and his eyes took on that troubled look again.

"She was sixteen years old," Erica said, "a juvenile, and in the company of her parents. I wouldn't be surprised if she is sentenced to community service."

Hunter caught her chin, so that he could look into her eyes. "How would you feel about that?"

"I think Jocelyn has paid dearly already. Like your mother, she's wrestled with a lot of guilt and she's made a lot of poor choices when the choice to leave the scene of the accident wasn't hers. A psychologist wouldn't have much trouble tracing her emotional problems back to the accident."

"How about my mother? You can't feel that kindly toward her."

"I'm sorry, I can't." With her hand, she brushed at dark hair falling forward on his forehead. "She's far more culpable than Jocelyn, but she's paid a dear price, too. I understand her fear of Morton, but it's still hard to forgive her."

His dark eyes searched hers intently. "I feel as if I need to get down on my knees and beg your forgiveness for the pain my family has brought to your life. All these years, I never had a clue they were hiding such a dark secret. I'm so sorry for what you lost. I'm so sorry that you weren't given the slim comfort of knowing the guilty were punished. I'm—"

She kissed him again to hush him. "Don't, please. It isn't your place to apologize. Think about this. When you learned that I meant to go to the police, knowing it would turn your mother's life upside down, would that have made you walk away from me?"

"Not in this lifetime."

"Well, then, why would I deny myself the joy of loving you because you happened to be Lillian's son?"

His hands clenched her waist as he stared at her. "Say that again?"

"Why would I deny myself the joy of loving you—"

He grinned. "That's the part I wanted to hear again."

"That I love you?" Slowly, she traced the shape of his lips with her finger. "I do."

"Then that's a good place to start," he told her, "isn't it?"

"The best place." She was smiling when he kissed her.

* * * * *

When does love deserve a second chance?

JEANETTE
BAKER

Two years ago, Francesca's husband moved out, leaving her with a hundred-year-old vineyard, their six-year-old son and her feisty mother-in-law. When a large corporation threatens to put the vineyard out of business, Francesca's already bleak world falls apart, again. Loyalty and family are tested when two generations of women are forced to take a hard look at the mistakes they've made, the dreams they still have and the possibility that love deserves a second chance.

A Delicate Finish

"Delivered with thoughtful exposition and flawless writing, this provocative book is built around Baker's personal experiences."
—*Publishers Weekly* on *Blood Roses*

Available the first week of June 2005, wherever paperbacks are sold!

If you enjoyed what you just read,
then we've got an offer you can't resist!

Take 2 bestselling novels FREE!

Plus get a FREE surprise gift!

Clip this page and mail it to MIRA®

IN U.S.A.
3010 Walden Ave.
P.O. Box 1867
Buffalo, N.Y. 14240-1867

IN CANADA
P.O. Box 609
Fort Erie, Ontario
L2A 5X3

YES! Please send me 2 free MIRA® novels and my free surprise gift. After receiving them, if I don't wish to receive anymore, I can return the shipping statement marked cancel. If I don't cancel, I will receive 4 brand-new novels every month, before they're available in stores! In the U.S.A., bill me at the bargain price of $4.99 plus 25¢ shipping and handling per book and applicable sales tax, if any*. In Canada, bill me at the bargain price of $5.49 plus 25¢ shipping and handling per book and applicable taxes**. That's the complete price and a savings of over 20% off the cover prices—what a great deal! I understand that accepting the 2 free books and gift places me under no obligation ever to buy any books. I can always return a shipment and cancel at any time. Even if I never buy another The Best of the Best™ book, the 2 free books and gift are mine to keep forever.

185 MDN DZ7J
385 MDN DZ7K

Name	(PLEASE PRINT)	
Address	Apt.#	
City	State/Prov.	Zip/Postal Code

*Not valid to current The Best of the Best™, Mira®,
suspense and romance subscribers.*

*Want to try two free books from another series?
Call 1-800-873-8635 or visit www.morefreebooks.com.*

* Terms and prices subject to change without notice. Sales tax applicable in N.Y.
** Canadian residents will be charged applicable provincial taxes and GST.
  All orders subject to approval. Offer limited to one per household.
  ® and ™are registered trademarks owned and used by the trademark owner and or its licensee.

BOB04R   ©2004 Harlequin Enterprises Limited